THE PRISM SERIES: BOOK TWO

EMERALD PASSAGE

ANETA TORCHIA

THE LUMINARY PRESS

"Success if not final.
Failure is not fatal.
It is the courage to continue that counts."
-Winston Churchill

EMERALD PASSAGE

ISBN: 978-1-7387687-7-6, 1st edition paperback, 2025
ISBN: 978-1-7387687-8-3, 1st edition hardcover, 2025
ISBN: 978-1-7387687-9-0, 1st edition eBook, 2025

Published by The Luminary Press
Mississauga, ON, Canada
info@theluminarypress.com
www.theluminarypress.com

Other books in THE PRISM series:
THE PRISM (Book 1)
FINDING AEONIA (Book 3)

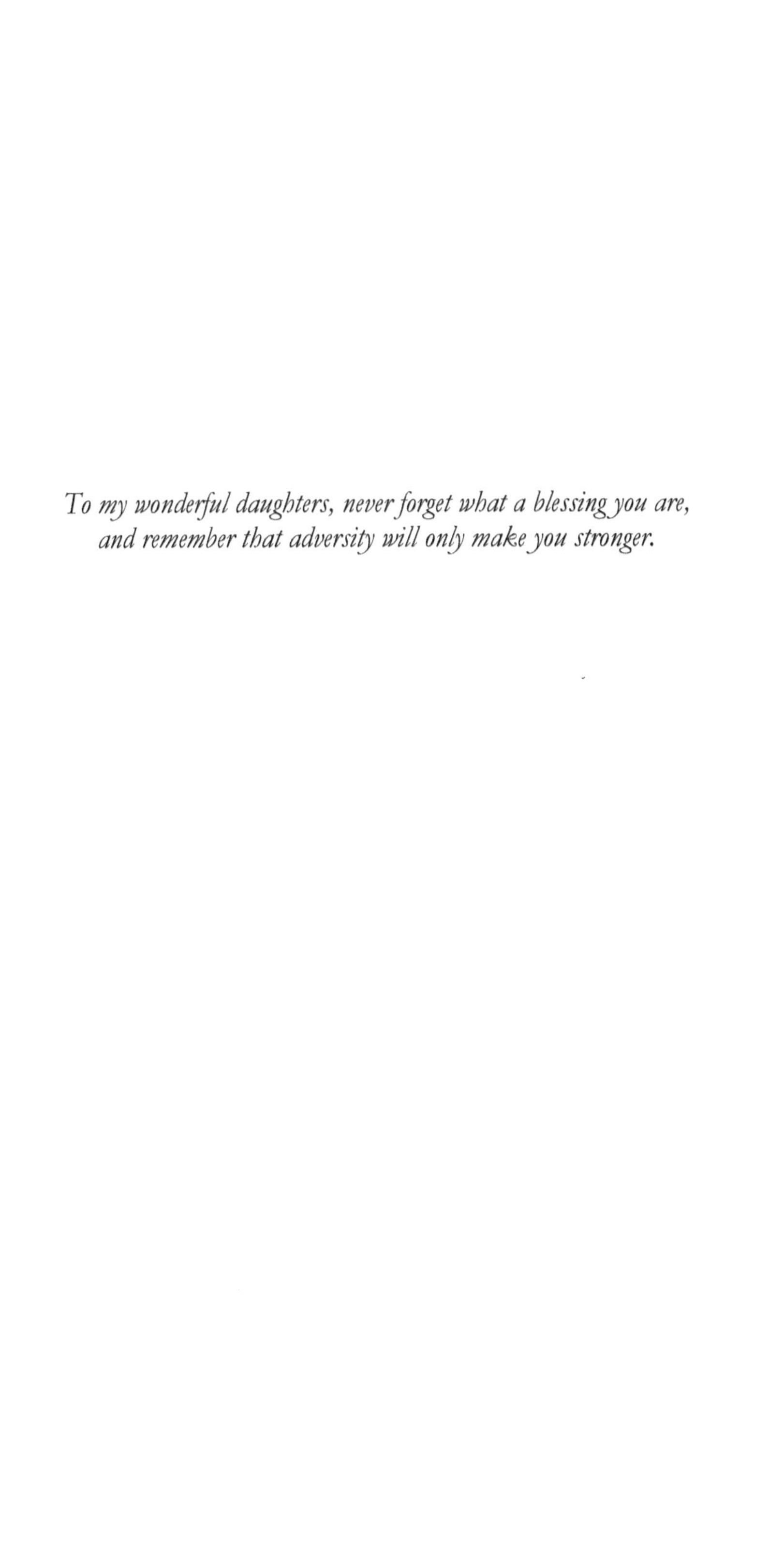

*To my wonderful daughters, never forget what a blessing you are,
and remember that adversity will only make you stronger.*

The most ironic thing about Sarah's perfect day was the horrific way it was about to end.

"Don't pull too abruptly on the control yoke," The flying instructor shouted over the plane engine. With his confident swagger, he exited the aircraft and circled around the back of the Cessna. "You gotta be smooth with it. And relax a little more," he added, reaching over to playfully jostle her arm. "I've been up there with idiots that almost killed me! You ain't one of 'em."

Marv Hannigan was the best kind of instructor: constructive in his criticism and not afraid to tell you the truth, but also willing to let you spread your wings without butting in too much. With his buzzed caramel brown hair and military physique, he wasn't bad to look at either. Sarah had to remind herself not to get distracted by his southern charm. She thanked him and smiled shily, brushing her brown curls away from her eyes, only to have a nearby propeller undue her work.

"Does that mean you're going pass me?" she asked.

"Now, that depends. You gonna bring me more of those fancy famuah cupcakes?" Marv teased in his Mississippi accent as he adjusted his aviators and butchered the French language.

"*Fram*boise?"

"I'm never gonna catch on to rollin' them Rs, am I? See you Thursday for your final." He flashed her his perfect teeth again before heading off duty. Sarah watched regretfully as he departed, letting herself daydream just a little. A little daydreaming never hurt anyone.

At least the Order couldn't take that away from her.

The sunset overtook the sky over the runway, the reds and yellows melting into each other. Sarah relished her high as she watched the planes landing. Her feet were on solid ground, but her heart was still soaring, as cliché as that sounded. Within the week she'd be licensed if all went as planned. It felt damn good to be this close. Flying had been a welcome diversion over the last few months and about the only thing that gave her a reprieve from hating herself and trying not to vomit. She loved every minute of being up there. She could escape it all and the clouds would just wipe the slate clean, even if for a few hours.

She headed into the women's changeroom feeling content but stopped dead in her tracks when she saw Basile leaning against the old lockers. One of the Order's bloodhounds. As usual, he was overdressed and wore a poorly fitting overpriced suit with pant legs that crumpled awkwardly over his shoes. He'd grown his black hair longer, and it was now slicked back and pulled into a short ponytail at the base of his neck. He busied himself flicking peeling paint off one of the locker doors.

"A little fancy for flying lessons," Sarah remarked, approaching calmly while her heart pounded through her chest at the sight of the Vulturian. It wasn't Basile she dreaded seeing – he was just a puppet, and as daft as they came. It was the person who pulled his strings, the person who could wipe someone off the face of the planet without a blink of an eye or shred of remorse she feared seeing.

And he was never far behind.

"We are not here on pleasure." His voice pierced the air behind Sarah's ear. She turned to lock eyes with the sociopath. If evil had a face: his lips curved in a spine-chilling grin above his newly grown facial hair. His head remained hairless and shiny, but he had a new scar below his right ear, courtesy of an explosion he didn't see coming the same night they killed the Vidal boy. A shard of metal had split his flesh open as his car burst into flames. *I hope it hurt like hell.*

But it was Irra's energy that was the most chilling. You could feel it the moment he entered a room, as if the grim reaper himself had brushed his boney hand over the nape of your neck. An almost ancient kind of energy, the kind from which all darkness evolved.

"We will give you a ride home today," Irra declared as he fiddled with the zipper on a pilot's jumpsuit hanging on a nearby hook.

Shit! Why?

Irra had never spoken to her before. Sarah had only seen him around the chapter house where the most they'd exchanged was a quick glance. And staying off his radar was exactly how she liked it.

"I have a car."

"Basile will bring it home for you. We make everything easy, yes?" Irra's grin widened unnaturally and cracked the parched skin on his lips. He wasn't asking.

Sarah's mouth went dry. There was no point arguing. She knew who Irra took his orders from and what the price would be for disobedience.

"Yeah, sure, great. See you outside then," she reluctantly agreed. Her hands began to tremble as she emptied her locker. She forced herself to steady them as she followed the two men into the parking lot where Irra's black sedan stood waiting.

Her stomach was in her throat, although she tried her best to hide it. For a moment, she considered bolting and taking her chances in a high-speed pursuit. She was a pretty good driver, and she had watched enough movies to know how not to hit the pedestrians or get stuck in a dead-end construction zone. They were outside the city, the streets were wider, she knew all the side roads. All she had to do was keep looking ahead. That was usually when the cars on TV ended up in a ditch – when the driver looked away. Television was so predictable.

This isn't a movie, she reminded herself as she handed Basile the keys to her hatchback. "Don't scratch it up." But he neither laughed nor replied, and simply stuck a piece of chewing gum in his mouth before striding off.

As she fastened her seat belt on the passenger side of Irra's sedan, she wondered if this was how she was going to meet her end. He'd probably drive her out to the country to kill her there, keep the car clean. On second thought, he would probably take sick pleasure in seeing her splattered brains on the headrest. She kept her ears alert for the sound of the door locking but heard nothing.

If this was the end, she was almost certain of the reason behind it. She searched her memories, trying to figure out where she had slipped up. *How did he find out about Everest? She had been so careful, told no one. And the girl had been missing for –*

"Are you good?" Irra asked, lighting up a cigarette.

Sarah looked over at him in confusion, ripped away from her blitz of panicked thoughts. "What?"

"Flying, are you good?"

Flying? "Uh, yeah, I think…I'm still learning, but I'm ok."

"Hmmm."

Still no locking sound. She couldn't take it anymore. "What is this about?" she finally asked, trying to sound assertive and indifferent at the same time in an even, measured cadence. The cigarette smoke filled the cabin and tunneled its way up her nostrils, the repulsive smell ripping through her throat and sinuses. She was desperate to open her window but held in her cough, afraid to make any uninvited movements.

"Why are you taking lessons?"

Sarah thought about her answer carefully, finally settling on half the truth. "Because I like to fly."

"Why," Irra mumbled, then paused, taking another drag before releasing more smoke, "…are you taking lessons?"

What the hell does he want me to say? What does he think he knows?

"Well, to be honest, I also want to have skills I can contribute to the Order."

That part was true too, although Sarah remained elusive regarding the complete nature of her motives. "That way I can be useful *and* do something I enjoy. Two birds one stone…you know? It's an American saying."

The countryside passed Sarah in a blur as the car navigated the winding roads from the flight school. Irra took another drag. "I do not like airplanes."

Sarah snickered on the inside. *I wonder why? Are you afraid of heights, perhaps? Is the psychopath afraid of something after all?*

"That's too bad. You're missing a rush up there."

Of course, she wasn't about to tell Irra that she wanted to learn to fly so she could eventually be tasked with transporting new recruits to their 90-day pre-membership assignments. She had overheard someone saying the Order needed pilots, and it had given her the idea. If she could get vetted into that exclusive role, maybe she could figure out the location of some of the Order's secrets – like where they kept the Arachna, the powerful tech that allowed it to track down and eliminate their threats: those with too high a frequency.

Sarah's thoughts raced back to her own time manning the Web, waiting for the Arachna to identify its next target. A shiver carved a path over her skin, like a snake slithering towards its prey. The memories haunted her and lived eternally in her brain – the people, the faces – and they weren't moving out anytime soon. The children were the most difficult to block out. She would see them on posters and in movies and passing her on the street. Everyone looked like them. Her conscience wouldn't absolve her so easily. It wanted her to feel like a piece of garbage, and it was succeeding.

She was no closer to answers about the location of the Arachna or the Order's coveted Skala than she had been months earlier. At this point, getting her pilot's license was her best strategy, and it didn't hurt that she enjoyed every minute and that it meant seeing more of Marv.

"It's not a problem, is it?" She glanced at Irra, hoping for some clue to his intentions.

"No, not a problem. We need pilots. That is why your lessons caught our attention."

Her master plan was bearing fruit, and she felt relieved that this interrogation wasn't related to Everest Cleary. Her cover was intact, for now.

It was dark by the time they entered the downtown core of Paris. "You've been with the Order for six months, yes?" Irra asked, even though he'd done his research and fully knew the answer. "We feel it is time to take your training to the next level." He pulled into an empty space in front of some townhouses in the 3ème arrondissement, then killed the engine and handed Sarah a small black stopwatch. "When I give the signal," he said, "you will have seven minutes from the time you leave the car."

Sarah stared at the stopwatch as she removed it from Irra's giant hand. It was too small to feel so heavy. A thin layer of sweat accumulated on her palms.

"Seven minutes for what?"

Irra reached in front of her and flicked the latch on the glove box. It fell open abruptly and gave Sarah a jolt. A chill ran over her body when she saw the gun, already fitted with a silencer. On top of it lay a key and a photo of a girl who looked so much like her at first Sarah thought she was staring at a picture of herself: caramel skin, curly hair, roughly the same age. She wore a mustard yellow sweater and held a tabby cat in her arms which she snuggled with her cheek. Such a pretty girl, with a bright smile and a beauty mark above her lip, the kind girls would paint on with eye liner.

"You worked in the Web, yes?" Irra asked.

Sarah simply nodded, unable to take her eyes off the picture – off the weapon.

"So, you are familiar with the term 'extinguished'?"

No! Not this!

She could never forget that word. She had hoped that once she left the Web she would be done with that part of the Order. Instead, those memories crept into every dream, turning it into a nightmare, and sent her conscious thoughts on a toxic spiral into a desolate valley of guilt and self-loathing.

But this wasn't the Web. She wasn't in the control room anymore – she was in the game now with the murderers and the plotters. She was one of them as far as they knew, and her life depended on them continuing to believe that.

Sarah knew what Irra was asking, and she also knew that

there was only one way to play this if she wanted to wake up tomorrow. The Order would have the neighborhood surrounded in case she tried to run. She'd be dead within minutes, and they'd kill the girl anyway. Even if she managed to escape, they'd figure out where her loyalties lied and she'd be on the run for the rest of her life, just like Everest. She could say goodbye to any plan of bringing down the Order from the inside.

Or she could do this incredibly horrific act – take an innocent life and live with guilt and self-contempt for the rest of hers; but at least she could buy time and possibly save countless others.

They had her exactly where they wanted her. It wasn't a choice. It was a death sentence no matter what she decided. A death sentence for the girl and a death sentence for her own soul.

Irra threw his cigarette butt out the driver's window. "Is there a problem?"

She was taking too long. He could grow suspicious and eliminate her too, just to be safe.

"The key works?" she asked, trying her best to fake confidence and buy herself a few more seconds.

"Of course. Stupid question."

"What's her name?"

"Does it matter?"

Of course, it matters, you evil bastard!

"And CCTV cameras?"

Irra proceeded to make a call. "Now," he instructed someone on the phone, then turned to Sarah and smirked. "No longer an issue. It's number 24. She's in the kitchen. Music is playing so she won't hear you come in. Seven minutes from when you leave the car." Then, he reclined his seat as if preparing to watch a movie and all that was missing was the popcorn.

Sarah swallowed the lump of saliva that had grown in her throat. She could feel the tears starting to well up in her eyes. If Irra noticed, she'd be blown, and he'd know that the desensitization sessions had failed and that she wasn't one of them, and her brains would indeed be splattered on the sedan's custom leather seats. She grabbed the contents of the glove box, concealed the weapon under her jacket and opened the car door.

Seven minutes.

A lone tear escaped and burned her cheek as it fell, but she quickly brushed it away. Every cell in her body screamed at her: *Just run! RUN! What are you doing? You can't do this. You can't do this!*

Her chest felt weighed down by a boulder as her shaking body struggled to take breaths. This was a decision that would define her forever.

There was no coming back from this.

Down the street, she saw a shadow watching. Waiting. She gripped the railing to hold herself up, pretended to be composed, and ascended the cement steps to number 24, Rue Marais. She could still smell the paint job on the newly refinished forest green front door as she struggled to retrieve the key from her pocket with her quivering fingers.

Maybe it won't work…they would have to abort if it didn't work.

But the key slid effortlessly into the lock. Dread settled into her chest and expanded like a balloon. She put a trembling hand on the knob and rotated right just as the stopwatch vibrated in her pocket.

Six minutes.

Inside the bohemian apartment she smelled something

savory cooking in the kitchen. The cat from the photo sat on the carpeted stairs and observed her with dull green eyes. It meowed once, but other than that it was useless as a security system, and Sarah found herself longing for the deafening bark of her childhood rottweiler. Nothing got past him.

She hugged the walls as she navigated the main floor, admiring the target's taste in décor; in particular, a painted abstract canvas with rich shades of red and orange depicting a barren, desert landscape. Ironically, it made the room feel warm and safe, and Sarah wished she could just lower herself into the velvet sofa and release all her emotions into the pillows.

Five minutes.

The target was in the kitchen just as Irra had said, preparing a meal she would never get a chance to eat. She sang along to a French song on the radio in a raspy but pleasant voice, a little off-key. Sarah watched her graceful dance steps with admiration. She was so young. So lively.

Four minutes.

It's one of us or both of us, Sarah reminded herself. Outside the living room window, the watcher stirred.

She positioned herself in a dark corner behind the dining table and pointed the gun, readying her finger on the trigger. Her heart was pounding. Her head was pounding harder. She felt paralyzed as a blurry haze veiled her eyes.

Three minutes.

Faces returned and filled the guilty vacancies in her mind. *We're here, Sarah. We see you. What will you do, Sarah?*

A coldness overcame her, and Sarah finally understood what it meant to feel the blood freeze in your veins. *What am I doing? I can't do this!*

Suddenly, it was too much. She made up her mind. She'd take her chances on the run. She began to lower her arm.

In that moment, the target turned. The glint of the lights on the barrel of the gun caught her attention. Her eyes grew wide, and a short, pitchy scream escaped her mouth. From her hands, a small bowl filled with green garnish fell onto the tile floor. The shattering sound startled Sarah and she reacted swiftly – the way her Vulturian training had taught her. She raised her arm again, pointing her weapon at the terrified face as their eyes locked.

Neither woman moved as dread overcame them both – for one a fear of dying, for the other a fear of living with her sins. They looked so alike; Sarah felt as if she were a pointing a gun at a mirror. Perhaps that was the reason Irra chose *this* target – maybe this wasn't only about extinguishing a high frequency, but also what was left of her own decent self.

"Please," the target pleaded in a shaky whisper, terror radiating through her voice as she held up her hands. "I have some money…I have some jewelry. I can get it. You can have it. *Please*…"

Two minutes.

Sarah readied her finger once more. Her face felt paralyzed, but the tears kept spilling out. The girl seemed to notice, and her gaze softened. "I have some food too, if you're hungry," she offered kindly, probably mistaking her for a junkie or homeless thief.

You're a good person, Sarah thought, suddenly wishing she was those things instead of what she was about to become. *You can't even conceive of the evil that has brought me here.* She wished she at least knew her name, but maybe that would be harder. It was easier not knowing.

A red laser danced on the cupboards. They would take two shots when the time ran out. That's how they operated.

Kill or be killed. I have no choice.

With one last look at the innocent girl, Sarah took a breath to steady her hand and tried to focus. "It's roasted potatoes," she mumbled to herself, recognizing the familiar smell of rosemary that so often filled her grandmother's house at Christmas and Thanksgiving.

A glint of hope appeared in the girls' eyes at the intruder's apparent humanity. "Yes! It is."

Another tear burned Sarah's cheek. "I'm so sorry," she whispered – to the girl, to the faces, to herself. Then, in synchrony with the final vibration of the timer, she pulled the trigger.

The doctor offered the woman the first smile he'd been able to offer in months.

"At least there's been some change," he told her, glad to be the bearer of positive news for once. Some new areas were lighting up on the scans. Not that it translated to much on the outside or made much sense to a layperson.

"What does that mean?" the women pressed. "All you say is 'some', there's 'some change', it's 'promising'. Just vague notions without any concrete –"

"That's all we know Ms Vidal," the neurologist replied, now ashamed of how little he actually knew and wishing he hadn't smiled at all. Doctors and distressed parents see progress differently. "I know you want more answers. Like you, we hoped it wouldn't take this long for Lise to come out of it. But it's something, some increased brain activity – it comes and goes it seems. It's as if she's fighting whatever is happening to her."

"I just want to know *when* she's going to wake up," Diane

Vidal sighed, sinking into the indented cushion of the armchair next to her daughter's bed.

"I know," Dr. Marchand replied. "I'm sorry I can't give you an answer to that."

He truly didn't have an answer. This case had perplexed him and tested his medical training. Every theory he had devised had been proven wrong, and he couldn't figure out what he was missing – what they were all missing. He wasn't her attending physician – that was Dr. Auclair – but he was nevertheless invested in Lise's case. All the staff were.

"How did this even happen?" the mother asked for probably the hundredth time. "When she arrived here, she was fine, she was speaking. And then she went to the psych ward, and they gave her some poison she probably didn't even need…and now she's in a coma! *How?* She was awake, she was fine…"

"She was experiencing some concerning symptoms of psychosis," the doctor explained. "You heard yourself the things she was saying – alternate dimensions, assassins – probably a psychotic break brought on by witnessing her brother's death. She was inconsolable. The intake doctor thought it best to sedate her, for her own safety. Unfortunately, sometimes medication can have side effects. The truth is, we just don't know what exactly happened."

The mother hung her head in defeat and wrapped her oversized sweater around herself. "That's the problem. You don't know what happens in your own hospital. How am I supposed to trust you?"

When she'd overheard the nurse mention something about 'promising change', her hopes had shot up, again. But her little girl was no closer to coming back to her than the day before. She didn't care about 'increased brain activity.' She wanted to see her daughter's eyes wide open, and hear her sweet voice ask a million questions. She couldn't stand the sound of the monitors and the paging over the intercom a second longer, or the smell of the hospital linens and cheap hand sanitizer. She had barely left the building since the day she buried Julian. Losing one child was unimaginable, but seeing another teetering on the edge of a cliff was another layer of torture.

Lise lay propped up on pillows, as still as a flower in a windless desert. She didn't appear especially ill, and her cheeks still retained a faint rosiness. Her tiny frame appeared lost under the large hospital gown and blankets, her lips dry and scratched from the never-ending parade of feeding tubes.

But her curious, quick mind was on another planet, and nothing the doctors tried so far could awaken it.

"Only time will tell," they kept repeating.

Stupid time, the desperate mother cursed. If only she could turn it back.

***

"You actually feel bad, don't you?" Maeve guessed correctly as she and Tristan Sarazen watched the hospital room feed in the Paris chapter house.

It was a tedious chore for them, and for the guards assigned to keep watch. It had been over three months and Everest Cleary hadn't taken the bait – no sightings of her near the hospital, no Arachna readings for weeks. There had been some activity in Paris the day she disappeared, then others in the days that followed suggesting she travelled east and crossed into Belgium, but nothing unusual after that. It was as if she had vanished off the face of the earth. If the comatose girl wasn't a sufficient lure, Maeve doubted anything was. Perhaps now the Ertu would finally give up on his obsession and cut Everest loose. Maeve, for one, would be quite content to never see her again. *Let's hope she's dead already*, she gleefully contemplated.

But Tristan felt different. Not about Everest, necessarily. He had never felt much for her one way or another. But there was something about the comatose girl – she was just a child, and it was the Order's doing she was lying in a hospital bed instead of playing in a schoolyard. For the first time in a very long time, his conscience was shouting at him that he was part of something hideous, even by his standards.

Tristan had never gone through desensitization sessions like the others. His father assumed he didn't need them since he came from a long lineage of Vulturian blood, groomed in the Order's ways from a young age. Tristan had always showed a certain detachment from normal human emotions and had mostly lacked empathy, so there was nothing to suggest he needed the sessions.

But lately, he had felt off, and if he happened to see a body being pulled out of a desensitization chamber into a recovery room, it left him feeling surprisingly queasy and a touch agitated – foreign feelings that were not going away with time as he had hoped.

He recalled a memory he had long buried of watching from the landing of his childhood Majorca vacation home as his father inspected a box with a severed hand and then handed an associate a wad of money. As a child, he had convinced himself it was a prank. But now, he knew better.

"Just mind your business," he snapped at Maeve. She was beginning to make him nauseous too. "Any news from Switzerland?"

"Nothing. No sign of her."

"You couldn't conceal your delight if someone paid you to," he observed, getting up to pour himself some whiskey.

"No, I couldn't. Pour me one too."

Tristan brought back the drinks and handed one to Maeve. She tapped a long black fingernail on the side of the glass, her deep red hair reflecting in the facets of the crystal. "It's not like we can't find it on our own. We don't need her."

"What, the Skala?" Tristan sneered. "It probably doesn't even exist!"

"But doesn't the existence of the Tiamat offer some assurance that is does? Why would the Aeonian texts lie about one and not the other?"

Tristan had to admit Maeve had a point there. Still, he had his moments when he wondered if it was all worth it – and for something that perhaps wasn't even as powerful as everyone imagined. "Has Tara found out anything about the Skala?"

As the current Sharur, Tara Bahar's clock was ticking. If she ran out of time without finding the Skala, she would be exiled in accordance with Vulturian custom and left to fend for herself in the deserts of the Middle East. A new Sharur would be named to take her place, and Maeve, for one, didn't want to be on the short list. "Nothing," she replied. "And on top of it, her cover's blown."

Tristan chuckled. "Daddy finally figured it out? Shocker."

"Seems that way. But it doesn't matter."

Sure, Tara had incentive – she needed to stay alive. But even if she failed, the Order had other resources. *Many* other resources.

"We have other cards to play," Maeve reminded Tristan, staring him down from under her thick curled eyelashes. "And I hope you won't hesitate when it's time to play them."

CHAPTER 1

Follow the Owls

EVEREST CLEARY

The mud sticks to my boots like a slimy glue as I trek through the rain-soaked woods. It's a 30-minute walk from civilization back to the compound, and once I pass the last gravel road it's just dirt paths through the brush following barely visible navigation markers.

Follow the owls.

I really didn't think I'd need to use them again – not after the time I visited my aunt when I was 13. I had just arrived in Paris and accompanied Uncle Tim and Catherine to Belgium on a bizarre journey into the middle of nowhere. We left the car in a small town and took a bus to the outskirts where we were dropped off on the side of the road, holding our suitcases and surrounded by dense forest. Then, when it seemed things couldn't get any stranger, Catherine headed straight for the brush and began following owl markers etched into trees, while Uncle Tim pointed out all the plants that could potentially give me hives. A half-hour later, we were at crazy Aunt Michaela's front door, and everything made a little more sense.

Bottom line, my family was messed up.

Even though my mother had just passed, Michaela was cold

and unsympathetic, letting insensitive comments slip about how her sister threw away her future for a man who never wanted her. "Johanna was the golden child and look where she ended up. A single mother living in a cheap rental, her brains splattered on the street." There were other horrible comments I've since deliberately pushed out of my mind.

Uncle Tim cut the visit short by two days when he saw how upset I was and chastised Catherine for not sticking up for me. I think both Catherine and Michaela were always jealous of Mom because Mom had something that her sisters didn't seem to possess: a will to be happy, no matter the circumstances. In any case, it was a relief to leave.

And yet, here I am, in the middle of a Belgian forest with a burner phone in my pocket, following owls etched into tree trunks that will lead me to a secluded compound inhabited by two miserable women who come as close to hating me as you could hate family.

A totally healthy situation.

I know the forest rather well by now, but things look different occluded by fog. The wet fallen leaves create a muddy earth soup on the ground. One clumsy slip and they serve as an efficient slide down the slope I've accidentally come upon. Before I'm able to grab hold of something to stop my fall, I'm being catapulted into a mossy mound of earth and hit the ground hard. It takes me a minute to stop seeing double and notice my shoulder throbbing from the impact.

"That's going to bruise nicely," I groan.

As I wipe mud off my cargo pants, I notice the massive boulder I thankfully missed landing on mere inches away. *Maybe my luck's finally turning around.* A marker catches my eye up ahead and I readjust my course.

After another ten minutes navigating the brush, Tru greets

me a half mile from the compound, his tail wagging wildly. I found him wandering in the woods with no collar or tags my second week here. Or maybe he found me. Those days are a bit of a blur now; I wasn't in the best state of mind. There were days I could barely get myself out of bed let alone take care of another living thing. But there was something about this animal bounding over branches in the forest – something about his playful nature despite the gruesome sores on his belly and cuts on his back. He should have been terrified of me, but he wasn't.

His eyes reminded me of Juno's eyes: trusting, loyal, perceptive. But if I stared at them long enough, past the rich hazel of his irises, I saw agony that infuriated me and left me in useless pieces. He needed me, and I needed him. I couldn't let him go. So, he stayed, and over time his welts healed and that pain behind his eyes softened. He's a handsome shepherd mix, reddish brown with a bushy tail like a fox and floppy ears shaped like fuzzy upside-down triangles. And while he's brought much needed joy to my life, I don't feel deserving of any of it.

Michaela was furious of course and said she wouldn't have a filthy creature giving her location away. But after I reminded her that he could be a good guard dog and hunt her some rabbits, she put up less of a fight and agreed to a "trial run." I had to train him to stay silent and not bark at the sight of every squirrel, so now he only barks when there's something novel around. The other day, it was the fattest possum I'd ever seen.

"I was only gone a few hours," I remind him, giving him the attention he's dying for. "Those two aren't that bad." Tru snorts and shakes his head dramatically, calling me out. "All right," I laugh, rubbing his side and making his leg twitch. "I lied; you caught me."

Michaela leans against the front door when we walk up to

the main house. She reminds me of a frontier woman ready to take on the wild west, with tall rubber boots over her faded jeans and a thick white wool sweater stuffed under a fur vest. All that's missing is the rifle – she keeps those inside. She's the oldest of the three Clearly sisters, and her long brown braid is threaded with grey. She has hazel eyes like my grandfather and his generous height. Even if someone did find her out here, at 5'9 and armed, I doubt they'd want to cross her.

Michaele scrutinizes the nearly bare trees. The approaching winter means less foliage and more exposure, so she's increasingly on edge. Finally, satisfied that I haven't brought along any uninvited company, she motions me to come inside.

"Not you," she snaps at Tru who tries to sneak his way in from the cold.

He retreats and tucks his tail. I kneel and rub him behind his ears. "I'll let you in soon," I whisper before leaving him lying on the outdoor mat.

Michaela takes the bag of groceries out of my backpack. "What if it's rabid?"

I roll my eyes while I pull off my muddy boots and place them by the door under the hanging rifle. "If he was rabid, I think we'd know."

Several weapons are scattered around the compound, which is basically a small cottage with an adjoining guest house and a fully stocked subterranean bunker that could easily sustain a few people for several months.

"Besides, no one's claimed him. There are no flyers in town…we can't just leave him somewhere where they'll put him down within a week. I thought you of all people would be happy to have a watch dog."

Michaela grunts. "I'm still not convinced it's a good idea. Just another way for someone to find us. You know how I live, and yet you still find ways to jeopardize all my efforts, always sneaking away to town to buy him food and…" She throws a bag of dog treats onto the table with a disgusted scowl.

"I'm careful, and we need to eat too. We were out of milk, I got some bread and fresh ham, and that jam you like."

But truth be told, I look for every excuse to get away – every possible reason to walk an hour, rain or shine, through shrubs and branches that scrape my face, then along a pot-hole studded road where one bus comes every four hours and sometimes doesn't even stop for me. It makes me feel normal again. I still can't tell anyone my name and conceal myself under a hood most of the time. But at least wandering out there and rejoining humanity helps me remember how life used to be.

How it could be again.

The only reason I come back to the compound is Tru. And there's also the fact that I have nowhere else to go and that an evil global cult is trying to murder me. Minor details.

"Where's Catherine?"

"Sleeping off another migraine. November ruins her. I'm putting on some tea," Michaela says between fits of coughing.

I try to avoid calling either of them "aunt" or "auntie." It implies some mutual affection that simply isn't there. I think they both prefer it that way. Michaela's built up a lot of walls to protect whatever it is she's hiding from the world in her off-the-grid bunker.

Still, sometimes I'll notice glimpses of Mom in both sisters – something about the way they eat their soup or drink their tea when it's hot, forming their lips into little funnels. Or the way they oddly love croissants with both butter and strawberry jam. Or how they hum while they cook, even though their civility is usually short-lived, and they return to insulting each other minutes later.

But in those rare moments I can see past the jaded cynicism to an innocence that still lurks somewhere deep in their psyche, to that secret desire for happiness they can never allow themselves to indulge – the one only Mom seemed to allow.

"My God, Everest, you smell worse than you look!" Catherine exclaims, coming up behind me. "What happened to you?" She's wearing a printed wool sweater, and her half ponytail looks disheveled and off to one side from being slept on. Her skin always appears radiant. Maybe it's thanks to the expensive creams she buys with the rest of Uncle Tim's money and my college fund. Or maybe she just inherited some enviable genes the rest of us Clearys missed out on.

"Just slipped. I'll change."

"Might as well have a tea first," Michaela adds, bringing over the pot. I smile at the surprisingly kind sentiment. Michaela isn't the nurturing type. "Warm up a little," she adds. "I can't afford you getting pneumonia and infecting us all."

Never mind. "Right, we wouldn't want that. Thanks."

Catherine dips her tea bag into her hot water repeatedly and stares at me from across the table. "So, Everest, when are you going to tell me why you're not in Berlin?" she asks, holding my gaze with her puffy eyes as she rests her left elbow on the table and props up her chin.

I try to hide behind the steam escaping my cup. "What?"

"Berlin? For that internship?"

Oh right! That little lie.

It's getting hard to keep up. I never went into much detail when I arrived about why I had made the "stopover." The days crept along, and we barely saw each other, each of us barricaded in separate spaces most of the time, not caring to spend too much time together. I thought I'd gotten away with being evasive. Most of what I've shared with them has been complete fabrication, for obvious reasons, and they seemed to buy it. I get the feeling that Catherine's a little softer towards me, like she might actually care if I'm in some sort of trouble. I guess it's nice if it's true. Of course, she's also the reason I can't afford to go to university anymore, so any fondness I have for her is tainted until she owns up to it and apologizes, at the very least.

"It wasn't what I thought it would be," I lie again. "Terrible work environment, that sort of thing. And I couldn't bear being alone in Montmartre without Uncle Tim, so I came here."

Catherine looks at her sister to get her take on things, but Michaela just shrugs. "I'm too exhausted to try and rip it out of you. But I'm not stupid, Everest," Catherine finally says.

Michaela takes the heat off me by erupting into another one of her coughing fits.

"Maybe you should go to Brussels and see that specialist?" I suggest.

But she shakes her head firmly, then summons a ball of blood-streaked phlegm from the back of her throat and spits it into a napkin. "They just take your money and poison you with chemicals. I'm fine where I am."

"Or they save your life, you know, sometimes."

"Don't waste your breath," Catherine advises, probably having failed at the same plea many times herself. It's the Cleary way – sweep things under the carpet and never talk about it. Don't even walk on the carpet or anywhere near it. And if someone by chance looks under that carpet, pretend you don't see what they see. Even Mom was good at that.

The room is a bit cold despite the fireplace blazing at full force. Dozens of blankets are thrown over chairs and couches and piled high in old chests to make up for it. It's a log structure with traditional carpentry around the kitchen cupboards and along the framing. We look like three creepy statues at a pioneer village wax museum, huddled around a tiny table in dim light, hoping Michaela's generator doesn't run out of juice.

"Well, thanks for the tea," I say, anxious to get back to Tru. I wash my cup, then grab Tru's treats and head for my room, but not before noticing Catherine's suspicious stare follow me out.

CHAPTER 2

Forgotten Memories

My room adjoins the guesthouse, which is connected to the main house by a narrow drafty hallway that always makes me pull my sweater tighter. Once inside, I lock the door and fire up the pellet stove.

All the doors have locks and a bolt. Sometimes I wonder if we're sitting on a stash of drugs or diamonds. I once asked Michaela how she came about owning this strange place, but she just gave me her stern side eye to signal that I'd overstepped. Still, if not for Michaela's paranoia I'd have nowhere to hide, so I guess I should be grateful she's as crazy as she is.

Tru immediately bounds inside when I open the window. He lets me wipe him down with a towel, then jumps onto the bed where he uses his snout to constructs a den in the blanket. I flop down beside him and throw him a treat. His scars are slowly becoming covered with new fur. I know I should be careful with the money I have left, which isn't much, but I can't resist spoiling him. I'm probably one of the few people who ever has.

The wood paneling in the cottage is dated, but cozy. Black

and white photos sit in dusty frames on a dresser. In one photo, Michaela stands in front of a Buddhist temple with a tall, bearded man. He makes an appearance in some of the other photos as well. There's even one with my grandparents – none of the sisters ever talked to them much for reasons that were always very vague. I never liked them much anyway. This family and all their drama.

The laundry basket sticking out of the closet catches my attention. I'm running out of the few clothes I have and can't put off the chore any longer. The basket catches on something as I pull it out. One rough tug and I create a small avalanche of Michaela's boxes and old musty clothes as they topple from the top shelf…along with a bag that causes my muscles to stiffen as it hits the ground.

The black duffle lays there like Pandora's box on top of the heap. I eye it with apprehension as if there's a ticking bomb inside, my legs suddenly feeling weak and wobbly. Other than unpacking my clothes when I first arrived, I'd never touched it again, choosing instead to stash it away and hoping that was enough to erase it from existence.

But the past is not that simple. There's no delete button – no trash bin you can empty when you're done with it. It's always waiting in the shadows, ready to pounce and haunt you again, often at your lowest moments.

I move some things off the top shelf to make more room for the duffle, but the worsening pain in my banged-up shoulder won't let me reach high enough to store it. I gather my strength a second time only to find my hands glued to the straps, unable to let go. *Just open it. It's just a stupid bag. Open it. You know you want to.* I stand frozen with indecisiveness. Finally, I give in and let it fall out of my grasp onto the bed, place my thumb and index finger on the zipper, and give a swift pull.

Tru is first on the scene. He curiously burrows his nose inside and retrieves a sock that I had overlooked. *That's where the matching one was.* I let him have it, and he immediately begins repeatedly chewing it and spitting it out. I reach in and feel around, retrieving objects one by one: the other burner phones Erik had given me…

Erik.

Not a day passes without his face entering my thoughts, eliciting tears I quickly wipe away as my heart shatters. I tried to shut him out; his eyes, his voice, everything that had passed between us. I tried to shut out the Prism, Lise, even Julian – shun them into the darkness of the closet where I could pretend that they never happened, like I had shunned Mom's death into that locked room in my brain. It was a solid plan along with numbing myself with distractions.

But it was easier said than done.

My first few days on the run I was in shambles, and within hours I noticed the light bulbs and glasses starting to shatter as I travelled on buses and stopped at cafes. It was like having a tracking device under my skin that would lead the Vulturians right to me, and I couldn't do anything about it.

Until I placed my hands into the pocket of my jacket and felt it. It had been there all along. Maeve had given me my ticket to staying invisible. *At least she was good for something.*

I twirl Maeve's prized weapon around my right ring finger, it's new home. Of course, initially I couldn't wait to destroy it. Every time I looked at it, I was reminded of the evil and pain the Vulturians had caused, of their diabolical agenda, of their heinous crimes.

But then I realized it was my key to survival.

As I ran from Paris, I thought my grief would rip me into a hundred irreparable pieces. I was too proud and hurt to turn back, and too emotional to stay hidden. I knew I'd lead the Vulturians right to me in a matter of days. So, I started to use the ring on myself.

It was just short intervals to start. I've increased the duration of contact over time, and eventually that familiar feeling of it ripping the essence out of me and turning me inside out lessened, until I became rather desensitized to it. I would never have imagined that I would conjure it up again of my own volition. Yet ironically, as despicable as it is, it's probably the reason I'm still breathing four months later.

After leaving Paris, I hid out in hostels, my bag always packed and one eye open at night. When I didn't cause any lightbulb explosions for a good five days, I knew the ring was working. Being halfway to Belgium and no one having found me yet, I figured it was safe to visit Catherine and Michaela without putting a target on their backs. It was the only place I had to go.

I look at Tru. The sock is dead, and he appears immensely pleased with the fact that there are more holes in it than Swiss cheese. "Don't get any ideas for my other socks," I warn him. "This was a one-time deal." He tilts his head, trying to figure out what I'm saying, then rests it on the dead sock and just stares up at me.

I reach inside the duffle bag again. My fingertips find something smooth and cold, and I pull the object into the light. Unlike the people I left behind, I haven't given the compass much thought at all. It's just a piece of metal I can't figure out. In a way I hate it and the role it played in Julian's death. Other than that, I have no emotional attachment to it.

But now, letting it rest in my hand, the feelings I experienced in the presence of that mysterious flame in the Prism come flooding back. They had been so intense, so pure. So indescribable. Whatever they were or whatever they meant, I don't feel deserving of feeling them again.

My hands tremble slightly, and I recall what they're capable of. What *I'm* capable of. I'm reminded that no matter what remote corner of the world I fall away to I'll never escape what I am.

I'll never escape my potential.

Since arriving at the compound, I've been careful to be as even keel as possible. Even a slight disturbance in my emotional equilibrium could alert the Vulturians, so I try not to feel. Maeve's ring helps, probably more than I care to admit. If I ever sense that I'm losing control, I simply apply it to my skin and let the suction do its work. I've defied the odds by lasting this long, but I know a storm will eventually find me, and when it does, I can't be here anymore. As much as they irritate me, I can't allow Catherine and Michaela to be collateral damage. I need to leave soon and figure it out on my own. I've already stayed too long.

My fingers travel to my neck in a preconditioned reflex that used to bring me comfort, but I find only by bare skin where I once found something else. I locate Erik's pendant in a corner of the bag, covered in lint and dust. Tru carries out his obligatory inspection and, realizing the pendant isn't very chewable nor a danger to me, rests his head back on the bed. As I feel the links of the chain entangled between my fingers, my feelings for Erik start to surface again.

Shut it down. I know my pounding heart won't lead anywhere good, so I place the necklace onto the bedside table and return to pulling things out of the bag: my old dead phone, and another phone I don't immediately recognize. Finally, I realize it belongs to Maeve. It's the phone I took off her at the Salle. I throw it back inside as if burned by it, determined not to let my hate for her make me do something impulsive, like turn it on and call her and tell her what an evil bitch she is.

At least not yet, and not here.

The only thing that remains in the duffle is one of the books I checked out of the Lumus. *Ancient Artifacts of Aeonia.* I'm not sure why I willed it out of the Prism but given the limited selection of interesting reading material at the compound, and the fact that I've now read an entire Encyclopedia Britannica P through S, I welcome the find.

"What do you think, worth a shot, right?"

Tru barely opens an eye. I rub his neck and lay down next to him, his back warming my legs. The book is soft and leather-bound, with gold embossed writing on the cover, and the leading *As* in the title larger than the other lettering, with swirly tails that sweep across the cover like strands of gold hair. I open it up and begin to read what appears to be the history of the Aeonian people, whoever they were, and wondering why I don't remember learning about them in history class.

There is no greater mystery than that of the lost realm of Aeonia – precisely because no one knows of its existence to begin with.

No book has been written about it – except the one you now hold in your hands.

And if you are holding it in your hands, it is not because you have found it...

It is because it has found you, Eridu.

I close the book and read the cover again, confused.

Is this fiction? There's no author. *Strange.*

I open it up again, pull the blanket from under Tru's heavy body to cover my thighs, then settle into the down-filled pillows.

Let us start at the beginning...
The Aeonians led a simple life. Unlike some ancient societies who placed importance on enriching their kingdoms, the Aeonians' primary objective was servitude to and protection of their most sacred possession:
the Skala of Elderann.

My throat goes dry as I do a double take.

The Skala of Elderann.

The Skala? *You've got to be kidding me!*

This whole time, clues about the Skala were right under my nose, in this book? This isn't fiction after all.

The Skala of Elderann.

How did I miss this? How did I not crack this book open sooner?

I haven't thought of the Skala at all, truthfully. I didn't want to be responsible for finding anything anymore – I was only interested in hiding. But now, I want to know everything so intensely that I can barely stop my eyes from skipping three lines ahead.

My pulse races with excitement. The book reads quickly, and I prepare my thumb and index finger on each upcoming page, anxiously awaiting the moment I can flip it over, salivating at the idea of finally knowing. By the last line of the first chapter, I know exactly why I'd willed this text out of the Prism, and why that duffle bag fell out of the closet...and why this book happened to fall at my feet in the Lumus so many weeks ago.

There are no coincidences.

I sit up on the bed, staring at the page to make sure I'm seeing what I think I'm seeing. The answers were right at my fingertips. I continue turning paper, my heart ready to burst through my chest, my brain soaking in everything at a speed I never realized I could handle. I feel my emotions escalating, the excitement pushing up against the surface, ready to erupt into a display of fireworks. I haven't felt this alive in months…

Damn it Everest!

How could I be so stupid? I take Maeve's ring, turn it into the inside of my palm and press it hard against my skin. That despised sensation overtakes me and empties me of everything that I am, of every spark, of every joy, of every desire. When it's done its work, I lie on the bed and stare at the chipped beams on the ceiling, weary and hollowed out. If not for Tru's warning bark I wouldn't even notice the space beside me splitting open, as if spliced by a supernatural knife. It expands to the size of an open door, a blinding light bursting through it. I can do little more than stare.

Am I losing it?

Tru stops barking. From the corner of my eye, I can see his puzzled head turning from side to side. I can't look away from the opening. Something pulls my arm forward to touch it and I watch as my hand disappears into the bright substance. I pull it back and find it's still intact as my pulse throbs in my ear.

Any normal person would be freaking out right about now. But then again, I'm not entirely normal, am I? And I've seen some things that are downright unexplainable, haven't I? I guess that's why I stare at the chasm in space with mixed emotions. Spinning the ring between my fingers, I notice there's something different about it. The suction's stopped. It takes a few more seconds to put the pieces together, and then I realize exactly where my hand travelled to and what's on the other side.

Just as Robert theorized!

My palms feel sweaty as they grip the book. But in moments like these I know there's only one decision I can make. It's the decision I always make, irrespective of the consequences – the only decision Mom and Uncle Tim would have approved of:

Go forth and figure out the rest later.

CHAPTER 3

Out of Place

When I was 12, I attended a charity gala with Mom, courtesy of my wealthy grandparents. Mom had been talking to them for a few months, trying to repair whatever was broken between them. The tickets were some sort of gesture of good will. My grandmother had some designer dresses sent over so we could look the part and not draw awkward stares while we sat at our $50,000 table.

Mom's dress fit perfectly – she looked like a movie star. Mine needed to be taken in a bit here and there, but it was equally gorgeous. I had never felt such exquisite fabric before and kept touching the raw silk and iridescent organza as if to convince myself it was real and that it belonged on someone like me.

The night of the gala, a Maserati picked us up outside our rental apartment and drove us to the hotel where the event was being held. I watched with excitement from behind the tinted window as the other guests arrived. They took photos with practiced poses like professional VIPs, chatting and kissing like they all knew each other – probably from the last gala or some luxurious vacation in St. Tropez. The girls laughed and coyly touched the elbows of the young men dressed in tuxes, while the older women brandished furs and jewels for days.

It wasn't what they had or wore that intimidated me; it was the confidence with which they carried themselves. They looked like they belonged, because they did, and they knew it. I couldn't say the same.

The minute my car door opened I knew I was in trouble. I tripped right out of the gate and was thankfully saved from embarrassment by the driver. We didn't stop for pictures, but just walked awkwardly and silently past the step-and-repeat to the main ballroom, Mom squeezing my hand in reassurance while looking just as uncomfortable as I felt.

I spent the rest of the night feeling like an imposter and barely eating, despite the abundance of expensive gourmet food. A natural conversationalist, Mom was able to carry on with my grandmother and the boho-artsy man sitting next to her. Every so often, my grandmother would flash me a forced smile and I would wait to see if her face would crack this time. My grandfather didn't talk to me at all, or even make eye contact.

At one point, a group of girls started talking to me in the bathroom as they touched up their make-up. They were around my age and told me they loved my dress. I mean, who wouldn't? It was a showstopper. For a moment I felt like I could be one of them. Like I belonged.

Until they launched into revelations about yachts and lake homes, extra credit courses in Tuscany, and frivolous complaints about the lack of low-fat options at their country club smoothie bar. I was instantly reminded that theirs wasn't a world I could come close to understanding. I was an imposter once again.

Mom and I sat uncomfortably through the auction, watching

diamond clad wrists raise paddles to bid thousands on fancy items that would be later recouped as tax write-offs. Our silence continued in the car-ride home after a cold goodbye from my grandparents. We never spoke of that gala nor saw my grandparents again. When we got back to the apartment, we cuddled up in blankets watching the first half of *The Sound of Music* before falling asleep, and wondering why we had wasted our time when happiness was so easy to find right where we were.

I often wondered what my grandparents' true motives were for inviting us that night. Was it out of kindness or was it a punishment – a cruel joke to make us feel misplaced and small. Whatever it was, it would be insincere to insist that night didn't leave a mark. Because every time I feel like I don't belong, that memory comes flooding back. I can even smell the roasted red pepper spread on the appetizer table and the cologne of the waiter who served us. I can smell the shallow hypocrisy of society's elite. But more than anything, I feel the sting of rejection.

And that's why it's on my mind in this moment as I find myself back in the Prism, feeling like an imposter yet again.

The enormous daffodil blooms droop and sway on their thick stems in the subtle breeze. The portal, or whatever it was, released me into a part of the Climbing Gardens I've never visited before. I had barely scratched the surface of the expansive maze when I first entered the Prism, and never had the opportunity to wander too far within it.

Maeve's ring rubs between my fingers. There's no doubt that its evil power is what got me here. All the potential I'd siphoned off over these last few months had to be stored somewhere. It was, after all, how Robert theorized the Vulturians were getting into the Prism – by harnessing the positive potential in others.

At least he'll be pleased that I proved his hypothesis. Of course, I'll have to face him first, and everyone else.

Like Erik.

I'll have a lot of explaining to do, including how I got here, which won't be easy considering I've already forgotten where I came in from. More importantly, I don't exactly know how I'm going to get back!

Leave it to me to create another messy situation.

***

I estimate it's been close to 30 minutes, but I can't be sure with the Prism's warped experience of time. After countless frustrating detours and dead-ends, I'm nearing my breaking point. *Will yourself out of here! Use your mind.* I try again, and after several more turns finally find the main entrance to the gardens.

In my haste to get out, I haven't really given myself the opportunity to appreciate my surroundings. But now, seeing the Prism unfold before me after all this time, my pulse quickens.

To cope these last few months, I tried relentlessly to rid my mind of thoughts or memories of this place and everything within it. It would have been too painful to remember everything I was giving up. But now, with the perfectly warm sun on my face and the vivid colors dancing on my pupils, I can't hold back the floodgates any longer. Weightlessness overcomes me and that sensation of unadulterated happiness explodes in the depths of my soul.

I'm back! I'm really back!

The book on Aeonia is still in my hands, and I protectively bring it close to my chest as I place one foot after the other on the lush carpet of grass. Weaving between the serene and joyful faces of the Wakers, I can't help wondering if they can see me for what I am. But if Maeve could fool everyone, maybe I can too.

Despite my slightly disoriented state, I manage to traverse one of the tunnels leading out into the Luminary courtyard where the sight of the impressive structure steals my breath just as it did when I first laid eyes on it. The blinding smooth white limestone seems to glow against the rich emerald foliage of the surrounding tree canopies. It all looks the same and yet feels foreign.

Because it isn't the Prism that's changed – it's me.

Inside, the Luminary continues to be a popular destination. I maneuver between excited Wakers and locate the small lecture hall on the far side of the interior courtyard. The ordinary brown door stands tucked behind a pillar, with no number or fancy plaque. Yet I know it leads to the jewel of the building where the secrets and mysteries of the Prism wait for me. The only question is, will I get in?

"Everest?"

I spin around to stare into the red frames of Gill Bennex's spectacles and startle to find him much closer to my face than I'd anticipated.

"Gill!" I gasp, jumping back. Then I smile, calm my nerves and in the next second impulsively throw my hands around his neck. He looks confused when I let him go. "Sorry," I say, "I don't know why I did that. Haven't been back in a while. It's nice to see a familiar face."

Gill grins awkwardly, narrowing his eyes at me a little. "Good to see you too Everest. I was wondering where you were. Everything is ok, I hope?"

I don't know, I answer silently. "Just, you know, life. But I'm back now."

His face brightens and he nods eagerly, then glances up at

the rows of balconies. "Well, I've got to get back to the Lumus. Say, did you ever find that book you were looking for? Something about a ring, I think." He motions to the book I'm still hugging tightly. "Is that it?"

Did I ever find it! "Yeah, I think I found what I needed. Thanks Gill."

"Oh good, good. Would love to read it sometime." He tilts his head sideways to read the book spine. "Aeonia…hmmm. Never heard of it. Maybe I'll pick up a copy. Well, I'll see you around Everest. Glad you're back!"

I doubt there's a copy of this book, Gill, but you're welcome to try.

I watch him depart with an aching sorrow in my heart. The last time I had seen him I was a part of the Sentry. I had a purpose. Erik and I were a team.

And then I ruined everything.

Protected from the threat of the Vulturians tracing my frequency, I finally allow myself to feel the weight of those decisions. It's all clear now. I blamed Erik because I needed a target for my rage. Since I couldn't hurt the Vulturians, I hurt him and ran like a coward because it was easier than staying. I allowed myself to be a victim just so I could justify my destructive thoughts and feelings. What a selfish and petty child I had been. *Will he even want to see me now?*

Inside the empty lecture chamber the curtains remain drawn, as before. One table lamp illuminates the lecture area. I close the door and wait for the clicking sound that signals it's locked behind me, then make my way towards the podium. It's been a while since I've decoded the labyrinth puzzle that will allow me access into the Citadel, but I'm confident I can remember it. It's etched into my brain like a brand. I move the pieces into place, briefly second guessing myself on the second-last one. *No, it's right, right? Yes, it's right.* I commit, then slide the last decal into place to reveal the map of the labyrinth, crossing my fingers that it hasn't changed since I've been gone.

To my relief, the podium slides aside. I release my breath as the staircase appears, each step darker than the last as it descends beneath the floor. Without hesitation, I step into the darkness and seal myself inside, scrambling the puzzle and returning the podium to its original place.

So far so good.

Having renewed faith in my memory, I take the turns confidently until at last, I come face to face with the Citadel doors. *Can I just walk in like this? What if I'm not welcome anymore, after all this time?* Behind that door are the faces I've missed. I can no longer relegate them to the dark corners of my closet or pretend they aren't real. I want them back. All of them.

But especially one.

My legs feel shaky as I approach the bulky steel handles. I suddenly realize that I've felt odd since arriving, experiencing more discomfort than the Prism previously allowed. *Probably because I entered through the Vulturian portal.* Desperate to stop feeling like a victim and face my past, I open the door a crack and listen to the hum of the conversation inside.

The group is seated. I see some new members, including Jenna, which makes me smile. *It's about time!* Robert is addressing the group. He's the only one standing.

"…going with the chapter houses and breaching their security?"

"We're getting close." That sounds like Shahina. "We have some ideas on how to get inside. And we've been able to track some of the activity coming out of the Paris chapter, thanks to Erik giving us the coordinates."

"And?" I recognize Jason's impatient tone immediately. I guess he hasn't lightened up.

"It's not that simple," Ethan answers. "There's a multitude of signals. But it seems the Paris chapter is some sort of hub. We've located signals streaming into France from several global chapters."

"Do you think they're tracking us from Paris?"

"I don't know. But they're definitely busy over there."

Robert prepares to sit, but quickly straightens when he sees me standing at the door. *Too late to change course now.* The other heads turn toward the sound of my footsteps. I walk slowly through the chamber and study the curious faces, finally settling on one.

Erik sits in his usual seat and stares at me wide-eyed. I can't help but stare at him for a moment, unable to decide which emotion to feel. I settle on relief that he's alive and emotionally well enough to find his way back here, then look away in embarrassment and head to the opposite side of the table where a beaming Jenna has already pulled up a chair for me. She leaps up and nearly suffocates me with a tight hug, speechless for probably the first time since we've met. I giggle as she chokes me. "Missed you too!"

Once she releases me, she switches to a stern expression. "You could have called!" she hisses quietly.

"Everest, finally," Robert adds as he approaches, one leg off step and trailing. *Why is he limping so much?* At least he looks pleased and not furious.

I eye the room with apprehension, unsure if I'm still welcome. "Is it alright that I'm here?"

Robert's smile broadens. "Of course! You're Sentry. There's always a place for you." His bright eyes look glassy. I feel like he wants to hug me too, but instead he touches my arm gently, then nods and allows me to take my seat.

The table is bigger now to accommodate our growing

numbers. I nod at the faces I know well, including Simon and Hadid. Petra gives me a rare though hurried smile that shows teeth, her hair still as light as I remember it.

"You've been busy," I observe, trying to break the awkward silence and hoping everyone will stop staring at me. Some give me welcoming nods while a few appear puzzled over who I am. I nearly laugh when I look at Jenna again, her lips spread into a smile so wide she looks as if she'll be ejected out of her chair out of pure delight, like on one of those slingshot rides at the fair.

Fox sits next to her, wearing a grin of his own. "It's good to see you Everest," he says. "Took you long enough." His long hair is tied up, and he still gives off that care-free surfer dude vibe with the collection of hemp bracelets around his wrists. I knew he and Jenna would be glad to see me. They weren't the ones I was worried about.

I meet Erik's gaze from across the table. His eyes still glow that brilliant blue, and physically he's the same person I remember. His hair still settles in subtle waves on his head, and just seeing him makes goosebumps appear on my lower arms. He's still so handsome, still has that presence about him.

But there's a change in his energy. It feels solemn and dampened, and the guilt eats at me as I realize I might be the cause of that. His lips move to a half-smile. I respond in kind, then quickly lower my eyes, unsure what message to convey to him, all the while wondering if my rapidly beating heart is audible to the entire room.

"This is Everest," Robert announces to catch up the new members. "She's been away for a while. But we're glad she's found her way back, hopefully to stay." Robert seems to plead, and I feel guilty again, this time for letting him down too. I smile weakly in return, not sure if I'm able to promise anything.

"I suppose we'll move along then. We were just catching up on developments," Robert informs me. "As you can see Everest, we've expanded. You know Jenna of course. We've also added Henrietta, Kalai and Dimitri…" Robert spits out at least five more names as I try to keep up and pair them with the faces. "We're working on identifying where the Vulturians are tracking us from and have some theories. Still in the dark about everything else, including the Skala or how they're getting in. That's a short summary for you."

The book rests on my lap. I'd almost forgotten that I had it with me. For a moment I'm terrified to reveal what I've learned. It chose me, and I'm wary of trusting anyone with it. Trust isn't exactly something I have a lot of these days.

But what the hell am I going to accomplish alone? At least the Sentry is a team, and no one ever won a war without an army behind them.

"I think I can help on that front," I offer with hesitation, placing the text on the table. "Um, it's nice to meet everyone new, by the way." I clear my throat. "Anyway, I um…came across this in the Lumus before I…took a break." *Sure, let's call it that.* "I think the Prism wanted me to find it. Do you want details or Coles notes?"

Petra scrunches up her nose. "What is a Coles notes?"

"Never mind. Details it is." I look at Erik again. He's studying the book. I long for him to look at me the way he did before, beginning to appreciate the extent of the void I've felt without him.

"The text speaks of a place called Aeonia," I continue. "It seems to be an Eden-like city that existed even before the time of ancient Sumer. It was an island, literally and figuratively, in that it is — *was* — protected from negative mind states by a powerful monolith stone and shield," I inhale and exhale a breath before finishing the sentence. "A shield known as the Skala of Elderann."

The room goes silent. I pause, letting the information sink in. The stunned faces say it all.

"You're kidding!" Fox cries. "That's the thing, right, the thing they want! Does it tell you what it is?"

"Yes, and it's a lot of things," I answer, trying to figure out the best place to start. "It was revered by the Aeonians as a mystical force and spiritual catalyst of some kind – a source of positive potential, or Aura, as they called it. They were the Skala's protectors as well as the keepers of another stone monolith of immense power – the Skala's nemesis and antithesis: the Tiamat." I look down at my finger – at Maeve's ring. "They were created together at the beginning of time – one for the darkness, one for the light. The book describes the Skala as being clear in appearance – so clear that the Aeonians were said to see into their very essence if they looked upon it and even see the past and future.

"The Tiamat, on the other hand, was composed of a kind of occluded pearlescent stone and had the power to drain potential when in contact with the human form. The Aeonians feared it could extract their spirit, so they kept it hidden – encased in a granite tomb. They buried it in the caves under the city where it couldn't harm anyone."

I catch Erik staring at the ring on my finger. He looks up at me with a creased brow as if to say, *What in the bloody hell, Ev?*

"In order to ensure the Skala's protection," I continue, ignoring Erik's puzzled expression, "the Aeonians had to lead very chaste lives, bound by a strict moral code. It was the only way they could ensure that the monoliths didn't end up being used for evil. They took their responsibility very seriously. That is, most of them did.

"A small sect resented this duty. They wanted freedom to experiment with the dark energy of the Tiamat, to act in ways that went against the code of Aeonia. The leader of this sect, named Parem, had a dark, powerful potential and wanted to unleash it in ways the Aeonian moral code would not allow. Parem and his followers escaped to Sumer one night, and returned months later with more followers and ships, poised to destroy Aeonia and take the Skala and Tiamat for themselves. The negative energy they brought into Aeonia was so intense that it created an immense earthquake, which broke the granite barrier that encased the Tiamat. Parem used his potential to manipulate the Tiamat to a smaller size, and took it with him, his plans to destroy the Skala thwarted by the earthquake.

"Freed from the limitations of the Aeonian code, the Tiamat fed Parem's power for years. It is written that he could even shape-shift, often taking a vulture form. But the Skala was holding him back, forever balancing the Tiamat, the ying to its yang. It would never allow Parem to fully channel all the Tiamat's dark energy. So, Parem and his followers plotted to finish the job and destroy the Skala for good, hoping that with the Skala out of the way, the Tiamat's power would help them dominate.

"Thankfully, before they could accomplish this, one of Parem's followers had reservations and warned the Aeonians. When the Aeonians heard of Parem's plan, they made the ultimate sacrifice. It's unclear how, but they created a powerful event which flooded the island and caused Aeonia and the Skala to be buried under water, never to be found. Parem arrived with ships to an open sea, and the book says his fury created a tsunami so devastating it wiped out 20 kingdoms along the Mediterranean coast."

You could hear a pin drop in the room as everyone stares at

me, no one daring to stir. And I haven't even gotten to the good part yet.

"With the power of the Tiamat behind him," I continue, "Parem created the Vulturian Order and devoted the rest of his life to seeking out the Skala, naming a successor – an Ertu – to replace him after his death. The Tiamat was placed in a secret location, manipulated back to its original strength and size, chipped away to make magical relics, and heavily guarded. The Vulturians have been looking for the Skala ever since, to finish what they started thousands of years ago."

Every single mouth around the table hangs open. Not surprising, considering I've just dumped a whole new chapter of fascinating ancient history and mythology onto their laps, teeming with references to alluring underwater lost treasure, super villains, and sources of immense power. It's a lot.

"The Tiamat is drawn to the same potential the Skala emits – the positive force," I add, tying it all together. "That's how it finds us. That's how they use it. The two monoliths are forever bound from the moment of their dichotomous creation. The Vulturians developed the Arachna technology to home in on this psychic connection between the monoliths and pinpoint the location of the potential source." I slip Maeve's ring off my finger for the first time in months and feel pressure ease in my head as I liberate myself from it. "These have likely been passed down through generations, used to drain the potential out of their targets. No doubt, they've helped Vulturians amass great wealth and power, win wars, gain influence – all things we already know."

"And you just happened to find this book and gain all this very specific information that none of us have ever found, just like that?" Jason wonders doubtfully.

"Actually…it found me," I reply, leaving out the part about

the book literally falling on me and not reading it until now. *No one needs to know that embarrassing detail.*

"Convenient," he huffs.

"Don't start!" Erik's first words of the meeting release a thick cloud of tension I have no doubt is felt by everyone in the room.

Jason straightens in his seat. "Ok, fine. It found you. And if it's all true then great, we know more of the puzzle. But what I still don't understand is, if they're as evil as this book suggests, how the hell are the Vulturians getting in here?"

"It's pretty obvious, actually," I answer. "Robert already figured that out. The rings – it seems the Tiamat can't handle too much potential once it's siphoned off. When it reaches a certain threshold the energy creates a chasm in space time, perhaps because the potential within is trying to connect with the Skala somehow."

"A chasm in space time?" Shahina repeats. "Isn't that a little far-fetched? How can we be sure about any of this?"

I lock eyes with Robert and hope I'm not making a mistake revealing my new imposter status.

"Because…it's how I got in."

CHAPTER 4

Hope Found and Lost

There's a lot of chatter from around the table, some members intrigued, others concerned by my use of a tool of great evil on myself.

Petra looks less than thrilled with me, but then again that's just her face. "You siphoned off your own potential with *that* thing?"

"I had to. I needed to stay off their radar and I couldn't control my potential on my own."

"Should we be worried that they can track you now, that they'll find us all?"

I didn't think of that.

"I didn't notice anything," I reply, feigning confidence and trying to calm anxieties. "If they didn't find me for four months, I don't think we have anything to worry about here. I also took something else off Maeve. Her phone." I look to Ethan. "If you can crack it, maybe we can get something valuable off of it."

Ethan nods. "But I don't have the equipment in the Prism. And not everyone can take things in and out of here like you can."

I forgot about that. "I'll get it to you," I promise. "You're in…"

"Stockholm."

"Oh."

"But I'll be in Paris tomorrow to work with Yoshi and Shahina on the chapter house scans. Can you get it to me there?"

Paris. Looks like fate is calling me home. I nod silently. It was inevitable, I suppose, and it's probably no longer safe for my aunts now that I've created a portal to another dimension in their guest house.

"This is excellent progress," Robert adds, his face bright with intrigue. "You bring us vital information Everest. Fascinating, truly. I wonder why no one's ever found that book before." His voice trails off as he asks the question everyone's wondering about: Why now? Why has this all been revealed now? Why me, again?

I recall the first page of the text: *It has found you, Eridu.*

Eridu. Is that me? *What am I?*

Despite the doubts and questions and apprehension, I must admit it feels good to be back in the fold contributing something. It won't bring Julian back or fix everything that the Vulturians broke – that *I* broke. But being useful is more honorable than wasting away feeling sorry for myself in a forgotten forest.

Robert does a round table and finally dismisses us. I hang around knowing he'll want to talk to me, and I see Erik rise from his seat. I wait like a desperate schoolgirl at a dance for him to find me, but he approaches Fox and Petra instead, leaving a wanting pit in my stomach.

"Everest," Robert says, causing me to turn around. His eyes convey joy and sadness. "Young lady, you had us all very worried. We thought they had taken you. *I* didn't…well, maybe a little. In any case, we're all glad you're back."

His sincerity comes through his kind eyes. Part of me senses that he cares about me differently than the others, although I still can't pinpoint the exact sentiment.

"Thank you, Robert. Me too," I reply, noticing his limp again.

"The Prism has been deteriorating Everest," he explains when he catches me staring at his leg. "Injuries, illnesses…we feel them more now. The more negative energy seeps into our oasis, the more the Prism will continue to decline. It makes our mission here quite time sensitive."

Deteriorating. I knew it had started, but it hadn't occurred to me that it could get worse. *That* much worse.

I look around the room. At least not much has changed within the Citadel. The stone walls look pinker for some reason, but that might just be the light or my memory catching up.

"Are you safe?" Robert inquires.

I laugh at the question. "Given the circumstances, probably more than most. My aunt lives off the grid in Belgium, near an obscure town called Bruine. We're literarily in the middle of nowhere. There isn't even a driveway. Just owl markers on trees."

"That's good. Maybe she's onto something all the rest of us missed." His gaze rests on the text in my arms. "Would you mind if I borrowed it for a short while? I'd like to have a read myself."

"Of course," I hand the book to him. "Keep it as long as you need. One more thing…"

He raises an eyebrow.

"The book, it speaks of another text. The guiding spiritual text of the Aeonians, said to hold universal truth. The *Anu Ki Zu.* Does that ring a bell at all?"

Robert wrinkles up his forehead in confusion.

"I guess that's a negative."

"Perhaps, it may be that way for a reason," he replies. "There may be knowledge contained within it that the world is not ready for, nor should have access to, given our propensity to use our powers for evil time and time again. *Anu Ki Zu*…no, I can't say that I've ever heard of it. The Lumus –"

"I haven't had a chance to look, but I'm not holding my breath. I have a feeling this one will be much more difficult to find."

I feel a tap on my shoulder, and turn to find Fox, Petra and Jenna. First thing's first – Jenna's second hug, which there is no escaping. She rocks me back and forth as she cuts off the circulation in my arms, and for her sake I try not to let my disappointment show as I watch the back of Erik's head disappear through the Citadel door without so much as a glance at me.

"Like Jenna said, you could have called and told us you were alive," Petra says flatly with some anger. Then her face softens a little and the wrinkles on her forehead even out. "But I'm glad you are alive Everest. The others had hope, but I admit, I thought you were dead."

She says it in such an indifferent manner I almost laugh out loud. Typical Petra. "I'm sorry. I wanted to call…" But I don't have a good enough reason, so I leave the sentence incomplete. "I don't know what the next day will bring though. I'm worried that if I use my potential in the real world, they may track me easily."

"Then use just enough and stay on the move," Petra advises stoically, forever the pragmatist. "If you manage things, you can outrun them, at least until you can control your potential or we find a way to stop them once and for all. Don't worry – we'll help you control it. It just takes practice." Petra pauses and looks down at the floor. "Listen, about Julian…we were all devastated. We are so sorry about what happened to him."

That's right. The day Julian died was the last time I saw any of them. "It wasn't your fault," I assure Petra, then recall how tormented she looked for not figuring out the danger sooner. "There was nothing any of us could have done."

I know that now. Deep down I always knew that. But I needed to be angry at something. I needed to punish someone, including myself. Erik was the other victim of my fury, and the last person who ever deserved it. No wonder he didn't hang around to talk to me. *What a fool I've been. What a complete fool.*

Fox reads me like a covert psychic. "You really broke him, you know. He's not the same."

I feel a jackhammer carving out a crater in my stomach. "I know."

He puts a comforting hand on my shoulder. "Well, now that you're back, please fix it. I miss my 'mate'."

I nod, looking down at my feet. "Will he even speak to me?"

Jenna takes my hand. "It's Erik," she says kindly. "What do you think?"

***

Cascada feels like an alien planet to me now. Gone are the whispers of the falls and the crisp greenery of the foliage. They exist, but just outside my experience of them. As I perch on the edge of the boulders next to the hidden entrance to the Citadel, all I can see is Julian's fading face. All I remember is the shock, the tears, the destabilizing fury. The beauty and magic of the Prism evades me, visible only through a fog of guilt and regret.

I remember as a child playing with one of Mom's VHS movies. I pulled out the ribbon and used it as a necklace, giggling at the sound of the crunching sound between by hands. It was a mangled mess. Even though Mom tried to stuff it back into the case, the film never worked again. What if that's all I'll ever be now: a mangled, unfixable mess of regrets and memories, static pictures on a crumpled-up film strip?

A delicate gust brushes against my skin causing something pure to come alive within me for a sliver of time. I try to stay in that feeling but can't hold onto it, and regretfully start to make my way back towards Castellum after wiping the wetness from my cheeks. As I turn to leave, I notice I'm not alone.

Erik sits on the opposite side of the waterfall, elbows resting on his knees, concealed by tall grasses that sway soothingly around him. For several painful moments we simply stare at each other. I try to make out the expression on his face, but he remains stoic, barely blinking as he looks straight through me as if I'm invisible. My pulse throbs in my ears, longing for his smile to light up his face and bring forth his dimples. But it never comes. Instead, Erik turns his head away to look at the clearing without so much as a nod or twitch of an eyebrow.

Stunned at how different he seems, I approach slowly and sit down nearby, flattening the tall grass to make a pillow. It pleasantly tickles my arms and the bare skin between my pants and shoes. I pull out a reed nervously, watching another immediately grow in its place, then finally find my voice.

"It's so good to see you." I've never meant anything more.

Erik turns his bright blue eyes in my direction. He seems to be deciding how to respond, opening his mouth then closing it again several times. Finally, he decides on a silent nod and looks away again.

That's it? "So, that's all I get, huh?" *What is happening? This isn't him.*

Erik breaks from his robotic posture and lowers his head.

"I'm glad to see you too, Ev," he replies, bringing his hands to rest on the back of his neck. "It's just…different than I thought it would be."

"Different?" *Different how?*

All this time I imagined I had been the one letting Erik go. I had always assumed that when I was ready – *if* I was ready – he would be there waiting, same as I left him. In my self-absorbed world, the painful alternative had never occurred to me.

Erik looks at me again. In his glossy eyes I can see my reflection, full of desperation and longing for that spark between us to ignite again. Yet his gaze seems empty and tired.

"I imagined seeing you again a hundred times," he says. "Finding you, seeing you here. It was the only thing that kept me going…the only thing that kept me coming back." He pauses and purses his lips. "But when I saw you…I don't know. Damn it, Ev!"

He runs his hand through his hair, then rests his elbow on his knee again. "You just left, with no warning! After everything we went through, you just trashed it like it was garbage – like it meant *nothing*! You treated me like you treated Maeve."

His facial muscles tense up. "When I saw you, I think I finally allowed myself to be angry at you for the first time. I spent all these months blaming myself for things I never meant to happen, or things that never happened at all – for things that were out of my control. But now…I'm just tired Ev. Emotionally drained. And all these months, you couldn't even give me a ring to tell me you were alive. Do you know what that did to me? Did you even care at all?"

The pit in my stomach I felt earlier has just grown exponentially, and I find myself wishing it was a black hole that could swallow me up.

"I'm sorry Erik."

Erik chuckles and throws back his head. "Is this the first time you feel sorry? It never occurred to you before that what you did was bloody awful?"

I don't know how to take Erik's tone. He's never been angry at me like this before, and I'm completely caught off guard. I know I took him for granted. I know what I did was wrong and spineless and stupid, and that I stole time away from him and relegated him to a state of unbearable limbo as he questioned whether I was dead or alive for months. I hate myself for it. I thought about myself and my feelings more than his. I'd wanted to bury the memories, erase the past to protect myself like a selfish coward when Erik deserved better. And now, all I want is to hold him and tell him I love him and have him kiss me and comfort me the way he used to. I want to touch his face and hear his infectious laugh and signature wit.

But I know I have no right to any of it anymore because I decided to place more importance on my own childish insecurities. I've really messed this up.

I'm scared to touch him and worried he'll pull away but find a small speck of courage and place my hand awkwardly on his arm. "You're right," I admit, my voice shaky, "I was so lost, so angry and selfish. I know I hurt you – but until now I didn't realize how much. You deserved better than that. Please, Erik…I thought of you every single day. I tried to forget you, but I couldn't. And I'm so glad to see you – you have no idea!"

Erik's frown lines seem to soften as he listens. "You could have called. You had the burner phones. No one could track you."

I let my lungs fill with air and breathe out loudly. "I know. I couldn't. There's no good reason. I just…I guess I wasn't ready. I was scared."

"You know," Erik adds, looking out at the place where Julian vanished, "I loved him too. I come here almost every day, to this very spot, where everything started to unravel. I stare at that clearing for hours, thinking of what else I could have done. Thinking that maybe if I force it, I can turn back time and prevent what happened. It's a stupid hopeless daydream, but it's gotten me through." He shakes his head a few times and picks at some moss. "I would have stayed by your side no matter what, you know."

I nod, feeling sick. "I know. I wish I had made different choices."

He continues looking ahead. "I'm glad you're ok. I know things are…awkward and complicated right now between us, but we need to put that aside for the sake of the Sentry. We both want the Vulturians punished. Let's just move forward and be friends, ok?"

Friends.

The word strikes me like a dagger, and suddenly that black hole in my stomach is made of fire and burning lava. *We can't just be friends! Why is he saying this?* Is our relationship as mangled and unfixable as that VHS tape? Did I really do that much damage?

"Right, yeah…." I recoil my hand, yearning for more of him yet too afraid to admit it to his face. "Are you going back to Castellum?" I ask, hoping we can at least walk together.

But he shakes his head. "I'm going to hang around here for a while longer," he replies, dashing my hopes.

"Ok. See you around then." I get up quickly and make my way through the grass, choking back tears as my heart breaks all over again. When I'm far enough away, I let the floodgates open.

CHAPTER 5

Reset

The Promenade hasn't changed much. It's still vibrant and buzzing with the boundless energy of its eager visitors. The beach umbrella canopies flutter ever so subtly. I take in the sea views and let my toes trace patterns in the sand, then wait for the waves to erase them before I repeat them again. People offer me cheerful greetings as they pass, and I once again wonder if anyone can see the scarlet letter of my pretender status.

I take a stroll and arrive at Stella's. As I peek through the bistro window, I glimpse Jenna and Fox sitting at a table on the patio. Thankful for some familiar faces, I walk in and over to them, noticing as I approach that Jenna's leaning in and giggling more than usual. Before I realize what's going on, Fox leans in to kiss her, the sweet moment abruptly ending when Jenna sees me staring at them uncomfortably.

I grin sheepishly. "Bad time?"

Jenna blushes. "Uh…no, of course not. Come. Sit. We were hoping we would see you. We were, um…"

"Oh, I think I got it. What took you guys so long?" I tease approvingly, giving her a wink.

"Why does everybody say that?" Fox asks, throwing up his arms. "Was it that obvious before?"

"What, that your childish banter was just shameless flirting? Yeah, it was obvious to everyone."

Jenna looks around the bistro. "Where's Erik? Did you speak to him? Tell me you spoke to him!"

She must notice my eyes well up because she instantly pulls me in. "I really messed this up Jenna. I'm such an idiot," I mumble into her shoulder.

"It's ok," she replies, "just give him time. He's been through a lot – with his brother, then you. And now you being here…We sort of figured this might happen. Erik, he gives everything of himself. It takes a toll on a person."

"Yeah, when he's let down, I think he takes it a little harder than most of us," Fox adds, looking disappointed. "Just be patient. He'll come 'round."

"I don't know," I respond doubtfully. "I don't know if he'll ever look at me the same way again. You should have heard him. It just feels so permanent."

Fox eyes me with that look of pity everyone hates to receive. "He'll get there," he assures me. "On another note, how does it feel, to be back?"

The Prismatic emits a gentle roar as the waves crash against the pier and the docks. I'd numbed myself and kept myself away from this place, partly because I didn't think I deserved it, partly because I couldn't risk feeling what I needed to get back to it. But being back is simply indescribable, as it always was.

"Do you have to ask?" I reply, allowing myself to smile again. But my smile quickly fades. "This is just for today though. Part of the reason I had to use Maeve's ring was so that no one would find my aunt's place. I couldn't put them in danger. They may drive me crazy, but I don't dislike them enough to lead the

Vulturians to their door. I guess I'll have to leave now, make my way home. But until I figure out how to control my potential, I don't think I'll have enough stored up to open that portal again. I don't even know how this all works – or how I even leave here."

Jenna squints up at the climbing balconies of Castellum visible in the distance. "Did you visit your dimension yet?"

"What? No. I mean, I haven't thought about it. Can I?"

"It's your potential that got you here Everest. Maybe it works the same as before. That's where I'd start." Jenna takes a bite of her margherita pizza. "It's still there, you know. That's how Erik knew you were still alive. He checked every day."

I cringe with guilt at the thought of Erik knocking on my door every day for three months only to be met with defending silence. "I'll check it out. Might be the only way I can get back."

"Are you really heading to Paris?" Fox asks.

"I promised Ethan I'd get Maeve's phone to him. And I need to go somewhere."

He alternates his gaze between my face and the ring. "Do me a favor, stop using that thing on yourself, will you? I can't even imagine what it's doing to you. And I don't want anyone to track you with it. It jeopardizes everything, and all of us."

I nod as I shift my weight uncomfortably in my seat, unwilling to promise anything out loud. Fox is right. But I may not have a choice if I want to stay alive, or at least get far enough away from the bunker.

Maybe just one more time.

***

Wakers drift in and out of the Forum portals in a never-ending stream. After parting with Fox and Jenna, I wander for a while on my own, exploring the familiar corners of Eden Hall. After that, I visit the Lumus, where my attempts to locate the *Anu Ki Zu* are predictably unsuccessful.

I lean up against one of the columns in the Forum, watching as the weightless mist envelops all who pass through the portals.

It's your potential that got you here.

Jenna's words replay in my mind like a dare. Would it even work, or would I be blasted back by some force field and exposed as the fraud that I am?

Let's face it – I'm too curious not to try.

Just a touch.

I lift my finger up to the mist and wait for the feeling of electric shock to signal the portal rejecting my presence. But to my relief it doesn't come. Inhaling for luck, I force my hand through and find no resistance. Then, with renewed confidence, I propel the rest of my body though the mist, focus on my destination, and step through the portal of Verding.

***

Machu Pichu is one of those places that seems to be on everyone's bucket list, so it's not surprising it would find a home in the Prism. The collective mind would have it no other way. I settle atop one of the ruins and stare out at the Andes, immersed in the high of being back and relieved by the Prism's acceptance of my presence.

So far so good.

"It's been a long time," I say under my breath, watching as an ethereal blanket of fog settles around the ancient settlement, making it look like it's floating in mid-air. "So much time wasted. So many nights."

A sea of regret rips through me as Maeve's ring rubs up

against my fingers. It has no place here. I've let her evil steal far too much from me already. In the end, she got exactly what she wanted – Erik and I apart, me out of the way. I even banished myself from the Prism, all of my own volition. It's time for her winning streak to come to an end. I pull off the ring and shove it into my pant pocket.

The sun dips over the mountains and ushers in the brilliant star-studded sky – the Prism's ceiling of galactic beauty.

Carpe Noctum!

A brilliant pastel aurora weaves in between the moons and rings of encroaching planets, and I find myself wondering if Juno could fly high enough to reach them. I've missed her too.

I'm back girl. Come find me.

Dark silhouettes of bodies and bobbing lanterns travel about the ruins, giving the place a haunted ambiance. Even with the long Prism days, my time atop the ruins seems to pass in the blink of an eye. I push myself up off the ground to head back to the portal and immediately feel a warm breath on my cheek, then a velvet nose nuzzling my neck. Juno's loyal presence seems to repair the hole in my stomach just a little.

"You found me. You always do, don't you?"

The regal animal lets me cradle her strong neck, my eyes welling up again for hopefully the final time today. I bury my face in her mane, grateful that she hasn't abandoned me, and she snorts and prances impatiently in place.

"How about a ride? Except this time, I might want to push the limits a little if that's ok?" I lift myself up onto her back and settle in between her massive wings. With my mental urging she lifts off the ground, and we take to the skies where the lanterns of Machu Pichu shrink to tiny specks.

The aurora calls to me, its winding ethereal highways lit with emerald and indigo ribbons. I urge Juno upward as far as I can take her, the Prism falling away until it feels as if I'm beyond the boundaries entirely – simply floating beneath the orbs and planets that dwarf me, above the clouds and completely vulnerable. I'm mesmerized by the night. *How did I not think to do this before?*

I let Juno tread air. There's a different kind of stillness up here, almost terrifying. There's no one else that's ventured this high, and we're completely alone in the dark void between the realm and the forever unreachable galaxy that comprises its upper frontier. I stubbornly refuse to come down, pushing Juno on further, higher. But the planets seem to always remain out of my reach, just as the mountains that enclose the Prism never let anyone reach their summits.

I take a moment to appreciate the mesmerizing beauty around me, not wanting to overreach like Icarus and tempt fate. "Thank you," I whisper to whatever power is listening. "Thank you for letting me come back."

I urge Juno into a descent toward Castellum, then lie my head down on her mane and let my eyes close. The Prism air weaves through my hair as we soar down through the atmosphere toward solid ground, and I begin to grow anxious about the possibility of this world deteriorating beyond repair.

Unexpectedly, Juno veers to the north.

"Where are you going?"

She sails over the dark waters of the Prismatic, for the first time ignoring my wishes and setting her own course.

This is new.

I hang on, hoping there's a good reason for the sudden change – that it's not just another glitch in the matrix. We fly for a long time, and my bearings tell me that we'll likely end up in Senna at this rate.

At last, I see shoreline. No lights. No people. Nothing else.

"Where are we?"

Through the inky night, I glimpse a structure. Or rather, half a structure, with beautiful steps that lead to nowhere. Steps that once led to laughter and dancing and masquerade parties. The Spectrum Palace looks like a ruin of Ancient Rome, the surrounding landscape deserted and dismantled.

Senna.

What happened here?

June sets down on the sand, and I recognize the feeling of it underneath my feet. *There was a marina here.* I've stood here before, with Erik, that night we finally told each other how we felt. Now, nothing remains but my memories.

The realm of Senna is no more.

I finally understand why Juno's chosen this place. She *did* read my thoughts, my memories, and my fears. She brought me to Senna to warn me that the future I dread is already here. The Sentry needs to act fast, or soon the entire Prism could look like this. Robert had warned that when the faith of the Wakers is shaken, the most fantastic elements of the Prism will vanish first, those that take the most belief and hope and imagination. Senna was always going to be the first to get hit.

My cheek falls onto Juno's. Her body is warm, her heartbeat reverberating through her body. "I'll try my best. I promise."

A powerful emotion begins to rip open my chest. *When does it end? When are they defeated? When is it enough?* My hands begin to tingle, and I step away from Juno as I begin to sense my potential taking control of me. I want to scream so loud that my anger finds its way to earth and shatters the foundations on all their chapter houses. Suddenly, I feel the ground beneath my feet mirror the trembling in my body. The earth cracks as my fury tears more pieces of the Prism to shreds, and I hear Juno neighing behind me in alarm.

Stop! What are you doing? Breathe. Stop!

The shaking calms and tears fill my eyes. This is not the way forward. Robert's words enter my mind again. *Don't make anger the source.*

I inhale and refocus, trying to fill my mind with love, and awe, and exhilaration; with memories of laughter and adventure and discovery, of creative endeavors, and life-long friends. Of all that is good.

Of all there ever needs to be.

I sense a smile move my cheeks, my potential still at my fingertips, longing to be released. I turn towards the still water and focus on what I want to see. No more destruction. It's time for rebirth.

It's time to start winning.

The marina unfolds inch by inch: each plank of the dock, then a few boats parked around it, bobbing rhythmically on the waves like they did that night, waiting to be sailed to unexplored corners. I may not be able to rebuild all of Senna, but maybe it will inspire others to follow.

We can rebuild. We don't have to accept our fate. We have the potential after all, and it starts with us.

✳✳✳

I stare blankly at my reflection in the shiny marble floor as I attempt to muster the courage to open my dimension door. The last time I saw it was also the last time I saw Julian. Would it make me unravel again and set me back?

Set me back from what?

There's nowhere left to fall. It's not like I've exactly moved forward all that much. I'm going to have to go in there at some point and rip off the band-aid. I shut my eyes, place my hand on the doorknob and rotate my wrist. *Keep it together. It's just a room.*

With a nervous inhale, I step inside.

"Less is more" is overrated in this case, I decide, scrutinizing my dimension. It looks exactly as I left it that night. Bare walls and a whole lot of white, kind of like my first day in the Prism. Lonely and lifeless, the way Julian last saw it.

It's not what Julian would have wanted. He would have wanted dinosaurs and elves and stars and jungles. He would have wanted adventure and to be awestruck and blown away every second he spent here. To have this husk of a space be the last place his spirit visited seems like a slap in the face to his memory.

The nothingness is only broken up by the terrace doors that gaze out onto the Avenue. The memories of my last conversation with Julian replay in my mind.

"We never truly die," he had said.

I wonder what he meant by it, and if it's true. Only he knows now, along with those who have taken the same journey. That truth hasn't been bestowed on me. All I've come to learn is that loss follows me like a curse, whether it's in Chicago, or Paris, or a parallel utopia where nothing bad is even supposed to happen. Somehow, Death manages to push its way in and play its cruel game, dangle that carrot and then snatch it away. With a sense of foreboding, I find myself wondering who it will visit next.

The creative energy I was able to harness in Senna seems to have faded. It's no surprise that in my renewed state of resignation and dread I can't find the strength to manifest even a bed in the room, no matter how hard I focus. I always thought it would come back to me effortlessly, like riding a bike. Yet manifesting in my dimension seems like a lost art now.

More memories flood in. This time of Erik – of our first

meeting that fateful Prism morning. "The Prism knows if you're ready," he had said when I had inquired about returning. The same can be said now.

The Prism knows if you're ready, and even I know that right now I'm not. As nice as a bed would be to rest on before I'm sucked back through whatever gateway brought me here, I'll have to earn that privilege again. For now, the bare, hard floor will have to do.

The only question is, where am I going to wake up?

CHAPTER 6

In Control

The cottage basks in the silence of the dawn when my eyes shoot open. There's no trace of the portal next to the bed. Tru's feet twitch as he experiences whatever qualifies as a dog dream. Perhaps most importantly, the compound doesn't appear to be on fire and that psycho Irra isn't standing over me with a revolver.

It's fine. I'm fine.

The Prism is suddenly mine again, the possibility of returning no longer a fantasy. It wasn't perfect and at times even torturous, but at least I know I can get back somehow. And after what I've learned about Aeonia and the Skala, there's more work to do than ever.

My hunger for answers returns. There are more mysteries to solve before time runs out and the Prism disintegrates beyond recognition. There's also my relationship with Erik to repair, and I can't do that from Belgium.

With trepidation, I use Maeve's ring on myself again. *One last time. Probably.* I can't risk being found, especially here. The note I write next is short and direct. There really isn't any benefit to waking up my aunts and all of us suffering through an awkward and half-sincere goodbye as I lie about why I'm leaving and how they might become a little dead if I stay. I place the note on the bedside table, finding the necklace Erik gave me lying there too. The necklace is a painful reminder I need to wear – a reminder of everything we had and everything I ruined. I fasten the clasp around my neck, then pack the black duffle with my few belongings and Tru's toys and treats. Finally, I step out into the crips morning air with Tru obediently following.

Outside, I tighten the scarf around my neck, caught off guard by the sudden drop in temperature as winter prepares for its stealth encroachment. The road into town isn't very busy. Every now and then a car drives by and Tru startles a little. I've never taken him beyond the vast grounds of the compound or out of the woods. I'll never know the details of his past, but it seems cars may be a painful part of it.

It's about three miles to the town of Bruine and a bus is how I'm planning to get out of it. The bus station is on the other side of town. I pass by shops and grocers on the way, stopping to purchase a few things to eat. I've already put on my baseball hat and tucked my hair away. The key is to be confident and sell the lie, believe wholeheartedly that I'm Melanie Gerault of Lyon and that I've lost my ID and am just trying to get home. I can travel relatively freely throughout the continent without being hassled.

I arrive at the bus station just after eight, and it's as busy as one would expect for a small European country town. By "station" I mean a lone yellow shed where a sour-faced middle-aged woman with a tight bun smokes a pungent cigarette and sells tickets. The waiting area consists of six orange metal chairs. The next bus leaves in an hour, heading East. The only question is, will they let me on with a dog.

Just as I'm contemplating how to get Tru on board, a man's

voice stops all thoughts instantly. "Do you have a Plan B in case it's 'humans only'?"

The amount of sleep I've had over the last few days is negligible at best, so I'm not surprised to find myself hearing Erik's voice in my delusional, sleep-deprived state. I turn to respond to the stranger, trying to conceal my eyes under the hat. He's wearing jeans and a grey hooded sweatshirt with the hood over his head. Something urges me to look up at his face. The piercing blue eyes are unmistakable.

How?

Tru must sense the shift in my emotions because he starts to snarl and inches closer to my leg, unable to read the situation or tell if I'm happy or afraid. I pat him on the back, still speechless and unable to take my eyes off Erik's face. He looks around, removes his hood as if to reassure me of his identity, then lets a weak grin turn up his lips. I want to throw my arms around him and bury my face in the warmth of his neck, feel him hold me with that desperate passion we once shared.

But how is he even here? How could he possibly know?

"You mentioned the name," he explains, eyeing Tru with some cautious admiration.

"What?" I can't believe those are my first words to him.

"When you spoke to Robert at the Citadel – you mentioned the closest town to you," he clarifies, once again prepared for the exact question that was on my mind.

"Oh…right. I didn't know you heard that. But how did you get here so fast?"

He looks down at his running shoes. The smile slips a little "When you ran, I didn't know where to look. But I knew you wouldn't stay in Paris. I remembered you had spoken about your aunt, that she had a place in Belgium, hidden away. I figured if I were going to hide somewhere, that's where I'd go.

"Of course, Belgium is a big place, so I pointed to a town in the middle of the country and decided to set up there – wait until you reached out, so I could be close." Erik looks around the station uncomfortably, digging the toe of his running shoe into the gravel road. "But you never reached out," he concludes in a softer tone. "I couldn't go home anyway, so I just figured I'd stay there for a while. And then that turned into a longer while. But now you're here, so I guess my genius plan worked in a way."

I don't know what to say. Guilt eats at my stomach until it chews through to the other side. "Wow. And I thought I couldn't feel worse about how I treated you. You did so much to find me."

He puts his hands into his pant pockets. "It's ok. Belgium's as good a place as any to lay low. I rented a room from a retired fireman." He rubs his abdomen. "Got a little fat from waffles and chocolate, learned some new swear words. Now I can tell Tommy to shut the hell up in Dutch and he won't even know it. *Uw bakkes Tommy!*"

Tommy. I wonder if he's ok. We break out into a chuckle at the same time, and for a moment we're back in the jungle, sitting on rocks by the waterfall in Erik's dimension, holding stars in the palms of our hands, walking giddily through the London night.

Erik looks down again to my disappointment, ending the moment. "Anyway, when I heard you tell Robert, I searched it out in the morning and saw I was just over an hour away. I took a chance, thought maybe you'd be passing through town at some point, since you said you were leaving."

I continue looking at him, trying to force him back to me. "You know me pretty well."

He smiles, then turns to study True with a puzzled

expression. "Didn't expect you to have a travel partner though. He's beautiful. Will he eat me if I get close?"

Tru's head turns 90 degrees at the sound of the word "eat". He's stopped his warning snarl, and I search my pocket for a treat which he happily devours. "I don't know. He hasn't been around other people that much. I'd be careful."

Erik crouches down to Tru's level and motions to the treats in my pocket. "Can I have two of those?"

I throw them to him. Tru watches the trajectory of the flying cookies with confusion, probably wondering why they aren't flying into his mouth.

"What's his name?"

"Tru."

"Tru. Hey boy." Erik places the treat halfway between them, then sits down on the gravel and waits without making eye contact. Tru sniffs the air and bobs his head as if trying to determine whether the stranger smells suspicious, then takes a cautious step forward and back again. After sniffing the air once more and apparently satisfied that Erik doesn't smell like a serial killer, he advances four steps, just enough to reach the cookie.

Before Tru can bolt back to my leg, Erik slowly extends his hand to reveal the second treat. It's like watching a movie in slow-motion. If Tru tries to eat Erik, that could set our relationship even further back. On the other hand, at least Erik would have something else to be mad at. Still, I know Tru's gentle spirit will win. After all, he never bit either of my aunts, and one could argue they deserved it.

Erik remains quiet and patient as Tru takes another step, followed by another. I watch as his velvet snout touches Erik's palm, and his slimy tongue scoops up the cookie. He pushes at Erik's arm, looking for more, and shockingly even allows him to rub the scruff around his neck and the soft fur behind his ears. He seems to be enjoying every minute. Eventually, he looks back at me with a silly face and lapping tongue as if to say, "Ok, he's cool. We can keep this one. He feeds me."

"Looks like you passed the test," I conclude. Erik appears more at ease now. They say animals are impeccable judges of character. Not that I ever had any doubts about Erik.

"Right, now that we're best of friends," Erik says, standing up and ending the cuddles to Tru's dismay, "we should figure out a plan. Are you heading to Paris?"

I nod. "I need to get Maeve's phone to Ethan. There's probably a gold mine of information on there we can use."

"And you were thinking bus?"

"Well…" I look at Tru, then suddenly realize that busy metropolitan bus depots usually come with CCTV cameras. "I'm open to other options."

"Good," Erik replies, "because I think I may have seen our ride on my way up here."

***

"I really didn't know it would be this bad."

Erik's apologized at least ten times already for the stench in the back of the transport truck. The odor has penetrated everything at this point: my hair, my clothes, the steel walls inside. It's probably some fancy cheese that's covered in layers of mold and will one day be eaten with ridiculously expensive caviar. I hope the rich person who eats it appreciates how much oxygen we had to sacrifice to get it to them.

"It's fine," I lie, trying not to gag. It's not how I would have pictured our alone time.

Tru, who sniffed the air obsessively for the first 30 minutes of our trip, now lies in a state of complete resignation, accepting his fate. I run my head over his smooth forehead and ears. "It smells a bit like my aunt's Limburger cheese."

"That's it! My Belgian friend bought that too once. It's vile! Stunk up the flat for weeks."

"That's the one. It grows on you once you try it though."

Erik grimaces. "I can't relate. I could never keep it down."

I can feel Erik watching me. I look up to see contentment on his face and realize that for the first time since we've come back into each other's lives, he isn't eager to break eye contact. That's promising.

"You know," he says, "this whole time, I didn't even have a photo of you. Just a memory. I couldn't turn on my old phone because, well, the obvious. Couldn't take a chance. It sucked." He presses his lips together. "I know things aren't how they used to be, but I'm glad we found each other. Friends need to stick together."

Friends. There's that dreaded word again. I really wish he would stop saying it.

"One more thing," Erik adds. He furrows his brow as he points to my hand. "That thing – I think we need to get rid of it."

I know without following his gaze that he's referring to the soul-sucking jewelry around my finger.

"I'm not going to use it anymore," I promise, leaving out the tiny detail of having already used it that morning. I take off the ring for what I hope is the last time and tuck it into the pocket of my cargo pants. "But I'm not going to throw it away so someone else can find it. Until we know how to permanently destroy it, it stays with me."

"And you won't use it?"

"I won't use it," I assure him, half-heartedly. "But..."

Erik's eyes widen. "But what?"

"What if I can't control my potential and I lead them right to us?"

"That won't happen."

"You can't guarantee that."

"You're right, I can't. But we'll keep moving, keep them on their toes, won't stay any place too long. Avoid cameras. There are other ways that don't involve you selling your soul."

I bite my lip, unconvinced. "Let's hope so."

"Look, I get it Ev. You've been through a lot."

"We all have," I reply, trying desperately to hold onto the way his voice sounds saying my name. He's the only one who calls me 'Ev' now.

"This may be a good time for us to practice," Erik observes. "You're a moving target and harder to pinpoint. Let me help you control it."

"What, *now*?"

"You need to know how to keep your potential in line, Ev. I should have already taught you. I just thought we'd have more time. Trust me on this."

Of course, I trust him. It's the Vulturians I don't want to underestimate. Moving target or not, it's still a big risk. What if he's wrong about outrunning them?

"Or...", he suggests, "we could start practicing once we've been captured. Your call."

I grimace. "Fine. You win. I'm your attentive student for the duration of this trip. Teach me your wise ways."

"Mocking me already?"

I grin. "Let's just get it over with."

"Now, that's the wrong attitude already," Erik replies. "This isn't easy. It takes focus and concentration and unrelenting resolve. I know you have a strong will because I've seen what you can do with your potential. Now you just have to use it to do the opposite: rein it in. You need discipline and patience for that because it takes time to perfect."

"How much time?"

"That depends."

I groan.

"Patience," Erik reminds me.

Patience is not my strong suit. "Fine. What do we do first."

"Close your eyes and focus," he begins, his voice calm and hypnotic. "Pretend you're in your dimension. Blank canvas, like when you first got there. Now fill it slowly with whatever you want. This part should be easy. You've done it all before. Keep building… Feel the world at your fingertips. See what's next before you create it. Become one with that desire."

The exhilaration of the exercise brings me back to my dimension, if only in my mind. I feel it coming to life, all the things I'd once created: the colors, the mountains, the emotions. My chest swells from excitement and anticipation, my blueprint of memories awakening the desire for more, feeding my addiction. The manifestations line up in the recesses of my consciousness, marching forward, waiting for me to bring them forth and pushing against the cage that holds them back.

Freedom.

Fulfillment.

Purpose.

The future tingles on my fingertips, teaming with possibilities. My liberation calls me again, like it did that first night in Montmartre as I raced from my own cage and into the light, not knowing what incredible things await. I reach for them with my mind, with my soul, feeling the power ripping through me, grasping at the light…

"Now, strip it all away."

What? The creations of my mind stop marching, crashing into one another and falling like dominoes at the sound of Erik's voice.

"Keep your eyes closed," he instructs. "Stop everything and take it back."

Why? Why did you do this to me? I finally felt free. I was finally myself. A self I'd lost.

"I know it seems wrong," Erik continues, "and goes against every instinct you have. But you need to learn self-control. Your potential is strong Ev. Controlling it will help you channel it and will protect you. Take it all away. You can create it all again. You *know* you can. Stop fearing loss and limitation and start dwelling in the world of possibility. When there is possibility the fear of loss has no hold over you. Strip it away willingly. Fight the desire for more now and you'll get the chance to have more tomorrow and every day. Isn't that what you want? A tomorrow?"

I had never thought of it that way. Isn't tomorrow the whole point – to move forward and to progress? I won't get to do that if the Vulturians find me.

Strip it away. I notice my heavy breathing. I want Erik to take my hand and calm me, but he doesn't. I guess he wants me to do this on my own.

But this is the way. Alone. Just me and my mind and my will.

An exercise of excruciating subtraction takes place next. One by one, they disappear – my memories, my creations, my dreams. Vacant space between pictures. At first, it burns like a real wound. But then, with each passing thing I remove, I remember Erik's words. It's just temporary. No more limitation. Think of tomorrow.

Control.

Breathe.

Calm yourself.

Discipline yourself.

Rein it in.

My chest rises and falls more slowly, the picture nearly blank. *You won't find me. You won't.* I sense a feeling of peace settle in and know it's not the end. I can control the intensity, like a dial on a stove – high to medium to simmer.

I can turn it off entirely.

"How do you feel?" Erik whispers.

I feel empty, but surprisingly fine. "I'm ok. I think I get it."

"Good. Now do it again. Except this time…" he pauses. "This time, I want to you to imagine things that make you sad and angry. The worst of it, Ev. It's the only way to test yourself. Build up the pain, the fear, the hate, the self-loathing. Build up every regret you've ever had. See it. Feel it rip you apart. And then strip it all away to nothing. To peace."

My serenity evaporates. "Do I have to?"

"If you want to learn how to control the power inside you, then yes."

"But you've seen what it does Erik."

"I've seen that you're capable of great things. Focus on the good. I know you can do this."

That makes one of us. To feel it all again, all at once, the worst of it…I wouldn't wish that on anyone. But I suppose I need to tear it down to build it back.

"I'm scared."

"I know," Erik replies with sympathy.

"What if I flip this truck over?"

Even with my eyes closed, I know Erik's grinning. He sounds different when he smiles. "You've never hurt anyone you cared about before. I think Tru and I are safe."

I sit in silence, paralyzed at first. *Just reverse it. It's temporary.*

Everything that will torture you is temporary. I steady my nerves and let the images come. The torment begins.

Mom. The shrieking tires. The blood. The funeral. The emptiness. Uncle Tim's turn is next. Shattered hope, a kindred soul ripped away, hollowness. Cambridge dreams dashed, family bonds broken, Catherine's coldness, Tristan's poisonous touch. The suction of the Tiamat against my skin. Fragments of my psyche littered around Montmartre as I frantically search for them among shards of broken lightbulbs.

My body feels on fire with all of it, ignited by loss and regret and what-ifs. An angry storm stirs.

Then come Julian and Lise. Their innocent faces, young and hopeful, not yet jaded by cynicism despite their tragic lives. I picture a hospital bed and a casket side by side, and suddenly the already fragile glue that was holding me together is liquid as I start to come apart. Julian's face is replaced by Maeve's. She leaps out of the coffin with a cackle but is pushed aside by Erik. His handsome face stares at me with sorrow and a sense of betrayal, until it too fades from my sight. The liquid binding me becomes thinner as all the images from the nightmare I've conjured blend into one horrifying demon shape. A fog sets in around me as I wrestle with my emotions and regrets, the demon pounding at the door to my mind.

"Don't fight it," I hear Erik whisper. "It's not real. It's passed. Let it be, and it will hold no power over you."

Let it be. It's temporary. It will pass.

"Take it away," Erik instructs. "Take it all away."

I reverse the process again, but unlike earlier, I feel liberated with each deletion, a piece of me returning to its rightful place, the binding glue hardening again and keeping me together. It's in the past. It's all in the past. Focus on tomorrow. Focus on what *can* be.

I imagine myself clicking the delete button on a keyboard, erasing the painful memories one by one, until finally there's one left. The shrieking tires that started it all. *It's done. She's gone. I can't change it.* She would want me to have a tomorrow.

I press the button one more time and wait for the sensation of inner peace to sink in. My breathing evens out and I feel my pulse decelerate. My hands don't fidget restlessly anymore. I've done it.

I'm in control of my mind.

I exhale loudly, releasing the final battle into the air.

"That's all you have to do to control your potential," Erik says softly. I open my eyes and stare into his. "It's that simple. Like a math puzzle: you add what you want and take away what you don't, and then multiply the good ten-fold when you want to wield it."

"Math was never my strongest subject." My heart beats loudly, but slower now.

We look at each other in comfortable silence for a few moments, not needing any words. The truck hits a bad strip of potholes that jostle us and dislodges the wood covers on a few crates, putting an end to our moment. Erik gets up to secure the crates again, pulling out some of the cargo and throwing it my way.

I catch the cheap scarf and cringe as the fabric snags on my dry hands.

"In case you get cold," Erik mentions. "At least it's not the source of the smell."

"Thanks…not just for the scarf."

He winks at me. "Don't mention it. You were due for that lesson."

My impossible brain is already fifty steps ahead. I'm not sure how Erik will react to what I'm about to ask, but I can't keep it to myself much longer. Maybe now that I can control my potential better, he won't be opposed.

I start with a soft ball. "Have you heard anything about Lise?"

He shakes his head and frowns, taking his seat again. "No. I tried calling the hospital. She's still there, but they won't reveal anything else."

She's alive. She's ok!

Time for the killer pitch. "Do you think we can go see her?"

I expect frustration and a debate about how stupid my idea is, and 'what are you thinking Ev,' etc. But Erik's face hardly changes except for the intermittent blink. The old Erik would have passionately told me exactly what he thought of my irresponsible idea, because he cared that I stay in one piece instead of being cut up into several. But this Erik takes it more in stride. As much as I thought I would appreciate that, I find myself wishing for the typical reaction. At least it revealed his desperation to hang on to me.

"Ok," he finally replies.

"What?!" I expected a "no". A calm "no" but still a "no" nonetheless.

"Isn't that what you want?" he asks, visibly confused.

"Well, yeah, but…you're not going to lecture me on how it's a stupid idea?"

"Oh good, we agree it's a stupid idea."

"No, wait…what are you doing? God, you're so impossible these days!"

He chuckles. "Sure, I'm the impossible one. You know, maybe I've just realized that there's no point trying to change your stubborn mind. You clearly feel strongly about this, and we both know you're going to get inside that hospital one way or another, regardless of what I say, aren't you?"

He stares at me, as if daring me to deny it.

"Fine, yes," I admit like a petulant child as I cross my arms, irritated by the look of satisfaction on his face.

"Why even ask me then?"

I shrug, a nostalgia building up in my heart. "Because we used to be a team."

Erik's eyes seem to develop a glossier coating. "Yeah…well," he replies under his breath, "I remember very clearly the day you decided we weren't."

Crap. I walked right into that one. These uncomfortable guilt-trips aren't much fun. It's not the Erik I know. "Fair point. Look, I'm sorry. I really am. I wish I could go back and do things differently."

"Me too. At least we agree on something."

"So, what, now you'll just do whatever I want, no more unsolicited advice?" I ask after a pause.

"Oh, you'll still get that. But something tells me that unless you find Lise, you're not going to be able to move forward. So best we just get it out of the way, hope we don't get captured or killed and just go from there. Sound good to you?"

If I'm being honest, it sounds like a suicide mission. Let's just hope I can control my potential under pressure.

"Sounds totally reasonable," I lie, knowing full well I'm being impulsive. Erik is right about the stupid part, and a part of my heart accelerates at realizing he still knows me so well. Maybe what we had is not entirely lost. And he's right – without seeing Lise or learning of her condition I won't be able to devote my attention to Erik, or the Prism, or frankly anything else. We need to find her, and ideally not leave the hospital in a body bag or tied up in a trunk.

"They'll be expecting you," Erik says, pointing out the obvious and giving me a dose of anxiety. "You'll have to be strong and calm. Disguises alone may not be enough. We'll need to think of a good cover."

"Yeah. I know."

Tru senses my energy shift and places his enormous heavy head on my lap. He stares up at me, the whites of his eyes lining his lower lids, and seems to telepathically send me a message that could solve our biggest obstacle.

"But," I think out loud, "they won't be expecting a dog."

CHAPTER 7

Warnings and Promises

The truck drops us off in a shipping yard outside the city where we emerge sore and photosensitive into a sea of stacked containers piled high like life-size Lego blocks.

"These places always give me the creeps," Erik says after he pays the driver. "There's probably dead bodies stuffed into drums and crates all around us."

"You've been watching too much TV. But yeah, let's just get out of here."

We prepared our disguises on the truck. I've got a dark brown wig on, which Erik already had packed in case he found me. The fake hair is beautifully curly – the kind of ringlets I would kill for on a night out. But it's unbelievably itchy and hot and I long for my plain old hair within 30 seconds of having it on. Erik opts for a hipster vibe with a plaid shirt and impressively realistic beard, finished off with spectacles and a fedora.

I wave my hand over his ensemble. "Is *all* of this necessary?" He looks unrecognizable and insufferable, but then again, that is the whole point.

He hands me a pair of fake cat-eye spectacles with deep

purple frames. "Here. Keep your face down whenever you can."

Leaving the shipping yard is easiest by taxi. We don't speak as we enter Paris, trying to appear boring and uninteresting to the driver, having barely convinced him Tru wouldn't be any trouble. Within thirty minutes, the old city begins to take form around us as we drive along one-ways and navigate dizzying roundabouts on the way to the Sorbonne, Tru panting in our ear and leaving trails of slobber on our legs. The entire time I wonder if there's a suspicious black sedan on our tail, but each time I check I'm relieved not to see one. Once we cross the Seine, I allow myself to relax.

The familiar grounds of the Sorbonne instill in me a sense of calm and comfort, even if the bare trees and grey November sky steal a bit of the magic and charm away.

"I made a copy before I left," Erik says, handing me a key to the door, "in case we ever needed to come back."

"You really do prepare for everything, don't you?"

"I have keys for every place I've ever stayed."

"*You're joking?!*"

"Yes, I'm absolutely joking. That would be insane!"

I let out a chuckle. "Ok, good. I was concerned for a minute there."

No one gives us much thought as we walk towards the storage room, and Erik blends right in with the hipster students. I've learned from sneaking around and hiding in plain sight that the more you believe your story the more others will too. If you feel like you belong, it's unlikely anyone will question you. Tru throws a bit of a wrench into our cover, but thankfully he's not as jumpy as I thought he'd be and stays close to my leg, drawing some attention but not arousing suspicion. Good thing therapy dogs have become so common. It makes the cover easier to sell.

Erik wiggles the key into the rusted lock of the storage room and turns it firmly. Inside, the place is just as I remember it, although dustier.

Suddenly, I'm not sure we should be here. It comes with painful recollections: it was the last place we saw each other before everything fell apart, the place we had our worst fight, and the place I ran from like a terrified child. The memories kick in: Julian, Erik…Maeve. All of it linked together by this tiny cramped, dusty room.

Why did we come here?

"This won't be a long-term solution," Erik says, putting down his bag. "We'll have to figure out a better place to stay. Do you want to visit the hospital today?"

I nod. "If we can."

"We should eat something."

"Ok. Eat, then go. And we need to get Tru's disguise."

Erik rubs his fake beard and grimaces. "Seems wrong."

"I know. I'm going to hell. But you must admit, it could work. And it's for a good cause."

He sighs and throws up his hands. "Fine. It *is* a good cause. But where on earth are we going to find a jacket for a seeing eye dog?"

***

"Therapy dog. He's a therapy dog." I tell myself.

"Are you trying to make yourself feel better?" Erik whispers as the automatic doors of Hôpital Sainte-Marguerite slide open in front of us.

My palms are sweaty. "Yeah. It's not working. I still can't believe you found someone online selling used guide dog jackets. There really is a market for everything."

97

Erik grins and reaches down to pet a cooperative Tru. "Luck is on our side. I also found out Lise is in the north wing."

I point at the floor plan displayed on the wall. "North wing…ok, pediatrics is fourth floor. Here."

Tru looks up at me with sad pleading eyes as if to ask why he's wearing an uncomfortable coat over his beautiful fur.

"It's just for a short while," I promise him. "Now, pretend like you know what you're doing. You're a big part of this, so work it!"

The north wing is relatively quiet compared to the main lobby and the packed x-ray area. Several nurses congregate at the main desk and giggle as they stare at someone's phone.

"Oh, mon dieu!" one of them exclaims. "Il l'a encore trompée? Amélie devrait être avec Jacques, sans doute!"

I know enough French to figure out they're watching *Saison de l'amour*. It's Catherine's favorite soap opera, and my afternoon nightmare. It seems everyone's favorite jerk Edouard has once again cheated on Amélie, who everyone knows should be with Jacques since, like, a decade ago. These dramas move excruciatingly slow.

A nurse in floral purple scrubs sees us and approaches. "Bonjour, puis-je vous aider?"

"Bonjour," I continue in French, faking my best native accent. "Therapy dog, for Lise Vidal." Erik smiles and stays silent, his knowledge of the language non-existent aside from *bonjour*, *merci*, and *baguette*.

"I don't have any notes about this appointment," the nurse replies, eyeing us skeptically. She looks over Tru with a scowl, as if to say, 'what is this filthy creature doing in my ward?'

Crap! We don't need a tough nurse. We need a nurse who's on her first shift on her first day, or the last five minutes of her shift before a long-awaited vacation. A nurse who isn't going to hassle us about visiting hours or silly things like unrecorded appointments.

"Dr. Behra sent us," I say as confidently as possible. "We have an appointment for 1:30."

The nurse has moved on to scrutinizing Erik and the fedora with a smirk.

"I know," I giggle, locking eyes with her. "Americans and their fashion crimes. Here is a referral letter," I say, hoping our moment of levity will work to our benefit. "We have two other appointments after this one. Balto is in very high demand for trauma patients. The patient's mother requested him."

The nurse raises an eyebrow, then looks at Erik again. "Hmmm. And he is…"

"The dog's trainer. He assists me."

The nurse scrutinizes the paper, the name seemingly ringing a bell. Erik lifted the letterhead from a nearby clinic as he flirted with the receptionist, after which I printed up the letter at the printing shop. It looked legit at the time. Adding forgery to our list of transgression seems insignificant at this point.

"D'accord," the nurse finally concedes, pointing us down the hall. "First right, then first left. Room 315."

I hold my hand out for the letter, unwilling to leave any trace of us behind, and smile sweetly at the nurse as she returns it.

"Merci." As we round the corner of the first hallway, I see the nurse whisper something to one of her colleagues. We don't have much time.

When we turn down the second hallway, I count the rooms mentally and realize that Lise's room is the last door at the end of the hall, with two men posted guard outside.

Of course. She's the bait, and I'm walking right into the sticky web they've set up.

The next few minutes play out like a slow-motion scene in

an action movie, the ones where a car flies off a ramp in a car chase and then flips over in the air, every second painfully drawn out as it plunges toward the pavement. As the men approach, I feel myself slipping out of that upside-down car, with only a seatbelt holding me in place, hoping we land on all four tires.

Sell the story. Sell it!

"Who are you?" I demand rudely in French as I approach, getting into character. My plan is to shock them into compliance with aggressive assertiveness and hope for the best.

The men look at each other. "Who are *you*?" one of them asks me. I can tell they're Vulturians. I can smell the stench of evil on them. But they must be low-tier because they don't have any jewelry yet.

"I'm the therapist…from the institut Broussais. I've brought the dog." I raise my voice after each sentence to convey my surprise over their ignorance. Upside-down, frozen in mid-air and mid-prayer is torturous.

The men don't blink and just stare at me. "A dog?" one asks, turning to the other, who just shrugs back.

"Je ne sais pas."

I throw the letter at the man on the right. "Quite an unorganized operation you run here," I snap. "The therapy dog – he helps comma patients! We really don't have all day, and I've already been held up at the nurses' station while they checked everything. I have many more patients to see after this one, so please, move aside," I demand.

The men stay put. "We are not supposed to let anyone inside," the man examining the letter insists. I rip it out of his hand. He takes a step toward me and right on cue Tru draws back his lips and emits a low menacing growl.

"He doesn't like you," I tell the man. "If I were you, I

wouldn't upset him further. Or we can call your supervisor, and you can explain how you prevented us from doing our work."

The men look at each other in confusion, then back at us. "And him?" one of them asks, motioning to Erik.

"He's the trainer. He goes where the dog goes. Now stop wasting our time. We only have 30 minutes."

The two men exchange glances while whispering something in French about "only 30 minutes" and the nurse having cleared us, then hesitantly move aside, allowing us to pass.

I saunter in confidently. The door to the room is a dark teal, on the same color spectrum as the lighter seafoam walls. The blinds are down. Inside, the divider curtain is drawn in the room, with only the foot of the bed visible from the doorway.

"Please don't disturb us," I instruct the men, "otherwise I will have to come back."

Erik sighs louder than I do when he closes the door. "Well played," he whispers.

My knees start to go weak as I clutch the leash with soaking wet palms. "I'm sweating buckets," I admit, giving Tru a treat and stepping past the curtain.

The first thing I see is a woman sleeping in a chair. She's covered with a beige hospital blanket, only one side of her face visible through her messy tangled hair. And next to her, immobile and strung up to machines, lies Lise.

Her pretty face is rosy, despite her tragic situation. The monitors beep at a constant rhythm, which I tell myself is a good sign. Still, I find myself wishing I knew more about medicine. Maybe I should have watched those medical dramas with Catherine and suffered through all the bad acting and awkward make-out scenes. Maybe then I could say confidently, "Her vitals look good," as I casually threw a stethoscope around my neck and wrote a bunch of numbers in her chart. But as it stands, I have no idea what I'm looking at, other than a girl who shouldn't be here at all.

I feel a sob crawl into my throat. "Lise," I whisper, taking her hand. It feels so small in my own, her skin dry and blotchy. "I'm so sorry," I mumble, trying desperately not to cry. Erik taps my shoulder and motions to the women. She starts to stir and opens her eyes laboriously, then straightens up abruptly when she sees us.

"Qui es-tu? Que faites-vous ici?"

I raise my hand up, at the same time easing Tru into a sit. "We're here to help," I say to her in French. "We've brought a therapy dog, to help Lise come out of her coma state. He's helped many children." *Well, he's helped one adult,* I correct silently. "Animals can be very helpful in dealing with trauma."

"No one said anything about this."

"Here is the letter from Dr. Behra," I say, showing her the paper but hanging on to it. "He called me last week to see if we were available. We had an opening and thought we would come by."

"I see." The woman seems puzzled by the name of the doctor. "And you think you could help Lise?"

"I hope so. Can you tell me more about her condition? I mean, we know…the medicine," I lie through my teeth. "But in your own words, what happened? And for the benefit of my friend, in English, if you don't mind," I add, remembering that she knows the language.

Ms Vidal nods and turns toward her daughter, looking flat and defeated, like she's cried her last tear weeks ago and all that's left is a hollowed-out shell.

"I lost my son," she whispers, the emotion rushing into her voice. Her face is pale and dark circles cast shadows under her watery eyes. I clench Tru's leash tighter to keep my composure.

"Lise saw him die, I think," she continues. "Asthma attack, in the middle of the night. Lise was in a state when they found her, saying things. They took her to the hospital, then to the psych ward. After that," she runs her fingers through her messy hair, "I don't know what happened, but she never woke up. They said her brain experienced a psychotic break."

Psychotic break? "But she was awake when she was brought here?" I ask, recalling the grim scene in front of the Iliad.

"Yes. She was fine when she got here. They said they gave her some medication to calm her down but that she had a reaction to it. The doctors were so confused. They couldn't figure it out, wanted to run tests. But the head psychiatrist that's been assigned to her case – Dr. Auclair – he wouldn't let them. He said it would destabilize her. Still refuses. I just don't trust him, but I can't do anything.

"The police said it's an active investigation and they need to keep Lise here. There are guards on her door all the time. They say it's for her safety – that someone was trying to take Julian the night he died, and they might come back for her. Who would want to take my boy?"

I glance at Erik who's trying his best to maintain a neutral expression.

"The doctors are convinced it was a hallucination. But a man and a woman come by a lot to check on her," the distraught mother continues. "Detectives, I think. They pretend like they give a damn, but I know they don't. There are so many questions, and no answers! No answers for my son, no answers for my daughter. How much can a mother take?"

I look at Erik pleadingly. He shakes his head, warning me not to do what he thinks I'm about to do. Then he shuts his eyes in resignation, realizing I'm about to do exactly that.

"Ms Vidal, can we talk outside?" I ask.

Erik mumbles something at me under his breath, but I can't make it out.

"Um, all right." The distraught mother looks again at Lise, then gives her a kiss on the cheek. When she's behind the curtain, I take one last opportunity to squeeze Lise's hand, not wanting to get too close and blow my cover. Tru nuzzles the bed, sensing our bond, sensing my pain. I'm afraid to say it out loud, so I make my promise silently: *I'll get you out of here. I promise you Lise!*

We enter the hall where I resume my cover. "You," I point to the guard, "you ruined the energy! The dog can sense it. I'm going to have a word with the hospital director. This is not a therapeutic environment! You have wasted our time!" I hiss as I lead a confused Ms Vidal away.

When we turn down the adjacent hallway, I pull her into an empty room and shut the door once Erik joins us.

"What is happening?" Ms Vidal asks, staying a safe distance away from Tru.

"Don't worry about him," I tell her. "It's the people outside Lise's room you need to be afraid of. You're right not to trust them."

"What do you mean? What do you know?"

"Ms Vidal – "

"Claudia."

Erik's head ping pongs back and forth as he watches our exchange in French. I can see him trying to decipher our body language and fill in the blanks. I switch to English again.

"Claudia," I pass Tru's leash to Erik, then step towards her and place my hands on her arms, "listen to me carefully, because we don't have much time. Lise's room may be bugged. Actually, it most definitely is. It wasn't safe to talk in there."

"*Bugged?*"

"Can you tell me about the woman and the man that you said visit Lise often? What do they look like?"

"Um…" Claudia blinks rapidly, probably still processing the bugged room, "the woman is tall, long red hair, pale skin, pretty face. The man is her height, early-twenties maybe, very handsome, more tanned, always smells strongly of cologne and wears very polished suits. They say they're with the police."

"They're not," I tell her. Detectives don't wear Versace suits, unless they're the corrupt ones. "Lise's favorite color was peach. That's her favorite fruit too. I know that because she told me the day I met her, at the build site of your new home."

Claudia's eyes widen. "You knew her?"

"Yes. My name is Everest. Lise may have mentioned me."

"Everest. Yes! She spoke about you, all the time!"

"Claudia, these people, they are not your friends. That man and woman, they are dangerous. In fact…"

Should I do it? Yes! She needs to know!

"They are responsible for what happened to your son, and they don't want Lise to wake up. Those things she was saying the night they sedated her are truer than you realize. I can't tell you everything now, but she *cannot* stay here. Do you know anyone who could help you move her safely somewhere else? Someone who could help you get away from under their watch?"

Claudia blinks at me in bewilderment. She closes her eyes after a moment, letting the bombshell revelation sink in. "No, no one. I'm completely alone. Oh my God…"

"It's ok. I'll find someone. But you must promise me something. You cannot tell them what I just told you. Claudia!"

She falters a little in place as she repeats "Oh my God," over and over.

"Claudia! Please, you must act normal. These people will

know everything. As much as you want to lash out at them and get revenge, you need to play it cool, for Lise. When the time is right, we will get Lise out of here, and then I promise you she will wake up and you will have your little girl back. And even get some answers, all right?"

She finally nods, eyes wide and frightened. "Ok."

"We need to go now. If anyone asks, it was just a therapy dog visit. Yes?"

"Yes, ok."

"The dog's name is Balto." I reach out to rub her arms. "I know this is scary. We just need some more time."

"Ok, ok, " she repeats. "This…this finally makes sense. Because nothing made sense before."

"You have no idea. Remember, act normal. Lise's life depends on it. Now go. Go, and say nothing. Nothing Claudia!"

She nods, glancing at Erik then back at me before whispering "ok" to herself several more times. We exit the room and watch her walk back to Lise's hallway, wrapping her sweater around her body. She turns and gives us a curt nod before disappearing down the adjoining corridor.

Erik mumbles his disapproval beside me. "You just couldn't help yourself."

I sigh, hoping I didn't just put Claudia and Lise in danger too. "She's been lied to long enough. If she's as strong as Lise, she'll do what needs to be done. We need to trust that."

"What if…"

"*Shhhhh!*"

A familiar voice echoes through the hall, the sound dampened by distance. "Now that Bolivia is up and running, we should have enough data to expand the project to other areas."

Erik looks at me uncomfortably, recognizing the woman's voice too. "Times up!"

Footsteps inch closer, coming from the nurses' station. It's a matter of seconds before we come face to face. At the end of the corridor, the stairway sign glows red. I grab Erik's hand and drag him and Tru behind me, pulling them through the exit and shutting the door. I'm tempted to pause and spy through the glass window, then emerge in a storm of fury to punch Maeve in the face. But it's too dangerous, and Erik's already halfway to the third floor. Tru leads the way, looking back at me occasionally and probably wondering what strange new world I've thrown him into where he wears clothes and climbs stairs instead of hills.

"The guards must have told them by now," Erik says, handing me back the leash when we reach the ground floor. "In a few minutes they'll figure it out. We need to move. Wait inside. I'll flag down a cab so we're not waiting in the open. Tru's easy to spot."

"Hurry."

Thank goodness for the small window in the exit door that gives me a reprieve from the nauseating seafoam walls. There are so many reasons people don't like hospitals. The smell of antiseptic mortality and helplessness seems to penetrate even concrete blocks, following you wherever you go. It's the same in every hospital, no matter the city. Same smell the night Mom died, and when we went to see Uncle Tim's body. I can't wait for the cab to arrive so I can escape it.

But that smell is also the reason I quickly identify a scent that doesn't belong: the scent of a cologne that probably costs $1500 a bottle. Even before Tru pulls back his lips into a snarl, I know exactly who's joined us in the stairwell.

"Tristan," I conclude without even needing to look behind me.

"So, you finally came."

I turn to face him without hesitation. That dread that used to eat at the inside of my stomach isn't a problem anymore. I've made my peace with the possibility of seeing him again, and I won't allow him to destroy what I've worked so hard to piece back together.

Tru must sense the tension between us because he catches me off guard and lunges forward, his teeth snapping at the air just a few inches from Tristan's arm. I manage to control him, but it's enough to send our uninvited guest a few steps back and erase the smirk off his face. He grimaces in disgust as he wipes droplets of drool off his suit.

I lock eyes with him again, refusing to back down. "Just let us go. Look what you did to that girl. Is it worth it, all for your father's approval – to be one of *them*? How do you stand by and watch? How do you live with yourself?"

I expect Tristan to laugh or roll his eyes or say something obnoxious and arrogant. But he remains silent, his eyes never leaving mine. There's something different about him. I can't quite identify what it is, but it feels a little like desperation. His face becomes sunken and tired before my eyes.

Before I can even entertain the ridiculous notion of having any concern for him, I glance through the window and see Erik motioning at me frantically from inside a waiting cab. Tristan remains still, as if bitten by some kind of poisonous insect that's paralyzed him.

"Ok," I mutter, unable to believe my luck. If he dares to make a move, I could try to use my potential somehow, but I'm not sure yet how well I could control it, and a hospital wouldn't be the best place to find out. "I'm going to go and you're not going to follow. Maybe you'll do what's right for once."

It feels as if we're in some kind of hypnotherapy session, with Tristan obeying my every suggestion. I look at him one last time, then hastily urge Tru through the door and into the waiting cab, holding my breath the whole way.

"What took you so long?" Erik asks impatiently.

I finally exhale. "Nothing. Door was stuck." As the cab pulls away, I glance back to see Tristan in the window looking after us with the same mystifying expression on his face.

CHAPTER 8

The Safe House

My pacing is making me dizzy. "I need to get Maeve's phone to Ethan," I tell Erik impatiently back in the storage room after we've liberated ourselves from our disguises. The hospital visit has me fired up and ready to act, although the details of my plan are still fuzzy.

"That'll be sooner than you think," he replies, gathering up our belongings. "We're going to stay with him. Yoshi, Shahina and Ethan got into Paris this morning."

"What? *Now?*"

"We can't stay here Ev. We'll be safer with them. We have some safe houses lined up."

"Are you kidding me? You're mister 'don't draw unwanted attention.' Right now, they're looking for us, and Tru's a dead giveaway, unless I paint him black or give him stripes or something. The Prism is the only place I can keep him safe, and I doubt I'll make it back there tonight…on my own."

Erik stops rummaging and sits on the floor with his back against the door. He looks tired.

"What is it?"

He shakes his head and looks around the room. "It's this

place Ev. I know you feel it too. I don't think it's good for us to be here – especially you. I'm worried it will only hold you back from the Prism…pull you back into that darkness again." He fiddles nervously with his fingers. "It's certainly not bringing back the most pleasant memories for me."

He's got a point there. Being around everything that brings back our painful past is not going to help either of us heal. I join him on the floor, my heart aching again and full of regret. Tru comes to sit between us, pushing us further apart as he curls into a ball.

"You should teach him some manners," Erik teases as he rubs the dog's fur.

"What if…we imagine a different ending?" I suggest. "The night we got here, remember we went to that Portuguese restaurant and then the gypsy street concert, which got rained out, so we walked along the river soaking wet. When we got back, we ate Raman noodles and you told me stories about Norway and then we fell asleep and saw each other in the Prism, where we cast off on a boat to explore Bora Borealis again. Then we woke up and spied on the Vulturians, found a secret entrance to the chapter house, set of a bunch of booby traps, escaped with our lives but destroyed the entire Order. The end. Better?" I wait anxiously for his response, longing for forgiveness.

"Yeah," Erik agrees. "That would have been preferable. If only we had a time machine, right?"

Time. That cruel master. The things I would change if I could travel back in time.

Time.

"Erik!" I jump up and resume my pacing, trying to put my scrambled thoughts in order.

"What?"

"Wait…give me a minute…I'm still catching up."

I try to remember what the Flame had said in Vieri's loft that night in the Imperium. *In time.* "The Flame had said 'find them both and conceal them well *in time*…the only way is *through* time.' What if I've been thinking about it all wrong? I always assumed the message was saying to be patient, to wait for the right time. But what if it was being literal? *Through* time, as in *time travel.* I think the Prism wants us to find the Skala, and the Tiamat, and conceal them somewhere else in time, so the Vulturians can't find them!"

Erik just stares at me. "That's crazy!"

"You said that the new physicist is exploring the possibility of time travel through past Prisms, right?"

He rises from the floor. I can see his own gears turning now, his eyes bright and brow creased in concentration. He looks around the room as if reading invisible clues on the walls. "Yes, the new physicist is Carmella Vieri. Where did you say you found that compass again?"

A smile spreads across my face so big it feels like I'll crack myself into a million pieces. It's all coming together. Finally, something is making sense! I can feel it in my gut.

"In Vieri's loft," I confirm. "We need to talk to her!"

After a pause, it's Erik's turn to smile. "We need to talk to her!" he agrees, his voice rising. We start laughing together in unison, shyly at first, like we don't want to jynx ourselves, but then loudly without inhibitions, looking a little crazy in the process. I bite my lip with anxious excitement, trying to wrap my head around the possibilities – or rather, the suddenly possible impossibilities.

"I don't suppose you have a time machine to go along with this theory?" Erik asks, reminding me that our excitement may be premature.

"Not yet. But I think I have something that might help find it. The Flame referred to the pendant as a compass. What if it's the key to Prism time travel?"

***

"Think about it! Some of the world's most brilliant minds have visited the Prism," I remind Erik, as he, Tru and I pile out of a minivan taxi and head toward the safehouse. We've spent a lot of money on cabs, but thankfully Erik's prepared for a life on the run, and the Sentry has its own stockpiles of resources. "They were inspired – linked to universal intelligence. Maybe they knew things, passed down things through their work to others, like Carmella?"

Erik motions me to keep my voice down as we pass a group of young people huddled around with their skateboards. "We're almost there," he says.

I'm a bit bummed he doesn't mirror my enthusiasm anymore. We used to feed off each other and find comfort in being so in sync. But it's different now, and after our momentary excitement, he's back to 'just business'.

The safehouse is accessed through the back of a dingy tattoo parlor. The 250lb tattoo artist gives us a perplexed look as we trudge through with Tru to the sound of buzzing needles.

"We're here to see Yoshi," Erik tells him, and he motions us to continue inside.

The air is saturated with a thick veil of cigarette smoke. Erik gives six coded knocks on a concealed door inside a storage room and is quickly let inside by Yoshi who bolts the door behind us.

"Good to see you man!" he says to Erik. He's wearing an oversized cargo vest over his sweater to match the oversized cargo pants, and his straight black hair falls over his eyes. When he sees Tru he backs up a little and gives me a nervous smile.

"Hey…Everest. Sorry, dogs and me, we don't mix. Erik told me you'd be bringing him, but just keep him on a short leash, ok?"

I nod. Dogs aren't for everyone, I suppose, even if they are as handsome and sweet as Tru. I tie the leash to the door. "He won't move. Let's chat with the others," I pat Tru and slip him a treat. "I'll be back. Sit tight. And don't eat anyone!"

"Do you have the phone?" Yoshi asks, tossing his head to one side to shift his bangs away from his eyes.

I search through the duffle to find it. "Hopefully in your hands it can do some good. Just be careful," I warn him.

"Don't worry, not my first time." He brings it over to Shahina and Ethan who are sitting at a table in the middle of the room surrounded by computer drives, monitors and cables. It's dark, probably because the one tiny window is covered by black board almost to the top. Cots are set up around the perimeter against the brick walls – just a pillow and a blanket, nothing fancy.

"Erik, Everest!" Shahina says, rising from her seat to greet us. "You made it! No complications, I hope?"

Ethan raises a hand in greeting from his seat but seems to be in the middle of something and can't pull his eyes away.

"No, not really," I answer Shahina, looking at Erik, who just grins and shakes his head at how easily I downplay trouble.

"I won't ask," she catches on. She's tall and slender, with her hair buzzed short. She wears two brilliant turquoise hoop earring that dangle as she walks and contrast with her dark skin. She speaks perfect English with an African accent.

"No," I change my mind, "you should know. Maybe you could help. We went to see Lise."

"Lise Vidal? The girl in the coma" Yoshi asks. "I thought she'd be heavily guarded."

Yeah, I know, I'm reckless. "We found a way around that. Sort of got lucky. Don't worry we weren't followed here. But that's not a coma she's in. Whatever it is, they're keeping her in it. She needs to get out of that hospital if she has any shot of waking up. I need to find someone I can trust to get her out. You guys think you could help with that?"

"You just got here and you're already asking for favors?" Ethan teases. "We're not even from here," he points out. "We don't know *anyone.*"

"What about the medical board? Could we find some records of doctors who have, I don't know…lost a license, need some extra cash? Maybe have a history of bending the rules?"

"Or nurses," Erik points out. "We just need someone with the right training to move her safely."

"That's…um…risky. Without knowing what th…they gave her, it could be dangerous to move her," Ethan observes. He comes across as a nervous recluse, hunched over his computer with his thick framed glasses, unkept brown hair and the occasional stutter. But I know behind the awkwardness lives a brilliant mind. "You could risk p…permanent damage." He notices our surprise. "I watch medical shows with my mom," he explains. "Don't tell Jason. He'll make f…fun of me until the end of time."

"Ok," I sigh, realizing Ethan reminds me of a more introverted version of Gill, if you substitute the love of books with computers. Back to the drawing board. "I'll try to think of something."

Shahina places a comforting hand on my shoulder and squeezes it gently. "We'll get her out," she says softly. "But time for some good news, yes? Have a look at this."

She leads us to Ethan's table where he's preoccupied typing code into his laptop. Next to him lies a small device the size of a flattened marble with a pinpoint black dot and a translucent-like shell.

"The outside is essentially a mirror," he says, "so it will blend into its surroundings s…seamlessly."

I study the strange object with intrigue. "What am I looking at?"

"It's how we're getting into the chapter house!" Shahina explains. "Well, not us, exactly. This is essentially a tiny drone spider, with some other features. If we can get it in, we can run a scan of the inside, get the lay of the land. Ethan's programming the blueprint tech now. It's small enough to fit under a doorway and from there it can travel and collect the data we need, be our eyes inside. We just need a way to get it through the front door – piggy-back it on something."

"Brilliant!" Erik exclaims, leaning in for a closer look. "It's practically invisible!"

"We may not have to piggy-back," I suggest. "There's a spyglass, remember? To one of the boardrooms inside the tunnel Sarah took me through. We could release it there without any suspicion."

"She's your Vulturian friend?" Shahina asks, crossing her arms protectively.

"She's on our side. We can trust her." I don't blame her for being suspicious. She hasn't met Sarah. She hasn't seen the regret in her eyes. All she knows is that Sarah works with the enemy, and that's the biggest red flag there is.

"That would work," Yoshi agrees, apparently more trusting than Shahina. "The program's pretty much ready. We could probably even get it in there tonight."

Ethan scratches his head and lets out a loud sigh. "Uh…let's aim for tomorrow. This is…taking me a little longer than I thought. Just focus on the blocker for now."

"It's ok," I tell them. "I can't get into those tunnels without Sarah anyway. I need to get in touch with her first. I'll see if I can figure it out by tomorrow." Ethan confirms the new deadline with a silent thumbs-up.

Yoshi sits down on a stool and eyes Tru from afar. "One more thing. You know he can't stay here, right? It's too risky. It's hard enough for us to stay in the shadows. A dog…."

Tru lies flat as a pancake, his head on the floor between his giant paws, his brown eyes looking up at us. "I know," I agree. "I have a plan. It just might take a few days."

Erik looks at me with a stern expression. He's always had an uncanny ability to guess my next move. He's probably figured out that I'm considering using the ring on myself again so I can bring Tru through the Tiamat's portal with me.

But I know I need to leave the past, and the ring, behind. I'll just have to access the Prism the good old-fashioned way and pray I have enough of my former potential to bring Tru and the compass along with me. It's the only place they can be truly safe.

Suddenly, a great deal depends on tonight.

"It will work, boy," I whisper to myself and Tru. "It has to work."

***

"I know, I know," I tell Tru as he tugs relentlessly at his tug rope. "You're a strong beast, I get it!"

I've taken him out in the cover of night so he can pee in a small park nearby. There's hardly anyone around. We're not exactly in the safest part of the city, so not many people are out walking at this hour, which suits me just fine. I wrestle Tru for the rope in the last of the fall leaves. *This almost feels normal.* He's like a puppy, and a resilient one at that. I'm proud of him. In a strange new city, he's remained calm and composed, and managed to land a starring role in a dangerous mission. I can't bear the thought of anything happening to him.

"I'm going to try, Tru. I'm going to try to get you in."

He lies down beside me and sticks his head under my arm, asking for a head scratch, which reminds of my own itchy scalp under my stupid wig.

"You'll love it. It will be your new home, for a while at least, until we can find something more permanent and, you know…real-world." We sit concealed by shadows in a quiet corner of the park until a rustling sound in the bushes startles me. It's probably just a squirrel, but it reminds me not to push my luck.

Time to go.

If tonight goes as planned, this will be our last walk in the real world for the foreseeable future. I still don't know if I'm doing the right thing. If anything happens to me, will he remain trapped in my dimension? Will the Prism take care of him? I shudder at the thought of abandoning him and things going wrong. But what's the alternative?

Once back inside the safehouse, I tie Tru to the door next to me and far away from Yoshi, and crawl into the cot that Erik's prepared for me. The blanket does little to absorb the cold from the hard tile floor.

"It won't be the most comfortable night," Erik says, handing me a deflated pillow.

I smile at him as I place it under my head. "Better than the truck. And it doesn't smell like cheese. How did we end up in a closet in a tattoo parlor anyway?"

"Blame Yoshi for that one. It's his cousin's contact."

"I went by the café earlier and left Sarah a message in the bathroom. I'm going to check back tomorrow for a reply."

Erik pulls a thin blanket on top of him. "Think she'll show?"

I sure hope so. I've been a ghost for three months. Part of me worries she stopped checking the café all together. "I don't know. I guess I'll find out."

I stare at the walls, trying to count the bricks and tire out my eyes. Tru repositions himself at my feet and sneaks on top of the covers. Yoshi and Ethan have packed up the last of the equipment and placed it in go-bags next to them. I watch as Ethan transfers something very carefully into a padded box, then stows the box in his backpack.

"You do this every night?" I ask.

"We need to be r…ready," he explains. "Wouldn't want this getting into the wrong hands."

No, we wouldn't want that. They've also barricaded the door with a filing cabinet and some chairs for added security.

Erik's sleeping on his side with his back towards me. I wish I could see his face before drifting off. I reach into my duffle and find the compass, then clench it tightly with fidgety fingers, willing it and Tru into my dimension and praying it works.

Please, God, let it be enough.

CHAPTER 9

Red Flags

Tru's slobbery tongue wakes me from a dream. I was skipping rocks across a stream in Vermont. Mom would send me to camp up there in the summer. She'd save for it all year. It was always the best week of vacation, and the perfect excuse to be wild and muddy. In the dream, the water sparkled like diamonds, which is how I knew it wasn't real, because the streams in the woods around the camp were surrounded by densely packed acres of trees which didn't allow the sunlight to lend sparkle to anything.

Tru doesn't give up and plants another kiss right on my nose.

"Come on boy, just wait a second." He starts pawing at me and making a whining sound. "Ok, ok. I'll take you out."

I open my eyes to find the leash, and freeze.

No way! It worked?

"It worked!" I shout startling Tru, who just tilts his head before resuming his frantic pawing of the covers, no doubt very alarmed at where he's suddenly found himself.

My dimension is exactly as I left it. White, and a whole lot of nothing. No wonder the poor dog is freaking out! He probably thinks he's going blind.

"Tru, we did it! You made it!" I grab him by the scruff around his neck and pull in his giant head, kissing him on the forehead as he stares at me, captive and perplexed. "You're going to be just fine now."

Holy crap! Maybe I really do have more potential than I give myself credit for.

My joyous moment of relief is instantly overshadowed by the memory of the last event that took place in this room.

Julian.

I pull Tru close to me again, this time for comfort, and just hold him. He seems to sense that I need him, because he just lets me be and snuggles his head further under my arm.

Surprisingly, the tears don't accompany the grief this time. I look around the empty space, remembering how disappointed Julian was when he saw it. It's time to move on from that day. It's already cost too many of us too much, and I won't let the Vulturians take anything more. Besides, Tru deserves better than four white walls and a window.

"Come!"

I head for the terrace. The Prismatic glistens like the stream in my dream, multiplied a thousand-fold and stretching out in front of me until it touches the horizon line. I breathe in the fragrant air as I marvel at the limestone walls of Castellum and jade green canopies of Cascada. As I enviously observe the Wakers moving about the Avenue, I calculate how much time I wasted being away from here.

For what? To feel sorry for myself? A lot of good that did!

Tru barks next to my leg. Maybe things are meant to happen. My time at the bunker allowed me to find him. I pat him on the head and lead him back inside, where I'm relieved to see the compass lying on the bed. I place the compass in the pocket of the jacket I find in the closet, then settle cross-legged on the bed and call Tru to snuggle up next to me. He refuses the invitation.

"Listen, you're going to be super freaked out in a few seconds. But a few seconds after that you'll be the happiest dog in the world. Just trust me." He sits on the floor looking goofy with his tongue hanging out but doesn't budge. "All right. Suit yourself. Here we go…"

Eyes closed. Deep breaths.

The images begin to flood in. A green plain, flowing grasses, gently rolling hills in the distance, perfect for some light climbing. A stream pushes through some boulders, flanked by mossy rocks and wildflowers and lots of things to sniff. Bursts of lavender spikes erupt around the perimeter of the meadow. The cottage takes shape, with the large stone hearth, the cozy kitchen, and ivory curtains that flutter in a welcome breeze.

Through my meditative state I can make out Tru barking. I open my eyes and smile. He's bounding through the meadow like a maniac, sniffing like he's on a mission and chasing his tail, then bounding off in another direction to do it all over again as he trips over his feet in excitement. It's safe, and welcoming, and stimulating. It's perfect, and it fills my heart with that unparalleled high that comes from creating something out of nothing.

Did I ever miss this feeling!

I'm about to join Tru outside the cottage when I hear two knocks on the door. When I open it, Erik's face transforms in seconds to display that same sense of pure joy – that childlike love of life I fell in love with. The corners of his eyes lift, and his dimples appear…finally.

"I knew you'd do it!" he exclaims. "I had no doubt. Is that Tru?" he adds, looking past me towards the meadow. "Hey big guy!"

Tru runs up and encircles us, smelling both our legs and making sure we're still the same people he knows. Once satisfied, he leans against my leg, then does the same to Erik.

"I think that means I'm part of the pack," Erik says. Our eyes meet for a moment before Erik looks mischievously towards the terrace. "It's been a stressful day. I could sure use a flight on Cass. Care to join me?"

My stomach flips. There's nothing I would want more. I glance at Tru with concern. Once I leave, he'll be the only living thing in this dimension, and it occurs to me that I'll have to arrange some company for him at some point if he's going to be staying here.

He'll be fine. It's the Prism. He'll be just fine. He seems to agree, and bounds off to explore his new world again, putting an end to my worry.

"To the Avenue!" I agree, turning to the door.

But Erik begins to move towards the terrace instead. "Why wait, when the sky is right here." Without warning, he runs through the doors and leaps off the balcony into the open sky, then succumbs to gravity, descending to the ground below with terrifying speed.

"*ERIK!*" I move swiftly with a pit in my stomach to look over the railing, only to find him settled comfortably on top of Cass, grinning up at me.

"You have so little faith!" he teases.

"You're such a jerk!"

Is it still safe, after everything?

But despite what's happening with the Prism and its deterioration, I know Juno won't fail me. I will her to me, and then, when I sense her near, climb up on the railing, refusing to look down.

"Are you coming or not?" Erik calls.

Just have faith. I close my eyes, and with an inhale for luck let my body tilt forward and off the railing.

I regret it instantly! The Prism spins in a terrifying spiral as I freefall. *What was I thinking!*

But my terror is alleviated when I see a whisp of ivory hair encircling me like a silky ribbon. I feel no pain as I land on Juno's back, grabbing onto her mane so I don't slip off.

"Brilliant!" Erik shouts from below, then motions Cass upward to meet us.

I glare at him, half exhilarated, half furious. "You're crazy!"

"Not my first time. Otherwise, I wouldn't have tried it. Where to?"

Where haven't we gone yet? "Ever see the Grand Canyon?"

"Just the Prism version," he replies.

"Well, one day we'll have to change that. But for now, I'll let you know how it compares."

***

The sun sits directly above us as we rest atop a rocky plateau in the center of the Prism's Grand Canyon. Cass and Juno keep each other company nearby.

"And the winner is?" Erik asks, reaching to the side to feed Cass an apple I've manifested.

"Huh?"

"Real world or Prism?"

"Oh…that's tricky. But I'd have to go with the real thing," I tell him. "It's a lot bigger. This is amazing but…it's missing something. Or maybe I'm just realizing how fragile this all is and appreciating reality a little more these days."

Erik lowers his head. "Yeah. Too bad reality can be so messed up." I can't disagree.

I see Erik's hand resting beside him on the brown dusty surface. I move my hand closer to see if he'll take the opportunity and brush his fingers against mine, but he doesn't.

"I wish things were the way they were before," I tell him.

He turns to look at me, his eyes soft and calm. I want the piercing eyes, the ones that would look at me full of desire and eagerness. The eyes that told me he had to have me and would stop at nothing to show me everything I could be.

But those eyes are gone.

"Me too," he simply says, offering me a sliver of hope before getting up and heading over to Cass. "We should head back."

That's it? That can't be it!

My heart sinks and I find myself wanting to hide under one of the giant boulders that surround us as I make my way to Juno. As we're getting ready to mount, the heavens suddenly open and the rain descends upon us. I catch Erik looking at me through the falling water. The rain works it's magic like it always does, cleansing me, freeing me. I feel Erik's fingertips find mine, and I ache to hold his whole hand. It's so close, I could just reach out and take back what I've lost.

The rain begins to slow, leaving me wanting more and reclaiming the promise of new beginnings. To my dismay, Erik withdraws, his face tensing up again. "We should find Robert, tell him what we've discovered," he says, then he mounts Cass and begins to ride off.

My heart splits in half as I watch him ride away. I bury my face in Juno's mane, trying to stop myself from feeling. After a few deep breaths I throw myself onto her back, once again angry at myself.

Move on. You ruined it. It's done.

***

Erik entrusts me with navigating the labyrinth so I can keep the way fresh in my mind. We're the first to arrive this time, aside from Robert. At least there isn't a room full of curious faces looking me over.

"Two days in a row," he observes as he smiles at me with fondness. "That puts my mind at ease."

"And this time I didn't need the help," I add.

"Good. I don't want you to ever use that on yourself again. You don't need it. You have enough potential within you to open ten of those portals in one night."

"I don't know about ten, but I'll take what I can get. How are Simon and Francine?" I ask with concern. God only knows what the Vulturians could be plotting now that they know I'm back in the picture. By now, Maeve and Tristan would have passed the information up the chain to the Ertu. That means all of us are in more danger again. Oddly, I can't seem to recall seeing Simon the last time I was in this room.

"Simon is fine. Missing his old life," Robert admits, "but there's enough to keep him busy in Montana. Uh…Francine…" Robert glances at Erik, who in turn shifts uncomfortably, then walks off to the side and examines some books on the shelf as if to give Robert some privacy.

"What is it?" I ask. "Is she alright?"

Robert's eyes begin to swim. He starts to open his mouth to say something but can't find the words, then quickly steps away as well, taking a moment to compose himself.

"Francine isn't a Waker anymore," he explains. "She never was."

Never was? "What do you mean? What are you saying?"

He turns to face me again, his eyes stern now, as if injected with ire. "She never belonged here Everest. She entered the way you did the last time you came here, as a Vulturian."

I feel my pulse quicken as I process what Robert's saying. *Francine?*

"How…how do you know?"

"Oh, the flags were always there," Robert admits, the sorrow written all over his face. "I just didn't want to see them at first. She was always uncomfortable in the Prism. I could see that she could feel discomfort more than the rest of us. The Prism could never read her thoughts, so she would never portal anywhere. She never let me see her dimension and demanded complete privacy, became…distant. Cold.

"When I couldn't locate her by name in Castellum, I confronted her about it. She said she used her birth name because that was her true name. Apparently, she had found her birth mother but never told me. I believed her. I'd heard of others using different names for privacy, so it seemed like a plausible explanation at the time, and I didn't want to upset her, in case she was going through something. With the Prism deteriorating and even my own earthly ailments catching up to me," he motions to his limp, "I assumed her discomforts were caused by the same thing. So, I buried my suspicions and put on my blinders. Deep down, I had concerns. But until I could prove something…well, ignorance was preferrable."

The tears balance on the edge of his lower eyelid as he appears lost in a memory. "She was my daughter in every sense of the word. Catherine and I loved her *so* much. But she didn't believe that, apparently."

"She told you that?"

He nods and sighs heavily. "She found me and Simon at our first safe house. It was too obvious in retrospect – an old family cabin that belonged to my uncle in the Poconos. When I saw her, there was just something about her. I knew immediately something was wrong.

"She told us to go outside. When I asked her why she came she wouldn't answer, then just grabbed Simon and hurled him towards the open door." Robert's face appears to age before my eyes in an instant as a painful frown overpowers his face. "The whole thing unfolded like a torturous nightmare. Simon's body travelled toward the door. She turned to me and…there was just this strange grin on her face, of evil satisfaction. I saw something on her wrist: that mark. *Their* mark. I couldn't believe I was seeing it on my own daughter.

"In a stroke of divine providence, Simon's shoe caught on an uneven floor plank, and he lost his footing. He fell forward, and the bullet that was meant for him grazed the top of his head and lodged itself in the wall. It was like an explosion of epiphanies went off in my brain. I started to connect all the dots, not wanting to believe any of them, each one a dagger to my heart. Everything made sense, even though I would give my life for it not to.

"I used my potential to knock her out, then took care of the two men outside before we grabbed what we needed and left." Robert swallows hard and sits down. "I haven't heard from her in weeks."

I let my stunned body sink into a chair next to him.

Francine?

I can't even imagine having your own family turn on you like that. I look at Robert with pity and feel another ache in my chest.

"I don't even know what to say."

He casts down his eyes. "There is nothing left to say. No words left to describe it."

"But *why* did she do it?"

"Francine came around as we were leaving. When I asked her that same question, she said we never loved her – that she always felt like an outsider. I couldn't even conceive of it. She was our miracle…our everything. How could her mind manufacture such a lie?

"And then I realized *they* must have poisoned her mind somehow. When the Vulturians came to her and told her of the Prism, she was probably resentful that she couldn't access it the way Simon and I could. So, she made a deal with the devil. She sold us out for a chance at paradise, and the Order took her soul in exchange."

Robert rises from his seat. "I don't know…maybe I did go wrong somewhere Everest. Maybe I could have made her feel more loved, done more to get her into the Prism with us."

"Don't do that to yourself," Erik urges, joining the conversation. I'd forgotten he was even in the room. "Sometimes, there are just things we can't fix, demons we can't cure out of people. They bring about their own ruin."

"Erik's right," I add. "She made her choices. We know you, Robert. I'm sure you did all you could for her. I'm truly sorry. If you need anything at all…"

"Thank you both, but I'm as good as can be expected. We all need time to deal with our losses. Simon is still a bit in shock I think, but the Prism is helping. I was amazed he even returned, although it took a few days. The last thing we need right now is to dwell on the past. We need to keep moving forward if we have any chance against this vile threat. The Vulturians want us to be slaves to our demons, to live in the wasteland of our deepest regrets and sorrows. We cannot let them win that easily."

I swallow the lump in my own throat. It's a lot to digest. This whole time Francine had another identify, another name.

Could that name have been 'Tara'?

"She followed her brother…." I look at Erik as I repeat

Maeve's words out loud. He inhales deeply, then clenches his fists and rests them on the table in front of him as he lowers his head. "Tara. Francine is Tara. She tracked Simon. That's how she knew about the Cascada access point."

"She led Irra and Basille to the glen that day," I finish. Francine had a part in Julian's death. Now there's a twist I never expected.

"Damn," Erik mumbles. "How did I misread both her and Maeve?"

"Well," Robert adds, "now *I* don't know what to say."

I shake my head, refusing to allow Francine – or Tara, or whoever the hell she is – take more than she already has. I've cried enough. I've darkened my own soul and robbed myself of light and love. I've screamed in pain at the night sky. I've hurt the ones that least deserved it. It ends now!

"Robert's right," I say. "We need to move forward. There is no other way if we want to win this war. Francine's deception, Maeve's deception…maybe more will come. Knowing the Vulturians, it's highly likely. But we can't let that derail us."

The other sentries begin to arrive. Jenna and Fox walk in together, shoulder to shoulder and blushing. A few new faces follow which I don't immediately recognize. Petra enters with her usual dispassionate expression, her spine straight and tall and her platinum hair glowing in the light of the floating energy orbs.

The new faces look suspicious to me now. I study them judiciously, trying to look for a tell. I turn to Robert to express my doubts, but he simply smiles reassuringly, somehow knowing exactly what I'm going to ask.

"We were *very* careful," he assures me. "No more blinders. Besides, the labyrinth would have scrambled by now if there was an imposter in our midst."

There is that. I hope he's right.

Erik takes his usual seat. "Ev," he calls out, and motions me to sit next to him. I know he's probably just being polite, but I'm grateful nonetheless to be back in my familiar spot. Jenna flashes me a hopeful look from across the table but tones it down when I subtly shake my head. At least Erik and I are on speaking terms now. But we have a long way to go to rebuild what we lost, if that's even still possible.

Robert gets started once we're all seated. "Good Prism morning to you all. First order of business – recruitment. Anyone have a new candidate?"

Corinne raises her hand. "I nominate Emmet Norberg from Salzburg, Austria,"

"Vetted?" Robert replies.

"Yes"

"Dimension?

"Active. Five separate tests."

"Potential?"

"Moderate, but inconsistent."

"Length of acquaintance?"

"Two years. No suspicious behavior to report."

"Seconder?"

Agnes raises her hand. "I've met him. He's solid. I second the nomination."

Robert sighs and pauses, no doubt reliving his personal tragedy with Francine and recollecting his own inaccurate assessments. "Very well. Bring him in," he concludes after no one objects. No other names are brought forward. "Round table then. Who's first?"

I retrieve the compass from my sweater pocket. If everyone has been carefully vetted, I need to have faith and seek help. Besides, Robert already knows about it.

"I have something," I say, placing the compass on the table and preparing for more puzzled stares and daggers from Jason.

"Surprise, surprise," he says on queue.

I ignore him. "I found this when I broke into Carmella Vieri's loft. Well, I didn't break in, the door was open."

"Maybe start at the beginning," Erik whispers, trying to help.

"Right. Ok, so, before I…took a break from the Prism, I went for a walk late at night in the Imperium courtyard. I saw a blue light coming from a third-floor window. When I entered the Imperium, I noticed there were only two floors, so I searched the rooms for a way up to the third. Carmella Vieri's office had a secret loft. That's where I found that same blue light."

And here is when I begin to sound crazy.

"It spoke to me."

"The light? It…*spoke* to you?" Jason jeers. "This is better than I thought it was going to be!"

Why does this guy dislike me so much? Has anyone vetted *him* lately? From the corner of my eye, I can see Erik shoot him a look, and Jason immediately raises his hands in surrender. "Go on," he says.

"I know how it sounds, but it happened. The light – more of a flame, actually – was just…there, burning in place. I touched it, and…I can't even explain the sensation. It was nothing like I'd ever felt, pure and powerful beyond words. It communicated to me through letters it wrote in the air. It said I didn't have much time." I have no problem recalling the message. It's been engraved into my brain since that night. "To fix the Prism and get rid of the unworthy, to give the Prism to humanity, you must find them both and conceal them well in time. We can help you. But the only way is through time. Listen to the whispers."

The room is silent as everyone waits for me to say more.

Petra raises an eyebrow. "That's it?"

"Unfortunately. We were interrupted by someone entering the Imperium. The Flame left behind this object, which it called a compass. I tried to sneak away but someone followed me."

I recall the events of that night in my mind: the faceless woman with the short hair, much like Francine's. *Of course!* I don't reveal what I suspect in front of the group to spare Robert.

"I lost her in the Climbing Gardens, but she saw that I had something. She must have seen the blue light and come for it, only I got to it first." Robert rises from his seat and comes over to inspect the compass again. "I'm not sure what to make of it. It must be a piece of the puzzle we need. And it would explain why I was chased in the gardens that night. But the Aenoian text doesn't speak of it at all. And I've read it front to back, twice."

"I don't recall anything either," Robert adds. "What's the symbol on the front?"

"Just a triangle. I'm assuming it symbolizes the Prism?"

"Funny, it's exactly the same size and shape as that pendant hanging around your neck," Callia, one of the new recruits, observes.

I bring my fingertips up to the pendant, letting them glide over the smooth edges and the stones.

Could it be that simple?

I turn to Erik. "Where did you say you got this again?"

He scratches his forehead. "Uh, just a shop…in the Isles of Edenia, that day we all went sailing. There was a woman inside. I was walking by, she stopped me, asked me if I knew anyone who might want it."

"How did she look like?"

"I wasn't really paying attention to her face. But she had long hair, really long, and some bracelets on her wrists."

Like the woman I met in Cascada the same night I saw the Flame.

The pieces fall into place in a slow cascade of still pictures in my mind, no longer disjointed and random events. It's an elaborate, frustrating puzzle, and I could be seconds away from solving a big part of it. "I often feel it become warm around my neck…" I mumble, more to myself, "like that night at the Imperium, or on the Sky Serpent."

"Well, aren't we going to test it? The suspense is killing me!" Fox cries.

I look up at Robert, who places the compass back into my hand. Erik's offers a short nod of encouragement, his lips drawn into a straight line as he waits with the others for me to place the pendant into the triangular depression.

It clicks into place without resistance, almost as if pulled in by a magnetic force. Instantly, a vivid cobalt light shoots out from the metal object, projecting an array of symbols onto the ceiling. They hover over our heads like floating stencils, never drifting. Circles and triangles, inside circles and triangles. Infinity symbols inside circles, infinity symbols inside triangles.

"Woah!" Fox mutters.

"Wait a minute, I recognize these," Erik says once the surprise wears off. He walks in a circle around the table, his head tilted upwards as he studies the ceiling. "The armor on the emerald guard."

"That's right! Each one has a slightly different pattern, just like these." Robert confirms.

"And the obelisk, in the Imperium courtyard," I add. "The same symbols are etched around it, in a repeating pattern."

There's so much to unpack my brain hurts. Compass, symbols, pendant, flame… and now the monoliths are in play?

Through time…conceal them both in time…

"The Flame's message spoke of time," I think out loud, recalling my earlier hypothesis. More still pictures litter my mind, along with words written in the air in sweeping strokes of perfect calligraphy. "It said 'the only way is through time.' I thought it meant to be patient, to wait for the right time. But what if it was asking me to hide the Skala and the Tiamat in *another time,* so they could never be found and used against humanity." I look up at the symbols projecting onto the Citadel ceiling. "What if the emerald guards are actually time portals? And it can't be chance that I found this compass in the loft of the physicist who happens to be studying this very phenomenon!"

No one speaks. As if the Prism isn't hard enough to understand, as if we don't have enough to worry about with the Vulturians and the Prism deteriorating around us – now we're throwing time travel into the mix.

Nathan, another newbie with a bed of curly hair that almost covers his eyes, looks about ready to launch himself into space judging by his broad smile and bulging eyes. He waits with twitchy fingers for someone senior to say something.

"It's certainly possible, I suppose," Hadid answers, causing Nathan to sit up straighter and smile even wider. The others also appear intrigued, no doubt grateful for some exciting news.

Time travel through pasts Prisms – it's enough to make the biggest skeptic giddy at the thought of it. Even Jason looks captivated as he tries to decipher the code that glows above his head.

"Well," Robert finally replies, "it's a good thing Carmella Vieri was vetted into the Sentry."

"She was?" I ask. "When?"

"A few weeks ago. I know her well and thought she would

be a good fit. She's a brilliant thinker and scientist, and a loyal Waker."

"Why isn't she here?"

"She is rather obsessed with her work," Robert explains. "She misses meetings on occasion when she's engrossed in a project. I'll make sure she's at the next one. But in the meantime, we should pay her a visit. A theory this incredible can't wait until tomorrow."

CHAPTER 10

Look Up!

We pass the obelisk on our way to the Imperium and study the ribbon of Prism symbols etched around it. I sense my stomach begin to climb into my throat, partly from excitement, partly from anxiety over the unexpected.

"Do you think she'll take us seriously?"

Erik chuckles. "Would you relax? You sound like you're going to a job interview."

I don't know why meeting Carmella Vieri intimidates me so much. Maybe because I could never come close to understanding the work she does. The equations and papers sprawled on her floor looked like an alien language to me. "She sounds brilliant. What if she laughs in our faces?"

"She won't do that. She's studying time travel, remember? If anything, she'll probably send you a bottle of wine."

"I don't need wine. I just need for all this to be over."

Erik sighs. "Well, *I* could use some wine right about now. I could really use a night away from all this – a normal night."

Like we always planned to have together. At least we got one, before the Vulturians turned our lives upside down. "You can say that again," I mumble under my breath. "She must really love physics to continue working here."

"For some people, work *is* their paradise. Like Robert. We're all wired differently. Not everyone finds that one thing that gets them up in the morning – that one thing they never want to stop doing. She's one of the lucky ones. Trust me, she won't laugh in your face."

Once inside the Imperium, we place our feet on the grey staircase which looks a little less dreary thanks to some sunlight creeping in through the four small windows at the front of the building.

"I think it was Francine," I say to Erik as we climb. "That's who chased me from here that night."

"Yeah, the thought crossed my mind. You think you know someone…"

By the time we reach the sixth door, Robert's already seated and waiting, *Ancient Artifacts of Aeonia* resting on his lap. I'm relieved to see that a little sparkle has returned to his eyes. Carmella Vieri stands over her desk, mulling over some papers. When she sees us enter, she extends her hand.

"You must be Everest, and Erik. Robert has filled me in. Come, come inside, come, please."

She looks more put together than her messy office would foreshadow. Her dark brown wavy hair is partly gathered into a twist, and her hazel eyes peer out from under naturally long eyelashes, the kind that Nina would stick on with glue.

Nina. I wonder how she's doing. So much of my old life feels so far removed, like it never existed.

With her chic grey shawl over a slim black dress and red belt, Carmella looks like she could be the dean of a university or one of those smart-looking people you see on the cover of alumni magazines, because they discovered a life-saving drug, or planet, or fossil. To say she's impressive and intimidating is an understatement.

I shake her hand. "It's nice to meet you, Carmella."

"Robert tells me you think the emerald guards could be time portals?" she says, getting right to the point.

"Thought I'd save us some time," Robert fills in as we take our seats.

I nod. "Does it sound crazy?"

But Carmella's eyes are on fire as she looks through her alien equations again. "Not at all. I think you may be onto something. Your theory corroborates my own research. Have a look at this…"

She shoves a paper with scribbles under my nose. I have no idea what I'm looking at. I show it to Erik, who pretends to read it, but ultimately turns to me and shrugs.

"Sorry, we can't read physics," he tells her. "You'll have to translate."

"Ah yes. I'm sorry, yes, yes, yes," Carmella apologizes, throwing up her arms. "I got a little ahead of myself. I assume everyone can understand my jumbled diagrams.

"What you're looking at are calculations based on energy field experiments. I've measured disturbances of energy throughout various parts of the Prism, and it just so happens that the greatest disturbances are consistently around the monoliths. Other areas hardly see any. But the monoliths…something very interesting is happening there, every night."

"Like a portal?" I suggest hopefully.

"Maybe, yes" Carmella answers, tilting her head back and forth. "Unfortunately, it's difficult to measure properly because these disturbances don't occur when we're here."

Erik leans in. "When else would they occur?"

"After we awaken on Earth." Carmella raises her finger in the air as if she's clued into something, then shuffles through her papers again. "I set up timed experiments, and all of them showed the disturbances happening *after* the Prism-day ends — that is, after it ends for *us*. Think of it as extra time in a football game, only it's the Prism's extra time."

Erik turns to me with a satisfied grin. "See, *football*. She gets it!"

I grin. I'm not going to convince two Europeans. "Have it your way. So, if the emerald guards are portals, you're saying they open when no more Wakers remain?"

"It seems so," Carmella confirms. "It's a mysterious time gap that we don't have much information on, and the monoliths appear very active in those hours. But not all. It's a different one each time. The one thing that remains consistent is the interval. The disturbance begins, on average, 47 hours and 20 minutes after the start of the Prism day, and it lasts about a Prism minute, with energy readings more intense than anything I've ever observed."

Intense is good. We want intense. It suggests something otherworldly — something unfamiliar and fantastic and paranormal. It suggests possibility.

"So, we just have to figure out which one opens and when," I conclude hopefully, sensing answers within my grasp.

"Yes, you need to know that, absolutely. But…" Carmella grimaces as she flicks a hair strand away from her eyes, "unfortunately, you'll never be awake to see it. My studies show that most Wakers fall asleep at the latest around 46 hours and 50 minutes. I've done multiple experiments on myself. I depressed a timer I designed in the Luminary. I held it myself at the end of the day. The idea was that when I *did* finally fall asleep, my finger would slip off the button and I'd stop the timer. The longest I ever stayed awake was 46 hours and 59 minutes, and I repeated it more than once. Sometimes, my day was slightly shorter, but never longer. So, it appears the length of one Prism day is just about 47 hours."

Erik throws up his hands. "Wonderful! We've got a compass, and maybe even a map – and potentially a time portal. But no way of staying up long enough to use any of them." He smirks. "How did we get so lucky?"

"Actually, our luck may be turning," I reply, digging through my memories. "I ran into a woman once in Cascada. It was the night I found the compass, which, now that I think about it, probably wasn't a coincidence either. She also sounds remarkably similar to the woman who gave Erik my pendant. Anyway, she gave me some tea to drink made from a leaf – the mekiza leaf, she called it."

"Mekiza?" Robert ponders the name, shaking his head and pouting. "I've never heard of it."

"Neither have I," Carmella adds, "but botany is not my specialty. It may be native to the Prism."

"Maybe. She said something about it helping me stay in the Prism a little longer. That could be how we make it to the portals – how we stay awake long enough."

Erik shoots me a puzzled look. "Anything else you want to share with the class?"

"I didn't think it was important before," I reply. "And we had bigger problems."

Carmella clasps her hands together, her pupils darting about, searching for inspiration among her calculations. "Good. This is good. We have a way. This is good," she keeps repeating.

Robert uncrosses his legs and leans forward. "It's a possibility. But beating the clock won't matter if we don't know where to go. How do we figure out which portal opens?"

Carmella's energy diminishes a little. "Unfortunately, I haven't figured out the pattern. I can't tell you if you need to go to Nevar or Arboran or Estra. And since the energy disturbance only lasts about a Prism minute, there's no room for error. You would need to correctly identify and travel to the correct portal before it opens and closes, otherwise you would miss your chance."

She reaches into her desk and pulls out a brass object that resembles a pocket watch. "But I *can* help with this. Another little thing I designed in the Luminary," she says humbly, downplaying her genius for invention. "It's a Prism clock – moves much slower, adapted to the Prism's time. I can make some changes and allow you to set a timer from the moment the Prism day ends. Then, theoretically, you would know roughly how much time remains to make it to the portal, once you figure out which one it is. You only have 20 Prism minutes from the end of the Prism day until the portal opening. *Potential* portal opening, that is. Remember, this is all still hypothetical."

The only way is through time.

"It must be the compass. It's the final piece," I mutter. "Why else would the Flame call it that?" I place my pendant on top of it and observe the lights illuminate the ceiling of the office.

Carmella's jaw drops as she studies the mysterious blue patterns. "Magnificent!"

"Yeah," I agree. "We just don't know what it means…"

I look at the text Robert is holding.

"May I?"

He passes me the book and I flip to the page I'm thinking of. "According to this, the symbols refer to four elements: the infinity symbol is time, the closed dot is earth, the triangle is potential, and the star is purity of spirit. The text speaks of all four elements being required to become the Master of the Skala.

That's why you see them carved all over the place – they were sacred to the Aeonians. The symbols are contained in either a circle or a triangle, symbolizing that all the elements must be present both on Earth and in the Prism. You need all the variables to be able to find the Skala."

"And each monolith has a different combination of those symbols," Erik points out. "There is only one combination per monolith – a total of eight."

I count the borders in my head. "There's nine borders," I remind him. So much for that hypothesis. "We're one combination short."

Erik grins mysteriously. "No, there are no monoliths between Nevar and Senna, only mountains. There are exactly eight monoliths and exactly eight combinations. No coincidences, right?"

"Hold on a minute" Robert suddenly jumps in, coming to stand beside me, then moving about the room in a circular motion, neck arched back as he studies the glowing pattern. "When you used this compass in the Sentry, it was a different pattern, I'm sure of it!"

"What do you mean?"

"It's like it's been moved around. There was a row of stars inside a triangle there, and…" he motions to different points on the ceiling, "a cluster of shapes up there. But I can't see them now."

"You think it changes?"

"Precisely."

"Maybe that's how we decode which portal opens," Erik suggests. "It tells you which portal is about to be activated. It's the key. The compass *is* our map!"

"A map with no legend," I lament. There's still a crucial piece of the puzzle missing – the one that ties it all together.

"We still don't know which symbol is the right one. Anyone know a code breaker?"

We stare at the meaningless collage of symbols, each of us desperately trying to crack the cipher, aching to cry out an epiphany that will put everything into perspective. But all we hear is heavy breathing and sighs. The chairs squeak across the floor as we squirm in our seats.

Nothing.

The muscles in our necks begin to ache, and each of us slowly begins to straighten our backs. Exasperated, I remove the pendant from the compass, clearing the light and meaningless map away, the room now appearing lifeless and dull by comparison.

"There has to be something we're missing..."

Carmella sits down and stares through us, the gears turning and grinding. "We'll figure it out," she offers, trying to stay hopeful. "We made excellent progress today."

I smile at her. "We did. Thank you."

Erik reaches to examine the Prism pocket watch. "Suppose we figure it out – which one opens. We go through the portal, if there is one, and into the past as we plan. Where will we end up, exactly?"

"I don't know," Carmella admits. "That you will have to figure out as you go. It may work like our portals, through the link to our thoughts and intentions. I can't be sure. But if that *is* the case, you would have to be very clear about your destination for the Prism to read your mind."

"That could be a problem," Robert admits. "We have no idea what this place is or how it looks like."

"Yes, you mentioned..." Carmella muses. "It may take several tries then, to get to...what was the name again?"

"Aeonia." I answer. "It sounds like an ancient place, far removed from our time, which means a lot of opportunity for things to go wrong. If we do miss the portal opening, and we're in a past Prism, what happens?"

Carmella sighs. "It's an unknown variable you won't be able to control until you're living it. I can only guess that if you miss your portal, you'll remain in the Prism of the past and awaken during that respective time-period on Earth, which could be very dangerous, depending on when that would be.

"Traveling to a utopian paradise is one thing. Waking up in another world where you're not supposed to exist is another. There would be many risks and things you would not be prepared for. To prevent that from happening, you would have to theoretically keep moving back in time through the Prism portals until you found your destination in one fluid series of portal jumps. That is your best chance at success."

Excellent. I'm not liking our odds. "So, no slip-ups. Never missing a portal. Not even once?"

Carmella nods. "I'm not a time travel expert, but it's best to be prepared for the worst and not test the past." She takes a seat at her desk, folds her hands in front of her and looks at us sternly. "There is… one other consideration. Even if we figure out this map, and you make every single portal in time, and everything goes exactly as planned until you reach Aeonia, from what I've studied, the portal will only be able to send you in one direction. I assume it's the past, because that's what others before me have hypothesized, based on their own calculations. But it very well could be the future, for all we know. I guess… what I'm saying is, I don't know if a return-trip is possible, regardless of where you go."

The mood shifts instantly. The progress we've made is dwarfed by the giant elephant that's just charged into the room.

Robert, Erik and I look at each other. There's no hope in our eyes, no excitement over chasing that adrenaline high that we've been chasing so far. This isn't an amusement park ride where you end up where you started and go on to the next rollercoaster. There may not be a next ride.

"So, if we go back…" Erik begins.

"You may never return to our time," Carmella finishes solemnly. "You may have to remain wherever the Prism takes you."

The elephant lies on top of us, compressing the air from our lungs and pushing it out of our bodies. We drop our eyes to the floor, reality sinking in.

Even if we succeed and the Vulturians lose, there may be no hero's welcome in the end, unless we find another magic compass to get us back. *And what are the odds of that?*

"Well," I say, letting out a nervous snicker at this new cruel twist of fate, "just another minor complication."

***

I can't bring myself to explore the Prism after our meeting with Carmella, and much rather spend my time with Tru. He looks content in his new environment, bounding through pastures and rolling around in the dirt yet never getting dirty.

We made progress today, but Carmella's last revelation has me rattled. The Prism chose me: it gave me the pendant; it gave me the compass. I know it needs to be me that goes through the portal. There's no guarantee that I'll come back, and it will be a lonely and terrifying journey, but I can't put anyone else through it. It needs to be me.

Only me.

Tru trots over and puts a paw on my leg, then a snout,

sensing my turmoil. He looks up at me with puppy dog eyes, like he knows I need the laugh. I kiss his soft head and bring my own forehead to rest on it. "Why can't things be easy for once?"

I think back to how great things could be if the Vulturians didn't exist – if it was just me and Tru and Erik and the Prism – and all the good stuff. I know what Erik would say. *It would get boring after a while.* Maybe it would. But boring sounds pretty good right about now.

I invite Tru up on the bed and turn the compass over in my hand, searching my brain for that 'aha' moment.

"Come on…"

It's at the tip of my brain.

Something calls to me – a silent voice from beyond the terrace doors, beckoning me back to the Nucleus, as if that's where the answers lie. They're so close, I can feel them encroaching on my thoughts, kept out by an iron black gate that refuses them entry.

What am I missing?

Tru's asleep, and I can feel my own head growing heavy. I head to the closet and retrieve the mekiza leaf from the pocket of the jeans I had worn in Cascada on the night I saw the Flame. It's still in one piece and hasn't dried up. I chop one half into tiny pieces, then steep it in some hot water, fighting sleep as I work. It tastes just like the tea the old woman gave me, and I down it in a few gulps.

Then I wait.

After a few moments my eyes feel less heavy, and the world outside calls to me again.

Maybe it's enough.

The Prism crowds are thinning as I make my way to Cascada. First, I set off to collect more mekiza since I'm going to need it anyway. There aren't many Wakers around, and I feel like I'm trespassing where I shouldn't be. I take the other half of the leaf and compare it to the flora along the pathways. It all looks the same. Boulders and trees blend into one enormous shadow, the stillness of the realm pierced only by the sound of falling water.

The stars help me see the details on the leaves. At last, I find a small clump of mekiza growing under a birch and collect a generous amount, stuffing the plants into the pockets of my sweatshirt as I watch the Prism magically replenish them.

Never gets old.

I start heading back when I hear it: a whisper hisses through the trees, the leaves rustle, the night moans around me.

Look up! Look up!

I cast my eyes towards the sky. It looks the same as every other night. Breathtaking, but the same. I recall what that old woman told me: If someone stands at the exact right spot in Cascada, the Prism will bestow upon them a secret.

And then later, the Flame: *Listen to the whispers…*

More sensations arrive: the pendant burning into my chest; the compass weighing down my back pocket. I retrieve it.

Look up!

I begin running my right hand over the compass engraving, letting my fingertips dip into the depressed triangle and over the etched letters.

Carpe Noctum. Seize the night.

Seize the night! *Look up…*

It's as if a flash of lightening has pierced my body. My legs spring into action, propelling me towards the Luminary, dodging branches and leaping over brush. I emerge into the courtyard and barrel towards the beacon towers, then push open the steel doors and rush into the centre of the Luminary.

Look up!

The *Galaxia* appears to glow at the peak of the dome as if the paint is infused with fluorescent properties. I bring the compass and pendant together and stand directly under the centre point of the painting, the compass map superimposing on Michelangelo's masterpiece. The Prism symbols find their places on the dome within the painting's parameters.

A perfect fit!

One of the painted orbs has writing around its perimeter, in an arc. It's so small I never noticed it before. Despite the Prism improving my eyesight somewhat, I need to squint, but manage to make out the letters.

In tempore.

In time.

A symbol is perfectly superimposed on the centre of the orb: the triangle with the infinity symbol.

I feel a smile lift my cheeks, butterflies thrashing their wings inside my chest.

The *Galaxia* is the legend to the map.

We have the final piece.

CHAPTER 11

The Test

It's the kind of news that can't wait until morning. But the day is nearing a close and I'm running out of Prism minutes, as all the Wakers are.

Erik, Robert and Carmella aren't just any Wakers. Their minds are infused with an endless curiosity that may allow them to delay sleep a while longer – just long enough for me to get to them and offer them a cup of tea.

I race back to Castellum, brew the tea, then head for Erik's dimension.

"Erik! Are you asleep yet? Erik?" About ten second pass before Erik finally appears before me, looking confusing by the unexpected visit.

"I was *nearly* asleep. What is it? What's happened?"

I shove the cup of tea in his face, almost spilling it. "Drink it."

"What is it?"

"Just, do it! We don't have much time." As soon as he takes a sip, I pull his body through the door and head for the elevator.

"What is going on?" he asks, stumbling behind me.

"You'll see. Just stay awake! We have two more house calls."

***

"Well, I'll be…" Robert mumbles.

I hold the compass on my palm facing up, projecting the map onto the Galaxia. Carmella's mouth hangs open, as does Erik's. The triangle with the infinity symbol glows slightly brighter than the other projections as it hovers inside the marked orb.

"I think this is it," I say, turning to Carmella for confirmation.

She locks eyes with me, her gaze radiating intrigue and hope. "I think it is!"

"It makes sense," I continue. "The Flame used the words 'in time'. *In tempore* is Latin for the same phrase. The symbol that's projected into the marked orb must point to the portal we need to pass through – the one that would be open tonight!"

Carmella appears lost in mental calculations as she paces around us. "And that specific one…I'm certain it's on the monolith on the border of Verding and Arboran."

"What about those?" Erik asks, pointing at three bright stars around the perimeter, one moving quickly clockwise, the second much slower, the third not at all. They all sit along tiny circular points that make up the map's border. "And why are only two of them moving?"

Carmella raises her finger and begins to count silently as the moving stars make their orbit around the masterpiece. "That's roughly the length of a Prism-day. Which would mean…" She looks back at us with a spark in her eyes, then bolts towards the rear exit. "I'll be right back," she shouts as she runs off.

Robert makes himself comfortable on the four steps that descend into the recessed inner courtyard. "Let's hope this tea holds up long enough to get her back here."

It better hold up. We're so close….

We just sit staring up at the display above us in silence, lost in our own thoughts, until finally, we hear a door open.

"I've got it!" Carmella yells, her footsteps echoing off the walls. I can see she's a little breathless. The Prism would have never allowed that before, which means sadly, it's still deteriorating.

In her hand she clutches the Prism clock she invented. "The moving points," she explains while inhaling short breaths, "may count down to the end of the Prism day and the portal opening. I think it's an hour hand, a minute hand and a second hand. There are just short of 47 hours in a Prism day, as many as there are points along that border. Meaning one full rotation of *that* star," she points to the one that appears stationary, "and a full Prism day has passed. According to this clock, the day comes to an end in…about three Prism minutes." She fiddles with the design of her invention in her mind, closing her eyes and whispering under her breath. "And – based on my research – the disturbance around the monoliths would begin 20 minutes after that."

Surprisingly, I'm able to follow Carmella's calculations. "Then this isn't the portal that's about to open after all. This was the one that opened last."

"Precisely! I think we are about to get new coordinates."

Three and a half Prism minutes might as well be three hours. I lie on my back to spare my neck. No one seems to breathe let alone speak. If Carmella's right about this, she's probably right about all of it. The test begins now.

Finally, three Prism minutes is up. When all three stars line up on the 47th point, the elements on the map begin to shift and scramble, like the pieces of the labyrinth. A new symbol settles onto the marked orb. A circle, and within it a triangle.

The Prism-day has ended, and we know the next portal.

My body starts to tremble, but after the rush of the moment wears off, I realize it's trembling for another reason. It's all beginning to feel very real.

"Estra and Azula," Robert points out, recognizing the location of the new symbol. "We have 20 minutes, I presume?"

I see Carmella looking up at the dome, lost in thought with a satisfied smile, the blue glow highlighting her face. Years of work and theories and late nights all bearing fruit.

"Nineteen minutes, 49 seconds," she whispers, almost inaudibly. "Give or take."

***

Robert looks nervous, while Carmella keeps checking the stopwatch. The border of Estra and Azula is deserted, which serves us just fine.

"How much time?" I ask our timekeeper impatiently.

"Four minutes."

The emerald guards that loom over us seem even more intimidating by night, with the top of the monoliths concealed by the sky, making them appear taller and somewhat menacing. Robert places a hand on one of the frisbee sized emblems on their stone tunics, a large emerald triangle in the center of the circular carving. "How will we know when it opens?"

"I'm not sure. But I wouldn't stand too close to the threshold," Carmella warns. "We need to send something through the portal to test it." She bends down and struggles to lift a small boulder. "Anyone good at discus?"

Robert chuckles and steps away from the passage between the two monoliths. "No one is throwing *that*. At least, not until the Prism is fixed. I like my spine functioning properly."

"We need something large enough to see from a far," Carmella insists. "We can't risk going through the portal ourselves to check where it lands and, God forbid, getting sucked into some rift in space time with no way of getting back."

"Don't worry," I assure her, wringing my hands together. "I think I've got this."

I close my eyes and focus on an image of two footballs – the elongated spherical shape, the soft brown leather, the white laces – then open my eyes again to find them lying at my feet. The color comes next. I pick one up when I'm done, admiring the vivid fluorescence of the orange I was able to achieve, and prepare my stance, trying to ignore Carmella's perplexed expression. Then I pull my arm back and release the glowing football, watching it sail through the night between the stone goal posts. It lands well beyond the border, on the Azula side, clear of the danger zone and glowing noticeably.

"Nice throw," Erik praises.

"Thanks. *That's* football."

"That's literally armball."

I laugh. "Agree to disagree. Time?"

Carmella manages to start blinking again and glances at the watch. "Uh…25 seconds, give or take. Are we going to talk about what you just did there?"

"I'll fill you in later," Robert replies, giving me a wink. "Everest has some talents that come in handy now and then. Let's get ready. This could be it!"

We all take a few more steps back away from the monoliths, careful not to get caught in the crosshairs of the portal, should it open. "12,11,10…" Carmella counts down. I can see her fingers twitching as she grasps the stopwatch. I steady the second football in my hand, my entire body shaking.

Four, three, two, one…

"Now!" Carmella cries, "It should be opening."

Stillness. Silence. The space between the monoliths remains undisturbed, with only the sound of the breeze reaching our ears. Maybe nothing happens. Maybe this is just a massive disappointment, a miscalculation.

Only one way to find out.

I pull back my arm, then propel myself forward into the throw, releasing the football towards the threshold and focusing on where I want it to land – right in between the emerald guards. A blinding flare engulfs it as it passes between the monoliths – the briefest of zaps, until the flash becomes absorbed again by the darkness like a momentary electric shock. The stillness returns, but only one football glows on the ground in the realm across from us. The original one. Goosebumps erupt over my skin, and I feel as if an earthquake has been set off inside my body. I can't stop the shaking, my eyes glued to the lone orange glow. Somewhere, someone is wondering why there's a fluorescent orange football lying at their feet.

Somewhere, but not here. Not now.

"It worked," I hear Erik whisper next to me. "It actually worked."

Robert crouches on the ground, hand over his mouth. Slowly, he rises and walks over to Erik and the two men start to laugh and pat each other on the back. "Amazing! Incredible!" Erik keeps repeating "brilliant" more times than I can count.

"All this time…I've been looking…" Carmella brings her hands to her chest and lets that last word linger on her lips, her hazel eyes blinking away water. "It's actually possible."

"It's not just possible," I reply, turning to her, my neurons still seizing with elation, "it happened! You discovered it!"

She smiles back at me, nodding and looking about ready to

cry. "We all did! With some divine intelligence guiding us, I'm sure."

Through the darkness I lock eyes with Erik and offer him a faint smile. But the joyous moment is tarnished by my realization that the very thing that could save us could also tear us apart. Once I go through, there's no guarantee I'll ever return. It's a responsibility I never asked for, but I can't ignore fate any longer.

I won't run again. It needs to be me.

I'm going to Aeonia.

CHAPTER 12

The New Place

"Everest! Wake up!"

My head rolls back and forth on the pillow as someone shakes me awake. I hear objects fall, violent pounding on the door. I open my eyes to see Erik's panicked face. Yoshi, Shahina and Ethan frantically gather their already packed go-bags. The pounding on the door continues, and I look over to see Yoshi's barricade coming apart, inch by inch.

"They found us," Erik says. "We need to go!"

Shit! I leap up from the cot, trying to untangle the blanket around my legs. "How?" Did they follow me and Tru from the park, see me on the cameras?

"Doesn't matter now. Grab your things. We're going to the new place."

I look for Tru, amazed that he's so quiet, but he's nowhere to be found. The leash lies on the ground, not attached to anything. Panic sets in for a fraction of a moment before it's followed by relief. He stayed in my dimension. It worked. He's safe. *Thank God!*

"I never unpacked. What else can I do?"

The room is basically vacant, and I assume we're not taking the cots and pillow. Shahina motions me to an opening under the floorboards, the hatch attached to the underside of a stiff rug. Yoshi's already below ground helping Ethan with the bags.

"Get in and stay quiet," Shahina instructs, opening the lone window, presumably as a decoy.

One of the chairs that forms the barricade topples over, and the wood around the frame begins to splinter as the door starts to come off the hinges. I grab Tru's leash from the floor and descend into the opening, after which Yoshi secures the hatch with a thick steel plate underneath, just in time.

We move stealthily through the dark, dusty passage under the floorboards, and I don't dare ask where it leads for fear of making a sound that could give us away. I hear the door to the storage room break off the frame and the sound of footsteps running into the room above us, sending dirt falling onto our heads.

A small crack in the floorboards offers me a view of the intruders, and the face of evil itself. Irra commands a group of five or six men, instructing them to check out the open window. I feel the hatred boiling up inside me again, summoning something dark from the underworld of my buried pain.

Don't give yourself away, I remind myself, trying to calm the inner storm the way Erik taught me. I hear Irra yell something in what sounds like Arabic. The voices get fainter as we move further away. Bullets penetrate the floor behind us. I don't know if it's Irra taking out his fury, or if he's trying to figure out if we're hiding underground. Either way, we can't stick around to find out. He could find the hatch at any moment.

Yoshi leads us down a series of sewer tunnels, and the smell of sewage and decay makes my stomach turn. When I think we're far enough away, I pat Ethan on the back.

"Where are we going?" I whisper.

"Another safe house. Thirty-minute walk," he replies, then turns to look at me and puts his finger to his lips. *Ok, I'll shut up.* Erik snickers and shoots me a smile, knowing first-hand how hard it will be for me to stop asking questions.

At least none of us seem to have caught a bullet. Shahina sprinkles something on the floor at the rear of our little caravan, maybe to throw off our scent in case they send dogs in to track us. I can't imagine Irra commanding a canine unit. He'd probably just release some poison gas. That seems more his style. In any case, I doubt he'll find us, considering Yoshi's doing a pretty good job of confusing the hell out of me. The underbelly of Paris is a complex maze of passages, abandoned quarries, sewers and subway lines. I've completely lost my bearings and feel as if we've gone in a circle three times.

On what feels like our fourth rotation guided only by the glows of Yoshi's cellphone screen, our guide stops, then turns to the right to face the stone wall. He proceeds to knock on it. *Tap, tap, tap.* The knocks all produce the same sound, except one – it's not as low. Two cracks in the stone travel on diagonals from the ceiling to the floor. Yoshi runs his fingers over the cracks, then bends down to remove a chisel from the front pocket of his pack. He begins to scrape at a narrow space between the wall and the ground while the rest of us watch with bated breath, hoping to hear only grinding and scratching, and no gunfire.

"Well?" Shahina finally asks. "Do you feel it?"

"No" Yoshi replies, letting the tip of the chisel feel it's way around under the stone.

"It's not here then. Let's keep going."

Ethan raises his hand. "It's here. Push it in further."

Yoshi brushes the scraped sediment out of the way, then

reinserts the chisel, moving it side to side. I hear it hit something. "I heard it, you heard that right? I need something longer, I think…"

Ethan takes off his own pack and starts to rummage through, until he retrieves a flat letter opener, of all things. "Try this." Within seconds of the letter opener sliding through the tight space, it clinks against metal. Yoshi pushes against it just enough, and suddenly the two diagonal cracks become the perimeter of a doorway as whatever Yoshi depressed causes a piece of the stone wall to push its way out.

"Pull with me!" Yoshi instructs. We position ourselves on either side of the stone, using our bodies and the tips of our fingers to try and nudge it forward.

Finally, we see the other side – another tunnel, this time much narrower, like the tunnel behind the chapter house.

"I hope no one is claustrophobic," Shahina mumbles.

Once we're all on the other side, Yoshi yanks the stone door back using an iron pull attached to the inside of it. It snaps back into place, held in position by a latch on the ground which can only be released by the lever Yoshi depressed with the letter opener.

"Clever!" I observe, wondering who thought to put this here. Uncle Tim loved stuff like this. He would have insisted on seeing it for himself.

"This tunnel was built before the French Revolution," Shahina fills us in. "The aristocracy would use these to move their wealth or other valuables."

"Or their mistresses," Ethan adds with a chuckle. "D…during the revolution, it saved some of their lives."

The tunnel isn't very long, and after about 30 paces we come to the end of it where a ladder waits to bring us back above ground.

"Where does it lead?" I ask nervously, wondering if Irra is in position, waiting to point his gun in our faces.

Yoshi is already on the top rung of the ladder, his hands on the circular wheel of a hatch. He strains to get it unstuck until he finally manages enough force to rotate. The wheel turns slowly at first, then faster until it's finally unlocked. He lifts the hatch and disappears as light from the world above floods the underground cavern.

Ethan and Shahina follow, and Erik motions for me to go on ahead of him. I place my feet and hands on the cold steel, climbing until I emerge into a beautifully decorated living room adorned in King Louis tables and chairs with curvy, gold legs. The paintings on the walls hang in thick gold-plated frames, and Persian rugs cover the polished wood floors. Juxtaposed to the posh and stuffy furniture is the taxidermy of deer, even a bear with his jaws open and teeth thirsty for a meal. Jade elephants crowd a display cabinet – at least 30 of them of various sizes and poses, trunks up, or down, or intertwined. Other priceless artifacts sit in other cabinets around the room.

Shahina puts her finger up to her lips, warning us to remain still and quiet. She proceeds to scout out the room, then opens one of the double doors and disappears into the hallway. We hear a thud and a groan. A voice speaks – a familiar voice...

"What are you doing you crazy woman?"

"Get up," Shahina commands, now with a heavier step. "Is it just you?"

"Scouts honor...it's just me!"

Shahina and the other body make their way toward us. "You know, this isn't how you should treat a host!" the voice complains.

Where have I heard it before?

Just then, Shahina shoves someone into the room. I can't

believe my eyes as I watch him ping pong off the door frame and almost trip over his feet.

"Tommy?" I ask bewlidered, still not entirely sure if it's him or an extremely impressive doppelganger. After my shock wears off, I run over to him and throw my arms around his neck, relieved to see that he's made it out of his ordeal in one piece. "What on earth are you doing here? How are *you* in Paris?"

When I release him, Tommy lets out a short grunt and rubs his rib. "Your friend's a 'ask questions later' kind of girl isn't she," he says, winking at Shahina. "Good to see you too, Eveline."

"Really?"

Erik comes over to give his friend a playful slap on the back. "He's just being a wise ass. You still haven't set foot in London, have you?"

"You joking, mate? After that crazy night?" Tommy replies, shaking his head and adjusting his tight dress shirt. His hair could use a lot less gel, and his belt could do with less studs, but I'd expect nothing less from his eclectic wardrobe. "I'm good here at my uncle's, surrounded by all his stuffed dead things and statues, and his many, *many* vintage weapons." He walks coyly over to Shahina. "I just need a lady to show me how to use them."

Shahina rolls her eyes before turning on her heel and walking out of the room.

"Don't worry," Tommy calls after her, "it really is just me. My uncle's still in India," he says, turning his attention back to his remaining houseguests. He collapses dramatically into a large chair, letting his left leg dangle over one of the arm rests. "Make yourselves at home!"

Ethan and Yoshi unpack the tech from the bags and get busy drawing curtains and setting up cameras at lightning speed.

I have so many questions. "So, you've been here, in Paris, the whole time?"

Tommy nods. "Erik's pal Eaton called my cousin, so I stayed with him for a few days after those gangsters roughed me up. My cousin's a surgeon – looked me over and said I was totally fine." Tommy scoffs. "Idiot. Did I look *fine* to you? Anyway, when I finally went back to the apartment it was bloody trashed. Who does that?" He pauses a moment. "Well, I mean, I guess ruffians would do that, but *so* rude, don't you think? Just so rude!" He tries unsuccessfully to get out of the armchair. "So, after I saw that bloody mess, I stepped outside to find a not-so-friendly gent waiting for me. Did his best to grab me. But I'm quick, see. I know how to dodge and weave – learned from my other cousin who was a pickpocket. He worked Piccadilly Square for years. I outran him, but there was no way I was going back there after that."

"So…you came to *Paris*."

"My uncle's a real estate collector, and he's paranoid about renting anything out to anyone. He's always travelling, so this place is vacant for eight months out of the year, at least. It's got some wicked underground passages too, as you just found out – I think it was used to smuggle 'ladies of the night' in and out of the red district back in the good old days. My uncle showed me the tunnel when I was a kid. Told Erik all about it. So, when Erik got in touch with me – "

"You offered it up as a safe house," I finish for him.

Tommy grins. "Anything for my mate."

"Yoshi figured out it was connected to the tattoo parlor by way of the sewers," Erik elaborates. "It was our plan B in case we ever got discovered. We just hoped the map Tommy found in his uncle's desk was accurate. Seems we got lucky."

"And not to worry," Tommy adds, still trying to squirm out

of the chair, "it's all on me! You don't have to pay me anything to stay here. Not a thing at all!"

"Because it's not your house, and you owe Erik and Everest for saving your life anyway," Shahina reminds him, re-entering the room and throwing a set of keys on Tommy's lap. "What do these open?"

"To the point," Tommy replies, grinning at her. "Sexy."

Shahina spins around to look at Erik sternly. "If the Vulturians don't get to him, I just might."

Erik chuckles in amusement. "He's harmless. Just a lonely romantic at heart."

"A romantic indeed!" Tommy agrees. "Like my man Shakespeare. I will bestow on you the most beautiful poems and sonnets," he promises Shahina, finally managing to get himself out of the chair. "You're the Juliet to my Romeo, the Isolde to my Tristan. When you took me by the arm in such a commanding way, I knew I had met my match and my muse. You will see it soon too. This is happening."

"This is never happening," Shahina replies, coming within an inch of Tommy's face. She lifts the keys out of his hand with one finger. "The keys. What. Do. They. Open?"

I can see the gulp travel past Tommy's Adam's apple and I try to contain my laughter.

"You're…beautiful…um, the keys, right…" Tommy tries to gather himself and resist the spell of Shahina's penetrating stare. "There's a shed outside, in the back courtyard. One of the keys is for the wine cellar. A great place to hide, almost as good as the panic room."

"Panic room?" Ethan interjects. "You have one?"

"A panic room is perfect. We can keep all our tech in there and not have to move it around." Yoshi adds.

"Oh, it's tricked out mate! See for yourself." Tommy leads

us through an opulent hallways adorned with paintings and hanging venetian masks to the main floor laundry room. He reaches behind a hanging ironing board and pushes against the wall. Immediately, a keypad elevates out of the marble counter.

"The code?" Shahina demands.

"37492."

"You sure?"

"Trust me, that's the first thing I memorized!"

She punches in the numbers and the counter lifts to reveal a staircase below ground. "Woah!"

"What does your uncle do again?" I ask, more curious by the second. *This is spy-level stuff.*

Tommy descends the steps, the rest of us on his heels with the bags. "What doesn't he do? He started in shipping. Now it's mergers and acquisitions, that sort of thing. This is where he keeps the gun collection. Check this out!"

At least 20 large guns lie in cases and rest on custom shelves, along with some smaller pistols and antique knives you would likely see in the Viking section of a museum. The space is about the size of three small bedrooms combined – massive compared to our last HQ. There's enough room for all of us to take a piece of the wall and sleep in complete safety. TV monitors show the feed from various angles inside and outside the property.

"Tommy, this is crazy!" Erik sputters. "The perks of having rich relatives."

"You said your cousin is a surgeon?" I ask Tommy, recalling what he'd mentioned earlier.

"Yup – the bone kind, I think. It's bones or babies maybe?"

Ethan snickers under his breath. "Two very different things, but ok."

My wheels are turning. What's that saying? The right people

come into your life for a reason. Maybe this is one of those times. I signal Erik off to the side.

"How much does Tommy know?"

"About…"

"All of it. Vulturians, Sentry, Prism…Anything? Nothing? Parts?"

Erik purses his lips, then grimaces and scrunches up his face. "Parts. Like a lot of parts."

"Wow! Really? You trusted him?"

"I sort of owed him an explanation about why he suddenly had to run for his life," Erik says defensively. "So, I told him some things, you know…to give him some context and make him appreciate the danger. He doesn't know about Aeonia or the compass, but he knows about the Prism, and the Vulturians. Surface level stuff about the latter. I didn't bother with the history lesson – he doesn't have the attention span anyway.'

"Clearly."

"As for the Prism, he probably thinks I was on a trip or something." He looks over at Tommy, then back at me. "What do you think? Are we toast?"

After the surprise wears off, I chuckle. "He *is* proving to be a useful ally so far. Not sure how he'd hold up in an interrogation though."

"He's a bit cowardly, but he is loyal. I can say that much," Erik replies, studying Tommy again. "It was kind of sad, describing the Prism to him, knowing he can't see it himself."

"Maybe he still will, once he works out his issues."

"If there's any of it left to see," Erik reminds me. We both stare at the wall ahead of us, silently pondering the likelihood of that happening.

"It can't come to that." I try to force the thought from my mind and wave Tommy over.

"Am I in a pickle?" he asks.

I grin at him and his ridiculous hair, picturing him using an entire bottle of hair gel that morning. "No, Tommy. Thank you, for all this. You have no idea how much you've helped us. But I need your help with something else now. The Vulturians are keeping someone I know in the hospital in an induced coma. A girl. I need to get her out, and there's no way I'll ever be able to get close to her. But maybe you can."

"You want me to break her out?" Tommy's eyes widen and he seems to lose some color from his cheeks. "Uh, no! Nope! Hard no! I'm good here. This is where I stay. I eat, I order food, I watch TV. I don't even date anymore, believe it or not. I keep to myself. I'm not getting face to face with those people again!"

"No…that would be very dangerous, and probably a disaster," I assure him. "I just need the name of the doctor who's ordering her medication. If your cousin could look at her file and find out, we can take it from there."

"We can?" Erik asks.

I ignore him. "I just need to know who he is and where I can find him – outside of the hospital."

Erik comes closer and whispers in my ear. "Ev, what are you doing?"

"Don't worry about it."

"Nerves! He does surgery on nerves!" Tommy suddenly remembers.

"Ah, so, he's a neurosurgeon," Ethan smirks, visibly amused by anything that comes out of Tommy's mouth.

"No – a nerve surgeon – I just told you, mate," Tommy replies. I see Shahina roll her eyes, but this time even she can't hold back a grin. "I can ask him." Tommy agrees.

"Her name is Lise Vidal. She's watched 24/7."

Tommy narrows his eyes at me. "Wait, are the same goons

going to come knocking on my cousin's door and start roughing him up?"

Lying used to be harder once. I avoid giving a definitive answer. "Not if he's careful. He can say he's doing research or something. I just need the name of the doctor. That's it. No personal health information. It shouldn't set off alarm bells."

Tommy thinks for a moment more, his cheeks pinking up slightly. "Ok. For you, I'll ask him. I'll call him later today."

"Thank you, Tommy!" *Finally!* Getting Lise out is a priority. I just need that name…

Yoshi and Ethan are almost set up, feeding cables into device ports at lightning speed, like mad scientists threading veins to keep their creation alive. It's convenient having our own in-house tech support.

"Ok. I think we're up and running," Yoshi says.

"The jammer?" Shahina asks excitedly, rushing over to the monitors.

Yoshi plugs away at his keyboard, inputting code that makes no sense to anyone but him and Ethan. "We should have a dome around this place. No signals in or out. I finally found the glitch that was messing it up. The vultures shouldn't be able to sniff us out this time."

"So, they can't track our frequency because of this…jammer you created?" I ask, skeptically.

Yoshi nods. "If it works like it's supposed to, then yeah, exactly. With so many of us in one place, we can't risk too many spikes in potential. That's probably how they found us at the tattoo parlor. But now, the jammer should hide the frequency." He glances over at Ethan, who's busy unpacking the small, padded box. "How's that thing coming along by the way?"

Ethan grins, taking off the lid carefully. "She'll be ready to go soon. Just need a little more time to work out some bugs."

Time isn't on our side. The Prism's deteriorating. Lise is still in the hospital, and I'm still foolish enough to want to go through the time portal. I don't know when my courage will run out. I need to go soon, and if I do, I need to make sure Lise is safe and that I have all the information I need to make the journey worth it.

"This is good. Really good. Um, I'm going to follow-up on Sarah – maybe she can give us some intel we can use. If I can get you into the chapter house, could you get that device ready today?"

"Today?" Ethan scratches his head and stares at his creation. "We were planning on doing a test run with Daphne first."

"Daphne?"

"She needed a name."

"Right. Well, you have this house. Do it here. Let's see if we can get Daphne into the chapter house tonight."

"Where's the fire Ev?" Erik asks as I fish out my dark curly wig, baseball cap and sunglasses out of my bag.

I keep my eyes down. "This is our chance to learn their secrets. Aren't you tired of waiting around and being in the dark?" Before Erik can reply, I reach for Tommy's arm. "Come on, I need you to show me the back door out of here."

CHAPTER 13

Reunion

The Petite Brioche café has a line out the door when I arrive. I cut through the customers and walk to the back of the shop, then down a steep set of creaking stairs to the sound of French jazz music. Once inside the women's washroom, I find the last stall and look for the wad of toilet paper I hid behind the toilet paper dispenser, hoping to find Sarah's reply and not my own handwriting. When I finally unfold the paper, I sigh with relief.

Fourth pew on the right, church one block east of the alley. Sit by the aisle. Five. Flush this

-S

Sarah's come through! She's still out there, and hopefully still on my side. I won't know either way until I face her. But when I do, it's time we exchange numbers. This bathroom communication system is ridiculous.

I glance at my burner phone. Only 2:15. I have time to kill. There's one place I've wanted to see again, but it would be foolish. Erik wouldn't approve.

They would be watching.

While I think on it, I navigate the Parisian streets, noticing the dirt, the graffiti, the run-down buildings. The homeless man sleeping at the doorstep of the laundromat, the used needle lying next to the waste basket. I never paid much attention to these things before. In my bubble of awe and admiration I focused on the good, on the beautiful – on the Paris of the postcards. But now I see the world through a different lens – a lens that sees beyond the surface to the darkness and decay that underlies society. A lens I wish I could rip out of my eyes. Denial was so much better.

Before I realize it, I'm standing across the street from the Hotel Iliad, strings of cars and tour buses in the space between us. My mind travels back to that night. I can hear the rattling wheels of the stretcher as it bounces on the cobblestone walkway, carrying the body to the van. Julian's little, innocent body, in a cold black bag. I hear his mother's scream tear through the night air.

Why am I here? This isn't going to help me stay under the radar. This is a mistake.

I glance one last time at the Iliad and realize there is nothing to be gained from revisiting it. He's not here anymore. He's long gone. It's just a building now, and that night is just a memory.

I invite the air to cool my flushed face, but it only gets warmer. My body is on fire, and I'm failing miserably at controlling it. I haven't released my potential since the Salle, and even then, there was so much more that I had yearned to unleash.

Don't make anger and hatred the source of it.

But how? How, when the anger seems to consume everything in its path?

Maybe if I release it, I can feel at peace. Or maybe I jeopardize everything the Sentry has built.

The angel and devil on my shoulder wage battle. *Release it…control it…release it…control it.*

Finally, the control wins. I'll live to fight another day.

"Rue Marienne," I whisper, the words spilling out of my mouth before I have time to rationalize them.

One more stop.

***

This time, a dark blue sedan stands parked near the crooked streetlamp. It appears to be a different model, older maybe. I can't see the driver. He may not even be inside. I try to blend in and head towards my old apartment building, nostalgia gripping my chest.

Control it. Control it. Shut it down.

The floral wallpaper in the hallway looks bearable now. I used to find it tacky and old-fashioned. But now, I wish I could see it daily. *Wallpaper.* Of all the things I thought I would never miss.

When I get to the front door of the flat, it's decision time.

Control it. Focus. Calm. The echo in my ears subsides.

Go!

I don't have much time. Before I unlock and open the door, I focus on the cameras. In moments like these, my potential is a gift. The lights in the hallway begin to flicker, then go off.

Sorry neighbors. No electricity for a while.

The clock ticks. *Make it fast.*

The apartment smells of musty old books and cinnamon. The aroma of Catherine's collection of perfumes and creams lingers in the air. Papers have accumulated on the floor, slipped under the door over the months: advertisements, mostly, and a letter from Ms Riene asking Catherine to watch her dog while she visits her mother. Catherine never did respond to those, and poor Ms Riene would always end up asking somebody else.

It's silent, eerie, like an abandoned planet. Once there was life here. Once there was joy. Then it all slowly evaporated until it was left soulless. But despite the emptiness, I can still picture Uncle Tim at the dining table, teaching me card games. I can hear the tires of the delivery trucks outside, the echoes of distant honking and bicycle bells, the hum of the neighbor's radiator through the thin wall. Every so often, a floorboard creaks, and I quickly take my weight off it, mindful of the bugs.

Make it fast!

I tip toe to the bedroom and into my old, simple world where my greatest worry was my grief, not going to college, and a few shattered light bulbs. My problems have evolved at lightning speed.

There are a few things I want and need. Some clean clothes wouldn't hurt. A deodorant that works. My warm boots. *Will I even need these if I'm trapped in a past Prism for all eternity?* I decide not to dwell on the details just yet and grab an empty backpack from the closet.

Then there are the things I *really* came for. My photos, mom's bracelets, Uncle Tim's journal that I snuck out of his study and hid before Catherine could toss it. Mom's perfume. I spray it onto my scarf and let it settle into the fabric before burying my chin inside it. She surrounds me, wrapping me in a comforting embrace. The door to the little room in my brain where I relegated all my grief opens a crack, and I know once I let it open fully, my location will ping like a beacon in the Vulturian chapter house, if it hasn't already.

Control it.

One more inhale and I turn on my heel, backpack over my shoulder. I feel my lungs tremble inside my chest as I approach the front door, hoping there's no one waiting on the other side of it.

To my relief, the hallway is deserted.

I look back once more at the life that was, wondering if I'll ever step foot in this apartment again, then shut the door and lock it before unwanted company arrives, my reckless mission a success as far as I can tell.

Maybe I'll get a lecture, maybe not. But it was worth it.

***

The mass doesn't start for another hour, and L'église Saint-Dominique is nearly empty when I arrive to take my seat in the fourth pew on the right at 5:00 sharp. The two people I've joined look nothing like Sarah, so it's a waiting game for now.

I was raised Catholic, but not the church-going kind. Still, I remember enough from the holiday masses to know proper church etiquette. I kneel before taking my seat, then wait patiently, admiring the stained-glass depictions of the stations of the cross and the smooth chestnut polish of the wood carvings. I say a silent prayer of gratitude and try to lose myself in the spiritual setting. A large crucifix with rays of light protrudes from the wall behind the altar, angels and cherubs carved into stonework and painted onto the colorful ceiling mural. Behind me, a massive organ springs from the balcony, showing off hundreds of shiny brass pipes of varying lengths. The smell of incense and old paper from hymn books lingers in the air.

Within a few minutes, the hymn book in the book holder in front of me starts to vibrate. I open it to find a burner phone, bringing it quickly to my ear.

"Hello?" I whisper.

"It's good to hear your voice Everest. Also…*where on earth have you been?*"

I smile. It's good to hear Sarah's voice too. "Everywhere, it seems. Sorry for not giving you notice. Are you here?"

"Leave the pew and look ahead at the confessionals when you cross the main aisle. Then lower your head as you leave."

"Ok, now?"

"Yes, now."

I look ahead to the confessionals before strolling back up the aisle towards the doors.

"Sarah? Are you still there?"

"Yes, I just had to make sure it was you."

"Where are – "

"Don't look back!" she snaps. "Usual spot. Give me a five-minute head start. I'll meet you there. Keep the phone. That bathroom is disgusting – we need a new way to communicate."

"You read my mind!"

When I arrive at the alley, I can see the roof of the Vulturian mansion a few blocks away, looming on the corner like a charcoal monster. It would be poetic if a sinkhole opened beneath it and swallowed it up. The thought puts an ease into my step as I approach the dumpster that's already been rolled aside. I knock on the door, and within seconds Sarah's familiar grasp is on my arm, pulling me violently inside.

"This part is getting old!" I grunt, rotating my shoulder, which is still bruised from that fall in the woods. "You could just say 'come in'."

"Sorry. Old habits."

I study her face. She looks the same. I had hoped for improvement, but her skin appears dry, and her lips chapped, maybe from a cold. The eyes reveal the most. At first, they look tired, but as we stare at each other, they become wet and coated, and within seconds the otherwise-strong Vulturian is a blubbering mess as I try to console her.

"Sarah, what's happened? What have they done?"

She sobs hard into my shoulder. Finally, she pulls away, squeezing my hand before proceeding to dry her eyes with the sleeve of her sweater. "I didn't mean to do that. I just saw you and…" She shakes her head like a dog trying to dry off after the rain. "Never mind. I'm good." She takes a breath, slaps herself on her cheeks, smiles faintly, then immediately furrows her brow and punches me in the arm.

"*Ow!*"

"Where did you go?"

I rub my arm as I think of the best way to answer. What is there to say? I ran away. I suck, and everyone has a right to be mad at me. "Look, I've beat myself up more than you know, so can we just skip it? I'm back now, ok."

"So, no explanation?"

I shrug. "I'm a coward. Is that what you want to hear?"

Sarah grins, then leans back against the wall, a little more relaxed. "No, you're not. You're just human. If I were you, I'd probably have run a long time ago, to be honest. You look good."

"Thanks. More importantly, you look…the same."

"You can say it. I look like shit."

"What's going on Sarah? You can tell me."

A few seconds pass as Sarah stares at the ground. "Well, the good news is I think they trust me more. I've been taking flying lessons. I may start flying new recruits soon. That could give us some clues about the Arachna. I've found some old writings about the Cypress Project too, but so far nothing that points to a location."

"Sarah, that's huge! You're a pilot?"

"Soon."

"And the bad news?"

"Well, they still want you, or the compass, and they're looking for more bait, in case you give up on Lise."

That's not going to happen.

"I know about Tara," I fill her in. "She's someone I know. She betrayed us. Julian's dead because of her."

"I'm so sorry Everest. When I heard about Julian..."

"It's ok. All I care about now is destroying them. I can't cry anymore. The tears don't magically fix the past. There's no point to them now."

Sarah nods, as if trying to make herself believe the same, and I weigh how much to tell her about the things I've recently learned. Deep down, I want to trust her. But then I think of Maeve and Francine – or whatever her name is now – and doubt proves to be stronger.

"I'm sorry about Lise too. That poor girl," Sarah adds.

"Speaking of Lise, I'm going to get her out of that hospital."

Sarah raises both eyebrows. "Everest, they will shoot you a block away! Are you crazy? They won't let you slip past them again."

I chuckle. *They already did.* "Don't worry, I've got an idea. But I need your help...to get a large working van."

"Should I ask?"

"Not yet. Can you get me one or not?"

A loud sigh escapes Sarah's dry lips as she gives in. "Yeah, ok, I'm sure I can find something."

"Good! Also, I need access to the chapter house, through the spy glass. We have some new technology that we want to get inside. It can scan the entire building and run a live feed, maybe reveal something that you normally wouldn't be able to see."

"That sounds promising. Um…I can check for a day that works – "

"Tonight, Sarah. We go in tonight."

Sarah's eyes widen. "*Tonight?* What the hell Everest! You can't just come out of nowhere and start making demands like that!"

"I don't have time Sarah."

"What are you talking about? What aren't you telling me?"

"I'm leaving!"

Crap. I wasn't supposed to go there. Yet. I guess I just decided I trust Sarah after all.

She stares at me in puzzlement. "Again? You just got back."

"It's not…I'm not *leaving*. I'm going back…in time."

It sounds comical, hearing the words come out of my mouth, so it's not surprising when Sarah bursts out laughing. "Girl, what game is this? Have you really lost it?"

I keep my eyes fixed on her. Time travel is something people fantasize about and marvel at. I never thought it possible, and now that it is, it's not the feeling I had hoped for. The risk is too great for it to be exciting. Sarah must sense my conflicted feelings because she stops laughing and stares at me, her brow furrowed again. "You're serious!"

I nod. "We found a way, through the Prism. It's how we find the Skala and keep it out of the Vutlurian's grasp, forever. The Prism's deteriorating everyday Sarah, so if I'm going to do this, I need to go soon, and I need all the information I can get before I leave."

"Everest…that's insane! It's *impossible!*"

"No, it's not. The Prism was impossible until it wasn't. It's happening Sarah. And the thing is, this may be a one-way trip."

"Hold on, like you won't ever come back, to like now-times, to present day?"

I nod slowly, the terrifying reality settling in more and more each second. "Something like that."

Sarah stares at me with surprise. "Woah! I'm glad I'm not you."

I smirk. "Yeah, I'm trying not to think about that part. Best to stay focused on what I *can* control. We need to get into the chapter house tonight, Sarah."

She lets her head rest against the tile wall. "Fine – but if this goes to shit –"

"It won't! It can't. We really need a win."

"Just you though."

"I need one more person. He knows the tech."

"Fine. No more."

"Deal. And go easy on him, ok? He's a bit quiet and, well, you can be – "

"A bitch?"

I grimace "Sometimes."

"Comes with the territory. I'm a Vulturian, remember?"

"No, you're not."

I expect her to grin back at me, thankful for the vote of confidence, but she doesn't, her eyes becoming coated again. I can feel that something is troubling her, and I'm about to ask about it when she starts to speak again.

"We'll have to be quick," she says, changing the subject. "In and out. If they find us, we'll be buried in these walls, and you won't get to try out your new time machine."

I reach eagerly for the door to the alley, my nerves jumpy at the prospect of discovering something vitally important in a few hours. "In and out," I nod to Sarah. "That's a promise."

CHAPTER 14

New Frontiers

The panic room erupts in cheers as Ethan displays the results of Daphne's mapping program. While I've been out scavenging through my past and meeting old friends, the tiny device has charted out every square inch of the main floor and provided a 3D rendering with incredible detail, down to the coasters on the coffee table.

"Brilliant! It looks exactly like the place," Erik exclaims.

"It has a video log as well," Ethan adds. "Everything it sees, we see. It can crawl vertically like an insect – a literal fly on the wall. And it can camouflage. Check it out: a camera on the underside captures the background and projects a similar pattern on the body so it blends in with its surroundings."

Shahina smiles proudly. "You really pulled it off!"

"Absolutely magnificent," Tommy whispers, stealthily appearing beside her and shooting her a flirtatious glance. Shahina promptly moves to another corner.

"Phenomenal Ethan," I praise. "This could change everything for us. And Sarah's cleared us to go in tonight. We can get Daphne in there and have a map of the chapter house within days!"

"More like hours," Ethan corrects, beaming like a proud father watching his son score a winning goal, "depending on how much ground she can cover."

"There can't be too many of us in the tunnels, so I'll take Ethan in. The rest of you stay here and download the footage."

Shahina raises one of her toned arms and stares at me sternly. "Hold on! No way! You think we're going to let you take Ethan and our prized tech to some Vulturian we've never met?"

"Shahina," I try to reason with her, appreciating her skepticism, "I wouldn't suggest it if I had any doubts about Sarah's allegiance. We can trust her. This is a perfect opportunity to get inside without being detected."

Erik nods to Shahina to reassure her, and I shoot him a grateful look for the support.

"Are you really sure about this?" she asks, feeling outnumbered as Yoshi casts his vote for our plan.

Finally, we'll get to see every inch of the demon's lair, and they'll have no idea. "Absolutely sure!"

***

"Are we *really* sure about this though?" Ethan questions as we approach the dumpster that guards the entrance to the tunnels.

"Got a better idea?" I reply, reminding him of our limited options.

"Not yet…but I'm still thinking. Give me a minute."

"Time isn't a luxury we can afford right now."

The dumpster is rolled aside, and Sarah wastes no time letting us in, thankfully without any arm pulling.

"Uh, Ethan, this is Sarah, she's –"

"The Vulturian," she finishes abruptly for me, extending a hand to Ethan who seems to have forgotten how to blink. "Might as well get it out of the way. Relax, I won't eat you or cast a spell or anything. I don't have fangs either, see." She shows off her perfectly human looking teeth, then flashes him a mischievous smile. "You must be the genius."

"Oh," Ethan stammers, still not blinking but managing to accept the handshake, "um, yes, h…hello."

Sarah chuckles. "I'm not hating the effect I have on people once they realize who I am. I could have some fun with that."

Ethan's face flushes. "Sorry, I just – never met one of you before."

"Oh, sure you have! You just didn't know it. You're a computer nerd, right? You have any idea how many of our people are on the net, chatting with you, watching you, surfing the dark web? Teaching at your fancy universities? You've met us all right. And that should worry you the most; not me or this creepy tunnel that smells like dead rats."

I can see Ethan clenching the straps of his backpack with white knuckles as he thinks about what Sarah's said. When I catch up to her, I push her playfully from behind. "Hey! Don't break my genius!" I warn her. "We need him functioning, not terrified and unresponsive."

"Sorry. You know my sense of humor. I can't resist."

We approach the false tile passage. "After you," I urge Ethan when Sarah pulls out the foam tile block. "I'm right behind you." He nods hesitantly, then gently pushes his backpack through first before crawling to the other side.

"Ok, listen up!" Sarah instructs as we continue walking. "When I say silence, it's not negotiable, got it?" She looks only at Ethan since I know the drill. He nods obediently, eyes wide like a baby deer. "The hole is this long and this wide," she says, using her two index fingers to demonstrate a width of about two inches and a height of one. "How big is your robot?"

Ethan smiles for the first time, no doubt eager to let his baby finally spread her wings and do some real work. "She'll fit."

"She?"

"Daphne. From Scooby Doo. Had a bit of a crush on her."

"Why am I not surprised? But I can't judge. I had a thing for Ken for years."

"From Barbie?" I tease.

She glares at me. "Tell anyone and I'll lock you in here."

We come to the narrow part of the passage, and Sarah instructs Ethan to leave the backpack and have Daphne ready. His hands are shaking as he retrieves the robot from the padded box.

"It's narrow," Sarah warns. "Shuffle sideways. And if you don't want that to break don't hit it on the walls."

Ethan nods. "What if they see us?"

"There shouldn't be anyone in the room at this hour."

Ethan looks down at Daphne. "Well, this is it. I'll probably never see her again."

"She's a robot," I remind him. "You can make another one. If she can camouflage as good as you say, she'll be fine. Worst case scenario, Sarah can try to retrieve her from the inside."

We squeeze our bodies through the tight dark passage one by one, and the further we go in, the darker it gets as the light from the hallway fixtures no longer reaches us. I feel my breath bouncing off the walls and the fibers of my sweater catching on the uneven surface. Sarah stops and locates the sliding brass plate. She puts a finger to her lips, then slowly moves it to the side, allowing a tiny beam of light to stream into the passage. She places one eye against it, then immediately backs away and slides the plate shut. A faint curse word escapes her lips. She holds up one index finger and mimics someone scrolling on their cell phone. There's someone in the room.

There goes our perfect window.

We wait in limbo as Sarah thinks for a moment. She decides to slide the plate aside again. When I see her lips curve into a smile, I know we've got our chance.

Sarah motions at her watch and then tries to make the action for "hurry." Playing charades isn't quite as fun when the stakes are this high, or when you can barely move your body two inches in either direction.

Ethan slowly brings Daphne in front of his face and shimmies into the spot Sarah freed up for him. He takes a moment to look around the chapter house boardroom, seeing inside the Vulturian lair for the first time. Sarah motions him to hurry again, and with a final glance at his creation, he lowers Daphne on to one of the books on the bookshelf, switching her on from the remote. He holds the robot in place, waiting until she engages her gripping feet, then sighs and withdraws his trembling hand. Sarah slides the brass plate into place, then urges us to retreat to the wider hallway.

Ethan groans, crouching down. "I want to throw up."

"You did good." Sarah reassures him.

"Do you think they'll find her?"

"That depends how well you made her. If you keep me posted on her location, I'll try to keep the Vultures out of her way best I can."

Ethan rises to his feet, looking a little less pale. "Thanks."

"Don't mention it." She grins. "I'd do it for Ken."

Ethan snickers. "We should get back to the s…safehouse, see what my girl sees."

Sarah nods. "Good luck!"

Ethan puts on his backpack and takes a few steps before

pausing. "Do you want to come? We could use you to guide Daphne. You know the layout."

I'm not sure how to respond to Ethan's offer, and I can tell Sarah doesn't either. She stares at him, caught off guard by his trust in her. "Really? You're not scared I'll give you away?"

"Well, I was thinking we c…could like put a hood over your head or something –"

"No!" I shake my head. "We're not doing that to her."

"Everest, it's fine," Sarah assures me. "It's actually a good idea. If for whatever reason they make me talk one day, I won't know where to send them. Not that I would do that but…Just put the hood on, for your peace of mind, and mine."

"I can't exactly walk you with a bag over your head to the taxi," I point out. "They'll drive us right to the police station."

She retrieves a pair of glasses from her backpack. "I can wear these. They're black-out lenses. The Order gives everyone a pair in case we need to be kept in the dark about something. I won't see a thing."

"Sarah," I eye her skeptically, concerned about her sense of self-worth and self-loathing. Being treated like a spy probably won't help cure whatever eats at her every day. "You sure about this? I don't want to treat you like the enemy."

She nods her head confidently. "And I would never betray you willingly Everest, you know that. But I sort of am the enemy, and we both know who we're up against. Use the glasses. I even have noise cancelling headphones in my car."

I hesitate before taking the glasses from her hand.

"And let's face it," she adds, "your friends won't be too happy you brought me, so this is the least we can do."

She's right about that part.

***

"This is a *really* bad idea! *Really bad!*" Shahina fumes when we explain who the guest is sitting in our panic room. "You can't possible think this is smart!"

I tried out Sarah's glasses earlier and know she's in the dark.

"Actually, it was my idea," Ethan replies.

"*Yours?*" Shahina questions. "You're the most nervous person I know. You check both ways three times before crossing a bicycle path!"

"They go fast, especially French people."

Erik laughs, but quickly stops when Shahina glares at him.

"Look, she knows that place. Who better to guide Daphne?" Ethan insists.

"I'm with Shahina on this one," Tommy jumps in, reclining in one of the office chairs.

I roll my eyes. "Shocker."

"Told ya they wouldn't like this," Sarah says.

Shahina rips the headphones out of my hands and places them on Sarah's ears.

"We need to trust her," I try to convince the others. "She's on our side. We wouldn't even have eyes and ears in there if it wasn't for her."

"Hey, hey, hey! Hold up! Back door – check it out," Yoshi cries, motioning us to the monitors.

"Well, that didn't take long," Shahina scoffs, sounding a lot like Jason now, "she led them straight to us. Quick, lock it down!"

"No," Erik interjects, holding up his hand. He studies the cameras, then smiles. "It's ok. They're here."

The monitors show three bodies standing at the door, their faces hidden under ballcaps and sweatshirts.

Erik releases the lock on the panic room and disappears up into the laundry area. "Disarm the security system. I'll be back!"

"Seriously?" Shahina huffs. Tommy tries to place a comforting arm on her shoulder, but he gets within an inch before Shahina swipes it away.

"Message received," he mumbles, giving her some space.

We wait in anxious silence for Erik's return or the sound of voices, or gunshots – anything that would signal whether we should feel relief or start arming ourselves. Footsteps propel Shahina to the bottom of the stairs with bat in hand, but Erik motions her to stand down as he returns with the three visitors, one of them limping noticeably.

The ball caps and hoods come off. A bob haircut emerges first, absent the usual sparkling eyes and exuberant energy

"Jenna?" I ask, stepping forward. "What are you doing here?"

"Surprised?" she asks, returning my hug.

I look to Simon next and immediately feel his sorrow. The smile he wears is cautious and weak, and I know better than to ask how he's doing. I simply squeeze his arm and nod to him, noticing how different it is to see them all in person, much like it was to see Erik that first day in London. Nothing quite like the real world, as messed up as it is.

"Our guests of honor," Erik announces. "Flew in earlier today. I sort of wanted to do a big reveal. Didn't have time to get the balloons though."

Everything is the same about them, except Robert's limp, which is much more pronounced.

"The Prism has it's perks, doesn't it," he explains, noticing me staring at his leg.

My face flushes from embarrassment. "It's good to see you, Robert. All of you. How did you even get here?"

"We snuck on board a cargo flight," Robert replies. "I know a friend in the postal service. Jenna met us in Boston and we left from there. Don't worry – there's no record. And I don't think we were followed."

He steps forward and looks at me with tired jet lagged eyes, then lowers his gaze to rest on my pendant, staring at it for a curiously long time. "Glad you're all safe," he says, squeezing my arm. I nod, hopeful that his calming presence will ease some of the anxiety in the room. He looks past me, and a puzzled expression comes over him as he notices Sarah sitting there, with the glasses and headphones on. "Are we interrupting something?"

"Crap!" I start toward her, but Shahina steps in my path.

"We weren't done discussing this," she says, her body language clear and the bat still in her hand.

"First of all, can you please put that thing down now? I'm not the enemy here. Second, I trust her. Third, we won't get far without her."

To my surprise, Simon steps forward. I wonder if his calm demeanor means he's just bottling the layers of conflicting feelings up like I do, coping however he can. He kneels in front of Sarah, removes the headphones, and lifts the glasses off her face. When she sees him, she smiles faintly, then blinks several times while her eyes adjust to the light again.

"Everyone, this is Sarah," I introduce.

"Sarah Jaqueline Bennet."

I lock eyes with her. It's the first time I've heard her full name. Our trust is apparently growing.

"Sarah Jaqueline Bennet," I repeat, giving her a nod of appreciation. "She's the Vulturian who's been helping me. She's on our side. Her involvement is non-negotiable." I look back at her. "If you want me on this team, then she comes too."

Sarah closes her eyes, like she's on trial and awaiting her verdict from the jury. I proceed to fill in the newcomers on

Daphne and Sarah's role in getting her inside the chapter house. "We have a double agent and a robot, and the Order has no idea."

There's 20 or so seconds of awkward silence before Robert finally breaks it. "Sarah," he says, limping forward and giving me a quick glance. "If Everest trusts you, I'm willing to put my skepticism aside and do the same. What do you think, everyone? Everest makes a good case. And Sarah's proved herself so far. We need allies."

I notice Erik shift uncomfortably, then lock eyes with me. I recall when he used that exact phrase. It was right before we had found out about Maeve's true allegiance and the trajectory of our relationship changed forever. He looks away awkwardly, perhaps wondering if history will repeat itself.

"Do you know her," Simon asks unexpectedly. "My sister, Francine. She'd be Tara to you."

I can sense his torment, as if he's unsure if he's supposed to love or hate the person who betrayed him and is searching for something that could tilt the scales one way or the other. He's probably looking for that elusive closure he'll probably never find.

Sarah shakes her head slowly. "No, not personally. I know she's the Sharur and she goes by the name Tara in the Order. Tara Bahar. That's all. If I knew more, I would tell you."

She looks sad. Simon looks sad. Damn it, we all look sad. Francine was one of our own, until she wasn't. It's just all around sad, regardless of how much anger we all feel towards her. If it wasn't for her, Julian would probably still be alive. I want to hate her with every fiber of my being. But I know where that ugly road will take me. For now, I'll settle on the anger – a healthy dose. The kind of dose that will keep me moving forward instead of weighing me down in the darkness.

Simon's next question brings the room to another awkward silence as everyone holds their breath for the answer. He crosses his arms as he observes Sarah.

"Did you ever kill for them?"

I see Sarah's face flush and her brown irises start to swim, and my heart sinks. I'd never asked her that before. I don't know why. Maybe I didn't want to know. She'd told me of the part she played at the Web. I had just accepted that as terrible as that was, informing the chapter houses of the Arachna's targets was the worst she had done.

Do I want to hear this?

"You don't have to answer that," I say, trying to protect myself as much as her.

But she stares right at Simon looking more distraught than ever. "Yes. Once. I had no choice. I mean, I did have a choice, but…" she corrects in a whisper as tears stain her cheeks, "it was me or both of us. She was dead either way. I did what I did to maintain my cover, to try to do some good another day. But I hate myself for it. I hate myself for it every day."

Damn it.

I stare at Shahina, expecting an 'I told you so' look on her face. But I find her unexpectedly moved by Sarah's confession and vulnerability, her irises glassy too.

"Would you do it again?" Simon asks.

Sarah inhales to regain her composure. "Maybe. If I knew that she would die anyway, and I had a chance of doing something to save others. Maybe. And maybe you would too. You're just lucky you've never been in a position where you were tested like that. Believe me, it's not a position I would wish on anyone. You can't even imagine how it breaks you inside. Everything you thought you were – it's all shattered instantly. When you see someone lying in a pool of their own blood by your hand, you're never the same. They took something from me that day – and I don't know if I can ever forgive it."

It's enough for Simon's emotions to finally surface. He nods, flushed and visibly shaken, but manages a kind and compassionate smile. "Ok," he simply answers.

Shahina surprises everyone by stepping back and putting down the bat, signaling she no longer sees Sarah as the threat she once did. Sarah looks surprised to have won over her biggest critic with the hard truth. Shahina walks back to the monitors but shoots me a warning stare. "Don't ask me why, understand?"

I nod. We all have parts of our story we don't share. Maybe Shahina's isn't so different from Sarah's. But I respect her wish – it's not my place to know.

Ethan has been rather silent throughout all the drama and sits in front of his laptop with an absentminded expression. But when his laptop pings, it's game-face on. He snaps his fingers to get our attention.

"Yes! Daphne, baby, you're amazing!"

"Is she transmitting?" Yoshi asks, coming to Ethan's side.

"See for yourself."

The ten of us try to crowd around the small computer and squint to make out the images on the screen.

"I'm feeling a little claustrophobic," Ethan admits. "We could really use a bigger screen."

"Say no more, mate," Tommy interjects, "I've got just the one! You've got like cables and stuff to connect things, like to a TV, right? Like you know, red ones, maybe black ones…"

"What are you talking about?" Shahina interrupts impatiently, Tommy obviously grating on her last nerve.

He holds up his hands. "Never mind. I'll show you. Come on."

Once out of the panic room, Tommy leads us to his uncle's media lounge where a massive projector screen faces three rows of cushioned armchairs.

"Now *this* is luxury!" Sarah observes.

"This will do," Ethan agrees, digging in his backpack for the right cable to hook the laptop up to the projector. After a few minutes of Ethan fiddling with buttons and input jacks, and the rest of us settling into our luxurious seats, Daphne's footage displays on the screen.

"This is chronological, since we sent her in," Ethan notes.

The first thing we see is the boardroom, with the gigantic hearth and mahogany paneling. We see the Vulturian come back in. No one I recognize. I look at Sarah, and she shrugs.

"I don't know everyone," she says.

Back to the show. We watch as Daphne maneuvers near the ceiling, with her tiny camera pointed downwards, scanning the room. The place looks pretty much as I expected on the inside. Stuffy and pretentious, with a lot of old furniture that looks like it's been lifted from a palace. Daphne finds the lounge and makes her way to a bar with several espresso machines. *I don't care what brand of coffee they serve. I want the juicy stuff.*

"Not many have access to floors 4 through 6," Sarah explains. "Honestly, I don't even know how to get up there."

Great.

"The Ertu's office is on the third though."

"I can give her a nudge," Ethan replies. I see Daphne change course and make for the stairs we saw her pass earlier in the footage. "Where on the third?"

"Um…take a left at the top of the stairs. Go straight down – I think it's down the right corridor at the dead end. It's a restricted area and always guarded. You'll know it when you see it."

I don't think anyone breathes as Daphne inches toward the dimly lit dead end. Sure enough, two guards stand at the double doors down the right corridor.

Erik leans in. "What if they see her?"

"She's in camo mode," Ethan answers. "She should be fine. I'll need to go slow though."

The next 20 feet take 10 minutes as Ethan guides the robot at a painfully slow pace to avoid attracting attention. Finally, she slides down the door next to the guards' feet, then underneath it and into the Ertu's office.

We're in!

The room is empty. "He's gone," Sarah observes.

"Good." I twitch impatiently. "Any way we can speed this up? That was excruciating."

"Don't listen to them," Ethan whispers to Daphne protectively. "Just do your thing. All right…what do you see?"

Daphne transmits images of the study with impressive clarity. A massive wooden desk with exquisite carpentry, the tabletop perimeter carved in a spiral pattern. A desk lamp and a stack of file folders. A closed laptop with a cigar tray next to it, a pile of ashes protruding from the center of the tray like a tiny volcano. In the top right corner of the desk sits a miniature replica of the ugly bird statue that guards the chapter house courtyard – Parem, in his vulture form. Mahogony panels cover the walls, and large stuffy armchairs face each other from opposite sides of the room. A wall of books towers behind the desk, and we get to work scanning the titles for the *Anu Ki Zu* as Ethan zooms in the camera. I grind my teeth impatiently. There has to be something important here. It's the Ertu's office. *If not here, then where?*

I examine the stack of file folders on the desk again and notice that they appear to be floating, as if resting on something.

"Can Daphne get a better look under there?"

Ethan nods and begins maneuvering. "Just give her a minute."

The robot crawls down the wall and across the floor, then up the wooden leg of the desk. Finally, she gets a clear view of the object underneath the stack of folders: a thin book bound in what appears to be suede, with a script of strange symbols burned into the leather on the spine.

"Do you think…" Erik mutters.

My lips curve into a smile. *I knew it was here. I felt it.* "It has to be."

"What?" come several voices.

"The text mentioned in the Artifacts book – the Aeonians' sacred text, said to contain secrets of the universe only Aeonian elders knew about. The Artifacts book stated that only chosen ones could decipher what was written within it." I jerk my head towards Jenna. "You're the history expert. Do you recognize the symbols on the spine?"

Jenna walks up to the massive projection screen and runs her hands over the zoomed-in wedge-shaped lettering.

"I am more of an art history enthusiast," she says regretfully. "Ancient history is not my area. But it does look like cuneiform, which makes sense. Everything we know about the Vulturians suggests that the Order was created near or around ancient Sumer."

"Can you read it?"

"No. But the internet could."

Yoshi is on it immediately, plugging screenshots into AI recognition software. I hold my breath, saying the name of the book in my mind and hoping whatever Yoshi discovers looks remotely similar. Within minutes, we have our translation.

"I've got something. I've found a Sumerian lexicon translator. Scanning it now…The first symbol is 'Anu', meaning God or heaven. The second…'Ki,' meaning earth. And the third… 'Zu' is to know, to understand."

A chill travels over my skin. *Anu Ki Zu.* A mysterious repository of secrets and knowledge and power, which could hold the key to finding Aeonia.

It's right there, in *their* evil hands.

Jenna is practically drooling as she studies the screen with hungry eyes. "They must have stolen it from the Aeonians when they tried to take the Skala. They've had it this entire time."

"Well, whatever's in it, I don't think they know how to read it. Otherwise, we'd all be in deep shit," Yoshi observes.

"Aren't we already?" Shahina pipes in with her predictable optimism.

I nod. "Yoshi's right. They would have probably found the Skala by now. Remember, only a select few can decipher it."

"Well, it's in that fortress now," Ethan reminds us. "Until we figure out how to get it out, we're not going to know what's in it either."

Everyone turns to look at Sarah, who immediately raises her hands and backs up a step. "No way! I wouldn't even be allowed in the Ertu's wing."

"It can't be Sarah," I agree, unable to take my eyes off the feed. "But we *need* it. I know it can help me get to Aeonia."

"Help *us*," Erik corrects me.

"Um, details please," Jenna interrupts.

"At the Citadel, my dear," Robert chimes in, leaving Jenna tortured and unsatisfied. "It's late. Let Daphne work while we get some rest. We'll debrief the rest of the Sentry in the Prism, see if anyone has any ideas on how to get our hands on that book." He turns to Sarah and looks unsure of his next words.

"Don't worry," she says. "Just put the glasses on and drop me off somewhere in the Latin Quarter. I haven't had dinner and I'm craving shawarma."

Erik steps forward, zipping up his sweatshirt. "I'll take her."

I grab hold of Sarah's arm as she walks past me. "I'll need you soon," I whisper, alluding to my earlier request. "Will you be ready?" Erik gives me a peculiar glance that I pretend not to notice.

Sarah rolls her eyes and grins. "Sure, what the hell. What could possibly go wrong?"

CHAPTER 15

Shattered Hopes

Seeing Tru so content in his new paradise brings me some much-needed solace. I know nothing can touch him here. I know he's sheltered from all the hideous monsters that roam the earth. The monsters that hide in plain sight, and the ones that emerge from the shadows only to feed the demons that live inside them.

As outrageous as it sounds, I miss the bunker in the woods, the silence of the forest, Tru curled up on my blanket, no murderous sociopaths on our heels. Of course, it was all a false sense of security. If the Order had known where I was, there would be no bunker in the woods, and the psychopaths would have come calling. They would have probably set the compound on fire while we slept or hit me with a sniper shot between the eyes. So, as much as I want normality back, I know it's not mine to reclaim yet.

At least Tru's got a friend now. I couldn't stand the thought of him being alone in the dimension while I was out, so now a sweet Dalmatian named Minny keeps him company as he bounds over logs and scales the hillsides. It's the least I could do for throwing him into the mess I call my life. But there are worse things than being stuck in the Prism and chasing your tail all day.

I watch for several satisfying minutes as the new friends dodge and tackle each other in a confusing game of tag and let-me-chew-your-face-off, then gather myself reluctantly off the ground and head for the door. Only a few days remain. Going into the past terrifies me. There's no way to know what I'll encounter on the other side. I wish I could have Erik by my side, but there's just no point in all of us getting stuck in the past. If the Prism chose me, then I go alone.

Before falling asleep in Paris, I had asked Robert if I could bring Gill into the fold. His brain is basically a library, and I can sense his devotion to the Prism, a devotion I know I can trust. My gut is giving the green light. I should have listened to my gut when it came to Maeve. Even Francine – there was always something off. That little voice is too often easily dismissed because it's not quantifiable in the same way tangible proof is. But that little voice often knows things that we don't yet know ourselves, like it's connected to something omnipotent.

Robert had agreed to the idea, so after quickly checking that Gill has his own dimension, I set out for the Lumus to give him the good news. Of course, there's always the off chance he won't want anything to do with the Sentry. But who wouldn't want to be part of a clandestine society that's been protecting the Prism for centuries and that meets in secret beneath the Luminary walls and fights the forces of evil.

Sure enough, Gill has the reaction I expected.

"You're serious?"

"Absolutely serious."

"This whole time, they've been meeting…like right down there?"

I grimace at him, knowing how much he prides himself on

knowing everything about our alternate world. "Stings a little, huh?"

He scrunches up his nose and looks up at the ceiling as if deep in thought. "Nah, I'm over it. This is wild!"

"Like I told you, this is serious. You can't say a word!"

"Oh, yeah, no, I know. I won't say a word. Scout's honor. I was actually a scout, so I take it seriously." He makes the scout pledge with his right hand to prove his point.

I fill Gill in on the Vulturians as we descend the orb-lit staircase beneath the podium. He looks absolutely bewildered and doesn't make a sound as I rattle on about the labyrinth, the same way Erik had done for me.

"You ok?" I check in. "I know this is a lot."

He nods silently, looking in all directions and probably trying to process everything – tying all those loose pieces together and attempting to remember the way at the same time. "So, the storm that day, that was because of them?" he asks.

"It looks that way. Their negative frequency disturbs the Prism's balance. As long as they're here, this world is a straw house in a forest fire. It could crash and burn at any moment. So far, our dimensions seem unaffected. But that may be because they're the last line of defense. You understand how important it is you don't say anything to anyone, right? Anyone, Gill!"

He nods, a little taken aback by the louder tone of my voice, and I'm satisfied that I've succeeded in terrifying him into eternal silence. We approach the Citadel doors. My hands pull them open, and the Sentry expands by one.

***

"Portals?" Petra asks skeptically after I've finished briefing the group about the plan and the monoliths. Petra is still limited in her facial expressions so I'm having a hard time reading how she feels about the news.

"We think," I clarify. "Carmella's calculations suggest it's possible. And we saw what we saw, with our own eyes. So, there's a good chance anyway. Of course, there are so many variables and unknowns, I won't really know until I go through _"

"You mean *we*," Petra interrupts, "because I'm going with you."

Fox's face breaks out in a grin. "Count me in too!"

I hold up my hands. "Wait! You don't understand – we just figured out how to go back through the Prism."

"*Yeah*. I heard it," Fox answers. "That's incredible!"

The room is alive with chatter and excitement. Eager faces turn towards each other, mirroring each other's astonishment and imagining how it would feel to step into the past. I don't blame them.

But they don't have all the facts. This isn't some thrill ride, and there may be no getting off at the end.

"But…" I yell over the noise, "we don't know how or if we can even get back…to present day." The chatter slowly dissipates like the fading ripples on a lake. "Whoever goes through may never return," I add. "It's a huge risk. That's why I've decided I'll go alone. It's obvious I'm the one who is supposed to go. And between the prospect of being trapped in the past and things going horribly wrong and waking up in the real past, I won't let anyone put their life at risk. No one else needs to come. You have work to do here."

The sentries eye each other, a cloud descending over the celebrations. They all have the same dejected expression – pity mixed with fear, mixed with a fear of missing out on whatever crazy adventure awaits me. Even Carmella, who's finally joined us today, looks uneasy.

"Like hell you're going alone!" Fox blurts out, rising from his seat and looking at me sternly. "It's time travel! I'll be responsible for the risks I take or don't take. There's no way you're cutting me out of this!"

"Fox…"

"I second that," Erik adds next to me in a calm, smooth tone, almost like he knew I'd try to pull a stunt like this. He smiles broadly, bringing forth his dimples. "Like it was ever a question, Ev."

"And me," Petra chimes in, no ambiguity in her tone this time. "I'm still interested. And you'll need protection." She gives me a surprising playful smirk. "I can be scary."

Jenna joins Fox on her feet. "A history geek could be useful." *Damn it. She's got a point there.*

"Everest," Robert adds, "even navy seals have backup. You shouldn't have to do this alone."

There's admittingly a weight off my chest at the idea of having some company. But too many people have been hurt, and I can't stand the thought of anything happening to someone else. Still, I know that the people standing around me are just as stubborn as I am.

I exhale loudly. "I plan to leave in two days."

Four heads nod without hesitation. "I'm ready now!" Fox cries, pulling Jenna close to him and kissing her on the lips. "Time travel baby. Let's *go!*"

I laugh, full of mixed feelings. "Ok. I guess 'thank you' then. I know it's a lot to ask."

"Technically, you didn't ask," Erik corrects.

Carmella bites her lip to my left. "It's not going to be easy," she tells the volunteers. "Each Prism night, a new portal will open. And only the person with the compass will know which one it is. You won't have enough time to try all of them. You miss it, you lose your window, you wake up in the past. The *real* past. Nothing can prepare you for that.

"The Luminary's Galaxia is the map – Everest will fill you in. Combined with the compass, it will point you to the portal that is active. You can never lose the compass, and you can *never* be separated from each other, or you may never see each other again! If you end up separated by time, and by Prisms, the odds of finding your way back will not be in your favor. I'll give you my research in case you can use it somehow for the return journey, but…there is no guarantee."

I nod to her. "I know. Thank you, Carmella."

"I should go too."

"No, the Sentry, and your family, they need you here. We'll be ok," I insist. I know she has two teenage sons. Robert filled me in. I wouldn't want to be responsible for their mother never coming home.

She smiles a little sadly, no doubt wanting to make the journey herself and see the outcome of her research. "I wish I had more time to figure out your return Everest. Such a pity the clock is biting at our heels. Perhaps one day."

"If," Jenna observes, "we do end up in a past Prism, will the Galaxia always be there? What if where we end up predates its creation?"

Carmella shrugs. "There may be other maps and legends, but the Galaxia is the only one we know of that aligns with the bearings on the compass. Just try to get to where you're going as quickly as possible. The emblems on the monoliths have presumably stood here since the Prism's creation. They should be a constant you can rely on."

After more details about Carmella's calculations, the

remainder of the meeting is taken up by updates on Daphne. I mention the fact that the Vulturians have the *Anu Ki Zu*, but we're unable to come up with a discreet way to get it out of the Ertu's office. At the end of the session, I'm left feeling frustrated over the text's inaccessibility and the new responsibility I have of keeping four additional souls alive on this journey.

As we leave the Citadel, Jason approaches, his clean-shaven boyish face looks vulnerable and soft. He doesn't appear combative and hostile, which is a welcome surprise.

"Hey, Everest," he says, "about Julian, and his sister, it's awful what happened to them. I know they were important to you. I'm sorry."

"Thanks. Yes, it's terrible," I agree, trying to figure out why he's being so decent and not knowing what else to say. Civility hasn't exactly defined our limited acquaintance.

He looks around at the people leaving, then steps a little closer. I can see him swallow hard as he seems to search for the right words. "I lost someone too," he admits, looking away. "Claudia. That was her name. We met here." His face contorts a little. "One day she didn't return, and then for months. And now, her dimension…it's gone now, so…"

I know his pain all too well – that realization that the person you're looking for won't ever be found.

"Jason, I'm so sorry."

He nods several times as if he's trying to push the vulnerability away so he can put on his defensive armor once again. "It's ok. I think, the worst is not knowing what happened to her, although, I think I know now. I feel it – I feel that she's gone. And I owe you an apology."

"For what?"

"For being a jerk to you and Erik. I like Erik. I like you both.

I think I was just a little…jealous, maybe. You had just found something that I had lost. Seeing you two together reminded me of that. It brought out a darkness in me. I let it consume me for far too long. Honestly, I'm surprised I've made it back to the Prism."

"Your potential must be strong," I offer supportively.

He lowers his eyes and grins. "I should put it to better use then. You know, the people we meet here are incredible Everest. Don't ever let them slip away." He looks towards the doors where Erik's chatting with Fox and Jenna. "I can see you two have something special."

I nod and smile in thanks, shocked at the change in him.

"Will you be all right?" I ask. "Can you move on?"

He shrugs while shoving his hands into his pant pockets. "As best I can. I offered to help Simon locate the Arachna. I'm in Greece, so I'll head over to Paris in the next few days. Probably best I stay on the move anyway. And…maybe, if we can figure out more about the Cypress Project, there's a small chance Claudia's still alive, a small chance I can find her." He shakes his head. "I know it's wishful thinking. I'm not getting my hopes up. But if she *is* 'extinguished'," his voice cracks when he says the dreaded word, "well…at the very least I can finally get some closure."

Closure. That cruel promise that seldom lives up to the hype. "Closure is overrated, Jason. Sometimes, it's easier to live in a fairytale and imagine all the things that cannot be."

He smirks and nods with understanding. "I'm starting to think fairytales are overrated too. You're making a pretty big sacrifice, going into the past, not knowing where the Prism will spit you out."

"We're all making sacrifices these days."

It's nice getting to know him better. We all have a story,

whether it's Shahina's mistrust or Jason's defensiveness, or Petra's hyperawareness, we're all shaped by our past and our environment in complex ways that we don't always immediately share.

Jason clears his throat and waves his hand. "I'll see you tomorrow?"

I smile, surprised to find in him a friend. People aren't always what they seem. "I'll see you then. And thank you Jason."

***

I'm exhausted by the time I get back to my dimension later that evening. After the morning at the Citadel, I've spent the day travelling to each of the monoliths. The Emerald monoliths now have a purpose – a reason for their mysterious existence. I've memorized each portal and the associated emblems, so that when it's time to decipher the map we can move swiftly to the right location.

Tru and Minny greet me with the expected amount of drool and enthusiasm, then retreat to lie down near the fireplace. My aching body has barely settled on the mattress when there's a knock at the door. When I walk over to pull it open, Erik's standing in the hall, hands in the pockets of his khaki pants. The last person I expected.

Neither of us speaks for several seconds. It's still awkward, but something's changed – like that magnetic force that pulls us toward each other is in play again. Finally, I step to one side and invite him in. There's so much I want to say, but more than anything I need him to say something first. I just need him to be *him*.

I need us to be *us*.

"The place looks better," he comments, stepping into the

cottage. "And Tru seems content. It would be tight in that panic room with a dog."

Enough banter. Just be real with me. He must sense that I'm in no mood for small talk and ends it there. "Are you alright, Ev?"

That depends on what he's asking about. I close the door and lean against the wall. "Yes and no. I've made my peace with going if that's what you mean. Not too thrilled about the size of the travel party."

"You really thought we'd let you do this alone? Don't you know us at all?"

I close my eyes and feel the tears accumulate behind my eyelids. "I don't want anything to happen to you Erik. I just can't –"

I sense him come closer and feel his hand brush against mine. He intertwines our fingers like he used to do, and my heart skips at the familiarity of his touch. I open my eyes and stare into his blue irises. *Time's running out. Just be honest.*

"Everything is about to change Erik, and I can't bear…should things go wrong – and there's a good chance they will – that this would be the end of our story, with so much left unfinished."

He brings his hand to my cheek and lets it cascade down to my chin, then brings his other hand up to tuck a strand of hair behind me ear before resting both palms on my cheeks.

"Damn it, Erik," I whisper, "can you please just say something! I'm sorry. What more can I say?"

"Ev…"

"I want us back! If this is the end, I want to go through that portal knowing we're us, the way we used to be!"

I see my reflection in his watery eyes. He leans into me and places one arm on the wall, his lips inches away. "There's nothing I want more. Nothing."

I close my eyes in relief, waiting for him to kiss me and for the scales to finally balance again. The magnetic field grows stronger, his warm breath leaving a comforting sensation on my face, his voice soft and gentle.

"But…" he adds.

My hope evaporates.

"…I want to hear you say that when you know we have a future, not when you think this is the end. I want you to choose me because you want me every day, good or bad, now and tomorrow. I love you Everest. I will always love you. But this isn't how I want our story to begin again, as some…last-ditch effort at happiness. You were about to leave me again and do this all on your own, weren't you? That's really what it comes down to, isn't it? When I think of us, I see beginnings. But all you see is endings."

He leans back on his heels, removing the weight of his body from mine, and with it carves another hole into my heart. The door opens and the lock clicks as he departs, leaving me shell-shocked against the wall. I sink to the floor and bury my head in my hands, just as Tru arrives to lend his comforting head.

The tears finally fall. *How do I always choose the wrong words? How do I keep messing up?*

If the dangers of our quest won't bring us together, what will? The fragile fabric of hope vanishes, like Julian into the light. But he's right – I was going to run away, *again*. Only this time it was to protect him, even if he doesn't see it that way.

A sense of hopelessness settles into my chest. No point chasing something I can never catch. What's done is done.

Just let it go.

CHAPTER 16

Crossing the Line

"**S**tupid piece of crap!" I snap as I try to figure out the fancy espresso machine in the kitchen. Finally, I push the right button, but then realize I've forgotten to put a cup in place. Within seconds, the pristine white marble countertop is covered with a lake of coffee that drips over the edge like a mocha waterfall.

Great!

"Sleep deprived or distracted?"

I jump out of my skin as Tommy's question buzzes in a creepy whisper behind my ear.

"Geez Tommy! You need to learn the concept of personal space!"

He backs up ever so slightly. "This better?"

I look down at the coffee I've stepped in, which now covers the bottom of my bare feet. I know I'm spiraling. It's always the same – one bad thing, then the next. I woke up in a mood over Erik and I've now taken out my frustration on Tommy and on his uncle's kitchen.

"So," Tommy continues, "I got that information you wanted about the doctor."

"Really?"

I grab the paper he's holding out to me and read out loud. "Dr. Simon Auclair. Psychology and Forensic Pathology. This is who's listed as Lise's doctor?" I ask, recalling that it's the same last name Lise's mother had mentioned.

Tommy nods, reaching for a towel to dry up the coffee as I make unsightly brown footprints on the white tile. "My cousin said his signature is on every order in the file."

"Thank you, Tommy! This is perfect. And…sorry about the coffee," I add, reaching for the paper towel. "I'll clean up."

"Don't worry, I got this," he insists, ripping half the paper towel out of hand. "You wouldn't believe how many times I've forgotten the cup myself." *That's hardly shocking.* "Oh, and…what's going on with you and Erik? You two in a lover's quarrel or something? You barely look at each other."

I soak up my half of the paper towels and watch them turn brown. "We're fine Tommy. Just a lot going on. Thanks again for the intel. I'll catch you later"

I head for the panic room. Everyone else is still asleep. I see Erik turned to the wall and try to forget. Facing him after our last conversation will be humiliating, so I'm glad I don't have to, yet. I make my way to Ethan's sprawled-out thin body and gently nudge him.

"Ethan, hey, are you awake?" My second nudge is more forceful. "*Ethan!*"

His eyes shoot open, then a second later he sits up with a jerk. "Get the bags!"

"No, no, calm down. No one's found us. I just need you for something."

He groans and lays his head back down. "What time is it? Can't it wait?"

"Not really."

I have two days. With new parts of the Prism compromised every day, it's only a matter of time before the Luminary is impacted, or the monoliths. The Galaxia and the portals – our tickets to the past – could be destroyed with it. But I need Lise out of that hospital before I go. I need to know she's safe and free and on her way to recovery.

"I'm going to give you a name. I need you to find something for me. Quietly. Please!"

Ethan grudgingly moves off the makeshift bed of blankets and pillows and settles in the office chair, pulling his laptop out of the packed go-bag. He punches in his password and opens an app, then taps his fingers on the bottom of the keyboard. "Ok, what's the name?"

"Dr. Simon Auclair. He works at Hôpital Sainte-Marguerite, Psychology and Forensic Pathology. I need to know about his family, specifically, if he has any children, and…if he's in the Order."

"Why?"

"Just…please. It's important."

Ethan yawns and doesn't press me, probably too exhausted to carry out an interrogation. "Ok. Give me like an hour. I'll get you a digital banker's box worth."

I look longingly at the cot on the floor, my limited sleep catching up to me. I remember when getting up at 4:00 in the morning was something I looked forward to. That's not really the case anymore. Thankfully, I no longer need to reclaim my soul and my sanity from Tristan or from the Tiamat in the early hours of the day. Of course, I have bigger problems now.

I glance at Ethan sheepishly. "Would you hate me if I slept while you worked?"

***

"Do you have the van yet?"

I know Sarah's dying to ask me why I want a windowless van, preferably an old recognizance vehicle tricked out with a bunch of equipment that no longer works, with a back door lock that conveniently jams. It's not exactly your everyday, run of the mill favor.

Her voice comes through the phone in a whisper. "I've got something in mind. What is this even for? Am I going to jail for this?"

A bolt of anxiety travels through me. "Let's not worry about that yet."

"And I'll ask again – what is all this for?"

I pause, thinking about the best way to sell my plan to Sarah. But there's really no way to phrase it that makes it sound any less crazy. "I kind of need to kidnap someone."

"*What?*"

"It's just temporarily."

"*Temp*…there is no such thing as 'temporary kidnapping' girl! It's just straight-up kidnapping!"

"Ok, fine, it's kidnapping. But it's for Lise!"

Sarah seems to relax a little and doesn't yell her next words. "Oh, so, you're just freeing Lise. That's totally fine."

"Um…not exactly. I'm just holding on to her doctor's daughter until he lets Lise leave the hospital."

"*What?*"

And we're back to full volume.

"It's just for a few hours Sarah."

"I can't with you Everest. Just when I think you're done acting like an impulsive lunatic!"

"Oh, come on," I defend myself, raising my own voice and hoping I've hidden myself well enough in the house so no one can hear my crazy plans. "I've thought about this for days. It's the only way. I need that doctor to wake her up safely, and he's not going to do it if I don't give him some incentive. He's one of them. Ethan confirmed it. He tracked his movements to the chapter house. I'm simply taking a page out of *their* playbook."

I can picture Sarah glaring at me with her angry, troubled brown eyes. "That's a very slippery slope, Everest. Trust me."

Her ensuing silence concerns me. She's a big part of this plan going ahead. "Look, she won't get hurt," I assure her. "Ethan found out her school schedule and did some CCTV recon. There's a coffee place she visits before her afternoon class. Then she spends the next hour at the park before class with her ear pods in her ears. She's in the engineering program – won a bunch of competitions. The girl loves to fix things, so, we just need to give her something to fix long enough to keep her occupied. All *you* do is babysit. It's not really kidnapping if she's there voluntarily. You just need to lock the back door when she's not looking, in case she's finished too quickly. Then pretend you can't get it open. Totally innocent. No one gets hurt, and she gets to fix something – just hopefully not too quickly. We send Daddy a deep fake of what appears to be his daughter tied up in a warehouse somewhere to get him on board, Lise wakes up, doctor gets daughter back, everyone's happy."

"And we go to prison," Sarah groans on the other end. "This could mess up my cover. You know Irra and Maeve won't stop until they find Lise."

"Just wear a disguise. No one will know it's you. And I don't think Irra would go after Lise twice. It would bring attention the Order doesn't want. Lise can recover in the safe house until she's strong enough to relocate. And also, can you stop being so judgy? I'm the only one coming up with ideas to get Lise out! And I'm pretty sure you would do the same if you were in my shoes. Now, are you going to help me get her out of that damn hospital, or not?"

My face feels flushed. Ten torturous seconds of silence pass. Sarah glares at me and pouts at the same time.

"Fine," she finally agrees to my relief. "I'll get the van. Get your nerd friends on the deep-fake stuff. I don't want to raise too many red flags. Also, Ethan just texted me. Daphne's stuck. I need to mobilize her. I'll call you when I'm ready."

Relief pours over me. "Thank you!"

Sarah chuckles. "Yeah, anytime. Just please try not to think of anything else criminal or suicidal, at least for the next couple of days."

The Paris chapter house was beginning to feel like a suffocating tomb. Stepping inside the gloomy building had always made Sarah nauseous, but the sensation went well beyond that now. She felt condemned walking the halls, like a cursed apparition of who she was – not entirely human anymore. She had done things now – things she didn't know if she could ever forgive herself for even if she could temporarily justify them. She was in no position to preach to Everest about kidnapping when she had done so much worse. Had the ends justified the means then too?

She navigated the mahogany hallway towards the north-west corner of the second floor, where Ethan said Daphne was stuck in a storage room, caught on some wire that had been hanging off a shelf. It took several turns down narrow aisles of densely packed ceiling-high shelves before Sarah located the wires.

She didn't immediately see Daphne, the camo working as intended. Finally, she glimpsed a slight imperfection on the wall. Something moved, and there she was. Ethan must have activated her remotely to give her a clue.

"Be very careful untangling her," he had warned. Sarah

steadied her hand, not wanting to be the one responsible for breaking the prized invention. She removed the wire from underneath one of Daphne's delicate legs, then from around the other, until the little robot was finally free of her bindings. She looked into the camera and gave Ethan a thumbs up. Ethan had instructed her to place Daphne on the wall near the door, so that he could maneuver her out. But the sound of the door knob turning brought that plan to a halt. Someone was coming. Sarah placed Daphne back on the wall, then turned off the light and retreated to the deepest corner of the room. She was still on the move when the door opened.

Footsteps. Two sets. One a women's, the stiletto tapping on the tile. The smell of perfume and cigarette's intermingled, and the light from the hallway cast shadows on the walls momentarily, until the door closed again. They didn't engage the light switch.

Oh no! Not that…

Her fears were realized when she heard the heavy breathing *Seriously?* She didn't need another reason to feel nauseous. Palms suctioned to her ears, Sarah tried not to listen. It would be over soon, she convinced herself. Just don't think about it. It was a musty and cluttered utility closet after all. No one would want to stay long. Finally, the humming in her ears was replaced my muffled voices. She slowly released her hands.

"What's going on with Bolivia?" the woman asked. She knew that voice, and that scent. It was Maeve's.

The man answered, and immediately Sarah identified the raspy nasal tone. The stench of cigarettes. The accent.

"Success, for now," Irra answered. "The water has been infused. We are seeing some dampening effects on the people from the Tiamat's properties. They are more docile. Stupid, pathetic sheep. Hermez is doing brain scans on some of them, but there have been no Arachna readings reported from that region in two months."

"So, it's really working." Maeve snickered. "Son of a bitch actually did it."

"Those idiots have no idea they are drinking Tiamat-infused water. I was skeptical myself, but the possibilities are endless now." There was a pause. "Let us go," Irra continued. "You need to stop by the hospital and check on the girl."

"Why don't we just kill the brat? We're wasting our resources."

"I couldn't agree more. Tell that to the Ertu."

"You'd like that wouldn't you? Get me to do your dirty work."

The door creaked open, then shut, and the two sets of footsteps retreated, leaving the stench of smoke and evil behind.

Sarah tried to settle her twisted stomach and vanquish the disturbing image of Maeve and Irra from her mind. She glanced toward the spot she had placed Daphne. *Did you get all that Ethan?* They had a much bigger problem now. A much, *much* bigger problem.

Sarah waited a few minutes before letting herself out of the storage room. One more stop before she had to commit grand theft auto, because the day wasn't eventful enough. She entered the lounge and took a seat in one of the armchairs and waited. Tara would be here soon. She had been flirting with one of the new initiates for weeks, so if he was there, she wouldn't be far. Sure enough, Tara arrived within minutes and took her seat across from the rookie, leaning in as the two of them engaged in flirtatious whispers.

The nausea crept into Sarah's throat again. None of these people deserved any happiness. *You're all despicable!*

She readied the phone Robert had secretly given her in the sleeve of her sweater and began to walk in the direction of the bar, slowing her step as she approached her targets. Tara's tote bag sat on the end table next to the chair, open just enough to allow the phone to slip inside when Sarah let it go. She looked back causally to see if anyone noticed the drop. No one made eye contact with her, too busy looking into smart phone screens or sipping brandy.

She let out a sigh as she left the lounge, her breathing shaky. *Now, moving on to kidnapping college kids,* she thought with dread.

CHAPTER 17

Disapproval

EVEREST CLEARY

I don't think I've ever seen Jenna completely gutted. Scared, sure, like that day on the dragon boat. Discouraged, yes, like the night before when she arrived in Paris without Fox. But never gutted. Not until today.

She sips a cup of chamomile tea and stares longingly at the world beyond the sheer curtains of the luxury apartment.

"It's so unfair that you can't be out there," I say to her. "You, of all people, shouldn't experience Paris in hiding from behind a pane of glass."

It's cruel irony. Jenna should be on her fifth museum by now. Instead, she's hanging out with me, looking miserable in a stranger's house.

"It is not that," she says surprisingly, blowing the tea to cool it down. Her Latin accent is lovely, and each letter rolls of her tongue like its own song. "Ok, maybe a little bit that. But it is mostly Fox."

"Oh. Everything all right with you two?"

She smiles shily. "Oh yes. Great. Everything is…great. But at least you and Erik got the chance to meet in the real world. We never got that chance. He was supposed to meet us in

Boston, at the plane, but he did not make it in time. And now, our relationship can only exist in some fantasy world. It may never be normal." She chuckles. *"El amor a distancia es para tonto*s."

The Spanish phrase sounds like candied poetry. "That's beautiful," I comment.

She bursts out laughing. "It means long distance love is for fools."

"Oh. I guess everything does sound good in Spanish."

"My mother said it to my sister when she fell in love with a boy from Panama. And, like she warned her, it did not work out for them."

"You and Fox are different. You have the Prism."

Her eyes light up a little. "Yes, for now."

I feel for Jenna, remembering how relieved I had been to finally meet Erik in London and assuring myself of his existence. There's nothing quite like the real thing.

"You don't have to come with me," I remind her.

"That is not an option! I am fine, really. But everything is just very strange now. I never thought this would be my life."

That makes two of us.

Our conversation is interrupted by the buzzing of my burner phone. "I'm ready," Sarah says when I answer, then gives me the coordinates.

"Give me fifteen minutes."

"Anything I can help with," Jenna asks when I hang up.

"Not yet. But I hope I can count on you all later."

***

Come afternoon, the panic room gets a lot chillier. Everyone seems to be staring daggers at me. I refuse to make eye contact with Erik, but I imagine there's smoke piling out of his ears like out of a cartoon character.

Robert finally breaks the silence. "This is the last thing I expected."

The plan had seemed so solid in my head, I didn't think it would be met with so much disapproval. Then again, it does involve a bunch of potential felonies, so in retrospect I should have anticipated the blowback. Robert's disapproval stings the most, and I'm surprised by how much his opinion has come to matter to me.

Erik doesn't say a word, Jenna looks even sadder than before, and Shahina looks as if she wants to strangle me in front of everyone.

"You have put all of us in jeopardy!" she chastises. "I'll be amazed if you even get back into the Prism after all of this. I bet it was Sarah's idea, wasn't it?"

"No, actually, she was against it too."

I lay out the events of the last 20 minutes. Dr. Auclair's daughter Jacqueline entered the coffee shop as expected. On her way out, she encountered a frantic and well disguised Sarah emerging from the working van, alarmed over her surveillance equipment not working and selling her a story about being a private investigator on an important job. As I hypothesized, Jacqueline Auclair couldn't resist the challenge of fixing Sarah's failing equipment. Once she was inside the van, Sarah locked the back doors. She had a chloroformed cloth ready in case she needed it, but it was a last resort, for Sarah's safety. This could be an innocent girl who didn't deserve any harm, or she could be a well-trained Vulturian. We had to be prepared.

"Someone should have told her not to get into creepy vans with strangers. Anyway, last I heard, she was still busy untangling some wires," I tell the group. "And we'll try to keep it that way. With any luck, she'll be sitting in class in a few hours with no idea of the part she played in Lise's rescue, her father will buy the deep fake Yoshi made and Lise will be free."

"This is madness Ev," Erik mutters, then glares at Yoshi.

"Well, it's done," I answer defiantly. If the plan goes awry, Jacqueline will likely have some major trust issues and need some therapy. But I tell myself crossing that line is justified. *For Lise.* "Jacqueline will be fine. Look, sometimes you need to go on the offensive. The Vulturians are counting on us playing by the rules. They'll never see it coming."

Shahina steps forward. "Ok. The girl is in the van. Plan is in motion whether we like it or not. What do you need us to do?"

"Well, for starters, I need someone to distract the paramedics so I can commandeer an ambulance..."

"Dear God," Robert mumbles while shaking his head.

"I can do that," comes a new voice. Fox stands on the steps of the panic room, rainwater dripping off the bottom of his polyester jacket onto the polished tile floor. His long black hair hangs free and is slicked back against his head. "Sorry, forgot to pack an umbrella."

I'm just as glad to see Fox as I am for the attention being off me for a moment. His face looks the same, but instead of his signature cargo shorts he's wearing pants, for perhaps the first time since I've met him. A Parisian November isn't as warm as the Prism.

"I told Ethan to watch for him at the door. My friend got him on the next cargo flight out," Robert explains, coming over to give Fox a handshake. "Glad you found your way kid."

Jenna approaches Fox slowly at first. She places a palm on his cheek to study him, and within seconds Fox kisses her. Someone whistles and the room erupts in applause, and the rest is history. I see Jenna's anxiety and sadness melt away as she starts to blush. We give them a few minutes to catch up while we try not to stare at them awkwardly. Finally, Fox clears his throat.

"So, this plan of yours," He says, resuming the interrupted discussion, "I could dazzle the masses with my potential of making things levitate, create a distraction that way."

Finally, someone who thinks I'm not going to hell. "You think it could work?"

"I mean, it's still crazy, but it's for Lise."

His eyes glaze over with a veil of melancholy. He was there when Lise and Julian were taken in the glen. *He gets it.*

"For Lise," I repeat, giving him a smile of thanks before turning to Yoshi. "I'll need you to help us get to Dr. Auclair unnoticed. We need to show him the deep fake video and demand he move Lise to the waiting ambulance."

Yoshi nods hesitantly and looks to Ethan, who's come down the steps behind Fox. "I guess we can hack into the security feed and guide you."

Now for the wild card. "It won't be me you're guiding. Since we snuck past them before, disguises likely won't work again. They probably know all the Sentry faces if they've been tracking us, so there's only one of us who is going to be able to get close to him without setting off alarms."

Shahina reads my mind, and her eyes grow wide with disbelief. "You can't be serious?" she scoffs.

Tommy looks around the room. "Who?"

"You, dummy!" Shahina groans. "We are totally screwed."

Tommy pulls his shoulders back and grins. "Me? Brilliant. Why didn't I think of that?" He maneuvers closer to Shahina with a confident swagger. "What? You don't think I can pull it off? I can do it. I approach people all the time."

"You approach women to hit on them," Erik points out. "I don't think the doctor is your type. Also, small detail, you literally ran away to *another country* the last time you met one of these people!"

"Now wait a minute, I can be scary," Tommy insists twisting his face into a comical snarl. I'm sure impressing Shahina has something to do with that.

I grab him by the shoulder and shove a phone into his left hand. "I don't need you to be scary. Just serious. He needs to believe his daughter is in real danger. So please, don't make that face. Just…poker face, ok?"

Tommy pouts for a moment. "Fine. I can be boring if you want. Question…are we going to kill her if he doesn't cooperate? You know, hypothetically of course? Can I say that?"

Oh boy.

"I'll work on a script with you," I reply, shocked that I'm considering it. "He needs to sense the urgency." Whatever gets the job done, I tell myself, then look to Shahina. "Can you get into the hospital and keep Maeve and Tristan away from Lise's room?"

She motions to the wall of collector guns and crossbows. "Can I bring a weapon."

"No. Not at the hospital. Distractions. Knock over a cart if you have to, fake a panic attack, but no weapons." I can feel the disapproval percolating in the air again as the extent of our illegal actions starts to sink in. "Look, you can all lay into me later and tell me what an irresponsible and impulsive person I am, and I promise I will sit there and take it. But right now, we have a very small window to get Lise out. It needs to happen *now!* Are you with me, or not?"

I look to Robert and breathe a sigh of relief when he gives

me a subtle nod. It appears to be the green light for the rest of the team, who make no objections.

"Thank you," I tell everyone, on the verge of tears.

"I'll only slow you down," Robert adds, "but I can try to keep Francine away."

It's my turn to raise an eyebrow. "How?"

"Sarah planted a phone in her bag. I've been trying to find a way to speak with her. Perhaps I can draw her away from the hospital long enough."

"You can't meet her Robert," Erik insists. "It would surely be a trap."

"I wasn't planning an in-person meeting. Just a call."

Jenna winks at Fox, still starry-eyed and blushing. "Every magician needs an assistant, right?"

I lock eyes with Erik for the first time since the Prism. "And I'll need someone to drive the ambulance while I make sure the doctor is doing his job. Could you hot wire the engine, like you did that night in Paris?"

He smirks and shakes his head, then runs his fingers through his wavy hair and over the stubble on his chin. Finally, he leans back against the wall and shrugs. "What's one more car theft?" He holds my gaze with an empathetic expression. "For Lise."

As she walked from her car to the hospital to check on the Vidal girl and scour the hospital footage for any sightings of Everest, Tara Bahar heard a strange sound and felt the accompanying vibration against the side of her body. She knew instantly that it wasn't coming from her Order-issued device.

She glanced inside her tote bag and saw an older model cell phone, its tiny screen lighting up green with each vibration. She had never seen it before, and the number was blocked. She knew better than to wonder how it ended up in her bag. In her world, the stuff of spy movies happened on a regular basis. There was only one reason for that phone to be in her bag.

Someone wanted to get a hold of her, off the radar.

Tara didn't like surprises. Whoever slipped that phone into her bag was able to get past her. She prided herself on being exceptionally vigilant, attuned to the slightest change in her environment. It was the product of years of Vulturian training, and she had been one of their best students. There was a reason they picked her to be Sharur.

How did I allow someone to get so close?

The vibrations continued. Whoever was trying to get a hold of her was not going to stop. She sat down on a bench outside the hospital, shoved her hand into the bag and pulled out the device with irritation.

"Who is this?"

Robert Crawford waited a few moments before responding. He hadn't heard his daughter's voice since the day she'd almost killed him and her brother. He had hoped, however foolishly, that the woman he had faced that day was not of sound mind – that she was some kind of glitch in the matrix – and that Francine was still alive and well inside the programmed Vulturian body. But when he heard her voice, his hopes evaporated, for he heard in her tone the same contempt and hatred he had heard that day at the cabin as she sentenced him and Simon to death by sniper fire without a hint of remorse.

"Hello Francine," Robert replied.

Tara froze. A tumultuous storm began to swirl inside her – a mix of anger, self-hatred, and denial. She had wondered what happened to her father and brother. She'd awoken in the cabin to a foiled plot and the ire of the Ertu. She'd come up empty-handed on Everest Cleary, and then failed at disposing of the Order's long-time nemesis, her father.

Although she couldn't admit it to herself, regret was seeping into her mind. It was the reason she spent her nights tossing and turning in a state of perpetual free-floating anxiety. It was the reason she often felt dissociated, like her mind and body were no longer in the same room together. It was as if she was two people, which she in fact was. Francine Crawford and Tara Bahar could never exist in the same body. They were of conflicting worldviews and ideologies, and her mind was growing weary of reconciling the drastic incongruency.

Although she told herself she had embraced her new

identity, her past was still a part of her. The desensitization sessions, while terrifyingly effective, could not completely erase who she once was. They could not completely erase the love and happy memories from her childhood, and the knowledge that she had meant the world to her loving parents. She knew this in the depths of her soul, regardless of the lies the Order had implanted. But she couldn't allow her conscious mind to recognize this. If she did, she couldn't be Tara Bahar any longer. She couldn't be a Vulturian.

"So," she replied, trying to calm the confusing emotions inside her, "you made it out."

"Of the forest, where you tried to have us murdered, yes." Robert meant to be frank and direct, hoping that maybe shocking Francine out of her identify crises with the cold-hard truth would be more effective than sentimentality.

"You got lucky," Tara replied, trying to maintain her persona. "But you won't be next time."

"Is that what you really want? To have the blood of your family on your hands?"

"You're not my family. You never were."

The words cut Robert deeply, and he wondered if she truly meant them or if she was just speaking from misplaced anger. Adopted or not, he loved her more than he could express, and she was his daughter in every sense of the word.

"Do you really believe that?" he pressed her. "We love you, Francine. We will always be your family. Not *them!* You cannot possibly believe that they love you or want you or value you. You're just a pawn – a tool to get what they want. How can you not see that?"

Tara struggled to find the right words to respond. She considered her father's warning, but her mind would not let her believe it. She had committed to the Order. She was a Sharur now. It wasn't a path she could turn back from, at least not easily.

"How did you get this phone to me?"

"That's not important."

"What do you want then?"

"Just to talk. To hear your voice. To see if there is any hope."

Tara laughed. "You are so naïve. You need to let me go old man. It will be easier for you to accept your fate if you do."

"No!"

Robert's firmly uttered reply hung in the air as more silence ensued. It was a simple yet powerful two letter statement of defiance. He would not abandon her, and no matter how far she fell, he would always hold out hope that she would claw her way up from rock bottom.

"Stubborn." Tara replied. But her heart fluttered for the briefest of seconds before she brushed it away. "The Order won't stop looking for you. Even the Prism can't protect you now. We have eyes everywhere. There is nowhere you can go where we won't find you. It's just a matter of time before one of you slips up, and we'll track you right to your front door."

"I'm aware," Robert replied calmly. The risk of being located by the Arachna was always at the forefront of his mind. For the time being, they had their jamming technology to keep the Order guessing, but their luck could run out at any moment. He had long made his peace with that reality.

"Whatever is meant to happen to me, I will not stop fighting for you Francine," Robert continued, trying to control the lump of sorrow that was expanding in his throat. "Whoever you believe yourself to be, whatever they've told you…I know my daughter is in there somewhere. I *know* you."

"You don't know me! You never did," she retorted coldly. "I was never one of you."

"You could have found the Prism on your own, Francine."

"Stop calling me that!"

"You didn't have to take their deal Francine."

"What do you know about it? You know nothing. You *don't know me!*"

"I know you. I love you, Francine. Don't ever forget that."

Tara felt as if the phone was burning the flesh off her ear. "Shut up!"

"I love you, Francine," came the words again.

She cringed. Why couldn't he just hate her, the way she hated him? Why did he have to be so virtuous and moral?

"My name is Tara!" she shouted at him, then hung up the call abruptly.

As she sat on the bench staring at the grey screen, she realized her entire body was trembling. Emotion overpowered her, and she threw the device across the courtyard, where it landed at the feet of an unsuspecting older man waiting for a taxi in a wheelchair. Her face was flushed and hot, her teeth clenched. He had wormed his way into her psyche, and she hated herself for allowing it to happen.

"Francine is dead," she murmured to herself, trying to steady her breathing. She walked briskly toward the man in the wheelchair and snatched the phone up from beneath his feet. She knew it was a burner, but maybe they could use it somehow. Without a word to the stunned man, she proceeded towards the hospital doors just as her Vulturian-issued device began to ring.

CHAPTER 18

Prison Break

EVEREST CLEARY

*I*t's a good plan. It's a good plan. That mantra is all I can think of as I wait for the signal from Tommy. The last time I saw him, he was heading into the hospital dressed as a doctor with a surgical mask over his mouth.

"Target is in the psych unit," Yoshi had informed us. "Take the west elevators, pass X-ray, then take a left after you pass Pediatrics. You should see him. Greyish-brown hair, black dress shirt. He's got his name tag on. He's writing in some charts beside a stretcher."

It still concerns me that I've left the most important part of this operation up to Tommy. Aside from Shahina, who thankfully hasn't sent an SOS yet, I have no eyes on the inside, and I've put a lot of friends in a dangerous situation. *Please, let this work.*

Around the corner, Fox and Jenna entertain mesmerized pedestrians with magic tricks. I've never seen Fox use his potential before. That goes for most of the Sentry. I wish I could enjoy the unbelievable spectacle of floating objects, but there's no time for that. I just hope that the portable jammer Yoshi crafted keeps Fox's potential off the Order's radar.

I stare at my phone, waiting for the signal. *He should be there by now…*

Erik hangs out near one of the ambulances, both of us disguised as paramedics and prepared for Fox and Jenna to pull the real paramedics away.

The phone buzzes. *'Going to room.'* That's the cue. Dr. Evil took the bait. *Good.*

I motion to Jenna to move in. She pulls off a stunning gypsy look as she approaches the paramedics, motioning with dancing arms for them to follow her. She points to Fox, who has turned it up a notch and is now spinning several small objects in the air. The paramedics start to gasp and exclaim. One of them calls over his friend from another rig. *The less eyes the better.*

The far ambulance now waits unattended. Erik gets in the driver's side and starts getting it ready to move. *Patience. Patience.* Tommy should be guiding the doctor to the elevators by now. But three minutes later I start to grow nervous.

Where the hell is he? Would it take this long?

Three minutes turns to five, then five to seven. *Come on Tommy!* If he'd been caught, Shahina would have sent word. But it's radio silence.

I signal Fox and Jenna to keep up the act when suddenly the back doors fly open. A stretcher rolls out. Dr. Auclair follows it, shoulders hunched, head lowered as if he's shielding his face from the cameras. He looks older than I imagined.

"All yours. I'm going back for Shahina," Tommy says behind him, then gives me a thumbs up and disappears back into the hospital. I curse under my breath. That's not part of the plan. He's supposed to get the hell out of there! But I can't stop him.

Lise lies on the stretcher like a life-size doll, tiny pink circles on her otherwise pale face. I touch her hand to make sure it's still warm, then glare at the doctor, determined to channel all my disgust and anger into one look.

"Get in!" I command. He glares back at me, at first hesitant. His eyes peer from under his creased brow and scan the parking lot. I clench my teeth. "No harm will come to your daughter if you just cooperate. *Get in!*"

He's a full head taller than me and muscular, but I grab his arm and force him inside without much resistance, paternal instincts working to my advantage. But just as I'm about to close the door, a hand pushes its way in and forces it open. A man's hand with a familiar ring on a familiar granite band.

"So close," Tristan says, using his other hand to pry open the adjacent door. "You almost got away with it."

My worst fears are realized. They're onto us.

I try to pull the doors shut but Tristan's stronger and counteracts my force. I know Erik's waiting for my three knocks to start driving, and it's only a matter of time before Fox and Jenna start losing their audience. I try to kick Tristan away, but he anticipates my move and blocks my leg, grabbing my foot and thrusting it back. I hit the foot of the stretcher, a warmth radiating through my injured spine and shoulder blade.

"Are you happy?" I ask him, rising from the floor. I study his face, searching for the evil that I believed he once embodied. But he let me go once. *Why?* Maybe there's a part of him that's capable of compassion, a part the Order hasn't infected. Maybe I can hack into that part and speak to his humanity.

I soften my gaze and lock eyes with him. "*Look at her!* Look at what you've done to her!"

"You have Tara to thank for that. Wasn't my idea."

"You mean Francine? The girl you brainwashed to do your biding?"

"We all make our choices. Francine is long gone, Everest.

Once the Order turns you, you're a lost cause. You'll never get her back."

I notice his eyes darting towards Lise, then looking away as if he's uncomfortable. I move aside to give him a better view. "Are *you* a lost cause then?"

He looks at the doctor. Then at Lise. "He'll kill you for this."

"Who, your father? Let him try!"

"I was talking to him," Tristan corrects, motioning to the doctor with a curt nod of his head. The doctor's face pales.

"We threatened his family," I explain. "I'm sure your father would do the same for you, wouldn't he?"

Tristan's eyes change. He glances at Lise again, but this time doesn't look away. I see the smirk slip from his lips. The seconds feel like minutes.

"Just let us go, Tristan. You've done it once. She's just a child! Find your humanity again, for God's sakes! You can kill us all tomorrow. *Please!*"

He stares at me, his tanned forehead glossy from perspiration, his lips drawn in a tight line. I hold my breath and fake composure. Inside, I'm panicking. I've put our lives and our entire mission on the line. And now everything comes down to what Tristan, of all people, does next.

I watch in astonishment as he releases his hand from the door and takes a step away from the rig. "No child should have to go through this. Some things cross a line. Just go. You have about two minutes before Tara notices. I can't stall her more than that."

I can't believe my luck as I watch him retreat another step. I gasp out a "Thank you" to the last person I thought would ever deserve one, then watch him head briskly back into the hospital. I allow the air to fill my lungs again as I secure the door latch, then walk to the divider wall and give Erik the signal.

"Finally!" I hear him say. The engine revs seconds later. *Here we go.*

I turn my attention to the doctor. "What have you given her?" He's almost the same shade as his lab coat now and looks worse than his patient. "Listen, just tell the Ertu I had a bomb, I was going to blow up the hospital, whatever you want. He won't hurt you."

He shakes his head manically. "You don't know him."

Oh, I know him. He's right to be scared. "Then run. Start over and don't look back. Think of it as a fresh start. You'll be doing your entire family a favor. Your daughter will have a better life. A *normal* life. Now, when is Lise going to wake up?"

"Should be a few minutes now. I gave her the antidote in her room, so it should take effect soon. It's a new consciousness inhibitor the Order is testing."

They were testing her, like a lab rat! "You people are messed up. Ok. And aftercare? What will she need?"

"Uh…it's, um, complicated. Like I said, we're in early stages of testing so we don't know all the side effects. But once she's awake she should be fine. I'd leave the IVs in for a few hours."

I reach for a nearby clipboard. "Write it down – everything I need to know and all the supplies I'll need. Once she's awake, I'll drop you off."

"And my daughter?"

"Just write!"

Erik said it would be best to leave the sirens off to avoid drawing attention. We maneuver Paris silently before pulling into the parking garage where our next ride is waiting. Just as we're guiding the stretcher off the ambulance, I feel a finger graze my arm and turn to see Lise's deep brown eyes staring at me, curious and tired.

"Everest?"

"Lise!" A tide of relief washes over me. "Oh my God! You're ok! You're awake!" I run my hand over her face and put my forehead to hers. "You're ok. You're ok!"

"Everest," she says again, smiling weakly. "Where's Maman? Where's Julian?" She tries to sit up and notices the ambulance. "Where am I? I feel…am I hurt?"

I take her hand and squeeze it, perhaps a little too hard. *How much does she remember?* "I know you have so many questions. You'll learn everything soon, ok? For now, just relax. We're just taking a different car."

Dr. Auclair sits with his legs hanging off the back of the ambulance, looking sullen and ill. "I had no choice," he mutters when I approach.

"We all have a choice," I remind him, harboring no pity for this man. "You took an oath to do no harm, and you broke it a hundred times over. I hope you think twice about it next time. If it was up to me, you'd never touch another patient again." I point to his ring and hold up an empty envelope. "I need one last thing. Put it inside."

He studies the object on his finger with a sort of conflicted longing. "You don't understand," he says, "It's not something you want."

"I know what it is." I inch the envelope closer to his face.

He struggles to pull the ring off his swollen fingers, but eventually succeeds, giving me a puzzled look in the process.

"They underestimated you," he says, then goes back to looking nauseous.

Erik opens the door to the rental van, and together we help Lise off the stretcher, taking the clipboard with the instructions, the IV, and the required supplies.

I bring the doctor another envelope, this time containing something he wants. "Inside are instructions on where to find

Jacqueline. Don't move for five minutes after we leave." Little does he know the envelope contains only the location of his daughter's next class, which she'll soon attend without suspecting a thing

I give him one more stern stare, but this time I don't want to convey my disgust. This time, I want to convey a message. A promise of what is to come – or rather, what isn't.

"And if you do decide to foolishly return to the Order," I add, "give the Ertu a message for me. Tell him he'll fail in the most breathtakingly karmic way possible. Not only will he never find what he most wants, but he will lose everything he has. We'll make sure of it!"

And with that, I climb into the waiting van and slam the back door, doubtful that my words could ever be true.

CHAPTER 19

Missing Piece

Shahida and Tommy managed to put their differences aside and successfully brought Claudia Vidal to the safehouse without detection. We set Lise up in one of the lavish upstairs bedrooms. Although less secure than the panic room, it's more comfortable.

I watch from down the hall as Claudia kneels by Lise's bed and tells her things no eight-year-old child should have to learn. Or nine-year-old child, I should say. Her birthday was two weeks ago. I succumb to my guilt again, hating myself for allowing all of it to happen.

If only they'd never met me. If only I'd never gone to that build site. If only, if only, if only…

But God has his own plan, weaved and mapped outside our awareness, bringing things into motion that we can never fully understand – an intricate blueprint that's not for any one person to know. I hate not knowing the 'why' of it all. It would be much easier to accept things if I just knew the 'why.'

Footsteps on the stairs bring me back to the present. Erik appears, looks down the hall at the open door to Lise's room, then comes over to sit next to me. He says nothing, and so I say nothing. I won't be the first to say anything to him again. I won't make that mistake twice.

"She's here thanks to you," he finally comments. "I was skeptical, but you pulled it off. It was a risky, crazy plan, but… it was brilliant, Ev. Lise is lucky to have you fighting for her."

I keep staring at the door, trying not to let Erik's words stir any emotion in me. The daylight slips away outside. Another Prism-day awaits. More strategizing, more last-minute preparations. More actions that will take me closer to leaving the world as I know it.

"Thanks for driving," I simply reply, then rise from the floor and descend the stairs.

***

I'm surprised to see Sarah inside the panic room.

"Don't worry, we picked her up somewhere else," Ethan assures.

"Yeah, cool. Hey," I greet her. "Thanks again for everything. What's going on? You here to check on Lise?"

Sarah shakes her head. "No. I mean, yes. I hope she's ok. Is she ok?"

I nod. "She will be."

"And Jacqueline?" Robert questions.

"She's fine. Everything went as planned. Sarah did a good job messing up that equipment. It kept Jacqueline busy long enough for us to get Lise to safety. She didn't even realize she was locked inside. She made it to class where dear daddy found her a short while later and probably realized he'd been played."

"The Ertu's furious by the way," Sarah adds. "And not happy with your friend, Tara. Apparently, she was supposed to be watching Lise when Robert delayed her. Glad it worked."

I smile sympathetically at Robert. "Was it a good conversation at least?"

He solemnly shakes his head, and we all know not to ask any more about it.

"I'm so grateful to all of you for everything," I say as Erik joins the rest of us in the room. "I know I asked a lot. I'll never forget this."

The energy in the room is upbeat and the smiles pour off faces as we all celebrate our victory. It's a step in the right direction.

"We saved a life today," Robert agrees. "There's much to celebrate."

"I'm so glad the plan worked," Sarah adds, "but that's not the only reason I'm here." She looks to Ethan, "I was hoping Daphne had audio so you could hear for yourself, but it appears it's just the video for now."

"Listen, I had to speed up my timeline," Ethan replies defensively "Excuse me for not getting in all the b…bells and whistles."

"Probably best you didn't have the audio today anyway," Sarah adds, running her hands over her face. "You owe me one by the way!"

I'm confused. What did I miss? "What exactly happened?"

Sarah stops her frantic face rubbing and inhales dramatically. "I overheard something today when I was trying to free Daphne. Let's just say Maeve and Irra had a little rendezvous in the storage room, and no, it wasn't a fight."

I feel sick thinking about it, and judging from the grimaces on the other faces, I'm not alone. "I didn't need to know that."

"Yeah, I didn't either. But I had no choice. I was stuck there…" she sighs again, then shakes her head as if trying to cast the memory from her mind. "Anyway, they had a rather interesting exchange about Bolivia. Remember that earthquake that happened there, back in the summer?"

I remember. I even remember where I was when I'd heard about it. It was the day I realized who the Ertu was, in Eaton's townhouse, waiting to head back to Paris.

"What about it?"

"From what I heard, the Order used it as an opportunity to mess with the water supply in the area. Irra said they had, what's the word he used…infused the water with the properties of the Tiamat. They're running some kind of experiment, doing brain scans. He said the Arachna hasn't picked up any potentials in the region for months."

Erik crosses his arms. "Are you saying they're exerting the power of the Tiamat through water?"

Sarah shrugs helplessly. "It looks that way. He implied the people in the region were a lot more docile."

"They're trying to find a way to wipe out human potential," I conclude. "They want to dampen the frequency on a massive scale, make everyone easier to control." I can't believe it, and yet it's entirely believable. The perfect method of transmission.

Water.

"Everyone needs water." How better to control the population than by using that which it can't live without.

The room is silent. Robert looks like he's been dealt a blow in a boxing match, eyes glazed over and distant. "They won't stop, will they?" he mumbles.

Fox holds Jenna a little tighter. Even Shahina looks rattled and seems to move closer to Tommy.

"Bloody hell," Erik whispers.

Sarah's frown deepens. "I'm sorry. I wanted to tell you earlier, but I didn't want to distract from Lise."

This was supposed to be a joyous day, a win – *finally*, a win.

And now the urgency has just increased exponentially. I try to calculate the days in my head. "They won't stop with Bolivia. How much of the Prism has been crippled already, Robert? If you could give a percentage..."

He ponders it a moment. "Twenty. Maybe twenty-five."

"Any of the monoliths? The Luminary?"

"Not yet, but – "

"We don't know what will be impacted next," I finish.

He nods. "Poppin is trying to work out a way for the Wakers to recreate what's being chipped away by the energy imbalance. But he's finding it hard to get ahead of it."

"Poppin is Sentry now?"

Robert shakes his head. "Not...exactly. He knows more than most, but I don't trust him completely yet. He enjoys power a little too much. I fear...well, let's just say I have a hard time trusting politicians in the real world as it is. His privileges are need-to-know."

I'm glad Poppin is working on restoring the Prism, but I can't depend on it. I address my travel party. "I know I said two days. But we can't risk something happening to the Galaxia or the portals. If the Prism deteriorates further by tonight, I want to go through the portal immediately. We can't risk the Vulturians finding the Skala first. I understand if you're not up for it."

Erik doesn't even flinch, a sign of his hallmark loyalty. It's like he's planned for this contingency. "What's a day when we can give the world a lifetime."

A day is everything. A lot can happen in a day.

Jenna and Fox nod their support. "You know we'll go anytime you're ready," Jenna says.

I glance around the room and make the final decision. "Ok then. I guess today could officially be our last night."

"Until we return," Erik corrects. "Until new beginnings."

I stare into his eyes and try to decipher the meaning of his words, hoping he's referring to us in some way. "Until new beginnings." I clear my throat and try to keep my tears at bay.

Tommy suddenly leaps over the desk, almost tackling Fox. "Then tonight we celebrate! We'll give you a nice send-off. I know where my uncle keeps the good liquor."

Robert snickers as Tommy disappears upstairs. "Your friend, Erik – what a character."

"That he is!" Erik agrees. "Right then, to the drawing room, shall we? We're not going to celebrate in this tiny box." He motions me to go ahead of him.

I try to avoid making eye contact again. This night could have been different for us, but he made his choice. "I'm going to say goodnight to Lise first. Meet you there."

***

The short climb up the stairs to the bedrooms feels like a trek up a steep hill. My legs seem to ache more with every step, and I don't know if it's real or if I'm making it harder on myself on account of my worries and fears. I'm almost out of breath when I reach the landing.

Breathe. Calm. Breathe.

The light is off in Lise's room. Claudia is asleep on the couch next to her, a step up from the hospital chair the poor woman's been living in for the last few months. I turn the hall light on to see better, cover Claudia with a blanket and head over to the bed where Lise lies. Rivers of salty tears have dried over her dry cheeks. She must have learned her brother was gone, forever. I've been able to process it, to some extent, but for Lise it is all fresh and raw. The news would have ripped through her heart and ate her up inside at a time when her body needed to heal and run and laugh. It was a cruel way to come back to the living, knowing someone you loved wouldn't be joining you there.

I place my hand on her arm, and she stirs. Selfishly, I want her to awaken so I can see her smile and catch up on all the time we missed. So I can tell her how much she means to me.

So I can apologize.

But her eyelids stay closed, and after watching her chest rise and fall for a few minutes, I plant a gentle kiss on her delicate hand and release it from my grasp. "I'm so sorry Lise. I hope we'll see each other again. Remember how special you are. You're safe now." But even as I say it, doubt pokes at my gut.

Laughter begins to make its way upstairs. I let myself out of the room and close the door, then sink to the floor, not quite in the mood for celebrating anymore.

Why is it that as soon as we make progress, the Vulturians snatch the hope and light away once again? It never ends.

I hear footsteps on the stairs and look up to see Robert perched on the last step, watching me over the banister. He doesn't have to say a word for me to know that he understands. The sympathetic creases on his face reveal the pain of dealing with his own loss. He motions for me to join him in the small study off the landing, and I gather myself and walk over to sit across from him in a large leather armchair. We sit surrounded by a stranger's art collection that's probably worth more money than we will collectively make in a lifetime.

"How is she?" Robert asks, offering me a glass of water. I take it gratefully and watch him pour himself some whisky from the liquor cart next to him.

"Sleeping it off," I reply. "She's free. That's all that matters. I just wish I could speak with her before tonight, in case…"

Robert lets out a belabored sigh. "I know. Timing is rarely

fair." He downs his entire drink in one shot, then retrieves an envelope from his jacket pocket and places it on the small coffee table that separates us. "There's something I've been meaning to tell you Everest." He furrows his brow in concentration. "Perhaps I should start at the beginning…" His face softens to an almost childlike expression of innocent content. "To 1998," he continues. "That was the year I met your mother."

CHAPTER 20

A Past Unveiled

I take my eyes off the envelope and focus on Robert, not entirely sure what to say. *What?* Did I just hear what I think I heard? *How?*

"You knew my *mother?*"

He nods. "We met in Nepal. I know it's probably hard to believe, but I was quite the adventurer back then. I was in a different country nearly every month, working on a graduate thesis, and never backed down from a challenge. At that time, I was at South Base Camp, preparing to climb in the next few weeks. Your mother arrived around the same time with a university trip.

"I remember the moment I saw her," he laughs and appears to blush, maybe from the drink, maybe from the reminiscing. "She was trying to put up a tent and the wind was fierce – she was no match for it on her own. The tent had detached from the pegs and blown right into her, and she was just walking about like a tent monster, flailing her arms, shouting for help." He laughs again, more heartily this time, and shakes his head. "I was admittedly laughing at her when I arrived to peel the nylon off her face. But then I saw her eyes."

He motions toward me. "The same eyes I saw in my lecture hall that day you walked in. When I heard your name, I knew you were Johanna's daughter. I just knew. And I thought…" He shakes his head again and waves his hand.

"Your mother and I, we spent almost every day together for those two weeks," he continues. "I had never fallen for anyone like that before. I didn't do much training, I just wanted to be with her. She left a few days before my climb, and I promised I'd call and write. I promised her I'd reach the top and send her a photo." He lowers his eyes. "I promised her a lot of things.

"On the second day of the climb, I began to feel ill. The altitude…it was getting to me. I was distracted, foggy, unbalanced. My lack of preparation didn't help either. I didn't see the crevice in the rock although it was clearly marked. My leg slipped inside, and I heard it twist and crack my kneecap well before the pain hit me – my dream of reaching the summit vaporized in an instant. The other climbers helped me out, but on my way back down I slipped again, this time hitting my head on a rock. I was knocked unconscious.

"I woke up days later with a head injury and a broken knee and was told I'd need extensive surgery that would probably not be successful. I'd never climb again, or even run. My brain was clouded, my memories…I'd lost some of the short-term ones. I couldn't keep my promises to your mother. I didn't even remember she existed."

As I watch Robert's eyes grow teary, I realize I haven't taken a proper breath since he started speaking. I inhale before the lightheadedness sets in.

There are no coincidences…

"It wasn't until months later," Robert goes on, "with some therapy, that I finally began to remember things. I searched frantically for the journal where I had written down her name and her phone number, but it had become misplaced at the hospital when they brought me in. They never located it. I just had a face in my mind, and no way of finding it. But the feelings were there, even if the memories were clouded. I just knew she was important in a life-changing way.

"Eventually, I came to accept that she had probably moved on and stopped thinking of me. I moved on too – accepted a job at Yale, met Charlotte, set down some roots. I gave up on regaining those last few memories that kept her identity a mystery to me. That is, until you walked into my lecture. You look *so* much like her. When I heard your name, the final pieces came flooding back to me. Johanna Cleary. I'll never forget her name again."

He places his hand on the envelope, then picks it up and holds it in the air for me to take. "Please."

I try to steady at least my hand as I accept, the rest of my body trembling. So many thoughts race through my mind. I do the math in my head several times, to make sure I'm not jumping to silly conclusions. A piece of my past begins to come into focus – the piece I've yearned for more than any other. An answer possibly lies within my reach. The answer to who I am, and where I belong.

My chest tightens and throat constricts. *Is this what a panic attack feels like? Don't have a panic attack! Not now!*

"Just to clarify," I ask, staring at the envelope, "the summit you were going to climb, was it Mount Everest?"

I look up into Robert's eyes and find them filled with water. He wrings his hands together nervously, slouching in the armchair, lips tight and tense. "It was."

My stomach leaps into my throat as I lift the flap on the envelope and retrieve the paper, unfolding it carefully. The letterhead reads "*Service de médecine légale de Paris*" followed by

"English Transcription of DNA Paternity Results." I start to feel lightheaded.

"I wanted to be sure before I came to you with this. My old college roommate now works in the forensics office of the Paris police department. He kept the names out of it."

…Donor X and Donor Y – 100% match - familial relationship. Paternal.

I blink a few times. 100% match. Paternal.

I have a father.

Robert Crawford is my father.

"I…" No other words come out. My mouth just hangs open, waiting for my brain to make up its mind about what it wants to say.

"I'm sorry Everest," Robert says, beating me to it. "I didn't know. I wish I would have looked for her. I wish…Please, don't hate me for giving up."

Tears fall down my cheeks. "I never hated you," I tell him. A smile breaks through my shocked expression. "I just wanted to know you."

He grins at me. "Well, now you know. I'm sorry it took so long to tell you. But once I knew for certain, I didn't want you to go into the past without understanding your own. I just wish we had more time."

I hang my head, remembering what the night may bring. Just when I've found what I've been looking for. Irony's finest performance yet.

"Our timing really sucks doesn't it."

"It really does!"

I laugh out of lack of a better response. "Can I at least hug you…Dad? Can I call you that?"

He gets up swiftly and I meet him halfway, throwing my arms around him and drying my tears on his shirt. His arms feel comforting and strong around my shoulders. "I'd be honored if you'd call me that," he replies, squeezing me tighter. "I always hoped…when we first met…I wish I hadn't missed out on so much."

All those moments between us where I'd imagined there was some hidden meaning in his words, a longing in his stare – it wasn't imagined at all.

"This is a really cool goodbye gift," I whisper, "even if it's bittersweet."

He steps back and holds the sides of my arms. "I know that if anyone can find their way back through time it's you. You're determined and stubborn just like your mother. This is not goodbye Everest. That much I know for certain. I *feel* it."

I picture my mother battling the tent at the foot of the mountains, intent on conquering it herself. My initial shock is now replaced by elation and disbelief. I hug Robert again before I hear Tommy's loud footsteps on the stairs. "Everest, you hiding up here? Oh, I found her, mate," he calls down. "You two are missing the party. They'll be time for tears and mourning after you leave, but not tonight. Come on!"

"I guess we should join the others," Robert says when Tommy descends. "One more thing…" He looks at the pendant around my neck quizzingly. "I have a vague memory of your mother having a similar necklace. I can't be sure…maybe it's my mind playing tricks on me. The stone was a different color, I think. When I saw you wearing it, it struck me as an odd coincidence."

"Are you saying she was a Waker?" I ask in astonishment. The thought of Mom being a Waker had never occurred to me. But why couldn't she be?

"I don't know for certain. If I had remembered her name while she was still alive, I would have looked for her in the

Prism. But…something tells me that she's connected to it somehow, and that at some point in the past, she had her very own dimension here." He sighs. "If it's true, she was so close to me all along. The irony."

A symphony of emotions course through me. "Why do I feel like we're being toyed with by a bunch of petulant Greek Gods, playing games with our fate."

"It's understandable to see it that way," Robert replies. "But I like to think of it as a greater plan. I have three children now, and I wouldn't have two of them if I'd never met Charlotte. It's a complex universe we live in, beautiful and meaningful despite its chaos and tragedy. The 'why' of it is not always clear, but maybe it's not meant to be. Perhaps if we knew the 'why', we would never allow things to unravel as they are meant to. Perhaps the 'why' is only for God to know."

"Another layer to the mystery of our lives."

"Another layer, and more to come. We can never know it all."

"Don't remind me," I say as we head downstairs.

More thoughts fill my head. My mother, the Prism, my father, the mountains…the pendant. *Are there still more connections to unravel?*

"I haven't told Simon yet," Robert reveals. "I'll chat with him in the Prism about it."

Right! 'Simon is my half-brother!" I exclaim. Never saw that coming – a half-brother and father all in one day.

Jenna dances in the middle of the living room with a drink in her hand, likely one of several judging by the amount of giggle coming out of her body, which is more than usual. Even Shahina seems more laid back as she laughs at a story Fox is telling about his time growing up in Amish country.

"I never stood a chance with that goat," I overhear him say.

I've heard the story before. The goat that chased him daily as he walked past the farm from school. "He was a menace. Gave me PTSD."

"It's nice not to be on edge for a change," Erik says, approaching. Robert squeezes his shoulder, then goes to seek out Simon, leaving us alone. The music is kept low, and the curtains drawn, but it's enough to ease the tension. I relax a little, trying to enjoy the moment despite the awkwardness between us. I'm glad when Sarah interrupts the silence.

"I'll try my best to get that book Everest," she promises, walking up to us. "I know you'd hoped to get it before you had to leave, but that place is a fortress for now. Ethan said he'll let Daphne hang out in the Ertu's office to see if there's anything else we can find out about it."

The second mission I had hoped to complete before leaving doesn't look too promising.

"Thanks for trying Sarah. I just thought it would give me a better idea of how to find Aeonia. I can't even picture it. If things work as we suspect, the portals will read my mind and my desire. How am I supposed to set a course for a place I can't even imagine?"

And bring people I care about into a potentially dangerous unknown with me.

"You'll figure it out," she replies confidently, saluting me with her drink. I wish I shared her conviction. "Maybe there's a way you could find clues about it in the past? I mean, it's ancient, right? It's been around forever."

I hadn't thought of that. I guess I could keep an eye out for it, wherever we end up.

Despite the strong drink Tommy thrusts into my hand, I find it hard to enjoy the evening. Much has happened today worth celebrating – getting Lise back, finding my father…

But more uncertainty awaits.

One by one, I study the faces around me – faces that have put their lives on the line for me, for Lise, for our cause. They're family. They're the reason we have no choice but to succeed and prevent the Vulturians from finding the Skala and wiping all that's good and pure from this earth. We must succeed for them, and all the others. And if we do, there'll be time for plenty of new beginnings yet.

With that thought, I put my apprehension on hold, and gulp down the disgustingly sweet liquor in the shot glass. I catch Robert's sympathetic gaze from across the room, plaster on a smile and raise my glass in his direction.

Cheers to all of us. Cheers to hope. Cheers to tomorrow.

Let's not mess this up.

CHAPTER 21

Transfer of Power

I don't expect Lise to open her dimension door. After all she's been through, it would take a miracle for her to return to the Prism so quickly. Even the strongest of us would find that impossible. I knock several times, but there's no answer. *She needs time*, I remind myself, then reluctantly make my way to the Citadel.

Outside, the grass looks even more vibrant than I remember it, the green melting into my eyes. Everything looks different today – feels different. The Prism places its addictive grip over my heart and injects a sense of unquenchable longing.

Perhaps that's what happens when you know you're about to lose something.

I try to push past the bitterness of my fate as I cross the courtyard towards the Luminary. Up ahead, Erik stands at the foot of the fortress steps. He's speaking to someone and looks happier than I've seen him in weeks, his eyes lifted at the corners as he laughs and gesticulates with infectious excitement. Curiously, I glance at the person he's speaking with, wondering who could bring about such a change in him.

Then I do a double take.

"Tanner?"

Erik and his brother barely notice me as I walk up to them. I smile at Tanner, wondering if his previous dislike of me has dissipated a little and a fresh start is in order.

"Hi Tanner. It's…um…so great to see you here. What a surprise!"

Tanner turns to me and I immediately notice the improvement in his appearance. His complexion for one. His skin is not as gray and sickly anymore – but that could just be the Prism working its magic. He stands with uplifted shoulders, occasionally looking around at the beauty around him and appearing lost and dazed. I no longer see outright anger in his eyes.

"Yeah, it's been far too long," he remarks, then looks back at Erik before the two brothers find their way into an embrace. I can see a tear lingering in the corner of Erik's shut eye. I can only imagine what this moment must mean to him – to have his brother back, no longer a slave to the darkness that previously consumed him.

Suddenly, I feel as if I'm intruding and start to back away, wanting to give them space and time.

"I'm so happy for you Tanner," I say softly before maneuvering around them up the steps.

"Ev, wait," Erik calls, then turns to his brother. "We have a thing, Tanner. Let's catch up later. Nevar? Usual spot?"

"You know it brother!"

"I'm out of practice though. You'll sweep the hills with me."

"I'd sweep the hills with you either way. Nice to see you again Everest," Tanner adds as Erik makes his way over to me. "I hope we can get reacquainted, properly this time."

I nod my agreement before walking with Erik into the Luminary. I have so many questions.

"Um…so this is kind of amazing! Did you even know? When did he get back?"

"Just now, I just saw him. We haven't been in touch at all. God, Ev," he lets out a loud breath, "you have no idea how relieved I am. He's here, he's back! At least I can go into the past knowing he's on his way to being all right."

The past. That could be tonight.

We enter the lecture hall and access the labyrinth. When we're sealed inside, I reach for Erik's arm before he can descend the steps. "I can't let you go with me Erik."

"What?"

"You just found your brother. I can't let you give that up. You need to stay."

"No!"

"Erik – "

"Don't you think I've thought of that? As soon as I saw him, within a half a minute I realized it. And within another half a minute I made my choice. I'm going. I'm not letting you face this alone."

"You have no obligation to me, remember. We aren't together. You have just as much loyalty to the others who remain here – you can do good work *here*. And spend time with Tanner. You've waited for this moment for so long."

I can sense his disappointment. "You really don't believe we're coming back."

I chew the inside of my lip. *Busted.* "I'm just being realistic."

"Well, sometimes it's exhausting being realistic. Try a little hope, Ev. It looks a lot better on you. Besides, you're not the only one who gets to be stubborn." With that he vanishes down the dark stairwell until I can only hear the dull echo of his retreating footsteps. "Are you coming?" I hear him yell. He certainly knows how to call out my hypocrisy.

Inside the Citadel I can't focus on much. I'm still conflicted over Erik's decision, even though I know it's not mine to make. Seeing Robert brings a smile to my face, and we nod to each other before the meeting starts, recounting the revelations and emotions and regrets we experienced mere hours earlier. I have a father now – a father I may never see again. Just as Erik may never again see a brother. The irony is cruel, and I snicker to myself over the absurdity of it all, which earns me a peculiar stare from Petra across the table.

Robert gives out new assignments. With the news about Bolivia, we have another objective – target the water plant that's allowing the Tiamat's infusion into the water supply. "It must be destroyed. We need to set them back," Hadid agrees. "I can go. I served in the army for many years. I can be useful."

Shahina is next to volunteer her skills. "Me too," she adds, leaving me wondering about her past again and the reason she's so good with weapons. Three others join, and Robert calls them Team Bolivia. It sounds like they're going to the Olympics, only with a bunch of explosives.

Team Cypress gets assigned next. The objective: determine the location of the Cypress project and, hopefully, the Tiamat itself. "Sarah would be an asset," I offer. "I know you're probably hesitant to involve her, but she's proven herself. She has Vulturian access, *and* she's a pilot."

Robert agrees to giving Sarah a need-to-know role, and she's made the first civilian member, while Simon is made the first Sentry. Yoshi agrees to be tech support for the mission. Agnes, Jason and Gill round out the team.

"I'm good with research," Gill insists with enthusiasm.

"The field is different than the library, my friend. " Petra observes skeptically.

Gill appears to consider this seriously, wrinkling his nose

under his spectacles. "I most definitely agree. I'll stay on the plane then."

Robert grins. "Just don't overestimate your strengths, and you should be fine. That goes for everyone. It's decided then. Ethan will work from here on getting intel from Daphne. I'll assist him however I can from Paris, as I'll only slow you down in the field. Three separate missions…but one gives me the most anxiety." He looks over at me, then at Erik. "Team Aeonia. But I suppose it can't be helped. We can't ignore the signs, telling us to follow this lead."

The room goes silent. Five of us will go through the portal tomorrow night and into a world of unknown wonder and danger. Petra looks unfazed, but I can see Jenna and Fox inch closer to each other.

"We have two more days," I tell my travel companions, both sad and intrigued by what's to come. "Let's make them count."

***

When our meeting ends, a sense of emptiness settles into my chest.

Make it count. The group has taken it to heart. Fox and Jenna walk off together, and Erik hurries off to Nevar to find Tanner. I can see Robert speaking with Simon, and as much as I long to speak to my father again and tell Simon I'm his half-sister, I don't want to get in the way in case Robert hasn't told him yet. *I'll find them later.*

The Prism day slips away faster than usual, and I spend most of it in my dimension with Tru. The warmth of his breath on my leg as he follows me around is the perfect antidote to the nagging emptiness. I've asked Robert to look after him and Minny while I'm gone. So many things to think of.

Like Catherine. I hope she doesn't head back to Montmartre. I hope she stays in the solitude of the forest.

The evening brings laughter and excitement to Eden Hall as Wakers prepare to dance and gather with friends in various social clubs and restaurants. I settle in the Gastronomique and order up three shots of banana lime giggle mist, then laugh to myself for what feels like hours for absolutely no reason at all. This time, my ribs and abs hurt, and I stop after the second shot. So when I hear the screams in my care-free state, I initially think they're rowdy party goers or enthusiastic children relishing the limitless world around them.

But as I stare out the window at the lush forest and winding paths, the faces I see tell a different story.

Terror. Fear. Disbelief.

Somethings happened!

I join a flood of bodies down the moving steps of Eden Hall. We pour out like a wave into the Luminary courtyard where a crowd has gathered in a circle around something – or rather, someone. A woman stumbles unsteadily, as if half unconscious, blood seeping through her white shirt around a large wound. A woman I recognize immediately.

Francine – or Tara Bahar, the Vulturian Sharur – wipes sweat covered bangs from her forehead to reveal a bruised, blood-stained face that looks as if it's been punched repeatedly for hours. Blood begins to spurt out of the sides of her parted mouth. She convulses, like she's choking on her insides, and no matter how much anger I have towards her I can't bear the sight of her battered body.

How is this even happening? How is this happening here?

The blood continues to course out of her mouth and wounds, and she collapses to the ground. After wailing in pain and holding her stomach as she unsuccessfully tries to rise, she gives up and rolls laboriously onto her back, staring up at the pristine sky.

I push through the crowd to get to her, not caring about her sins anymore. I don't want this for her, even after everything she's done. Maybe she deserves it, but that's not for me to decide. She could have been my stepsister. We could have been family if she had made different choices. I don't hate her. I pity her.

When I reach the inner semicircle, I see Robert has gotten there first. *Don't look! Don't watch this!* My heart breaks for him. Tara's betrayal was torment enough. This is unbearable. Barbaric.

How could the Prism allow this?

I can't stomach the thought of his anguish and join him silently at Tara's side. His face looks completely frozen as he tries to comprehend what's in front of him. He says nothing, just kneels beside his daughter's body and places a hand on her abdomen, watching as it rises and falls less and less with each breath as her final minutes tick away. His words are hoarse and barely audible, like a haunted whisper through a fog that blankets your skin in shivers.

"Francine. My darling girl…"

I kneel beside him and wipe the strands of hair away from Francine's face so he can see her better, too stunned to cry at the horrific sight of her. Her skin is both crusted and wet from old and fresh cuts. They took their time inflicting their brutality. The sun's rays sneak in through the canopies and settle in speckled patterns on the ground, as if calling to her. Her fading eyes shift to stare into her father's. An ever-so slight twitch of her swollen lips attempts a smile, as if asking for redemption.

Or maybe that's just what I want to see.

The speckled pattern shifts, until a ray of light rests on

Francine's face where a lone tear from Robert's eye joins it. The hand he placed on her abdomen stops moving, the shine from her eyes dimmed as if someone's flipped a switch. Robert lets out muffled sobs in between the haunting whispers.

"No, why, Francine, *no…*"

No one in the courtyard utters a sound. I feel my own tears about to join Robert's but look up in time to see Erik standing with Tanner around the perimeter. He speaks to me silently to be strong, comforts me, even from afar. I can hear his voice in my head, soothing me, calming me.

As we stare at each other, willing the other to push through the pain, my gaze settles on a movement behind him – a body travelling away from the crowd, towards the gardens.

A giant body with a hairless head – and an unmistakable scar down the back of it.

"*Irra!*"

I feel the scream rip me in half. My temples throb as my blood-pressure spikes. Robert jolts next to me, but I have no time to apologize for my outburst, my legs already in a full sprint across the courtyard, pushing through bodies who part for me as they see me barreling towards them. The bald head moves quicker, disappearing down a path to the gardens.

"*Irra, you son of a bitch, you coward!*"

My instincts guide me, perhaps recalling my own unauthorized entrance into the Prism. I slash away branches and blooms, failing to notice their brilliance. They feel like a maze of thorns, shielding something evil. After several turns, I come upon a dark corridor, absent life or color. It's as if we're getting close to something ominous. He comes back into my sights and his body turns 90 degrees. He stares me down with a cold, wicked smile that emits the essence of all the tragedy he's ever inflicted. It oozes out of him like puss out of an infected wound. He's proud of his latest kill, his eyes gleaming with ravenous hunger for more of it.

"I will not need four months," he yells, his words reaching me like a dozen piercing daggers.

Four months? Does that mean he's the new Sharur?

The ground beneath our feet begins to move, and when I look back up Irra's vanished again, only this time I'm not balanced enough to follow. The branches around me thrash and snap, the clouds billow and form menacing shapes and swelling spirals. The wind awakens with vengeance.

It's not like the previous storm – it's much worse.

The Vulturians have brought death and malice to the Prism and put on a spectacle for all to witness. There's no hiding the true danger from the Wakers anymore. The threat is known. The already delicate balance irreparably shattered.

The Prism's last days inch closer, just as Francine's breath did, until it finally escaped her. We were already chasing time, and now Irra just sped up the clock.

I shield my head from falling debris as I run for shelter towards the Luminary. I eventually see the back of Eden Hall obstructed by a fallen free. The grass is faded and covered with a strange ash-like coating. Limestone slabs slip off the Luminary's exterior and smash to pieces on its stone steps. Screams trickle in from Cascada, from the gardens – from everywhere.

The nightmare continues inside the Luminary, where startled Wakers seek shelter in lecture halls. I glance up at the Galaxia and am relieved to find it still intact. *Please don't crack! Please don't crack!*

My fingers tremble like the building around me as I sneak into the small lecture chamber, slide the labyrinth puzzle into place, and run towards the Citadel trying to stifle my dread.

Everyone's fine. They're all fine.

But they're not fine. Some Sentries tend to scrapes and bruises, others valiantly deny they have obvious concussions. Hadid looks like he wouldn't walk a straight line if his life depended on it. Erik…

Where's Erik.

"Who else needs aid?" Simon shouts, running around with water and some towels. We don't even have a first-aid kit. No one thought we'd every need one here. This was supposed to be paradise.

I struggle to manifest a pack of ice and bring it to Jenna and Fox who are trying unsuccessfully to urge Hadid to lie down. The door opens and Erik rushes in. There's no room for awkwardness anymore. I run to him, relieved to feel his arms take hold of me tightly. I bury my face in his neck and listen to him breathing. "I was worried."

"I had to make sure Tanner didn't follow," he explains, tightening his hold.

"Is he ok?"

"Yeah. He's fine. I mean, physically."

"After all this time, to come back to the Prism only to see this." I pull away and he gathers my hands in his. "Bloody timing, right?"

"When will we finally catch a break?"

"I think we're going to have to wait a little longer for that."

I scowl. "You're still insisting on coming?"

"Yeah, Ev. That's not up for debate."

"Even if that means we go tonight?"

He looks at me with a firm resolve. "Even if it means right now."

We don't even notice Robert enter the room. We just hear him bang loudly on the table. People take their seats as Simon collects blood-stained towels, each of us staring at Robert with shock and worry. He struggles to gather his thoughts and stumbles through some incoherent sentence fragments. His face is sullen and gutted, and he finally gives up on making any sense and sinks crest-fallen into his seat.

What's happened to Francine? Where is her body? Is she really gone?

We all have the same questions though dare not ask them. But Robert knows what's on our minds just the same. The silence is uncomfortable as everyone waits. Finally, he begins to sit up straighter and lifts his chin a little higher. He attempts to speak again, shutting down the sob that creeps into his throat from the demon that's eating at his gut.

"Francine is dead," he says at last.

Shivers erupt over my skin. I had hoped, however foolishly, that perhaps something miraculous had happened once I ran off, and that perhaps I'd come back to tales of her awakening – to tales of hope and promise and redemption.

But Robert's words put an end to my wishful thinking. His face should have made it obvious enough. He stares ahead of himself with grief-stricken, vacant eyes. Eyes that feel nothing, want nothing, fear nothing.

Eyes that are simply tired.

"We all know loss. It's something we have many words for, and yet, there isn't a single word that truly captures the complexity and awfulness of it. Whatever my daughter's choices, I loved her very much. And I will grieve the Francine that I knew – the one that I believe was still somewhere inside her.

"But I will do so after we are victorious." He raises his voice on the last syllable and infuses it with fire. "There will be time to mourn everyone – to mourn our world. But today is another turning point." He waves his hand above his head, and the Eye shows the live feed to the Luminary courtyard. "I don't need to turn around to know what you see. The Vulturians have brought war to our doorstep. And in times of war, we must cast aside our emotion, our desires, our needs. We must be of one mind and one goal. Survival! We must *end* them and their hold over this earth, over its resources, over its institutions and leaders. We must *bring them to their knees!*"

The ire emanating from Robert unsettles me. He's always been the voice of reason among us – the calm lighthouse to call us into port when things got rough. But today he's the violent, tumultuous ocean. And he has every right to be.

Outside, the negative disturbance has left the Prism in shambles, far worse than before. The room is silent as we all study the images. They represent a mere slice of the Prism, the full extent of the damage unknown. The Citadel door opens, and Jason runs in, pale and gasping for breath. "It's gone!" he cries, pointing behind him. "The Promenade, even a piece of the gardens. It's…vanished! It's *gone!*"

Robert rises from his seat. "Gone? *Completely?*"

Jason's head bobs up and down weakly. "I didn't believe it either. But it's gone Robert. I saw it with my own eyes!"

Robert spins to the Eye. "Show me!" A fog encroaches on the mirror and lingers, then slowly evaporates to show the next scene. A synchronized gasp is heard from the entire table.

Stella's, the shops and restaurants along the Promenade, the beach canopies – they are no more. The main entrance to the gardens sits further back from the shoreline, the majestic gates also missing. The remaining terrain is abandoned and lifeless.

No Wakers. No laughter. No life. It's unrecognizable.

"That's just here," Jason elaborates. "I heard others talking who flew in from Verding – buildings and monuments reduced to rubble. It's never been this bad. Not like *this.*"

"And it will only get worse," I mumble, but it's loud enough for all to hear in the eerily silent room. "After seeing this, the faith of the Wakers will destabilize rapidly. It could cause more damage to the Prism – damage we can't even begin to prepare for. If we are to go into the past, we need to go tonight," I make clear to the others, "otherwise, we risk the monoliths disappearing, the Galaxia…our maps, our portals. Without them we have no way into the past. No way to find the Skala before they do. They have the *Anu Ki Zu*. For all we know they have clues we don't. If they get it and destroy it, there is nothing standing in the Tiamat's way. They will cripple the earth. We can't wait."

I feel Erik find my hand under the table and squeeze it hard, and I'm sick to my stomach for him. He probably thought he had at least one more day to celebrate his brother's return. Jenna had just met Fox in the real world for the first time, and now their relationship would be thrown into a world of danger. The only one who's probably fired up is Petra, with her terrifying nerves of steel.

"Why would the Vulturians do this?" Jason wonders, staring at the table in front of him. "They must have known what could happen. Don't they want to find the Skala as much as we do? If they cripple the Prism, they're no closer to that aim. It's foolish!"

"Maybe," Erik agrees. "Or…maybe, they want to force our hand. Maybe they want to see how close we are, and if this spurs us into action so we can lead them to the Skala. Maybe it's all by design."

"Then the Ertu is desperate," Simon notes, looking pale. "Francine still had time. Unless it was payback for allowing Lise to get away."

"Irra is the Sharur now," I add. "He feeds off misery. Hell, he might even be a demon. I wouldn't be surprised at this point."

Robert rests his fists on the table and casts his head down.

"I'm sorry Robert," I begin, finally able to express my sympathy. "I'm so sorry."

"No!" he replies, straightening. "We'll have none of that. If you are to go – which I…I'm sorry to hear is so soon – but if it is to happen tonight, you must stay focused. There is no room for error. The Prism is delicate, but our potential is strong. If others waver and lose faith, if their negative frequencies hasten the Prism's disintegration, perhaps we can do something on our end to slow it down, to buy you and the Aeonia team more time. Buy us *all* more time. So no, there will be no tears or grief or sadness. We will have to wait for that."

"How long?" comes a voice. I don't even recognize it, too dazed and overwhelmed to notice anything but the humming in my ears.

"Let's hope not that long." Carmella walks into the room, the Prism clock she's invented tucked into her hand, pieces of hair falling out of her braided twist. She approaches me and hands me the clock, signaling she's finished the tweaks she promised, then squeezes my shoulder. "Let's hope you find your way back to us, and that we're all still here when you do."

CHAPTER 22

Final Preparations

I lose track of how long I've been burying my head in Tru's furry neck. He lies beside me on the wooden cottage floor completely still, as if he knows I just need him to be next to me. Minny tilts her head in our direction, not understanding why I'm holding her playmate hostage, but I can't bear to let Tru go.

I call Minny to join us, and she approaches and settles nearby. She's my manifestation. She does what I want. But Tru stays because he senses I need him. He stays because he wants to.

"I'm sorry I have to leave you."

What if I'm stuck in the past for all eternity, and Tru thinks I've abandoned him? "I'm doing this for all of us, understand? I'm not leaving forever. I promise! And Robert, he'll take good care of you. He needs some companionship too right now. You be there for him, ok? You'll be staying with him while I'm gone, so no chewing on anything. Or maybe, chew away. He can just replace it. Whatever makes you feel better."

With "tea-time" inching closer, I gather myself off the floor, then proceed to brew the mekiza tea – enough for one. I pour it into a thermos and fill another thermos with green tea, then throw both into a sac along with some cups and Tru's favorite toys.

Will my dimension exist in the past if I don't technically exist in it? Likely not.

I glance around the space that's been my second home, neglected for so long, finally reclaimed only to be lost again. Outside the cottage windows it's twilight, the Prism sun setting beyond the terrace doors. I keep it bright inside, refusing to bring forth the night. It feels too much like saying goodbye for good. The dogs obediently follow me into the elevator and to Robert's dimension. The door opens quickly after the second knock.

"I thought you weren't coming," Robert says, no amount of smiling able to hide the pain that eats at him.

"I didn't think it would be that hard."

"Leaving?"

"Yeah."

"It's not forever."

"Yeah."

He ushers us in, looks over his new dimension-mates and laughs. "Well, I'm sure these two will keep things interesting. Maybe it will do me some good."

I know he said not to get emotional, but I can't stop myself from reaching out to embrace him. I'm finally getting to embrace my father, only a second time since finding him, and maybe the last. It feels for a moment as if I'm holding my mother, that desperate feeling of never wanting to let go, like on the first day of school. Or that day on the street when they rolled the stretcher away towards the ambulance and wouldn't let me follow.

Or in all those dreams I've had of her ever since.

Robert gulps loudly as if trying to bury his emotions. "It's like I'm losing two daughters in one day. I know you'll be alright, I know it, but…it doesn't make this any easier, does it?"

The last tear I have left begins to trickle down my cheek. It hangs briefly in a suspended drop at the bottom of my chin before falling onto Robert's shoulder. "There is nothing easy about this." I imagine how difficult it must be for Robert to hold it together, with what happened to Francine being so raw and fresh. I know he hasn't allowed himself to grieve, and all his pain is still bottled up, the pressure growing with each passing minute.

"You're remarkable my darling girl," he says to me. "You have so many gifts and hold so much promise. You *will* save the Prism and fix what the Vulturians have broken. But sometimes…" his inhale is labored and loud, "sometimes I wish you weren't Sentry. Sometimes I wish you were just ordinary and that you didn't have this burden. It's selfish, I know."

I hold him a little tighter for a moment, then let go and take a long inhale of my own. "We all have our purpose. I'm the descendant of Luminarians. As unfair as it all is, I can't imagine making a different choice."

He brings his hand to my cheek. "My goodness, I have another daughter," he whispers. "How did I ever get so lucky. I wish I was going with you."

Damn it. Hold it together. "The Sentry needs you here. We all have our place."

"That we do. I'm glad Erik will be with you. He loves you Everest. Don't ever doubt that, no matter how much life tests you both. The most precious things in life are the ones we must fight for the hardest."

I look away, more hopeful than a moment earlier. "I'll try."

He reaches for something beside the door, then hands me

the *Artifacts of Aeonia* text he's been holding on to. "Here, you might need this."

"Right. Thanks. I wish I had the *Anu Ki Zu* too. I was hoping for some solid images of Aeonia, to help me imagine it and navigate to it. I just *know* they're in that book. I can *feel* it. But as of right now, we're travelling blind. Just vague descriptions of a land that no longer exists, that sounds like every lost civilization known to man. Except there's nothing other than this stupid book to even prove it existed at all. No general location, nothing that I can envision and say, '*that's* where I'm going'."

"You'll find a way. And you'll find what you need wherever the Prism takes you. The great intelligence will guide you. Trust it, Everest! It's never wrong. *Listen* when it speaks to you."

Listen to the whispers.

The Flame reached out before. Then Cascada spoke to me and brought me to the Galaxia. It could happen again. I've believed in guardian angels all my life. Maybe they'll show up for me.

"I'll be back to catch up on old stories. Dad."

He smiles a sad smile again. "I like the sound of that. All of that." His gaze falls to my bag. "You have everything you need?"

I nod, retrieve Tru's toys, then bend down to kiss him one last time, trying not to drag out the goodbye for my own sake. "I love you boy. I'll see you around. Be good." I give Minny a quick kiss as well, ushering her inside to her new home and watching with conflicting emotions as Tru joins her.

Robert holds open the door. "Come. They'll be waiting."

I walk backwards past the threshold, unable to take my gaze away from Tru's tilted head and the brown loyal eyes pulling me back.

***

I haven't told them.

It's easier that way. They wouldn't understand.

The Luminary sleeps, the Wakers now settled back in their dimensions. Only a handful of us remain: me, Erik, Jenna, Petra, Fox, Robert and Carmella. Six of us will wake up tomorrow in the present time, and four will wonder why.

I can't let the others come. I can't bear them risking everything without knowing where I'm taking them and what awaits us: certain death, being lost in space and time for eternity, a life of endless limbo in God knows where…the dangers are endless.

So, I've decided: I go alone.

There's only enough mekiza tea for one. They'll drink the green tea and I'll wait – wait until they shut their eyes and their consciousness travels back to Earth. Then, I'll go to the portal. Alone.

Carmella paces beneath the painted dome in the inner courtyard, head tilted back so far it looks as if it will pop off. At the very least it will be unpleasantly stiff tomorrow. She studies the images and draws shapes and lines in the sky with her pointer finger, mumbling things, probably words or numbers in Italian translated into Prism English. Robert approaches her and the two of them start to speak in whispers.

The others sit on the steps with their backpacks at their feet. "I filled up on pastries at the Gastonomique," Erik reveals, throwing me a bag. "We each get our own, cuz I'm not sharing!"

Typical Erik, thinking of others. *He's going to be so mad at me tomorrow when he realizes what I've done.*

I study his face, the face I love. I wish I could say goodbye without giving away my plan, feel his heartbeat against my chest, a rhythm that's forever part of my own. He looks a bit like a vagabond in his faded khaki travelling jacket and jeans. An incredibly handsome vagabond.

"Ok, gather 'round. Let's drink up before we start to drift." I pull the cups out and fill them one by one from the decoy thermos, handing them out to the group. Lastly, I pour my own from the alternate container, careful to shield the switch behind the sac. Robert and Carmella join us, worry all over their faces as they wonder if we're all being foolish.

"Well, here goes nothing," Fox says, throwing back the tea first.

I study them, wondering if they suspect something, but they each drink the tea without hesitation.

Petra grimaces at the taste. "Would it have killed you to add a little sugar?"

"Sorry."

I feel the hot liquid burn a path down my throat and settle at the top of my stomach. *This is really happening.* Panic grips my chest. I'm really doing this alone. What am I thinking? What if I fail?

Erik places a hand on my arm. "Ev, you ok? You look petrified."

"Do I?" *Don't give yourself away.* "Sorry. It's just getting real."

"Everest!"

Simon steps out of the shadows and runs up to us. He looks at me intensely. I can't read him. What's happened? Does he know I switched the tea?

Suddenly, he smiles. Then frowns again like he can't decide what to feel. "Dad told me. He told me about your mom."

"Oh!" I sigh in relief. "Yeah, who would have thought right."

"We're family," he beams. "It's pretty cool actually, to have you as a sister. I just wanted to tell you…" He takes my hands and looks unsure. I pull him and his wavy golden retriever hair into a hug.

"I wish we had more time to get to know each other," I reply.

"You will," Robert adds, approaching. "Come now, we agreed – no grief. No tears. What we think of we attract. We must be of one mind now. We must all believe that we will find our way back to one another."

"He's usually right about these things." Simon lets out a nervous laugh. "Just…be safe, Everest. All of you," he adds turning to the others. "It's going to be boring in that citadel chamber without you, and pretty gloomy without Petra's sunny disposition."

Simon receives a playful glare from Petra, who then extends her hand to him. "Good luck my friend."

He shakes her hand firmly, then proceeds to say his goodbyes to Jenna and Fox. The embrace with Erik is emotional as Simon looks on the verge of a breakdown. He turns away and goes to join his father.

Carmella approaches next with a small folder and hands it to me. "Here is all my work, every calculation, if you can make sense of it. I've put some notes in there, in plain language for you. Maybe it will be of some help.

"Remember what I said. You *must* keep moving through the portals. Don't risk waking up in the real world. This is not tourism. You survive by moving quickly and not making mistakes. And wherever you end up, leave the past alone as much as you can. Focus on your goal."

"No pressure," I sigh, taking the folder. "Thank you, Carmella. Without you, we wouldn't have a way."

"We all complete the puzzle, my dear. Use the clock I gave you. It will help you time your journeys. Stick together. You are stronger in numbers."

Yeah, about that…

"It's time we let them go," Robert adds, hanging his head as the last round of goodbye's begins. "I know you'll figure this out Everest. The Prism is on your side. We live in a friendly universe."

A friendly universe. That famous quote that hung on the postcard from Uncle Tim, that later came from Erik's lips, now arriving in a broken whisper from my father.

There are no coincidences.

"Remember, make love the source," he reminds me. "Let it fuel you – empower you. Call upon it when you need it most, and it will give you potential stronger than any other you have ever experienced. If there is any advice I can give you on this journey, it is that."

I silently pray for it to be that simple, then embrace him a final time, noticing a slight tremble in my arms as I raise them. "I'll try to remember that."

"We should leave now," Carmella interrupts, hesitantly. "Our day will come to an end soon. God speed, all of you! Find a way. There is always a way!"

Robert, Carmella and Simon begin to depart, turning occasionally to look back at us and offer a wave. It's torture. One look at the others and I know they feel the same way I do. Nauseous, nervous, afraid, excited. Unsure of everything yet determined to take on anything.

The three bodies finally disappear into the shadows and are soon followed by the thud of the Luminary doors closing, leaving the five of us inside. Carmella's watch weighs heavily in my left jacket pocket, the compass in the right. I retrieve the clock and look at the time, doing some quick calculations in my head to determine when the next sequence appears on the Galaxia.

Several minutes pass. I study the faces of the others, trying not to make eye contact with Erik out of fear that my guilt will give me away. My fellow sentries seem to be engaged in the same exercise. In fact, all of them seem to be staring at *me*.

Are they waiting for my signal? Why don't they look tired? They should be tired by now…

Erik grins at me and takes a step forward. "It's not going to happen."

I furrow my brow at him. "What?"

"Whatever you're waiting for. We're not going to sleep anytime soon. See, we found some mekiza and had a little tea party of our own before coming here. Had a feeling you might try to pull something."

I look at the others. Jenna and Fox smirk at me. Petra just stares daggers, unimpressed.

"You figured it out."

Jenna shrugs. "We had a hunch. You're stubborn, and you have a terrible poker face."

"Yeah, I've been told," I pout, embarrassed, angry and relieved all at the same time. I had it planned perfectly. But the only thing I didn't plan for was my predictability and Erik's uncanny ability to read me like a book. It sucks. My plan is foiled. My travel party in the same predicament I'm in. But at least I won't have to journey alone. That brings some comfort.

"Last chance to back out. You sure you all want to do this?"

"We've answered that already at nauseum," Erik says curtly, reaching for his pack.

"You may not be able to bring that with you," I point out.

"We'll see, won't we."

"Yeah, we'll see about a lot of things." I retrieve Carmella's clock and calculate again. "We have about 15 minutes until the Prism day ends for everyone else. Then we can check the Galaxia and…"

A thud stops me mid-sentence. We all turn to see Jenna sprawled out on the floor. Immediately, Fox is at her side, checking her vitals frantically. "Hey! Jenna? *Jenna!*" His finger is on her throat, searching for a pulse. "Ok, she's alive. What's happened? It must have been the tea, it did something to her. Jenna, can you hear me?"

"It wasn't the tea."

The voice emanates from the depths of the shadows, and it's not one I immediately recognize. "I'm sorry," it says again.

Tanner emerges slowly from beneath the staircase, hands in his pockets, slouching sheepishly like a child busted for stealing cookies from the cookie jar. "It wasn't the tea, because she didn't drink it. I did."

It takes a moment for the rest of us to process what's happening. Jenna lies on floor, her body fading to rejoin the real world. I'm not sure what I'm seeing, or hearing. Tanner just got here. How does he know *anything?*

"What do you know?" I whip my head around to face Erik. *"What did you tell him?"*

Erik's baffled expression tells me I won't get an answer. He simply shrugs at the question, staring wide eyed at the last person we all expected to see.

"I heard Erik talking to Fox earlier." Tanner turns to his brother. "I heard enough to know you were going somewhere and I might never see you again and…then about the tea, how you needed it. When you steeped it in the Gastronomique, I switched Jenna's cup. I knew it was the only way I could go with you."

"*You asshole!*" Fox lunges at Tanner like a hungry gladiator, fists knotted into balls, ready to strike. "Do you know what you've done? You can't come with us!"

Erik pulls Fox back before he reaches Tanner. "Stop it!"

"He's not one of us! He can't be here!"

"He's my *brother*!" Erik yells back, holding Fox back by his shoulders. "Doesn't that count for something, mate?"

Fox frees himself from Erik's grasp and unclenches his fists. "Jenna." He stares at her fading body. "Shit! She'll think *I* did this. She'll never forgive me."

Seeing Jenna fade away is eerie and unsettling, and immediately Julian comes to mind. He vanished the same way. Only Jenna will wake up safe in a panic room, while Julian awoke to Irra. I try to shake away the disturbing memory and focus on the heated conversation taking place in front of me.

"I can explain," Tanner offers, resembling a trembling deer as he inches closer, his thin frame still months away from regaining a proper weight. "It's my doing. I didn't think, I…I just knew that I had one chance to go with you and I acted on impulse."

"Did you have something to do with this?" Fox snaps at Erik.

"Are you kidding? He just showed up, literally today!"

"And you just expect to tag along?" Petra asks, narrowing her eyes and trying to decode Tanner like a human lie detector. "You've been gone a long time from here. And instead of enjoying paradise again you want to come with us. For what?"

"For what? Oh, I don't know…maybe I don't want to lose my brother again! Like I said, I heard you talking. You said you might not be coming back! Besides, maybe I can help."

Petra scoffs. "You have nothing to offer. You will probably get us killed."

"Now, wait a minute, that's not fair," Erik interjects. "It's not like we know what we're getting into either. We're all going in blind. Listen…" he looks at Fox pleadingly. "I promise you mate, I had nothing to do with this. I wouldn't do that to Jenna. To *you*. But it's done," he motions to the clock in my hand, "and we're coming up on time. It's better he comes with us. He knows too much now anyway."

Tanner raises an eyebrow. "What kind of spy shit is this?"

Erik glares at Tanner in response. "Not now. You've rocked the boat enough. Shut your mouth and let us talk."

"Right! Decide my fate then!" Tanner jeers, putting up a thumb horizontally. He pretends to point it up, then down, then up again, imitating a Roman emperor. "Just let me know before you have to use your fancy watch."

I glance at the clock again. "We have two Prism minutes before we have a portal location. Who knows how long this tea will last. We need to get there on the first try."

Petra looks around at the ground. Jenna's gone. "She's disappeared."

"She'll return in the morning," Erik assures Fox, who's body begins to tense again.

"She's probably safer anyway, don't you think?" Tanner adds. "Don't you want her safe?"

Fox just glares at him. "You're lucky you're Erik's brother, *mate*." He says the last word with palpable disdain. "Don't expect me to make this trip pleasant for you."

I can't believe this is happening. Not a single part of the plan has gone right so far. At least Jenna will be spared the unknown dangers of time travel. But now we have a wild card.

Tanner.

"We can't afford mistakes," I remind Erik.

"I'll keep him in line," he promises, closing his eyes as if trying to convince himself he'll succeed. "He won't get in the way."

"Whatever you tell him is need to know."

"Agreed."

"And he does what he's told. *Every* time!"

Tanner nods his head vehemently to my right. "I won't be any trouble. You won't even know I'm there."

Too late for that.

"Fine. Let's get this started before something else goes wrong."

The clock tells us it's time. I retrieve the compass from my pocket and place the pendant on top of it. The blue light flashes upward to illuminate the Luminary dome, the symbols transposed onto the painting, pointing us where we need to go. I try to ignore Tanner's gasp and mumblings and read the legend. A star inside a circle. I've memorized them all.

"Senna and Oransen. Come on!"

Fox, Erik and Petra begin to move as Tanner continues to stare at the ceiling. I remove the pendant from the compass and launch us back into darkness.

"Keep up big brother," Erik calls out, already at the doors.

I look back at the obscured silhouette of our new teammate. Memories of awkward dinners enter my mind. "I'm glad you and Erik get to spend more time together," I say to his shadowy frame. "But this journey is more important than you could possibly imagine, so you better stay out of my way. Understand?"

In the pitch blackness I can see only the outline of his head move up and down in confirmation. He says nothing. I turn on my heel, adjust my backpack shoulder strap and cast the Luminary and Citadel into the little locked room in my brain, knowing I may never see them again.

***

We decide it's best not to take the portal, on the off chance there's anyone still hanging around the Forum that could spot us. Instead, we summon the Pegasi and swiftly make our way, riding in silence to the sound of loud flapping wings and quickened heartbeats.

At last, we set down a safe distance from the passage between the monoliths where another heartbreaking goodbye takes place, this time with Juno. "Like I told Tru, girl, you'll see me again. Maybe you'll even see me in the… wherever this thing takes us." I laugh nervously and she seems to take it as a signal to perk up. "Go now. Go, before I change my mind." She obeys and joins the others in a gallop, her wings finding the wind.

The pant legs of my jeans make a rustling sound as they brush against each other. Heavy panting, swaying trees, creaking branches, crisp grass crushed beneath the soles of eager feet. Every sound is amplified and sharp, scratching against my ear drums amidst the silence of our deserted paradise. Five small, terrified-looking humans stand at the foot of the immense emerald guards, waiting desperately for something to happen.

"We just go through," I say, remembering the night of our test. "Nothing happens until we pass through." It hits me hard – the responsibility, the burden, the unknown. "I don't know where I'm taking you." My throat closes, my breathing halts. I bend over to keep the nausea under control and hold my stomach. "I can't do this."

The shuffling of feet brings a body to my side. Erik straightens me up and lifts my chin, then pushes my shoulders back. I know he's trying to hide his fear, but I can sense it. "Where is your gut and your heart telling you to go?" he asks.

"Get yourself to that feeling, and then we go from there. We trust you, so trust yourself."

Trust yourself. Maybe it's that simple.

"Alright."

The wide grassy passage between the monoliths is cloaked in a sea of black with the stars illuminating a faint path. I approach the edge and motion the others to join me in a line.

"Hold hands. Hopefully that's enough to stay together."

Erik takes my left hand, Petra my right, and the others connect to form a chain. I point my eyes at the passage, my pack hanging off my shoulders, the seconds ticking away. I may not be able to imagine my destination, but maybe I can feel my way there.

"When I move you follow. Don't let go of each other!"

My focus narrows to the path ahead, little else in my awareness. With my legs planted firmly on solid ground, I start with the feeling. *That* feeling. The only one anyone ever wants to feel. I close my eyes, and it brings forth images of Erik. I squeeze his hand tightly without thinking. Then I move on to Uncle Tim, Lise, Julian, Tru. Finally, I allow myself to think of Mom.

Within seconds I sense the tension evaporate from my face, taking the fear with it. Weightlessness sets in, along with ease, peace, and acceptance.

Guide me, I whisper, letting the last bit of emotion I'm holding back take control. My legs twitch with eagerness and I shift my weight to the left leg as my right leg stretches forward.

"Now."

CHAPTER 23

1988

The green foliage of the forest disappears. Everything is white, except the illuminated path under our feet and the faint emerald gems shining around us like stars from somewhere in the distance.

The minute our bodies enter the passage, terror grips me, but only for the smallest sliver of a moment. The nothingness lingers as our senses fail to catch up, until grand pillars of light appear to flank our path, shooting up higher than our eyes can see like a pale, iridescent borealis that winds and stretches on indefinitely. Within the dancing pillars I see moving pictures – faces, maybe – but they change so quickly I can't be sure. The sense of peace returns, and I lose all concept of time or space or sanity. It's otherworldly, and I find myself wishing our journey would end in this mesmerizing ethereal place where everything and nothing exist at once and nothing else seems to matter.

Slowly, I become aware of the hands I'm holding – the others around me. *We're still together. Thank goodness!*

The pillars seem to dance less and shrink around us, the path ahead constricting, as if walls are closing in. An endpoint appears and seems to rush toward us, making up ground quickly. Instinctually, I try to turn around and run, but my feet remain planted.

No, I don't want to run. I want to stay right here.

The pillars evaporate and a grey thick mist settles in, weighted with something indiscernible. It begins to thin, fading in substance and color until our eyes set upon the massive stone feet of a familiar statue, emerald ornaments adorning its carved tunic.

We're back where we started, only the sky is blue and bird songs ring in our ears. The border of Senna and Oransen looks unchanged.

Was it all for nothing? Was it a massive failure?

No. Something happened to us in there. I can feel it.

"Everyone good?" I call out.

"Did you all see that?" Fox asks, letting go of Petra's hand to stare behind him, around him, and in all directions. "We all saw that, right?"

Petra looks up at the sun, with no need to blink or wince. "Yeah. But what was it?" She takes a seat on the ground, and it's the first time I've seen her composure rattled. Her stoic, unreadable eyes are lit from within like beacons, her face full of wonder.

Fox's head continues to jerk in all directions. "Gotta say, it was way cooler in there. Where do you think we are?"

"Hopefully in Aeonia," I answer.

But I know we're not. It feels too familiar – too close to home. Whatever Aeonia is – *wherever* it is – it's not here.

Tanner looks spellbound and stands speechless next to Erik, who simply smiles at me nervously. "Just give him a minute."

"And you?" I'm still squeezing his hand, probably a lot tighter than he wants me to.

"All in one piece. At least we made it out."

I let go of his hand and give Tanner one more worried glance. "Now we need to figure out where we *really* are. See anyone around?"

Fox inspects the brush behind the monoliths. "Negative, unless they've all been turned into trees."

The emerald guards exude their intimidating power, rising far above us like the statues of gods in Greek temples.

"The Luminary," Erik suggests, shaking Tanner's shoulder to get him to snap out of it. "That's where we need to go. The Citadel could still be there."

The Citadel. "Of course! Is there a portal we can take?"

Erik looks past me towards something in the distance. "We can ride!" he replies. To my disbelief, Cass stands on the far side of the passage. The Pegasi have always been a part of the Prism. Of course they would be in whatever version we found ourselves in.

"Why am I not surprised?" I summon Juno with a sense of relief coursing through me.

But does this mean we never left?

"Tanner, you can ride with me again." Erik instructs.

It doesn't take long for Juno to find us. "I had a feeling I'd see you again," I whisper to her as I run my fingers through the strands of silky mane. "Let's see where we've ended up, shall we?"

***

The monoliths fall away, the sapphire waters of the Prismatic beckoning us in the distance. We weave between the clouds to see it, and it doesn't disappoint. Regal, vast, sparkling in the sun; it calls us home.

Assuming the same geography as our starting point, we veer south, flying just above the surface of the water. Juno's wings dip into the sunlit liquid, sending a refreshing mist sprinkling through the air every time she raises them. The freedom of riding calms my nerves. Fish zigzag beneath the surface, dolphins leap from beneath the waves along the horizon. The Prism looks intact, unspoiled, as it should.

As we near Agora I see that the gardens and the Promenade have been restored to their original form. There's no trace of the violent storm that left its mark. Is this really the past, and the Prism is yet to experience the full extent of the Vulturian influence?

"Did we miss a fashion update?" Fox calls out as we dismount on the Avenue, placing our feet on the familiar cobblestones.

Petra observes the Wakers with ridicule. "What is happening with their clothes? Why do they look like this?"

"A festival?" I suggest, noticing it too. Neon textiles, big earring, bigger hair and lots of perms. The Wakers study us with equal curiosity as they pass.

"Guys, I think *we're* the odd ones out here," Erik points out

Tanner finally utters his first words since the portal. "What do you mean?"

"Look around, mate. There's no festival. They're not playing dress up. This is their normal. This is…"

What year is it exactly? There's no question this isn't Aeonia. *So where did I take us?*

A young girl walks by wearing a pink mini skirt and some knee-high boots. "Excuse me," I stop her, "Um…I'm trying to imagine what life will be like in the future. My math is terrible. Could you tell me, how many years would I have to live to see the year 2066?"

The girl looks over my clothes, but thankfully seems far more concerned about getting the math right. "Uh…I guess, that would be…78 more years, right? Yeah, 78."

"Yes," I reply, fishing for more information so I don't have to do the math myself, "makes sense, because this is the year…"

"1988."

"1988?" I exclaim, forgetting my plan to appear inconspicuous.

"I don't think you're going to make it that long, no offense," the girl teases.

If you only knew…

"No, I don't think I will. Thanks anyway!"

She looks me up and down one more time, then does the same to the others. "I hope they don't dress like *that* in the future," she remarks before walking away.

I turn to face the group. "We did it. We time travelled! We're in 1988! I know it's not Aeonia, but this is incredible! The portal worked!"

"That it did," Erik agrees, still staring at the Wakers that pass us. "We're in a past Prism. It's like a time capsule. This is something else!"

Petra seems less impressed. "But why 1988?"

It's the question on all our minds. "I wish I knew. I must have wanted to come here for some reason, but I haven't the faintest idea why." There's nothing significant to me about 1988.

1988, 1988… I wait for an epiphany that never comes.

"We won't get any answers standing around," Erik notes, jostling Tanner out of another daze. The guy is like a cat chasing a laser pointer. Everything distracts him.

"And we won't blend in unless we find some new clothes," Petra adds. "We can pick up something from the shops."

I release Juno from her duties and watch her retreat with mixed feelings. "Let's hope it's still on the Prism tab."

***

"I look ridiculous," Petra whines, looking herself over in the mirror. She tugs at the polyester blouse with contempt and disgust. The busy pink and blue hexagon fabric reminds me of the games on the back of cereal boxes, where if you looked at them long enough and made yourself go cross-eyed, a 3D image would emerge. "Why did I let Fox pick this for me? This is perhaps the most hideous blouse I have ever seen."

"Trying to brighten you up. And at least we'll never lose you," Fox teases.

I opt for acid wash jeans and a printed orange t-shirt with a graphic of the Statue of Liberty.

"Here, add these," Erik says, handing me a pair of oversized retro brown sunglasses. "We might as well have some fun! It's 'radical!'"

The boys choose jeans with graphic t-shirts as well, with Fox adding on a neon blue jacket with a bright yellow zipper.

"I thought we were trying to be low-key?" I chuckle.

"Are you kidding? It's the 80's – my absolute favorite decade. I am experiencing *all* of it!"

I inhale a deep breath before we exit the shop. "Remember, we belong. If you believe it, they'll believe it. Don't be weird!"

The walk to the Luminary is awkward. No one says a word, too concerned about saying the wrong thing or making a sound that gives away our identities (or generation), and far too busy marveling at the 80's vision of the population.

"It feels like a movie set," Tanner sputters, adjusting his own large sunglasses. "Too weird."

"What if they're watching?" Fox asks, referencing the Vulturians. "They were probably here in the 80's, right?"

Erik gives Fox a shove to signal him to keep quiet. "Later mate." Not everyone in the group is up to speed on the Vulturians now that Jenna's been replaced, and for the time being it's better we keep certain information to ourselves. I'm glad Erik's playing ball, although I imagine keeping so many secrets from his brother must be difficult.

Ahead, the cliffs of Cascada jut up from the hillsides beyond the limestone brilliance of Castelum, with its climbing balconies and hanging vines. Aside from the fashion, not much has changed.

We continue moving, taking the entrance through the garden and wrapping around the side of Castellum to emerge into the Luminary courtyard.

"What is it about this building? Every time I see it, it seems even grander," I remark.

Blankets thrown across the grass, groups sitting, chatting, eating. No garbage, no agony, no deterioration – it's just as it was. Our perfect paradise before it was thrown into ruin. The Luminary's towers brush the canopies of the tall oaks and maples. The pristine limestone steps beckon us to climb them, to go within, to learn, to see the Citadel of 1988.

"I'm shaking," I whisper to Erik.

"I know. At least we didn't die in a ball of hellfire."

"You actually thought we would?"

"No. I imagined coming out missing an arm for some reason. I dreamed about it more than once, oddly enough."

I laugh. "That would not be ideal."

Inside the Luminary, we find the inner courtyard and immediately look up. The Galaxia is as we left it decades in the future. Unaltered. Magnificent. Then, four pairs of eyes dart to one unsuspecting door. The Citadel access point.

"Wait here," I tell Tanner firmly. "Don't move an inch!"

"Can I sit down on the floor at least?"

"Yes, of course. But here. Right here!"

The rest of us begin to move towards the small lecture chamber that goes towards the Luminary, but suddenly, Erik pulls Fox back. "Wait. We can't go in there."

Petra rolls her eyes and huffs impatiently. "What do you mean? Can you think of a better place to go? It's the Citadel. We are Sentry."

"Yes, we are Sentry in our own time, but not here. If someone sees us and doesn't recognize us, we could blow our cover, endanger the Citadel even. Not to mention the labyrinth puzzle could be different. We risk the Sentry suspecting a threat."

"Erik's right," I agree. *There goes that plan.* "Remember what Carmella said. We leave the past alone."

"Hey, check it out! Is that who I think it is?" Fox hisses, motioning with his head to a young man walking along the outer corridor. His hair falls in blonde waves almost to his shoulders. He wears jeans and a navy-blue polo shirt. But it's his eyes that give him away.

I feel a warmth travel through me. I'd almost forgotten that long before I discovered the Prism, Robert was already here. Is that the reason for 1988, to see my father again?

"This is too weird," Petra says. "He's so young!"

He's seems barely changed, other than the hair length, the normal wear and tear of aging and the marked absence of a limp. He walks fluidly towards the door of the small lecture room that will bring him to the Citadel.

My mind is racing. Maybe I could speak to him. Just a few words, nothing history-altering. When else would I get this chance?

"I'll be right back," I tell only Erik in a whisper, putting my oversized sunglasses back on.

I hardly notice the ground beneath my feet as I stagger forward. Robert looks around the Luminary for signs of anyone following him, and I hope the others are smart enough to avoid staring and acting like stalkers. He pauses at the door to the lecture hall just as I reach him.

"Excuse me," I begin. My mind becomes an empty space, and in the next instant is full of swirling lines that form no coherent thought or question.

Now what? Say something not suspicious!

"Um…I'm looking for a class about rocks. Fascinated by them. Especially the, you know…sparkly, rare ones. Do you know of any classes on…rocks?" *Rocks? That's what I go with?*

He blinks a few times as he stares at me, probably caught off guard by the strange question and the hysterically large lenses over my eyes. "Rocks, uh…I'm not sure. Professor Jacobs, maybe? No, that's more seismic activity. But he may know of something. You can find his courses on the main board, over there," he says, pointing to the class schedule that's obviously displayed. "New?"

"I'm sorry?"

"Are you new?" he repeats in that familiar soothing low tenor of his voice. I can't stop staring at the youthfulness of his features. He's maybe in his early 20's, not that much older than me. Life is so extraordinary. We grow, we age, our lives unravel in unknown ways. *You have a daughter. You have a family. You are a leader.* I can't tell him any of it. It's not for me to reveal. So, I gawk instead.

"Um, yeah. Sorry. I'm a little overwhelmed."

He smiles sincerely. "It won't pass."

"I figured that."

"You have a magister?"

"Yes, yes, uh…he's just…eating. Um, thank you. I'll have a look at the board."

Get out before he senses something.

He laughs a little, probably at my awkwardness. I look at him one last time through the tint of my sunglasses, trying to burn his image into my memory, then slowly turn on my heel. I wait to rejoin the others, fighting the urge to run into the room after him and ask where I could hear a lecture about toads, just to hear his voice again.

"What were you thinking?" Petra hisses in annoyance when I return. "We can't go to the Citadel, but you can talk to Robert? What if he recognized you somehow?"

"Relax. I haven't even been born yet, remember? He hasn't even met my mother. Plus, I had these," I remind her, pointing at the glasses. "I just *had* to speak to him."

"What are you talking about?" Petra asks, looking genuinely confused. "What does your mother have to do with anything?"

Fox raises his eyebrows. "Right, you don't know. Robert's Everest's dad."

Petra's eyebrows shoot up next. *"What?"*

"I just found out," I add. "I told Erik and Fox in Paris. Sorry, it's been an eventful couple of days. I'll catch you up later."

"We can't hang around here all day," Erik reminds us. "We'll look too suspicious. Might as well explore the past a little."

"Your *dad?*" Petra says to herself in disbelief as we walk. "Seriously?"

Tanner springs up off the floor. "Where to first?" he asks, lighting up. He may annoy me, but we do have a few things in common. We love Erik, and the Prism. And he's here for the ride, whether we planned it or not.

Make the best of it. I give him a faint smile as a gesture of acceptance. "You've been away for a while. Why don't you pick first."

***

It's not enough time. It's never enough time.

The sun hangs low in the sky of the Prism, 1988. The end of the day approaches, and with it more unknowns – the excruciating, mesmerizing journey through time inches closer, the outcome a mystery once again.

It's been a treat to see the past, to experience the Prism as it was meant to be experienced. We've touched down in Bora Borealis and Azula. From gliding in boats to feeding dingoes, the Prism has felt like the haven it was designed to be. I almost considered giving the Sky Serpent another chance.

Still too soon.

Our final stop is Senna, which is still magical and out of this world. It's different, colored by the dreams and expectations of the 80s. More space exploration-related attractions. A lot of bright colors. *Far* too much neon. Rock concerts, video game arcades, fashion that continues to fascinate me. Funny how some trends are buried, and others revived.

We manage to get a taste of Atlantis before our day runs out. It's majestic, floating off the Senna coast, with pyramids connected by intricately carved bridges, gardens that defy gravity and test the senses, marble clad buildings, *so* much gold. I never got the chance to visit in our time, so it's nice to finally see it. We haven't even scratched the surface when it's time to leave. *More for another time.*

The clock weighs in my pocket and reminds me it's time to start heading back.

"I wonder if we have our own dimensions here," Fox thinks out loud as we approach one of the regular portals back to Castellum. "We should find out. Doesn't hurt in case we need a place to hide out."

"Would be nice to have something constant linking us on this time jump," Erik agrees. They have a point. It wouldn't hurt to test the theory.

Castellum's marble Forum buzzes with eager bodies anxious to lock in one more experience, one more visit to Eden Hall, one more portal journey. But outside, the light dwindles.

"The elevators look the same too," Petra observes, entering first. The rest of us file in for a tight squeeze. "Petra Starzik."

"Nice to know your last name, mysterious one," Fox teases.

"You must forget it."

"Or what?"

"Just forget it."

'Tell me, how does someone as paranoid as you manage to get into the Prism? You're literally the opposite of 'love and light' and all that crap."

"I ask myself that every day."

The elevator remains motionless. "We haven't moved. Nothing's happening," I observe.

Petra shrugs, as if getting exactly what she expected. "Well, it was a nice idea."

"Fox Huong," comes another attempt.

Nothing. "Erik Halvorsen" only yields more silence, as does Tanner's name.

I inhale, imagining how incredible it would be to walk out into that Castellum hallway, open the door to my own dimension and find some comfort in familiarity. "Everest

Cleary." But the elevator doors remain tightly sealed. There's no dimension here for us. We're visitors, that's all.

"At least you got to see your father," Petra says. "Maybe that's why we came here. I guess you kept your mother's last name then?"

I nod. "Cleary was my mother's name. Johanna Cleary."

The elevator seems to awaken, giving us all a jolt. Only a second passes until the doors slide open. I've barely had enough time to realize what prompted it to move.

"Ev, look," Erik points into the hallway, to the nearest door on the left. The lettering on the gold plate is big enough to read and causes my breath to catch.

Johanna Cleary.

CHAPTER 24

A Life Changed

I had a probability test in math class that day. I was going to fail, without a doubt. My fingernails were chewed off from the stress. I just didn't get it, and no matter how much I stared at the numbers and repeated the questions in my head, the answer was always wrong.

"This is the worst day of my life!" The cereal was soggy now. I'd forgotten about it as I poured over my study notes.

"It's just one test, honey. Don't get so bent out of shape over it. Let me see those." Mom pulled my hand away from my mouth to examine it, then gave me a stern look. "Stop biting them! It's not going to make you learn any quicker. I'll get you a tutor if you want, but I don't want you stressing yourself out about math."

I groaned dramatically. "Easy for you to say. How about you just take the test for me?"

Mom threw an orange into her lunch bag. "You're a smart girl Everest. You've got this. Just take a breath."

"I don't 'got this'. Not even remotely."

"So, math isn't your strong suit. I'm sure billions of people can say the same."

Billions of people didn't have their hearts set on Cambridge, and every grade is going to matter.

"Want me to walk you to the bus stop?" Mom asked, wrapping a baby blue sheer scarf around her neck. Some days we would walk together, and Mom would catch her bus at a stop further up the street.

The numbers blurred on the page. I looked up to rest my eyes and smiled at her. "It's ok. I'm going to study right up until I need to leave. Maybe I'll have some miraculous epiphany, and everything will make perfect sense."

"Stranger things have happened," she answered, coming over to kiss the top of my head. Her perfume had saturated her scarf. She always smelled like a spring day. "After school I need you to clean your room. It's disgusting."

"Seriously! I just cleaned it."

"In your dreams, maybe. I want it clean Everest."

I groaned and thought of the pile of clothes I'd been putting off folding, and the pile of unmatched socks underneath that, and the slew of magazines that cluttered my desk. It would be a fun afternoon. "Fine!"

"I'll see you tonight. I'm making fajitas."

"Well, at least that will make up for the cleaning. Feels like a bribe."

She laughed and grabbed the keys from the pocket of her other jacket. "Love you. Good luck!"

"Love you, Mom."

The door shut. The lock clicked. I tried to work out the number of favorable outcomes to 'A' divided by the total number of possible outcomes as I listened to Mom's shoes clank in the stairwell through the thin walls.

Seconds later, shrieking tires.

A loud thud from an impact outside.

A shrill scream poured in through the open window. Someone was shouting. More shouting followed.

An accident? Maybe a scooter hit a cyclist. There had been a lot of those recently.

I walked up to the window and moved the delicate curtain aside. People were gathered in front of a bus. A crumpled body lay on the ground, a stream of blood on the asphalt flowed towards the curb.

A baby blue scarf turned purple.

A life ended.

A life changed.

The worst day of my life, just as I had predicted.

***

"Ev."

Erik stands beside me. I have no memory of leaving the elevator and making my way to the door. *How long have I been standing here?*

"Ev."

The others stand behind him with puzzled faces. They must be wondering the significance of all this.

My mother.

The Prism.

1988.

She was a Waker. *My mother was a Waker.* If it's even the same Johanna Clearly.

The Prism reads our thoughts. It's the same one. It has to be!

Even the Prism can't tame the rollercoaster of emotions inside me. Is she behind that door? If I knock, will she answer? Will I see my mother, *alive?*

"Are you ok?" comes Erik's voice.

Am I ok? What am I? It's hard to pinpoint what I feel, exactly. My hand comes up to meet the door and I make two slow knocks from what seems like outside my own body.

Muffled steps. The doorknob mechanism clicks loudly, and the knob rotates. A young woman appears and smiles shily; late teens, with hair that falls angelically in highlighted ringlets around her rosy freckled face and down to below her shoulders. Her eyes swim like the shallow waters of the Caribbean. A small mole adorns her lower left cheek.

"Hello," she says. *Her* voice. *Her* eyes.

Words escape me, all knowledge of language erased from my memory. Finally, something registers.

"Hi."

"Are you looking for someone?"

You. I'm looking for you. I'm always looking for you.

I can only stare, unable to pull my eyes away from her. The youthfulness of her features, the kindness that dwells within her eyes and permeates everything around her. I want to touch her, hold her.

Don't!

Erik steps in to save me. "Sorry to bother you, we...were looking for our friend but got the wrong door, didn't we?"

"Ah," Johanna says. "Happens. Not to worry. Maybe I can help you find them."

"Robert," I blurt out. I bite my tongue before I utter *Crawford.*

"Sorry, she's new," Erik interjects.

"I figured. The doe eyes kind of give it away," she replies, winking at me. "I don't know a Robert. Or a Bob, even. Sorry. But try the elevator again and be very clear about who you're looking for. It usually gets it right. Or maybe it's one of these other doors. The names are on them."

Her eyes suddenly travel down to my pendant and her smile widens. "Did you get that here?" She reaches under her sweater to pull out an almost identical pendant in the shape of a mountain, with an ivory pinnacle and a gemstone base, except hers is green, like a spring meadow on a rainy day.

I gasp. "They're so alike."

"At least we can have fun with some pretty things here," she says, and gives me a wink. "Hope you find your friend."

Don't close the door. Don't go.

Impulsively, I extend my hand in thanks. It's the only thing I can think of. If I can't hug her, maybe I can at least touch her, feel her warmth for a moment.

I stare at her awkwardly. "Thank you."

She smiles again, eyeing me with curiosity and perhaps amused by the astonishment on my face. Then, instead of taking my outstretched hand, she reaches up to her neck and removes the pendant, then places it in my hand, using her other palm to cover it. "Here, I know where to get another one. Keep it. Maybe they belong together."

A warmth electrifies my spine and my chest. Memories of holding her hand as she walked me to school, of holding her hand while she read to me in bed. Of holding her cold hand at the morgue. I shake the last image away.

I can tell she's studying me. "You remind me of someone," she says. "I didn't get your name."

A name. I need a name.

"Betty."

"Betty," she repeats, still holding on to me, "enjoy the Prism. It's a gift." She starts to retreat, taking her warmth with her. I stand there paralyzed.

The door clicks. The footsteps retreat into the depths of her dimension. What does it look like? What does she dream about?

Is the room covered in bangles and trinkets, or does she create a life of secret desires even I never knew about?

Erik stops my hand mid-air before I can knock again. We lock eyes as I turn to him and he shakes his head slowly as if to say, 'leave it alone.'

Tears fill my eyes as I nod back. I've been given the gift of seeing my parents in 1988. I summoned it through my love of them — a love and a loss I had never fully given into. The Prism had called me to face it, and now I had. It's more than I could have asked for, and now it's time to let it go — to move on from the grief and look toward something new.

New beginnings.

I smile, feeling her warmth still on my hand as I hold the new pendant within it. "I guess its tea-time," I say to Erik, as we all walk back to the elevator in stunned silence.

***

We're on the move again after reading the new coordinates on the Galaxia. Juno trots off and I face the monoliths. Edenia and Estra this time. Images of my parents take up my thoughts. I'm not ready to leave 1988 behind, but the Prism clock ticks in my hand.

What do I intend this time? Where do we end up next? I thought it would be clear, but it isn't. Nothing is clear. I should have prepared more for this, figured out where to channel my intentions. I panic, looking behind me for a way out. But there's no way back until we reach where we're meant to go, or so we hope.

Twitchy, nervous hands join. Faith propels us into the unknown. Pillars dance. Blinding, hypnotizing light penetrates our eyes. The illuminated path winds beneath our feet.

Faces, colors, emotions, weightlessness, bliss. Everything and nothing, until it fades again.

A new world awaits. But is it the right one?

CHAPTER 25

The Luminarian

"I'm not trying to put pressure on you Everest, but *why* the Renaissance exactly?"

Jenna's taught Fox well. He recognized the time-period immediately. We concealed ourselves after emerging between the monoliths as a group of Wakers approached. The clothing gave it away. We had jumped several centuries into the past this time.

"Damned if I know."

Exasperation is the only thing I'm feeling. The adrenaline of the time jump has passed. The reality of our new predicament sinks in. Yet again, this isn't Aeonia. Just another opportunity for mistakes and miscalculations.

The Prism's deterioration sped up the timeline. Necessity took over. But maybe going so soon was a mistake, especially when the fate of others was in my hands. I needed the *Anu Ki Zu* to tell me what to focus my desire on. Without that missing piece, we're just shooting blind and hoping we get lucky and hit the target.

"I'm sorry," I say, looking pleadingly at the others. *Please don't hate me.* But I know they never could.

Petra seems intrigued and not the least bit fazed, which puts me at a much-needed ease. "It's fine. We just try again. At least we are moving in the right direction."

"Petra's right. And maybe there's a reason we're here," Erik adds.

Fox snickers. "Yeah, maybe we'll meet Everest's great great great great great great grandmother."

Epiphanies. They come at peculiar times. "That must be it!" I remark, observing the Wakers from the shelter of the forest. "Ciavutti!"

"Who?" Tanner asks.

"Maybe we should get him up to speed," Fox suggests. "All the 'who, what, why' questions are getting irritating."

"No!" Petra is quick to answer. "It's not for him to know. He hasn't earned it." She holds us with that stern Slavic stare you don't talk back to.

Tanner pouts like a child whose new toy has been ripped out of his hand. "You're a little harsh," he complains to Petra.

"I'm aware."

Erik ponders my idea with a pensive expression. "How are we going to talk to Ciavutti without arousing suspicion? We can't exactly enter the Citadel."

"Let's just find him first," I answer, settling on the ground and closing my eyes to focus. "But first, we need to blend in."

***

Castellum pierces the clouds, but its width is less generous. The result of a smaller population perhaps. The natural elements remain unchanged, but the Promenade has been replaced by an alley of quaint pubs and cottages and some grander structures with palatial architecture and grand steel doors. It's a very different beach vibe. No bathing suits, no umbrellas. A handful of Wakers give into the thrill of the waves and submerge themselves completely, while others mostly wade or go ankle deep. Small ships bob out in the water, brilliant white sails pulling against the imposing masts, wood sterns impressively carved out to resemble dragons and sirens. Ladies pass in velvet dresses and embroidered sashes, hair braided and styled with gold pins and satin bows. Men wear interesting things. Lots of leggings and long jackets, some jackets too short, some leggings too tight. The non-Europeans walk by with colorful tribal garbs and beaded leathers, feathers, corals, saris, kimonos, moccasins, absurdly opulent head pieces, jewelry on every wrist, every finger, every ankle.

Imagine knowing there were other people on this earth, continents away, and no one believed you.

I suddenly feel especially awful for Jenna. What she would give to be here, history throwing itself at her feet, begging to be unwrapped like a long-awaited present. Tanner robbed her of that opportunity. Instead, she's in hiding, wondering why we abandoned her.

I know I'm supposed to like Tanner – he's Erik's blood after all. His return means everything to Erik and fills that void in his heart that even the Prism can't fill. But it's taking me a while to warm up to him. It's true what they say about first impressions. I know I need to try harder and give him another chance.

Petra looks surprisingly comfortable in her elaborate velvet outfit, poised and regal, like a goddess who belongs in a royal court with her stoic aristocratic face and her perfect posture. Fox, on the other hand, pulls at his leggings with dramatic annoyance.

"How did people wear something like this? What's wrong with them? This is torture!" He pushes the giant feathers that sprout out of his hat away from his eyes. "Does anyone actually enjoy wearing a bird on their head?"

"I'm sure they'd feel the same way about wearing surfing shorts and flip flops, mate," Erik points out. "It's what you know."

"No, they would feel liberated." He eyes the promenade shops. "I'm going to pick something less awful. No offence Everest."

"None taken. We'll wait."

The rest of us eye the string of bodies piling in and out of the gardens and floating down the Avenue steps.

"Do we know what he looks like?" I ask Petra.

"No."

"Not even like a sketch or something?"

"No."

"Cool," Erik remarks. "Who's ready to do some major networking and bullshitting?"

"I can help," Tanner offers. "What do I say?"

"Nothing!" Petra and I say in unison. "Just, talk about food or pinecones or something, if absolutely necessary," Petra adds.

Tanner retreats to hover around Erik, occasionally staring daggers at his nemesis.

Fox returns looking much more at ease, rid of the hat and leggings and wearing a white linen shirt, suede vest, and some looser trousers. He looks as if he just walked off the set of a Robin Hood movie. "Alright," he says, releasing his hair. If he had a moustache, he'd make a good musketeer too. "Now that I can breathe again, I believe we have a gentleman to stalk."

***

Priorities change with the decades. The Renaissance Wakers

have no interest in having a swimming pool as the focal point of Eden Hall's main floor. The pool has been replaced with what essentially became the third-floor museum at a later time – art, sculptures, canvases, costumes. A buffet of food, large round wooden tables, seats fit for royalty with plush velvet cushions. A quartet plays. Music fills the room. A lute, a flute, a viol. The mood is serene and calm. In another corner, a different vibe. Colors, dancing, drums. A different slice of Earth.

A burly gentleman walks by us and snickers as we listen to the quartet. "It's livelier upstairs, at the pub. This music puts me right to bed." He takes a sip of beer and his eyes dance with mischief. He proceeds to ascend the stairs, although there aren't very many. Unlike modern day Eden Hall, these climb a mere six stories. Another byproduct of a different time, with different dreams and desires and understanding of what is or could be possible. How things change.

"I'm going to follow him," Tanner asserts, eyeing the departing beer pint with longing.

Erik reaches for his vest and pulls him back. "Not a chance."

"Come on! We have all day."

"We can't afford any detours. And *you* certainly can't afford any setbacks."

Tanner pouts but ultimately listens to reason, agreeing not to endanger his recovery. I gain a little more respect for him.

Outside, the Luminary is surprisingly unchanged. The architecture, the courtyard, the towers – all the same.

"This is the original structure, as Ciavutti imagined it." I marvel at it again. *How did he create it?* "He must have had the power to manifest and alter the Nucleus as well," I observe.

"Him and whoever helped him," Erik adds. "Robert said there was a group of them who pulled it off."

Fox eyes the crowd when we enter the building. "What I'd give to have a quick chat with him. No picture, huh? We got nothing."

Suddenly, he turns to a young man walking by and asks, "Enzo! Enzo Ciavutti?"

"Uh, no, no," he replies, giving Fox an odd look as he shuffles on his way.

"Sorry, my mistake lad," Fox notes, turning on a British accent.

Erik chuckles. "Why do you sound like that?"

"Figured I'd fit in more with the accent, like those actors in the history movies. Taking a shot someone may know him or *be* him. You never know."

"Not a bad plan, I guess."

"Enzo!" Fox tries again, this time yelling out the name for the whole building to hear. No luck. "Enzo Ciavutti!"

From the corner of my eye, I see a head whip around quicker than the others to the sound of Fox's repeated calls. The man walks with an older Waker, robes down to the floor over their clothes. He has a neatly trimmed reddish beard and almond shaped, wise-looking eyes that pear out from under bushy eyebrows. He stares at the noisy Asian man with puzzlement, then raises his finger to his companion as if signaling him to wait.

"I think you need another plan," Tanner says disinterestedly from the floor where he's resigned himself to being useless, as instructed.

The man approaches to the ignorance of the others who haven't yet noticed him, and I see Fox take a breath to get another good bellow out.

"Enzo Ciavutti!"

"You don't have to shout," the man replies, finally within

earshot. The others turn, amazed that Fox's half-baked shot-in-the-dark plan actually worked.

Petra remains skeptical. "*You* are Enzo Ciavutti?"

"I am. Not who you were expecting?"

The others seem stunned into silence. Tanner's eyes dart back and forth between the five of us as he tries to piece things together.

I motion the group to step further away from Tanner and see him roll his eyes as we settle out of earshot. "Signore Ciavutti," I begin, "we didn't know how else to find you."

He smiles. "Well, the Prism has a way of bringing people together," he says. "Do we know each other?"

"No. But we know *of* you, and what you're fighting against. The Vulturians."

His facial muscles tense and his temples twitch at the mention of the Order. His faint smile slips away, and he quickly scans the crowds, perhaps to assure himself the wrong ears are not listening. "Who are you?"

"We're friends," I reply, hoping I haven't made a mistake by being so forward. "And we need your help."

"You haven't answered my question."

"It doesn't matter who we are."

"It does to me," Ciavutti insists. "I've worked hard to rid myself of them, hide from them, protect my loved ones from them. I've built this Luminary here to spread truth rather than their poisonous message. And now, here you are. Rather odd timing. Clothes put together strangely. A most peculiar company," he pauses as he gives Fox another once over. "So, yes, it does matter. It matters a great deal to me."

"We didn't think this through," Fox mutters.

"Obviously," Petra hisses in response. We imagined it differently. How exactly, I'm not sure, but in retrospect we probably should have expected some kind of interrogation. Ciavutti is right to be protective.

Think!

"How is your wife?" I blurt out.

Fear comes over Cavetti's face at my unexpected question. "What did you say to me?"

"Your wife," I repeat. It's the only thing I can think of to gain his trust. "She's in danger. They *will* kill her."

I feel Erik nudge my arm as he whispers in my ear. "What are you doing, Ev? We can't mess with the past!"

I face him, trying not to let my own doubt rattle my plan. "You got a better idea?"

Erik opens his mouth and freezes.

"You once told me that some Wakers believe that every time we awaken back on Earth we enter another parallel reality, that we never return to the time we came from anyway. And if there really are billions of parallel realities happening all around us, maybe we can give him back his wife in one of them."

Erik mulls it over. "Ok. But we could still alter history in some unforeseen way."

"We don't know anything for sure. I just need to trust this right now."

I turn back to Ciavutti whose brow is increasingly furrowed from suspicion. "You don't know us, and we can't tell you who we really are," I continue. "But what we *can* tell you is that the Vulturians are our enemies too. We are risking a lot to tell you this, but we're doing it to prove you can trust us. We want to stop them, and we need your help. And in exchange, we hope you believe us and go somewhere safe where they can never find you or your loved ones. Run. Hide. If you want your wife to live, trust us!"

I can't tell if he believes me or suspects me. He simply stares at me, then the others, one at a time, methodically calculating the chances that what we're saying is true. The Prism seconds drag on as we wait for his reaction.

Finally, his lips curve into a flicker of a smile, although his eyes retain a sadness. He settles on me. "It's nice to see others dedicated to the triumph of good over evil. That dedication and the energy that stems from it can always be trusted."

I let out a sigh of relief. "You believe us then? You'll listen? You'll go somewhere safe?"

The sadness from his eyes now spills over to the rest of his face, and the faint smile vanishes again. "I'm afraid it's too late for me. It's too late…for her."

I recognize the sadness. It's grief. Agonizing, all-consuming grief. "It already happened."

Ciavutti nods. "They took her months ago."

An icy fist grabs at my heart. I know his pain. For a moment, I thought I could spare him from it. For a moment, I thought I could prevent the Vulturians from taking at least one thing. "I'm so sorry."

"So sorry," Erik repeats behind me softly.

Ciavutti studies him, then allows a weak smile to return, and I appreciate just how difficult it must be for him to muster it. "We're just passing through, my friends. We can only leave this world better than how we found it before we too walk through a door which we can never come back from. I had hoped it would be some time before my wife had to make the journey. But God had other plans."

"Then please, at least save yourself," I plead. "The Luminarians need you."

He jerks his head towards me. "What did you say?"

Shit! "Nothing. At least…nothing I can easily explain."

"You know. But how? We've told no one."

Think! How do we get out of this one?

Fox steps forward to my surprise. "Because time and the universe are mysterious. And because one who comes after you believed in us and trusted us. I know how it sounds, but that's all we can tell you. That's the truth."

It takes a moment for Ciavutti to grasp what Fox has just said, and for the rest of us to get over the shock of him saying it.

"I see," Ciavutti says thoughtfully. "So many mysteries we cannot fully understand."

"I'm sorry we can't reveal more," I add.

"Do not apologize. You have given me something more precious: hope, that there are means to achieve beyond that which we know. That there are still Luminarians in the future."

"We may be too late to help your wife, but we can still help you."

"I don't fear death, my lady," Ciavutti replies. "I will not run from them."

"But then – "

"Yes, I've come to terms with that possibility. Tell me, when you first spoke to me you told me you needed my help, yet I have still not learned how I can assist you."

Would he even know about Aeonia?

"There's a book we need to save the Prism – to save the world, actually. It could help us find a place we're looking for."

"And you think *I* have it?"

"Not exactly," Erik answers. "We think *they* do."

"I see. And what is this book called?"

"*Anu Ki Zu.*"

"Hmm," Ciavutti answers, meditatively. "Maybe I know, although I cannot be sure it is the exact one you seek. Did it have strange symbols on its spine, by chance?"

"Yes! Have you heard of it?" I ask with relief, excitement pulsing through my arteries. "Do you know where we can find it? Is it in Paris? The Vulturian chapter house, we saw it there, back in...," I bite my tongue. Best not to reveal just how far in the future we're from. I want to avoid too much surprise. "We couldn't get inside the chapter house to get it before our journey. We were hoping you could help us find it, or at least tell us where we could find a certain place we're looking for – an ancient place we'd never heard of until recently. It's significant to the Prism somehow."

"You speak of Aeonia."

Finally, we're speaking the same language! I can feel the missing pieces within my grasp. *"Yes!"*

"When we built the Luminary," Ciavutti explains, "we had tremendous power concentrated into that effort. The Lumus was born out of that energy. Books and manuscripts flooded in. It was an incredible moment in time. I remember a book, Artifacts of Aeonia. None of us had heard of Aeonia before. Nevertheless, we were all able to read it in our own language, as with any book in the Lumus. But the book we found beside it... it was very strange. Written in a language we couldn't decipher. It looked like Sumerian, but inside none of the symbols made sense, like it was...some cryptic code. In fact, most pages were entirely blank. One of my fellow Luminarians had a unique potential to take things out of the Prism, so he took the book out in hopes of showing it to an acquaintance skilled at deciphering ancient symbology."

"And did he decode it?" Petra asks impatiently, barely waiting for Ciavutti to finish the last syllable.

"Sadly, no. He was killed. The Vulturians got to him first. Clearly, they knew he had something of value. I don't know what happened to the book after that, but we never found it."

Damn it! "Were there illustrations, anything describing Aeonia that you could tell us about?"

Ciavutti thinks for a moment. "I remember only symbols and blank pages. I'm sorry."

"And no one can even read it; not even you," Fox realizes glumly. "So much for our brilliant plan."

"I'm sorry I cannot give you the answers you are looking for. But that book is not in the Prism."

Suddenly, an idea enters my mind. A reckless idea.

A downright crazy idea.

"When did this happen? Your friend, taking out the book?"

"Well, let me see…" Ciavutti considers, "about a year and a half ago, perhaps a little less than that."

"And where was your friend – where was he killed?"

"He lived in Florence. In the countryside."

"Is there a Vulturian chapter house there?"

"A rather large one," Ciavutti confirms.

"And do you think the Vulturians still have the book?"

"Possibly. I imagine they would keep it there, unless it has been moved. But it would be death to enter a Vulturian nest."

"We know," I reply, nodding my head as my thoughts become increasingly concerning. "But where could we find the chapter house, if we just wanted to have a look." I can feel Erik's eyes boring into me and I can't face him. He knows me. He knows exactly what's in my head, and that it's suicide. It's exactly what Carmella told us *not* to do.

Ciavutti studies me with a deep frown. "It is easy to find, though not many know what it is. In one corner of the Piazza della Signoria in Florence, there is a street that branches out from the north side. I cannot recall the name. But if you reach the end of the street and look across a smaller square, you will see a dark grey, almost black, menacing looking place. You will know it as soon as you lay eyes on it. You will *feel* that it does not belong. *That* is the chapter house. Locals call it *la casa nera*."

I begin to imagine a monstrous, terrifying structure, jutting out of the earth with spiked towers and venomous snakes slithering out of windows, perhaps with a moat of blood around it. I hope I'm exaggerating.

"My lady," Ciavutti adds, taking my arm, "whatever quest you are on, I can sense it is an important one. And I pray that you are successful; that you and your friends return to wherever you have come from safely.

"But I also sense a danger that follows you. Those of us who have particularly strong potentials can sense these kinds of things. And I regret to say it, but your path will be most treacherous. Where you are going – what you are thinking of doing – is not an easy task. On the contrary, it is a death wish."

I meet his gaze and see his eyes full of tears, memories, and regrets of his own. I see my own regrets. "We understand. Success sometimes requires risk and sacrifice."

"But not foolishness. Be wise. Be prepared. And keep your potential from paranoid eyes. Wherever you are from, this is 1525. Perceived witchcraft can land you on the gallows."

1525. I'd forgotten to ask about the year.

"Thank you," I reply.

"I know someone in Florence who may be able to help you," he adds. "His name is Angelo Macardi. If you run into trouble, he is a loyal Luminarian. Seek him out at the Piazza San Jacopino. He is an apothecary. He looks…" Ciavutti chuckles to himself, "unusually surprised all the time. That should help you identify him. Also, there is a small blue triangle painted on the top right corner of the door to his shop."

"We appreciate that," I reply with gratitude. "But we'll try to do this on our own. The last thing we want is to put more people in danger. You've been very helpful Signore Ciavutti. We are indebted to you."

Ciavutti inhales a labored breath and looks at us all again, pausing on Tanner and no doubt wondering why he's in a time-out. "Your presence has given me a great deal to ponder. If your mission is as important as you say, then we are all indebted to *you*. God Speed on your journey, wherever you come from. Or should I say, whenever."

With a respectful bow of his head and a sly smirk, Ciavutti departs to rejoin his friend and the two men enter the small lecture room, no doubt headed for the Citadel.

As the door closes behind them, the information Ciavutti conveyed begins to sink in. The fact that we talked to Ciavutti in person begins to sink in. My suicidal plan begins to sink in.

"Ev…" Erik starts but doesn't finish.

"I know. I'm not asking you to go," I reply.

"Hold on!" Petra interrupts. "How would we even *get* to Florence? We've jumped through time now more than once. What happens when we awaken? We have no way of knowing."

"No," I agree. "That's why I need to do this part alone. I can will myself there. I know I can."

"Not a chance!" Erik insists. "We all go, or we don't go at all. We stick together, remember?"

No sense going through this song and dance again. I know I'll lose. "I suppose I could try willing all of us out. I've done it with objects, and Tru. Never people though. I can't guarantee it will work. I would never force any of you to go. But it would have to be a unanimous decision. Erik's right – if we split up, we may never find each other again. There's too many variables and uncertainties."

"And you think this book will lead us to Aeonia?" Petra asks. "It's really worth the risk?"

"I don't know," I admit. "I don't even know if it'll be there. But I don't know if I can get us to Aeonia without more information. I can't see it. I…don't understand what I'm trying to do. I'm sorry. I feel like I'm letting you all down."

"You're not," Erik assures and takes hold of my hand, his touch soothing me. His blue eyes find mine and I wish I had the luxury of losing myself in them without a care in the world.

We all stand in contemplative silence, thinking the crazy idea over. Where we'll end up, what could go wrong.

Everything could go wrong!

"Let's just do it!" Petra finally says. "If we keep jumping aimlessly with no idea where we're going, at some point our luck will run out anyway. At least this way we have a chance to get our hands on something that could help us."

Fox sighs. "I guess I'm the only one who has slight reservations, but ok."

"You? You always jump into things head-first and think later," Petra observes. "You choose now to become cautious?"

"What can I say, I'm getting wiser with age. What about Tanner. Shouldn't he get a vote?" Fox points out.

"I'll talk to him," Erik adds. "His best chance is with us. It was his decision to come." He looks at me and smiles that daring, mischievous smile he flashed when he first met, when he took me on thrill rides around the Prism and opened my eyes to a world of possibilities. How I've longed to see that look on his face again.

I smile at him. "I'm surprised you're on board with this."

"I guess you're rubbing off on me."

Petra snaps her fingers at Tanner, instructing him to get up from the floor like she's commanding a dog.

"I wish there was a Stella's here," Fox adds. "I miss Jenna. She would have been on cloud nine."

"Then take as many mental pictures as you can so you can tell her all about it," I reply, sympathetically. If she was here, Jenna would be on a high that would be hard to top. "And while we prepare to do something completely irresponsible tonight, maybe we can find a Renaissance version of Stella's to kill some time. Erik will just have to keep Tanner away from the ale."

"I can manage that," Erik agrees.

"We're really doing this, huh?" Fox questions again. "The *real* past."

"Yeah. We're all totally nuts. Think it'll work?" I reply, hoping he'll reassure me.

But he just stares off into the distance with a blank expression, standing eerily still, like a robot that's lost power. "I guess we'll find out, won't we," he finally answers, switching back on. He places a hand on my shoulder, then slumps as he walks away, his thoughts perhaps occupied with Jenna or the dangers of altering history in some unforeseen way.

We spend the rest of the day in Cascada, trying to steer clear of other Wakers. It's harder to blend in this far into the past, and staying off the radar seems smart. The evening comes far too quickly. No one mentions the pub. We all sit around a campfire with conflicted expressions, our minds ablaze with questions and anxieties. The air hangs heavy as we barely utter a word to each other. It feels like we're strangers, completely out of our depth, anxiously waiting for the clock to run out. There's a real chance that a lot could go terribly wrong tomorrow. There will be no portal tonight. We'll just fall asleep and pray that I can bring us all to the same place, and that we're not separated from one other for all eternity. That's a lot of faith to put into one person. That's a huge responsibility.

A river of ice begins to flow through me. *What have I gotten us into?*

CHAPTER 26

La Casa Nera

It worked! It *actually* worked! I got us out. *All* of us! Even Tanner. I was worried about him because our connection isn't as strong. But there he is, in a snoring heap next to Erik. I can barely believe it. I imagined us waking up in a barn, and that's exactly where it seems we are, sprawled out among bales of hay and farm tools, the walls of the city visible on the horizon of the countryside, a few hours walk away. It was so easy. *Could the compass be amplifying my potential?* Whatever the reason and however it's possible, and despite all the challenges and detours we've faced so far, it's reassuring to know I can at least count on my potential to be consistent.

I'm standing at the cracked barn door, staring out onto the horizon with a foolish grin on my face. I have yet to confirm it, but it feels like we've succeeded. Even the air smells different, like we're not in Kansas anymore.

This is the Renaissance. The *real deal* Renaissance! Florence 1525. I can sense it.

And if it is, then this is actual time travel, not just through past Prisms or dream realities, but through the real, physical world. It's beyond incredible! Of course, if it wasn't for the danger of being discovered and potentially killed, I'd enjoy this time-jumping business a lot more.

The barn is more of a large shed, and rather dilapidated. Some of the wood inside is rotting. A lone pig peers at me curiously from one corner. A donkey sleeps standing up in another. A few chickens wander about, pecking at the remnants of some grains on the ground. It smells awful, as a barn should smell. But it's warm and as good a place as any to wake up in.

The others begin to stir, and a symphony of gasps and cheers erupts.

"This is wild, mate," Fox exclaims, running to the barn door to get a glimpse of another century. "You did it, Cleary!" He takes me by the shoulders and hugs me abruptly. "You fricken got us here. Holy cow!"

"Shhh…" I urge him. "Let's not let the whole village know we're here."

Tanner and Erik mirror Fox's awe and excitement, Tanner's face alight with wonder. Erik looks over at me and laughs. "You're going to have a hard time topping this, you know."

"Don't celebrate just yet. I still have to get us back, remember?"

"Yeah, but you've brought things into the Prism before. This…," he looks toward the walls of Florence and sighs, "is on another level. 1525. Damn…"

Throughout all the jubilation, Petra is just quiet, but she has those same day-dreaming eyes I noticed when we first came through the time portal. She doesn't need to speak words to describe how she feels. We all get it.

Thankfully, no one seems to see us leave the barn, and we set off through the Tuscan countryside towards a road that's visible in the distance. It's cooler than I expected, but there's an absence of clouds in the sky which will eventually lend itself to a warm day on the open plains. Tanner complains about smelling like livestock the entire journey, but at least we made our debut into the past without prying eyes – or rather, without prying human eyes. Good thing animals can't rat us out.

"I still can't believe we're here," I say to Petra as we shuffle along, sounding like a broken record. We've bonded a little on our hike as we sweat in corsets and velvet, the sun now climbing higher in the sky. Petra's even revealed details about her family, including that she takes care of her younger brother. Fragments of her past are slowly emerging into the light.

"It is truly amazing," she agrees. This is the first time I've seen her outside the Prism, and her eastern European English accent is very prominent and suits her perfectly. "You read about it, dream about it, but to really travel back in time…I never thought it would happen in our lifetime. I never thought it was even possible."

"No regrets about coming on this suicide mission?"

She snickers and glances behind us, maintaining her vigilance. "You may ask me tomorrow."

The city walls grow taller as we draw closer. Carts pass us down the dirt path, layering us with dust the wooden wheels kick up. We're among an eclectic mix of people: merchants and families, guards on horseback donning flags and banners, gypsies, noblemen, clergymen…time travelers. We keep our eyes down and speak to no one.

Everyone in our travel party wears the same expression on their face: a blend of astonishment, anxiety and awe. "I feel like I'm on a movie set, or at one of those historical fairs, like none of this is real," Erik mumbles. "This is crazy, Ev."

But it is real. These are real people that lived centuries before us, the technology of our day unknown to them. *Unfathomable.* Planes, spaceships, cellphones, refrigerators, modern medicine, electricity. None of it exists yet. Here, things get done not by robots, but by the blood and sweat of the citizenry. Cathedrals build over decades, more extravagant and majestic than any church built in the 21st century. Clothes sewn and washed, and books written and illustrated by hand. Human potential and determination at its best, showing what can be achieved with only imagination, time, and pure will.

And in between all that is admirable are the things that are tragically broken – poverty, illness, injustice, brutality of war. Children wander dirty, hungry and diseased, begging for scraps on the side of the road. Orphans, the elderly, the disabled, the pickpockets, the ruffians. What a sad verdict for our times, that even with planes and spaceships and robots, we still haven't been able to fix those sad and awful parts of life which remain constant across the ages. Perhaps we can never escape them.

Finally, we pass through the city gates, trying to blend in with the locals. The stone walls enclose us and tower above like prison walls. In the open countryside we were invisible. No prying eyes, no swords, little risk of being found out. But here, I'm suddenly very aware of the fact that one mistake could mean a death sentence.

At least it's beautiful!

With its ancient Greek and Roman influence, the architecture teams with classical symmetry and proportion. Orderly columns and pilasters and semicircular Palladian arches abound. Domes sit upon the rooftops of brick and plastered buildings, meticulously carved moldings frame windows and doorways, and sculpted figures adorn niches.

I'm not even remotely finished admiring the architecture when I notice a structure that doesn't belong from the corner of my eye. Against the backdrop of the picturesque city, the gallows stand out like a thorn. From the top wooden beam, three bodies hang. Two older women and a gypsy man, their necks broken and bodies limp, eerily swaying ever so slightly on a thick fraying rope. A priest sings beneath them, pacing back and forth and splashing holy water on the gawking crowd. A chill travels through my body as I listen to him.

"What is he saying?"

"It's a mixture of Italian and Latin," Petra replies. " 'Let your souls be cleansed of their evil', something about redemption, evading the devil's spell."

We study the scene with nervous expressions, knowing that our potential puts as at risk of a similar fate. Magic. Witchcraft. Potential. It's all the same here. The Renaissance was the beginning of more enlightened times, but there was no lack of ignorant minds afraid of things they didn't understand.

"Come on," I say, not wanting to draw the attention of a crowd of fanatics who might accuse us of something if we look at them the wrong way. "Best to blend in." Fox has already received a few curious stares. There probably weren't many Asian visitors in Florence during this time. Hopefully, he'll pass for a merchant.

Petra uses her knowledge of Italian to ask the right questions and avoid suspicion. "Piazza della Signoria? Si. Piazza della Signoria." She fits in, even with her intimidating Amazonian height. She even manages to confirm that it is indeed 1525. It still hasn't really sunk in.

Fingers point us down alleys and narrow cobblestone streets of what seems to be an endless maze. We sometimes walk in circles, afraid to ask too much too often, and hopeful that eventually we'll just happen upon where we're meant to be. It's all too surreal, and none of us speaks more than necessary as we experience a form of culture shock. Or perhaps time shock would be a better term for it.

At last, at the end of a narrow alleyway, an open space. The Piazza. The political center of the city. Arched entryways line the perimeter of the square. More uneven cobblestones ripple under our feet. More symmetry, more beauty, more history.

"David," Petra mumbles, almost incoherently.

"What?"

"David," Petra points at the statue at the center of the square.

"*The* David?" I gasp. Is this the right era?

Erik gawks next to me. "Is that…?"

Petra nods. "It is. And he still has both arms."

We move closer to admire the authentic version of the iconic masterpiece, as it was created, before riots and earthquakes, and the elements took their toll.

I notice Fox glaring at the David with less enthusiasm than the rest of us. "We don't have to tell Jenna about this," I remind him. "No sense rubbing salt in the wound."

He nods and continues glaring as if angry at the statue itself, even though I know his anger is directed at the uninvited guest standing next to him.

"Ok, let's keep moving," Petra reminds us. "But which street is it?"

"Ciavutti said north side, I think," Fox replies.

"Yes, but which way is north?" Petra studies the piazza, then rests her gaze on a beggar woman sitting against a brick wall to our left. We follow as Petra approaches her.

"Scusi, casa nera, que la? Casa nera?" She makes a rudimentary drawing of a house with her arms.

The beggar woman stares at her blankly. Next thing I know, Fox is throwing down a bag of coins onto her lap. She picks up the bag with a dry, bruised hand and spills out the silver circles. She gasps as they catch the sunlight, then frantically collects them back into the little cloth sack and brings them protectively close to her chest, looking around as if to make sure no one else saw what just happened.

"Allora, laggiù, da quella parte."

We turn to follow the woman's arm, which points to one of the streets across the square.

"Grazie!" I tell her, glad to know at least one word in Italian. "Muchos grazie."

"I think that was half Spanish," Tanner points out.

"Good enough." I turn to Fox. "Where did you get that money, by the way?"

His eyes sparkle mischievously as he wiggles his fingers. "Being able to make things float in mid-air has it's perks."

"*Are you crazy?*" I hiss. "What if someone saw you and thought you were a sorcerer? Then we'd all be toast!"

"It's crowded enough, no one saw a thing. I got a stash for us too," he adds, motioning to his pocket. "We need to eat and survive the day here, remember? Don't worry – I lifted it off a total jerk who looked like he had plenty to go around and treated his servant like garbage."

I let my panic subside. "Ok. But let's just keep our special talents under wraps from now on and get through this day."

The narrow road leads us around several bends, past shops with pretty shutters, the smell of fresh bread, and the sound of blacksmiths hammering on steal. Then past several doorways that look uninviting, with splintered wood and doors coming off hinges. As we travel further down, the energy drastically shifts. Our path narrows as the buildings close in around us. The smell of bread vanishes. We no longer hear the laughter coming from the lively piazza. Blood covered clothes hang from ropes, drying next to laundered sheets. Rats scatter around our feet. A woman with disheveled hair and a half open corset eyes us flirtatiously from the shadows, then is pulled through a doorway by a man's arm. She stumbles over the threshold before the door slams. Eerie silence returns. We try to step lighter, but we're the only ones on the street, and we stand out.

A different smell surrounds us now. It's more than just the smell of an old city. It's more than dirty clothes and rotting vegetables from last night's dinner. It's a smell that burrows its way into your soul and consumes it, suffocating it as it settles in. It's open wounds. It's rat feces. It's death and decay. It's the smell of hopelessness, and it surrounds us.

Warning signs flash before my eyes. *Turn around. Dead end. No-go zone.* But we press on, attracted to the danger, fueled by curiosity about what lies around the next ominous bend. And the next. And the next.

Until we finally see it.

We don't need to ask anyone if we've found the right place. It's just like Ciavutti had said: we can sense it doesn't belong in a city like Florence, although its presence has been foreshadowed by the route we've taken. We can sense the evil. Its menacing dark exterior, complete with the hideous vulture statue, is void of beauty. The mansion has spread its poison to the streets around it, attracting the decay, the immorality, and the shady practices of the underworld to its doorstep.

Even if I was blind, I would know I was standing next to it. The structure has a terrifying energy, like a silent scream that reverberates in my ears, a screeching whistle gnawing at my brain and tearing the flesh off my skeleton. It's almost as if all the damned souls of Hades are calling to us from within its walls. This is the place where light comes to die, and where evil is born. This is the Vulturian nest of Florence, 1525.

La casa nera beckons us with invisible bony fingers. *Step into my darkness,* it calls in a forceful whisper. *There's nowhere to hide.*

/ CHAPTER 27

The Nest

I f not for Erik pulling us all into the shadows, we would
have been spotted. He saw the guards before the rest of
us. Three, to be exact: two on the roof, one at the front
door, all clad in black tunics and brandishing swords.

"Just once, it would be nice to just walk right into one of
these dens of evil without a whole brigade of bloodthirsty orcs
in our way," Fox groans.

I supposed it's too much to hope for a secret tunnel that
leads us directly inside, that we happen to miraculously come to
know about in the next few minutes.

"Damn it!" I mumble.

Wait a minute! Just walk inside…

I ruffle through my canvass sack which contains my
belongings. We'd made sure to bring carry bags that looked
unextraordinary, made from canvas and material that could be
found in earlier times. At last, I find the pouch. It contains two
rings: Maeve's and Dr. Auclair's.

I brought them because I thought they'd be safest in the
Prism where they couldn't hurt anyone. I also hoped Aeonia
would have answers on how to destroy them . I cover my palm

with the fabric of my skirt and carefully spill them out for the others to see. Everyone – minus Tanner – catches on. I just need a volunteer to be my partner.

Surprisingly, Erik's eyes light up. Maybe he really is coming around to my crazy plans. They do work out sometimes. "Looks like we're walking right in after all," he says.

****

It's a quite straightforward plan, really. This is 1525. There's no technology. No cameras. No facial recognition. No immediate means of communication. Even with superb record-keeping, there's no data storage or backups. But there are floods and fires, and time delays, and all kind of ways records could disappear or take time to be collected. So even on the off chance that the Florence chapter house has a record of all Vulturians from every chapter in the world (which is highly unlikely), we should be able to fake our way in. We know enough about them to act the part, and the rings are our golden ticket.

"Remember, if things go wrong, I'll create a diversion," Erik remarks as we approach the door, the others watching from a hiding place.

I nod. "Light it up."

"In and out, Ev. Let's get what we need and get the bloody hell out of here. I feel like I'm dying just wearing this awful thing."

"Just don't let the stone touch you."

"I know."

As far as I can tell, the granite band is harmless. But it's the Tiamat we need to be cautious of, and its destructive power to drain anything good and pure it comes in contact with.

The street is quiet, aside from a few drifters and drunks that stagger about. No one respectable would venture here. It seems the Vulturians moved up in the world over the centuries, blending into society's elite and owning prime real estate, the fruits of their treachery and deceit.

The guard becomes more alert when he realizes we're headed straight for the door. He speaks to us in an intimidating tenor and warns us to turn around with a motion of his head. I can only guess at what he's saying. *What business do you have here? Get away you filthy rats! Don't step another foot!*

Our plan relies heavily on the guard not speaking French and not catching onto my accent. "We're from the Paris chapter," I say, trying to sound as Parisian as possible. "We are here to tour your chapter house, as visiting guests. Our Ertu advised us to find a manuscript we seek."

The guard stares at us blankly, and doesn't seem to understand a word except "Ertu," at who's mention his ears perk up. I hold up my hand to show him the ring and narrow my eyes to match his, trying to convey that we're ruthless and diabolical and not willing to take 'no' for an answer.

He raises an eyebrow and looks me up and down. "Donna?"

"Si. Donna." Now there's a word I understand. Woman. I guess there weren't many female Vulturians back in the day. I narrow my eyes further. "By the will of Parem, let us in," I command assertively, trying not to let my body shake like gelatin.

It must be the mention of Parem, for the guard finally steps aside. Erik holds up his hand as well, displaying his admission ticket. The guard says something else to us in Italian, approaches the door and pulls up the iron latch, granting us entry.

"Grazie." I saunter in decisively, like I belong among the evil filth. My stomach turns and I try to stop myself from throwing up. To pretend to be the thing I despite most in the world is torturous. I hadn't realized how a simple game of make believe could be so dehumanizing. *This is how Sarah must feel all the time.*

The door closes behind us and I shudder. *Now what?*

I look at Erik who gives me a nervous smile. "It's your plan."

I shut my eyes and inhale. "I hate that we're here."

"I know. This place makes me sick too. Let's get what we need and get out."

We're met with a staircase on our right that leads to the top floor. The walls are stone. The floors are stone. The air is cold. We try to tread lightly as we look around the east side of the main floor. The place is eerily deserted. An icy current travels through my body

The rooms we explore all yield similar results. Furniture, tapestries, gold and silver dusty trinkets, swords piled on long wooden tables or displayed on walls. Chairs draped in silks and hides. Dozens of hideous Parem statues made from bronze, jade, and stone. I check the desk drawers but find nothing. The rooms are all connected with adjoining doors. In one room, a door begins to creak open, so we scurry into the adjacent study to evade detection. That's when we begin to hear voices and footsteps echoing in the west end of the building.

"So that's where everyone is. Let's try the second floor," I suggest.

We climb the stairs hurriedly, hoping not to run into anyone on our way up. A long fresco covers a wall, depicting an ancient battle in faded colors. The building itself resembles a miniature medieval castle, thankfully without the bloody moat. It's more gothic in style and décor compared to the classical symmetry found elsewhere in the city.

Footsteps approach, and with nowhere to immediately hide

Erik spins me around and presses me against the wall, then leans in as if we're in an intense, intimate conversation. I feel his breath on my mouth, his lips millimeters away. I ache for him to kiss me and bring some light into this awful nightmare.

The footsteps pass, and I see from the corner of my eye as they give us curious looks. Perhaps women are not often seen inside. When they round the corner, I expect Erik to pull away. But he doesn't. He stares at me, his body pressed on mine. I notice how heavy his breathing is from the adrenaline. Or maybe it's something else. I so badly want it to be something else.

But not here. It's not the right time. It would only be tainted by this evil place. I bite my lip and begin pushing his weight away reluctantly, feeling him trying to hold on to my hand as it slips out of his. *Our timing really sucks.*

Ahead, a door stands ajar. Even from down the hall I can see the spines of books. My pulse accelerates. Could this be the room? I try not to get my hopes up in case we leave empty handed again, but something pulls me toward it, whispering to search every crevice. When we step inside…books!

Finally! I count at least fifty of them. A solid wood table sits in the middle of the room with several open manuscripts sprawled out on top of it, handwritten on thin, aging paper bound in soft calfskin, and beautifully illustrated. I don't understand the language they're written in, but I know within seconds that they're not what I'm looking for. I'm not looking for an alphabet I recognize. I'm looking for one I don't.

Erik inspects the books that rest on some shelves.

"Anything?"

He shakes his head. "Nothing that resembles what we saw in the Ertu's study." He examines the thick curtains that hang next to him, then peers out onto the street warily.

I keep scanning the books, my frustration building, my patience evaporating. "It has to be here! It just…" But it doesn't. It was always a gamble we knew might not pay off.

I sigh loudly but refuse to give up. "Even if the *Anu Ki Zu* isn't here, maybe there're something we could use. Keep looking. I'm not leaving empty handed!"

Luckily, no one enters to interrupt us as we scan the remaining manuscripts.

"These are mostly religious texts," Erik notes, admiring the illustrations, "created after the birth of Christ. They're assembling quite a collection, probably from monasteries."

"You're not seeing any cuneiform either?"

"That's a negative."

I let out another dramatic sigh and abandon the shelves, then turn my attention to the last place I haven't checked. A low, dark walnut cabinet stands under the window on curvy legs, with round iron door pulls on each of its square doors. Conveniently, a key has been left in the lock. With time ticking away, I march over with a racing pulse and pull them open, finding inside a linen scroll the length of my torso and a small, leatherbound book, too small to be the one we seek. There's nothing else.

I secure the scroll under my skirt with the velvet sash that hugs my waist. If it's kept under lock and key, it must be important. Maybe it can give us a clue.

As a last resort, I start tapping and pushing at the walls and peering under furniture, trying to find secret passages or hiding places. But after several minutes of looking anywhere and everywhere I can, I finally accept that we've struck out.

"Let's get out of here before our luck runs out," Erik says. He offers to take the small leather book, but I shove it down my blouse.

"Less likely to be searched," I say as I reach for a small bag of cold coins lying on a side table and add it to my haul.

Erik chuckles, then looks away blushing. "Valid point."

It's awkward to walk, with the scroll shifting and scratching against the inside of my thighs, but there's no time to adjust. The halls are abandoned. It's the right time to leave.

I pass the tapestry where Erik drew me close to him, a depiction of the Tuscan countryside, with cypress trees jutting towards the sky from rolling hillsides. For a moment I want to pull him back there and end things the way I really want them to end.

No time. Not here.

We descend the stairs, tiptoeing as we go, and quickly remember why the place is deserted. Voices echo through the inner chambers, radiating from somewhere deeper within the building. *What if it's there? What if we're close?* We both inch closer to the sound. The voices reach their peak volume near a pair of double doors on the west side of the main floor. Words repeat phrases I don't understand, with the occasional "Parem" or familiar sounding Italian.

They're all in there. Something insidious is happening inside. *What are they doing?*

"I don't like this," Erik whispers. "We need to leave Ev. You can't exactly run with that scroll under your skirt. This is the perfect time to get out of this place!"

We have what we've come for. I nod and take a step back just as a door opens unexpectedly. A stout, heavily bearded man emerges and stares at us with disapproving eyes. His hair escapes in unruly waves from beneath a beret. His black tunic is buttoned up high on his neck. A spiral trim is embroidered on the shoulder in a red and black alternating pattern, and a red "V" is embossed on the right side of his jacket, just under his collarbone. His trousers balloon out at the thighs, and an unmistakable Vulturian ring adorns his right hand.

The chanting grows louder momentarily, then becomes muffled again by the shutting of the door. He looks at us, right through our charade, and I can see him put two and two together instantly. We don't belong, and he knows it.

Imposters!

His chest lifts in a deep inhale as he prepares to bellow out the alarm. But within a fraction of a second, Erik is on top of him, putting him in a headlock. I watch as the two men struggle. Where's a heavy vase sitting on a conveniently located pedestal when you need one? But to our advantage, the man is much older than Erik, and Erik is able to neutralize him with a chokehold. A limp body falls to the floor in front of me.

"Clean up time," Erik says without hesitating, looking around for a place to conceal the body. He grabs the man by the arms and drags him to another room, checking first to make sure no one is inside. I watch the man's legs disappear, and it sinks in how close we came to being made.

"Is he…did you…"

"No, just unconscious."

We move swiftly towards the exit. "Act normal. Walk normal."

I do both, barely breathing. The guard sees us exit and watches us retreat the way we came. Thankfully, he remains at his post. I dare not look in the direction of the others and give them away. As we disappear around another building and out of view, I sense the chapter house's hold lessen, that suffocating energy losing its power with every retreating step. A few minutes later, I check behind me and see Fox, Petra and Tanner following, all of us on track to reconvene at the barn where we started from this morning.

We were so close. We were *inside* the nest. And yet we still don't have what we came for. It's frustrating and disheartening, to say the least. But we did breach the Vulturian lair and managed to come out the other side, with bounty! My scowl begins to soften. It's not the worst outcome, if we ignore the unconscious fat man lying in a closet. Maybe things are starting to go our way. Maybe we'll learn something from the loot we took with us. Maybe we can try again.

Consider it a win.

I reach for Erik's hand and find it, receiving a comforting squeeze in return. He intertwines our fingers, and the world begins to feel right again. Hope is back on the table. Relief washes away my disappointment as we move further away from the soul-sucking darkness.

Then, I hear the low bellow of a horn, and all the light is extinguished.

CHAPTER 28

Locked In

The city gates are only 30 steps away. I watch the guards mobilize in front of me through a veil of disbelief. Each horn blast signals another to join in a prescribed pattern: one long blow, followed by a pause, and then another two in quick succession. The last reverberation lingers eerily in the air before the pattern resumes and overlaps with the echo of the previous alarm.

Imposters!

The guards activate locks and pull-down beams. Loud clicks and bangs tear at my ears. A dozen or so men arrive wearing black tunics, their heads on a swivel, looking for something.

Looking for us!

They control the city, though most don't know it, and they're calling in their favors.

An arm pulls me off course and away from the exit that's no longer viable. Within seconds, that long awaited feeling of relief and hope is snatched away, derailed yet again by another obstacle.

Petra looks back at us, then motions with a subtle tilt of her head for us to follow her. She takes several turns into narrow passages before coming across a doorway. She peers inside, then tries the knob, which to our relief rotates in her hand. I doubt any of us care where the door leads, so long as it can conceal us.

The pungent odor sends Tanner into a coughing fit as we shuffle in. The room is dark with only one tiny window that's covered in a disgusting coat of grease. Pieces of flesh hang on ropes from the ceiling beams, pink skin stained with dried blood.

"An appetizing little butcher shop," Fox muses while pinching his nostrils shut and peering into the lifeless eyes of a large pig carcass. "I thought I'd seen the last of these at my old neighbor's farm."

Petra looks nauseous herself. "It's just until things calm down outside."

"There's a back way out," Erik informs us, appearing from around a column.

Tanner darts past him, eager to escape. But Petra extends her arm and nearly knocks him to the floor. *"Not yet!"* she hisses. "They are looking for us!"

"Yeah, them two probably," he replies, pointing to me and Erik. "They're not looking for me."

I raise an eyebrow at how readily he would abandon his own brother, and any respect I may have gained for him quickly evaporates. Fear of death always ousts the cowards.

"Sit down!" Petra commands, blocking his path. "We can all suffer through some disgusting smells for an hour. A 16th century dungeon, on the other hand…now that's somewhere you don't want to find yourself."

"Fine!" Tanner slinks away to a corner, looking paler with each step.

We settle on the cold floor and Petra shuts the door. The

stench of animal flesh and mildew lingers in the air. We wait for the sound of a door creaking, boots on the ground, swords clanging against armor. But all we hear is the typical clamor and bustle of the city outside.

There's no way to know how much time passes. We left our modern watches in the past as they would only lead to questions. But when the light that outlines the wooden door vanishes and signals nightfall, it appears safe enough to move.

"I'm not staying in here another minute," Tanner insists, rising from the floor.

I wait for Petra to give him permission but hear nothing. We all join him at the door, more than ready to leave the foul stench behind.

"Petra, what's our next move?" I ask.

She doesn't reply.

"Petra?"

Only four of us wait at the exit. In the recesses of the cold room, I see the silhouette of Petra's body curled into a protective ball under a stone archway. The body quivers slightly, and rhythmic gasps escape from it at the speed of a fast metronome, controlled yet full of terror.

I stumble through the dark and kneel beside her. "I think it's safe to go now." I keep my voice low, trying to sooth her. My body seems to absorb her torment, leaving me feeling anxious and scared. "Are you ok?"

I can make out the outline of her face and her wide, terrified eyes. "It's so cold," she says, rocking back and forth.

Her behavior is unnerving. She was always our calm harbor in the storm, our voice of reason amid the chaos. Nothing could shake her stoic composure. There was no vulnerability or weakness – not even a hint of it. This isn't the woman I've come to know. But then again, I don't really know her at all.

"It's a little cold," I agree. "I'm sure we can find something warmer to wear. Can you walk?"

Suddenly, her head jerks to the side to stare at me. I can see her eyes grow even wider. Her blonde hair seems to glow in the darkness, as if electrified. "He'll be coming soon! *He's coming! He's coming for us!*"

The panic and desperation in her voice send chills over my body.

"*Who's* coming? Who are you talking about?"

She jerks the other way again, then begins crawling backwards like a crab, her head hitting a skinned rabbit that hangs from a low beam. She stops only when her back violently collides with the stone wall, then cries out in pain, covering her head before resuming the rhythmic breathing. "He's coming…soon… there's…no time…"

Petra's broken!

I frantically rifle through my canvass bag and take out some matches. The flame wavers as it ignites in my trembling fingers. I bring the match up to illuminate the space between us.

"Petra! Look at me. *Look at me!*" Her head lifts and her light eyes reflect the warm glow of the flame. "It's me. It's Everest. You're ok. No one's coming. You're ok."

"Everest," she whispers, then closes her eyes. "Everest." She inhales deeply and begins to slow down her breathing. "I'm sorry. I'm sorry."

"It's ok. It's fine. It's all fine. Just tell me you're alright."

She begins to rise from the floor, and when she lifts her head fully, I see the familiar face of my fellow Waker. It's as if whatever possessed her has been vanquished, like a switch has flipped. She stands tall, although her vulnerability remains. I've seen it, and now I can't unsee it. She's revealed a telling piece of that cryptic side of her, and now I want to know more.

"Who did you think was coming?" I ask as the match dies.

Her cold, clammy palm connects with mine. "We don't need to go back to the barn. We just need to find a place to hide until we can return to the Prism," she says, evading the question as she makes for the door. "A few hours. Somewhere we can sleep, somewhere safe. Let them shut the city down. We just need to stay hidden until tonight – until Everest can bring us back into the Prism."

I can't see Erik's face, but I sense his confusion. My cards were on Tanner to be the first to lose his mind. No one expected Petra to have the first breakdown. It creates a strange energy among the group.

"Right, just a place to lay low. Should be easy enough," Erik agrees.

"Somewhere else," Petra repeats as she cracks open the door. "Just…not here. Remember, do not talk to anyone. I will go ahead. Walk behind me in pairs, a comfortable distance away. But do not lose sight of me."

She's back to her commanding ways. I look around at the others, noticing their reassured expressions. Our ears listen for the sound of horns and chaos, but we hear only the distant humming and muffled sounds of a tiring city.

Time to move.

CHAPTER 29

The Ice Queen

The moonlight streams inside the butcher shop, illuminating our faces and the animal corpses that sway eerily around us. We pull cloaks over our heads and emerge into the night air.

To the left, I can see the top of the city gates that lie a few turns away and tower over the inner structures. Petra heads right with determination, like she's navigated this historic city a hundred times and each step falls on familiar ground. Tanner and Fox follow next. Finally, Erik and I are last to leave.

We just need to lay low for a few hours. Simple enough. Just a few hours…

Just not here.

What dreadful, horrifying memory did that room conjure up that it could pierce Petra's impenetrable armor? I suddenly realize I don't want to know. Nothing that does that to a person can be good. Nothing that does that should be relived. I promise myself to never ask her about it.

Torches and lanterns light up stone walls, casting eerie shadows. Petra moves swiftly away from the perimeter and into the heart of the city, away from the guards that pace at the gates.

We pass beggars and prostitutes, noblemen and priests. I try not to look at faces, keeping my eyes down and focusing on cobblestones, shoes, robes. Trying to look as uninteresting and ordinary as possible. Smells escape from open windows – the aroma of roasting meat and hearty stew torture my empty stomach.

Our guide peaks in through another window, then shakes her head and continues down the street. She tries another door, but it's locked. Finally, her third try yields something promising. After peering through the window, she fiddles with the lock and lets us into a blacksmith shop, abandoned for the night. An enormous forge stands at the back of the room, a brick chimney protruding from it toward the ceiling. Several buckets are piled to the top with coal. On the walls hang axe heads, swords, and several other iron tools I can't name.

"At least we have weapons if we need them," says Fox.

Let's hope we don't. *It's just a few hours. No one will find us.*

We settle in front of the forge, soot and ash transferring from the floor to our clothes. No one seems to want to be the first to speak. A heaviness settles in the air, made more palpable by Petra's earlier setback.

"Try to sleep," Petra says.

Fox sighs. "I think it's pretty early."

"I wasn't talking to you." She gives me a nod. "You can bring us all back, like you got us out?"

Right. Only I need to access the Prism. No pressure. "I hope so."

"Then get to work."

"I don't know…I mean…" My chest begins to flutter. "I need time."

"Of course," Petra replies, her frown softening to a weak smile. Pain lurks behind it, forever unmasked. "Sorry. Do it your way. I did not mean to force things."

Fox gets up to inspect some of the blacksmith's handywork. He's joined by Erik, while Tanner slumps in a far corner and mumbles, "I sure picked the wrong trip to tag along on."

Petra rolls her eyes, and I can't help snickering under my breath. She stares at me with her bright irises, her tight braid now messy and coming apart. "I never got a chance to tell you Everest, how much I admire what you can do. How much I am grateful for it."

I squint at her as I remove my stolen bounty from under my skirt and from underneath my blouse. "What do you mean?"

"You've helped the Sentry in so many ways. Without you, we would not have the leads we have. We would not have been able to come here. We would have no tools to use against them. Your potential is very special. You must be the Eridu, like that book said, whatever that means. Your light is stronger than their evil, no matter how much power they wield and amass. Remember that. Even if they try to break you, even if life tries to break you, there is an army of a hundred thousand men within that light that burns in you. *Use it.* Do not be afraid of it."

I don't exactly know how to handle all the gratitude and compliments. She's the last person I expected this pep talk from. She's surprised me in so many ways today, and I once again realize that I don't really know her at all.

"I never asked you what your potential is," I blurt out, hoping it's a safe topic.

Petra continues to stare at me. The pain returns to her eyes, and I regret my question immediately. "I do not speak of it," she replies, turning to look towards the small shop window. "Only one person ever knew. It is not like other potentials."

"What do you mean?" I can't stop myself from probing and feel slightly guilty about it. But I sense Petra wants to say more.

She rises and moves closer to the small window. "Do you see that girl out there?" she asks, motioning me to join her.

A child sits on the top step across the street. Even from a distance I can see she's very dirty and disheveled, her brown hair matted together, her pale, sickly skin layered with dirt. On one side of her face, I can make out a deep, purple bruise. She has no shoes. Her scarlet dress is ragged and dusty. But before my eyes her sad face appears to brighten.

"She hasn't eaten in two days," Petra says, bringing her palms to her abdomen and closing her eyes. "Up until a few seconds ago, it felt like there was a giant machine boring into her stomach."

"How could you know that? Is that your potential? Telepathy?"

She smiles. "No. That would have been preferable. But no." She grimaces, reaching for her bag. She pulls out an apple we found earlier on the road, and bites into it savagely, devouring it in under a minute. "I absorb pain, Everest. I can take it from someone and make it my own. *That* is my potential. It's not as fun as Fox's." She manages a chuckle. Slowly, her hands fall off her abdomen.

"You mean, you took away that girl's hunger? Just right now?"

She nods, laying her head back. "The pain of it at least. She is still malnourished and neglected, and very ill, but at least she will not feel it for a little while. It is a blessing and a curse all at once. To help someone, that initial realization that you've eased their pain is wonderful. But it's followed seconds later by…well, it depends on the ailment. It is not pleasant."

I'm speechless. A shiver runs over my body. I have so much admiration and so much sorrow for her at the same time. "That must be incredibly difficult. I can't believe you do that!"

"It is my choice to do it, ever since I knew I could." She opens her eyes and stares at me again, but this time I don't see Petra. I see the same girl I saw in the butcher's room. "When I was eight years old, I went on a trip to Turkey to visit my older cousins," she reveals. "My father's brother had moved there from Estonia for work. We were there for several weeks. One morning, my mother went out to get some groceries with my father, and I was bored at the house. I was just a child. I saw other kids my age playing outside and wanted to join them. My mother said it was not safe for me to go out alone, but of course, I did not listen. It was a decision that forever changed my life.

"I stepped outside, and they all stared at me, maybe because I looked different from them. One of the children yelled something loudly in a language I did not understand. Then he and the others ran away until I was the only one left on the street. I knew instantly something was wrong, but I just stood there, confused. By the time I was ready to move, it was too late.

"I heard the car tires first. Then the car pulled up beside me – dark forest green with a broken headlight. Paint was chipping off around the doors and side mirrors. A bearded man in a red sweater jumped out and put something over my face. I remember feeling faint and my legs dragging on the pavement as he shoved me into the back seat. My next memory is the room I woke up in. It was like…*that* room."

Her eyes fill with water, but she doesn't cry. Instead, she folds her arms protectively and brings her knees to her chest. I can picture her as a child in that same position, waking up in an unfamiliar place, violently taken away from everything she knew.

"My legs were free, but there were ropes around my wrists,"

she continues. "Thick ones. Each rope was connected to a metal ring on the wall so I could not go far. No windows. Just…darkness. The floor was cold concrete. The room smelled very strongly of urine and sweat. I'll never forget the terror that gripped me in that moment, like all the demons and monsters of my nightmares were right there in the room with me. I started crying, screaming for my mother, for my father. I yelled and cried until my throat felt like someone had run a cheese grater over it, until I could not scream any longer and my chest ached from sobbing. It was then that I heard the whimpering.

"It came from another part of the room. Muffled and delicate, like a wounded animal. I tried to move toward it, but the ropes kept me from going too far. I called out, 'is anyone there?' And then a voice, so soft I thought I was dreaming it, joined mine. 'Don't bother' it said. 'No one will hear you. No one is coming.' A defeated, hopeless, almost lifeless voice. I was desperate to know it and hear it again, but it said nothing more.

"I sat in that dark room for what seemed like hours, waiting for someone to rescue me. Waiting for that voice to speak again. Finally, I heard the sound of a door opening. A light flooded the room, and I saw where the voice had come from. There was a body in the corner – a girl, several years older than me. She was lying on her side. Her red curly hair fell around her on the floor. The one eye that wasn't swollen stared through me like I didn't exist. I could see blood on the floor around her and on her skin, some fresh, some dried. Her face was bruised and beaten badly. She had chewed off her fingernails so much she had barely any left. She lay there with just a thin gown on her body with no dignity."

The water begins to spill out of Petra's eyes, and I notice that my own cheeks are wet. I don't even know when I started crying.

Her voice cracks as she continues. "The man brought us a few scraps of food, then left. I wanted to ask the girl if she was alright, but I knew she wasn't, so I asked her name instead. It was Alina. She sounded…" she pauses a moment, "she sounded terrible. She told me she had been there at least a month, but one time, she had lost consciousness from the beatings and wasn't sure how many days had passed, so that was only her best guess. In that moment, my heart sank. If no one had found her, no one would find me either."

Silence replaces Petra's voice. I can hear the boys whispering and rummaging with tools on the other side of the room., but all I care about is Petra. I can't wrap my head around what I've heard. My mouth is dry and I realize I've been clenching my teeth.

"I was younger, so they used me for housework. Alina never talked about what happened to her, but I knew even as a child that it was something horrifying. She fought back every day, that's why they beat her. I fought them too and tried to escape from the main house when they would bring me up, but they beat me too."

My stomach begins to tighten, and it feels as if I could be sick at any moment. A pulse begins throbbing in my head and my entire body starts to burn with rage. I have to remind myself to control it. There's no Arachna in the Renaissance tracking my potential and no light bulbs that can explode, but I could still cause something significant to happen and draw unwanted attention.

"At least we had each other," she goes on. Oddly, she's more composed than I would have imagined, almost as if putting words to her pain is having some kind of liberating effect. "We spoke every day when we weren't apart, about our families and where we were from. She was from Romania. She had three sisters and a pet pig, and her family lived on a farm. I grew up in the city. I would tell her about the city and she would tell me about the country, and I would imagine that we were running free through meadows around her family home, with her pig and her sisters, and the birds in the sky. And there was no one around for miles that could hurt us.

"We could never hold each other or keep each other warm. The ropes never allowed us to touch. We could only come within a few feet of each other. And when the door would open, we would scurry off to our corners, so they did not make the ropes shorter. Over time, the ropes burned holes in my skin. The weight fell off my bones. I refused to eat, hoping they would discard me if they had no use for me anymore. But it continued, for both of us."

Petra inhales deeply. I'm sensing the next part of her story will be even worse than the first, and I'm not sure I'm ready to hear it.

"One day, they brought Alina back in a terrible state. She had been beaten so badly she was unconscious. I saw the blood dripping from her head and her clothes as they dragged her inside. They threw her in the corner like a piece of trash and shut the door without even checking if she was still alive. I cried and shouted for her to answer me, but she didn't move. She didn't…" Petra wipes the tears from her cheeks and throws back her head. "I knew I would not survive in there without her. I did not even know if I wanted to survive, and wondered if it would be better if we were both dead. The thought had crossed my mind so many times I had lost count. But in that moment, I wanted her to live. I wanted to save her. I couldn't stand the thought of her suffering or in pain.

"I remember feeling as if my entire body was being pulled apart, as if I was drawing her toward me with some strange force. A light filled the room for a fraction of a moment, and I fell to the ground in agony. It was as if someone had beaten me for hours. Every bone ached; every muscle burned. My flesh felt torn apart. On the outside I hadn't changed. But inside, I felt butchered. I didn't understand it. I heard her speak to me through the fog, but I passed out. When I woke up, her body was still beaten up and bloody. She said she felt no pain, but mine was excruciating. It was then I realized that I had absorbed the pain for her somehow. I didn't how, but I just knew it. The pain tortured me for about a day before it passed."

My body is shaking as I listen to Petra recount her harrowing ordeal and the discovery of her potential. "It's incredible that you can do that. Your friend, was she alright then? What happened to her?" Petra doesn't answer me for a long time. "I'm sorry," I add with guilt. "You don't have to tell me."

She clears her throat. "Eventually, Alina healed. I told her about what I thought had happened, thinking that she would call me crazy. But she believed me without question. She said, when the pain left her body, she thought she had finally died. She couldn't believe that after what she had endured, she no longer felt anything. She told me I may have saved her life, that she felt as if she would have died from the pain alone that day.

"But she made me promise never to do it again because she didn't want me to suffer. I made the promise knowing I would break it every time if it meant saving her life, and I did.

"It continued for several more weeks. They always beat her more than me. The man that took her was a pure sadist. But even though I took away her pain, I could never take her memories. Those remained and tortured her soul. And every time the door opened, and the light flooded in, I could see her eyes were more and more lifeless. And then, one day, she never returned."

Petra drops to the floor and hides her head between her knees so I can't see her face. I know she's sobbing silently because I can see her body rise and fall as she chokes on her tears. "I didn't know…what happened to her, but…I knew she was dead. I…I felt it. And part of me felt guilty for…for keeping her alive so long. What was the point of it, if she died anyway? I just made her endure all of that…all over again and again, thinking we would somehow eventually escape. It was all for nothing!"

I make my way to her side and hold her as she sobs, sensing that I'm the only one she's told any of this to. I'm glad she felt safe enough with me to tell me, but my heart feels like it's been pulverized.

"My God, Petra." I gasp, wiping my eyes so she doesn't see me. "I'm…so sorry." What else can one say? What words of comfort could ever be enough? "How did you escape?"

"I didn't," she admits. "Police raided the house a few weeks later and found the rooms. There were other girls there. My mother flew back from Estonia when she heard. My father had stayed in Turkey, searching for two months. I went to therapy when I returned to Estonia. I never told anyone about my potential. But my soul was tortured, my guilt unbearable. I started absorbing the pain of others to make myself feel worthy again. I made myself incredibly sick and weak. It took years for me to make peace with myself, to forgive myself. I took self-defense classes and started meditating, joined the army. Over time, my mind came into balance again, and I learned to only absorb what I could handle if I wanted to help others. Once I made peace with myself, that's when I found the Prism."

It all makes sense to me now – the hard shell, the stoic composure, the protective wall she built around herself. It was the product of a horrifying past that she hid from the world.

And now, she had been forced to relive it all again.

"I don't know what to say."

She looks up at me and takes my hand. "We cannot change the past. And we cannot eradicate all evil from this world. I wish we could, but we cannot. I have seen too much of it to believe that fairytale. But what we *can* do is give human beings a fighting chance, by stopping the Vulturians, by preventing more evil from seeping into our world, by giving people an opportunity to find their potential before they use that awful Tiamat to steal it away; before they target and kill people like us. We do ourselves and others no favors by playing the victim and wallowing in self-pity and regret. What's done is done. We must focus on what must *now* be done and survive!"

"Bloody hell!" I hear Erik cry out, struggling to lift a sword near the forge. "How do they use this to fight? It's heavier than a bowling ball!"

"Imagine being a physiotherapist in these times?" Fox observes. "You could make some good money fixing everyone up after their back gives out."

"Yeah, not sure that was a career back then, at least not a lucrative one. Tanner, come check this out."

No one answers.

"Tanner," Erik repeats. We all look around the room but see no sign of him. "You've got to be joking! That little weasel."

"He is a terrible listener," Petra says, with an unamused 'I told you so' expression.

"I'll go find him," Erik huffs, charging at the door. "He's my bloody responsibility."

"Wait," Petra insists. She gives me a weak and grateful smile, squeezing my hand as she rises from the floor. "Thank you, for letting me get that off my chest," she whispers to me. "I feel a little lighter now. I think…it was time I told someone the whole truth." She walks over to Erik and inserts herself between him and the door. "I will go too. I need some air."

"Well, alright then. Just don't scare him too much. He's already petrified of you," Erik jests.

"Obviously not petrified enough, otherwise he would not have left!" Petra pulls the hood of her robe over her head and turns the door handle. "I'll go left, you go right."

I rise from the floor and watch them depart through the window, still processing Petra's unbelievable story. The little girl still sits on the stairs. I couldn't see it from my vantage point earlier, but at the foot of the stairs lies a body. It looks to be a man, her father perhaps. His beggar's cup lies empty on its side. He doesn't move. I can't tell if he's dead or sick or sleeping.

Petra heads straight for him.

She says something to the little girl and the girl nods her head up and down. Then Petra bends down and puts her hand on the man. I can see only the back of her, and the platinum hair spilling out from under her hood, freed by the breeze. Several second pass. A bright light illuminates the scene momentarily, and seconds later, the man appears to stir.

She's done it again.

Joy and sadness overcome me as I watch Petra use her potential the only way she knows how – for others. The mysterious ice queen has turned out to have the gentlest and kindest heart. I begin to feel the anger I felt over Petra's horrifying past fade, just a little. Petra remains at the man's side, seemingly having forgotten about her mission to retrieve Tanner. I move to the doorway to get a better view.

The aromatic smell of 16th century dinner no longer lingers in the street outside the window. Something shifts in the ether. The sensation is akin to the cinematic effect of switching on the fog machine for a scene in a dark cemetery.

Something's coming.

Petra's head jerks suddenly, as if she's felt the same shift. Goosebumps blanket my skin instantly. A man's voice calls out across the cobblestone street, snatching away the calmness from my soul.

"Guarda! Strega!"

CHAPTER 30

Taken

A shadowy swarm of bodies descends upon Petra almost instantly, as if they had been watching and waiting for their moment to pounce. The man's words hang in space like a frozen echo. My knowledge of Italian is limited, but a Sicilian neighbor we had in Montemarte a few years back used to call her mother-in-law by a certain endearing term almost daily, so I immediately recognize it.

Strega. Witch.

Perhaps it also meant demon, or sorceress, or pain-in-the-ass, but I know the implications. Whatever the man intends by his description, it isn't good for Petra, or any of us. But especially for Petra if anyone else saw what I just saw.

Several bodies surround her, grabbing at her and shouting. Instinctively, I run to the door and take a step outside, but an arm pulls me back in before I can take another and a hand covers my mouth. I succeed in ripping it away. "Not now, Erik!"

"*Think!* You'll just be taken with her!"

I spin around in surprise to glare at Tanner. *Where did he come from?* He reluctantly loosens his grip on my cloak. Fox has returned to marveling at weaponry, completely unaware of what's transpired. Tanner takes hold of me a second time. As I struggle to free myself from him, I can hear Petra speaking in English outside. "I am not a witch. I was not performing any dark magic here. I do not know what you saw."

She knows Italian. Why is she speaking English?

When she makes eye contact with me, I understand why: it was for my benefit, so I could know the accusations against her.

She proceeds to speak to the swarm of angry men. There are even a few women in the mob, pointing fingers and making a racket with their shrill voices. But it's the man with the hoarse voice that is the ringleader. I see him more clearly now as he stands closer.

"Silencio!" he cries. "Vai, portala nelle segrete!"

Two black beady eyes pop out above his sunken cheeks. His shoulder length grey hair is balding in a perfect circle at the top of his scalp, and an exquisite jeweled cross falls from his neck and over his long black robe. He gesticulates dramatically, spitting and seething as he barks orders.

"Why are you taking me to the dungeons?" Petra asks in English as our eyes meet. To her detriment, her striking pale irises seem to glow like beacons, and, along with the brightness of her hair and the fairness of her skin, make her look a magical sorceress straight out of a story book. We stare at each other across what seems like an ocean, although it is merely 30 feet, give or take. She shakes her head subtly, forbidding me from following her.

No! This wasn't the plan! We were hours away from getting out of this place. I could have tried to sleep. I could have gotten us there quicker. Why did I wait?

I watch helplessly as Petra is dragged away by the mob and the darkness obscures her silhouette. Tanner pulls me back and secures the door. By this time, Fox has noticed the commotion. One look at my ashen face and he's at my side, launching himself at Tanner and shoving him up against the wall.

"You've been waiting to do that, haven't you mate?" Tanner hisses.

"I'm not your *mate*. What's going on?" Fox demands. *"What did you do?"*

I try for the door again without answering, but Tanner pushes Fox off and plants his hand across the wooden planks. "Where will you go? How will you help her, running like a lunatic through the night?"

Someone tries to open the door from the other side. I hear Erik's voice, and Tanner steps out of the way to let him in, raising his arms up for Fox to signal that he's not a threat.

"Petra's been taking by a mob of fanatics that think she's a witch," I fill the others in. I look at Erik pleadingly. "She's gone! They've taken her to the dungeons!"

Erik brings his hands to his head, then covers his mouth, stunned speechless. "When? How did this even happen?" he finally asks.

"Quickly. I would have gotten to her if not for your idiot brother! It's because of him she was out there in the first place!" My dislike for Tanner swells. "He should never have come!" I stare at him with anger again. "And then he stopped me from saving her. Keep him away from me so I can go after her!"

"No!" Erik interjects. "He's right. You can't just run after them. You'll be treated like an accomplice – or another witch. *Damn it!"* He yells his last words and smashes his fist against the door, then glances at the table of deadly metal weapons next to us.

Fox reads his mind and hands him a blade, which Erik secures behind his belt without hesitation. Fox takes a sword for himself, then conceals a shorter blade into one of his boots.

"There's no way we're leaving her with those fanatics. Arm yourselves," Erik adds, placing a hand on my shoulder. It brings me no comfort. My head is spinning with worst case scenarios. "We *will* find her!"

I nod and head to the table to pick my own weapon, glaring at Tanner deliberately as I conceal a knife under my cloak. "We will find her," I hiss, silently wishing it was Tanner who had been snatched off the street. *This is all your fault.* If it wasn't for him, Petra would be perfectly safe, awaiting her transition to the Prism. But instead, she's God knows where with God knows who, awaiting God knows what!

"Wait a second, didn't Ciavutti talk about a friend he had in the city?" Fox recalls out. "What was his name again? Angelo, something?"

"Macardi," I complete the name. "Good thinking Fox. He could know where they took her. I think we could trust him."

"And just how exactly are we supposed to find this man in a giant city where we can't even speak the language, oh and where we're being *hunted?*" Tanner scoffs.

I don't care what he thinks. He can stay behind for all I care. "He's an apothecary," I reply, securing the scroll under my skirt and the Vulturian book in my corset I haven't even had an opportunity to study them with all that's happened. "Ciavutti told us to look for him at the Piazza San Jacopino, and to look for a blue triangle on his shop. So, that's where we go."

I step toward Tanner and lean in close until my face is a mere inch from his. My resentment of him grows with each passing second. Jenna would have listened. She would've been an asset, not a liability. She would have put the interests of the group above her own selfish whims.

But instead, we're stuck with Tanner.

His thin body looks frailer and sicker now, his eyes more vacant and unreadable. Maybe he left to go get drunk or high. Who knows. All that's clear is that he's ruined everything.

"If you're going to follow," I warn him, "keep your mouth shut and never lay another hand on me again."

***

The temperature drops as we move into the evening hours. An old peddler informs us that it's "otto e mezza." Eight thirty. When Fox asks him about the Piazza San Jacopino, he looks him over, corrects his Italian pronunciation with disdain, and then directs us in the opposite direction with a wave of his hand.

"You know, he probably saved you from the same fate," Erik says, referring to Tanner as we walk ahead of the others. "You could cut him a break."

My teeth clench again. I don't want to cut him a break. I don't like him right now. Of course, I don't want to tell Erik that I deeply detest his long-lost prodigal brother, but if it wasn't for Tanner, Petra wouldn't be in danger. She's suffered enough. She doesn't deserve this.

"He's a liability. Anyway, I don't want to talk about it," I insist. "Let's just find Macardi and get Petra back."

My palm is clenched tightly around the handle of the blade that's tucked under my cloak. We hug the walls as we maneuver the city streets, trying to fade into the shadows and stay invisible.

"Hey!" Fox bellows behind me.

Erik and I spin around in unison. "*Shhh!*"

"Sorry. Are we lost yet?"

Erik stares down the length of the street. "Hard to tell.

Sixteenth century signage sucks. Sure miss having GPS right about now."

We take turns approaching strangers for further directions to refine our course, trying to hide that we're travelling in a big group. There could be orders to watch for us. Thankfully, the piazza is relatively easy to identify as most people mention a *fontana delle sirene*. When we finally come upon it, it's clear we've found what we were looking for.

The fountain is the focal point of a smaller square, the sculpted busty mermaid resting on a boulder in the center, holding a trident in one hand and wrestling a sea serpent with the other, her long hair falling whimsically around her body and reaching down to her scaled tail. Around the square, several windows flicker with the glow of burning lanterns. And on the far side, a wooden plaque creaks as it swings back and forth in the night breeze.

Farmacista. Italian for 'apothecary'.

We circle the fountain and arrive at the apothecary's shop. On the door, in the top left corner, someone has painted a small blue triangle, so small you wouldn't even notice it unless you were looking for it. It's just as Ciavutti described.

"This has to be it," I exhale, running my hand over the wood. I grab hold of a steel ring door knocker and let it fall heavily three times.

No answer.

I try again, another three knocks. The nervous breathing of my travel party echoes through the silence behind me.

Finally, a panel slides aside to reveal a small opening in the door, and a man's face appears. Unkept brows sit atop his large round eyes, and I immediately understand why Ciavutti described him as looking surprised all the time. I don't see much more of his face.

"Sono chiuso. Torna domani," he says with a hint of annoyance in his voice.

"Domani," I recognize as "tomorrow." But we may not have until the morning. For all we know, Petra's life could be in danger of ending within minutes. There's no time.

"Angelo Macardi?"

"Sì, ma – "

"Per favore, signore," I plead. My mind goes blank. I don't know how to form the sentence with my limited knowledge of the language, and our only translator is locked up in a dungeon. I don't even have a pen and paper to draw a picture, although I doubt that would help given my lack of artistic ability. Desperate, I say the only other words I can think of and pray he'll understand.

"Enzo Ciavutti."

His eyes widen to an even more exaggerated size before he abruptly slides the wooden peephole closed.

"*Please*," I bellow on the verge of tears with my fists pounding against the door, "per favore, we need your – "

But before I can finish my plea, the door creaks open.

CHAPTER 31

The Apothecary

Angelo Macardi is a mysterious man. He occasionally spins in half circles mid-walk as if indulging a compulsion, all while rapidly muttering to himself. He hasn't said a word to us since he ushered us inside, right after he scrutinized the piazza with a suspicious eye and secured the latch on the door with a sense of urgency.

The shop is a bit of a mess, with rows of tightly packed jars lined up on rickety wooden shelving. Small vials of different colored powders, reeds of varying lengths, and piles of vegetation litter the tables and benches. The room is saturated with a powerful odor of cinnamon and herbs.

I approach the shelving unit to examine one of the jars more closely, and nearly gag when I realize it contains a tiny brain floating in brown sludge. Almost immediately, Macardi saunters over and throws a cloth over the jar, repeats his strange spin move and wanders off to find a chair. Without a word, he encourages us to find a seat and join him. After finding a place to rest our legs, an awkward silence ensues.

"Bloody hell," Erik mutters, "I wish one of us knew Italian."

"English," Macardi replies, unexpectedly. We all startle a

little. "But, uh…some of you speak a different, not like a my brother-in-law. He from England." He speaks very slowly and with a heavy accent, but it's understandable.

"Oh, um…," Erik stutters. "Yes, that's…brilliant. Um, some of us are probably from a different part of England than your brother-in-law," he says, trying to avoid more questions about where we've come from.

"He is a from the north," Macardi elaborates. He has a kind, rosy face with a short beard. His brown hair is pulled back into a ponytail, and the suede vest he wears over his tunic fits a bit snug around his belly.

Suddenly, he throws up his arms and strains to get up, walks out of the room and disappears without explanation. The four of us stare at each other nervously. Is he going to sound the alarm? Did we make a mistake trusting him? Fox shrugs his shoulders just as Macardi waddles back into the room with a plate in his arms. On top of the plate, rectangular slices of a yellowish-colored cake are arranged like building blocks in the shape of a pyramid.

"My sister make. Limone. Mangia."

He shoves the plate under Erik's nose and doesn't have to ask twice. Each of us takes a helping and devours it in seconds. It's delicious. Homemade, moist with a hint of nuts, and – most importantly – edible. We haven't eaten much since the morning.

"You look like you travelling," he observes. "From England?"

I nod. *Sure. Let's call it that.* "Grazie," I reply, wiping crumbs off my mouth. He offers me a strong-smelling drink in a tiny cup which I politely decline. We need to stay lucid, and that smells like it could knock me out for days. Macardi drinks it himself and his cheeks turn a deeper shade of pink. He shakes his head and spins before finding his seat again.

"I can tell you, uh…affamato. Hungry? But, that is not only thing you need, is it? Medicine? Potions?" He raises one of his bushy eyebrows. "Poison?"

"No." I assure him. *Poison?* Do people actually ask for that? I hope it's for rats. "None of those things, signore. We just need information." I convince myself I can trust him. I have no choice at this point. He knows the city and is our best chance of finding Petra. "We need to find someone. One of our friends was taken today, to the dungeons."

"Dungeons?"

"Yes."

"Oh, that is no too good," he mutters.

"They accused her of being a witch. Strega."

"*Witch?* Oh, that is no good. No, no."

I sigh in frustration. His pessimism isn't helping.

"Yes, well, we want to rescue her. We don't have much time. We need to get out of the city tonight, but we won't leave without her."

"And how do you plan on rescuing her from guards and steel bars?"

He makes a valid point. With our potentials, I'm sure we could figure it out. "We have our ways," I say, leaving out the details. "But we don't know the city. We were hoping you could help us."

Macardi rubs the sparse beard on his chin thoughtfully. "Do you know who take her?"

I shake my head. "An angry mob. There were several of them and…they all looked the same. The man who accused her though…" I proceed to describe the beady-eyed man in the long cloak with the jeweled cross, and Macardi appears to grow ashen before my eyes.

"This…this is very no good," he exhales after I've finished.

Can he please stop saying that?

My heart sinks. "Why? What does it mean? What will they do to her?"

He releases another labored sigh. "There are two, uh…" he searches for the word momentarily, "inquisitors who investigate the witchcraft. Balsom, he works the daylight hours. An unpleasant beast man." He gesticulates to describe Balsom's giant form. "But he was a soldier, one day, long time ago. He has some honor. At least he gives a trial, asks the questions, takes a time. He does not like to be…uh…wrong."

My palms are drenched in sweat. "And the other?"

"The other," Macardi replies, looking at us sympathetically as if Petra is as good as dead, "is Lazaro, the man you saw. A corrupt, evil man of the church. Bastardo! He runs a shadow court of death like a dittatore. He does not care for truth. It is all a…a big show. A spectacle! He is blood-thirsty and…uh… ossessionato…how you say…"

"Obsessed?" Fox guesses.

"Si! Obsessed with power, and the devil. He is not a man of God. I would rip that cross off his neck if I could!"

This really isn't good.

"Before he gives…uh…*la sentenza*…ah, si! A sentence," Macardi recalls in English, "he take all the money the accused have. Some time, he let someone go. But most time, he kill them anyway."

My stomach turns. I clutch my hands so tightly I think I might bruise them. This can't be happening!

"When is the trial?" I hear Erik ask through a fog of panic.

"Trial?"

"You said she would get a trial. When is it?"

Macardi grimaces and starts to wring his hands together. He looks incredibly uncomfortable, like he would rather be anywhere else. "I sorry if I misled you. But…with Lazaro, there is never a real trial. It is a public display and execution, at midnight, usually a same night he catches his victim, in la Piazza Carmine."

Something registers. I remember the name of that piazza written on a decrepit shop we passed on the way to the Vulturian chapter house, in the underbelly of the city. Fitting that this psychopath would hold his theatre of death close by. He's probably a Vulturian himself. I shudder at the thought, realizing how true it can be. Just because they're not tracking potentials doesn't mean they can't find us and kill us just the same. The method is just different.

"If your friend lucky, Lazaro wait for tomorrow. Some time he like to give crowd a few to choose. But your friend will not get a fair trial. That is for certain." He frowns deeply, and I can see sorrow blanket his face. "I knew a few who met their end by that demon's hand. Maybe, one day, he come to knock on my door as well. *Bastardo!*"

"Why don't you stop him, then?" Fox blurts out, accusingly. "If he's such a menace and terror to the city, aren't the people tired of it? Can't he be stopped by the mayor or something?"

Macardi chuckles as he studies Fox's different appearance with puzzlement. "Lazaro has…power here. Even our rulers fear him. No one challenge him. It would mean death. *Morte!*"

Fox's face is tight with anger. He throws his cloak aside to reveal the sword he's packing. "We're not afraid. We've been up against evil before."

"What will you do with that, *ragazzo?*" Macardi asks, motioning to the sword with a nod of his head. "You do not even carry it right. And you want to fight trained killers. I do not mean to insult. But this man…he has an army on his side…an army that will make your blood run cold. No one knows where they come from, but he has used them before. And the dungeons are well guarded by them."

Tanner has stayed silent during the entire visit, not a single word rolling off his tongue. Barely a gasp or a sigh. Maybe it's because I've been intermittently glaring at him. I did tell him to keep his mouth shut after all. He finally learned to listen a little too late.

From what Macardi's told us, Petra's fate hangs in a delicate balance. "So…we have a small window," I inhale deeply. "We need to get her out of that dungeon before midnight then. Where is it?"

"Did I mention," Macardi replies, looking at me like a concerned grandfather, "that you would be tempting death if you go there?"

"Yeah, yeah, we heard all that," Fox huffs. Macardi eyes him with curiosity again. Aside from not looking or sounding like the Brits did back then, Fox is not the most eloquent speaker when he's agitated.

"We know," I reply, hoping Macardi is still buying our cover story. "We don't care. Please, we just need to know where to go. We won't ask anything more from you."

The apothecary scrunches up his forehead into several deep lines and purses his dry lips, then shuts his eyes and makes the sign of the cross as if bestowing a blessing of protection on our doomed souls.

"Ciavutti, you know him?" he asks without opening his eyes.

"Yes," I confirm. "A little." I make no mention of knowing Macardi is a Luminarian. It will only lead to more questions we don't have the time to answer.

"And how is my friend? I have not seen him in many… many months."

"He is well," I lie. I have no idea how a man I've ever only met for five minutes is doing right at this moment. I only hope Macardi's questions end soon. "He told us we could trust you," I continue. "He said, if we needed anything to seek you out. We need this, signore. Please, where can we find the dungeon?"

Macardi opens his wide, surprised eyes and holds my gaze with them, wringing his wrinkled hands together in his lap with obvious unease. An unnerving silence blankets the room as we wait for his reply.

"Bene," he finally whispers, still holding me with his eyes, as he makes the sign of the cross across his chest. "Per Ciavutti. *Mio Dio!* May God have mercy on your souls. And may He send you all His angels for the battle, for I fear it is not one you will win."

CHAPTER 32

Tempting Fate

I tug at Erik's sleeve impatiently. "Are you sure this is the place?"

"Doesn't it look like the place?"

We have two more hours until midnight. It's not a whole lot, and we can't afford getting lost. But the structure we're staring at does look exactly like the place Macardi described, and we followed the directions to the letter.

We've travelled back to the underbelly, close to the square where Petra's "trial" could be held. In fact, we passed it on our way. To our horror, three stakes were sticking out of the ground beside the gallows. I felt the ice fill my veins as I looked at the stakes, trying to figure out what part they played. The ice must have frozen my feet too because Erik had to urge me forward. He placed his hand soothingly in the small of my back, pulled me towards him, and nudged my chin in the other direction.

"Don't look."

But it was too late. Now, the image of the stakes haunts me. And what's worse, it feels like my anxiety is somehow speeding up the clock and making the seconds tick faster, while filling my chest with lead and sucking the air from my lungs.

How did we get here?

It all happened so quickly. One minute Petra was telling me her life story, the next she was at risk of being executed. All within a span of 15 minutes.

I promised to keep her safe.

I promised to keep *all* of us safe.

I can't fail her.

The doors Macardi described loom eerily before us, and the fog that's pushing in gives the illusion that they're floating above the ground. "Steel, rectangle doors with a pattern, like this." He had drawn a horizontal zig zag pattern with his finger like he was writing a pointy "M" in the air. "Two stories high. Two guards will be outside, and more on the roof. No windows. It is like tomb. *Impenetrabile.* They march the prisoners to the piazza when it is the time."

Torches sit inside steel brackets on each side of the entrance. The doors are manned by two guards, just as Macardi described. On the roof, I make out the faint swaying of shadows. We observe from a safe distance, our gears turning as we plot our attack. Tanner stays further back. I refused to divulge too much to him. I don't know anything about his potential, and I'd prefer he know as little about ours as possible. Besides, if he uses his irresponsibly, he could get taken too.

"Once we reveal our potential, we'll expose ourselves," Erik says. "We have to move quickly, use the element of surprise to our advantage."

I bite my lip nervously. "At least it will make less commotion than the clanging of swords and a blood bath in the streets, which we'd probably lose! A sword fight isn't exactly in our wheelhouse."

"Speak for yourself."

I raise an eyebrow curiously. "Really? Story for a later time?"

Fox looks a bit disappointed at the prospect of never getting the chance to wield his shiny new toy. But after heated discussion and debate, we finally settle on a plan that gives us a better chance of staying alive past 30 seconds.

"Stay here," Erik instructs Tanner, who proceeds to move out of sight without protest. "Whatever you hear or see, don't move. We'll find you here later." In case we get separated, we agree to meet back at Macardi's shop.

"Whenever you're ready, mate," Fox says to Erik and extends his arm. "It's been an honor."

Erik takes it firmly and grabs his shoulder. "You won't be rid of me that easy. We can pull this off."

"Wish I had your confidence. This better work. Although, I'm still going to use my sword if the opportunity presents itself."

"No doubt you will," Erik chuckles. "Just don't cut yourself on the blade. I don't have a first aid kit."

Fox playfully punches his arm. He turns to me next, and to my surprise, pulls me into a hug. "Be a badass, ok. Just do your thing. I believe in you. Jenna would too. I need some good stories to tell her when I get back."

"Don't worry – we'll give you some good material."

He lets go of me and gives us a decisive nod. "All right then. Let's get this over with and live to tell about it," he says as he departs to position himself under an archway closer to the entrance to the dungeons.

As I stare at the doors feeling unprepared for what lies within, I sense Erik reach for my hand. "Ready?" he asks softly.

I look up at him, surprised not to be shaking as we're about to tempt fate. "No." I squeeze his hand tightly. His fingers fit perfectly in mine like pieces of a jigsaw puzzle. "Promise me you won't hold on to the light for too long."

He touches my chin, then brushes my cheek with his fingertips. "Don't worry about me. Just promise me you'll be careful, Ev."

I can't tear my eyes away from him and hate myself more than ever for destroying what we once had. "Promise."

His gaze betrays the fear that's gnawing at us both. I can barely let go of him. But I can't get distracted. There's a job to do.

I ready myself. *Focus. Feel it.* Robert always told me not to make anger the source of my potential. I never knew how. Anger seemed to summon it so easily, so consistently. I could rely on that rage to propel me into action. But I've done things I'd never imagined I could, and Erik's prepare me well. He's the best magister I could have ever asked for. I'm suddenly filled with a strange peacefulness that encircles me like a protective bubble. As I walk to my position, it feels as if I'm gently bobbing inside that bubble in slow motion. I've blocked out every sound and every stimulus, my mind focused on something else now.

Love.

Joy.

Light.

Don't make anger the source of it. Don't be like them.

Erik gives the signal by putting out the torches. Phase 1: Kill the Lights is complete.

Now for the tricky part.

Nothing happens for a moment, but then, the panicked cries ring out like music to my ears. I can just barely make out the silhouettes of bodies floating in the darkness near the gate, and others above the roof. Fox has succeeded with Phase 2: Make the Bastards Fly. It was a long shot, but he nailed it.

You got this, Fox! Keep them treading air.

Phase 3: Tear it down. That's where I come in.

Fox has never attempted to levitate this many people, so I need to move quickly in case his potential wanes. All my energy is focused on the door. I don't need to rip my heart in two and scream at it this time. I'm diving deeper now, feeding off something bursting inside me, something transcending and pure. Something bigger than all of us. The pendant burns into the skin on my chest, and the heat of the compass emanates from my satchel and warms my waist. I let that euphoric feeling reach the summit, and like a burst of magma that explodes from a volcano, I allow it to pour out with purpose.

Tear it down!

The formidable doors fall with a loud thud on the inside of the building as the floating silhouettes become entwined with clouds of dust. I run for the doors, Erik joining me mid-sprint just as Fox launches the two guards against the stone walls forcefully. They don't get up. Maybe they're dead. I know the pure part of me should care, but all I can think about is Petra and getting her out, along with any other innocents Lazaro and his band of seething fanatics have imprisoned here.

We step onto the fallen doors together. The sound of shouting starts the clock again. More will come. Erik immediately gets to work putting out the torches inside, blasts of light shooting into his palms.

"Release it!" I plead with him, witnessing his face contort with pain. "You're holding too much."

"Not yet. Get everyone out first!"

An arm sticks out from underneath one of the iron doors, a tattoo that we know all too well inked on the underside of its wrist. I grab at the boys and direct their attention to the body as lightbulbs turn on in my head. "The pattern on the doors…it's not M's. It's V's. This is Vulturian territory."

How many witches have they murdered that were, or could have been Wakers? It's been happening for thousands of years. They've been hunting, torturing, murdering. This is them.

"Lazaro is one of them," I realize, my suspicions vindicated. "We need to get to Petra, now!"

Stairs recede below the stone floors, guarded by iron locked gates. Fox reaches under the fallen door and rifles around in the pockets of the dead Vulturian. I hold my breath. "Hurry!"

The adrenaline kicks in again as footsteps and the clanging of swords echo above us, along with the clanging of keys Fox has finally found. I look at Erik. It's earlier than he wants, but we have no choice. He nods in understanding.

Phase 4: Light 'em up!

While Fox tries the keys in the lock, Erik and I move wooden furniture into the passageway. We step back before Erik turns in the direction of the approaching bodies and casts out the light he has stored in his palms, setting the barricade and a nearby hanging tapestry ablaze. "Hopefully this holds."

"Whatever buys us time. I'll find Petra and come back."

Fox is nowhere close to getting the gate open. "There's too many keys!" he shouts in exasperation, pulling at the gate desperately.

I pull him aside and focus on the gate. Now, it's easy. I know where I need to go to get what I need. I channel my potential until the gate flies open.

"Shit!" Fox mumbles. "Why didn't you just do that to begin with?"

"Still getting used to how this all works."

We run down the steps and into a massive cellar. It's empty, and my heart hits the floor like an anvil.

"Petra!" No one answers. *"Petra!"*

"Chi sei?" The voice is delicate and soft, as if spoken by a tiny butterfly. Eyes peer from around a column. It's the girl we saw outside the blacksmith shop. The one Petra helped. She looks frightened and alarmingly thin from up close.

"Hi! Are you alright?" I ask, approaching her. "Sta bene?"

She nods but looks down at her feet. Her father lies there, curled into a ball, clearly very ill.

"What did they do to you?" I mumble, knowing she won't understand me. I kneel in front of her to look her over, gently brushing her matted hair away from her dirty, tear-stained face with my fingers. She's so fragile and innocent. "We're going to get you out! Um…ragazza, bionda?" I ask, hoping to get information on Petra. "Dov'è?"

"Gone." The girl's father attempts to speak, his voice cracking and weak, as if he's on his last breath and the next words out of his mouth will cause his bones to break. "They asked what she did to me. I said I did not know." Tears fill his eyes. "But I do know! I know. Angelo! Lei è un angelo!"

"Si! La ragazza. My friend. Please, where did they take her? Where is she?" I look at the little girl. "Bionda ragazza. Dov'è?" But she shakes her head as tears start to fill her eyes.

"They took her a short time ago," the man answers. "The angry man…he took her away."

"Where?

"I do not know. But I think, Carmine."

Piazza Carmine? But that would mean…

"They will kill her," the man says bluntly. "That is what they do. That is always what they do, to give the crowd a show."

Smoke fills the cellar. "Come on!" I tell the girl, as Fox tries to get the father to his feet. Normally, I'd be panicking that we could be trapped and burnt to a crisp, but I have renewed faith in my potential now, faith that I can do more than I realized with it, even carve a path through hell itself.

We climb the steps while covering our mouths with our cloaks, but the smoke burns our eyes mercilessly. My panic for Petra grows with each passing second, but I use what I can of my waning potential to blow some of the smoke out of our path.

Upstairs, the flames rage. I can hear shouting behind the fiery curtain as Erik tries to hold the guards off with fireballs. He looks spent when I run up to him.

"That's enough. Let's go."

The shouting intensifies behind us as more bodies arrive to fight the crackling flames and intruders.

Not today. I stare at the enemy with stubborn resolve. *Today you lose. Today, your dungeon of terror burns to the ground.*

Erik sends a final blast of light that ignites the approaching guards, allowing us to escape.

"What kind of historical blowback do you think this will cause?" he asks as we run away from the chaos.

It's just one Vulturian dungeon, and unlikely to alter the course of history in our favor.

"Sadly, not enough."

CHAPTER 33

A Spectacle of Death

Tanner's eyes are wide with fear and awe at what we've left in our wake. He stares at the scene unfolding behind us as if not really sure to believe his own eyes.

"Take your father somewhere safe," I say to the girl. The man is nearly falling over. Whatever ails him, I doubt he has much time left on this earth. What will become of the girl when he's gone? The question torments me as I convince myself to let go of her hand.

"His wife is dying," the man says to me. "He took your friend to try and save her."

"So, maybe he will spare her a trial?" I ask hopefully.

But the man shakes his head. "Even if she succeeds, he will kill her. I overheard him tell her to make peace with her death, because she's filled with the devil's magic. He's a hypocrite, using magic for his own purpose, yet murdering those who wield it. That is what he is known for. He will stand by his mandate, and after he is done with her, he will dispose of her like all the others."

I feel as though I've been punched repeatedly in the stomach as I process the man's words.

"Uh, a little help," Tanner says, propping up Fox. An arrow protrudes from Fox's right side, and another from his lower left leg.

"I'm ok," Fox insists. "Just a scratch…or two." But with every movement he winces in pain.

"You're not fine, mate.," Erik argues, rushing towards him to examine the damage. "They must have got you from the roof. Tanner will take you back to Macardi. He'll know how to help."

"No chance! I'm going to get Petra, with you."

"You're not going anywhere except back to that apothecary," Erik insists. "Everest and I will find her. You can barely walk. You need medicine. I wouldn't be surprised if these arrows are poisoned. We need you alive more than we need you with us."

"Erik's right Fox," I agree, bending down and touching his leg. It's alarmingly hot. "The arrow is lodged pretty deep. Tanner, get him to Macardi as quickly as you can! We'll meet you as soon as we have Petra."

"Please, go *now!*" Erik urges.

Before Fox can protest again, Tanner pulls his arm over his shoulder and starts dragging him away. It's not easy, as Fox is heavier and taller, and Tanner's skinny body is still in the process of doing its own healing. I see Fox try to turn back to look at us, but the pain in his side prevents it. He cries out instead in frustration. "*Damn it!*"

They'll get there. I convince myself. *It'll be fine. Fox will be fine. Macardi will know what to do.*

The little girl eyes me with intrigue. "Who are you?" she asks. "Who is your friend?"

"Sorry?"

"You're not from here, are you?"

"No, we're from – " Suddenly, it dawns on me that I can understand her just fine. "Wait a minute, do you speak English?"

The little girl bats her eyes quizzingly. "No."

"But…I can understand you. How are we speaking?"

"You have been speaking to me and my father this whole time. Do you not remember?"

I have? I stare at Erik. "What did you hear?"

He scratches at the stubble on his chin, and looks as puzzled as I am. "I was surprised myself. I couldn't understand a word out of your mouth. Could you have tapped into something?"

"Speaking in tongues? Seriously?"

He shrugs. "We've seen stranger things."

The distant moaning of a bell pushes my contemplation aside. The sound lingers in the air until the echo fades, repeating three times in succession, long and drawn out, like a summons.

"It is time," the girl's father says. I guess I can understand him too. "They'll be starting soon. If you want to save your friend, go now!" His eyes are sympathetic, like he thinks we'll find only sorrow.

I nod, then glance at the dirty little girl with sadness, wondering again where she'll end up. Back on the streets, hungry, caring for her ill father, then orphaned. Maybe, if I had more time, I could figure out a way to help her. Maybe I could take her with me. *No that's insane. What if moving back through time means death for all of us?*

"What is your name?" I ask her.

She looks to her father as if to ask his permission to reveal it. He nods. "It's Antonia."

Desperate to quench my guilt, I hand her the bag of gold coins I took from the Vulturian chapter house.

"That's beautiful. Antonia, here, take this," I say, turning to her father. The welts on his skin look infected. "Make sure she is taken care of. If you need any care or medicine, go to the apothecary at Piazza San Jacopino. The man there can help you. You can trust him. Mention the name 'Ciavutti.'. But be very careful. There is evil in this city. Stay far away from it, if you can."

Before they can ask questions, I grab Erik's arm and tear him away, leaving the two pale puzzled faces glowing against the inky backdrop of the night as I swallow away my guilt for not being able to do more.

I fill Erik in on Petra's potential and on my conversation with the girl and her father. I can sense the tension in his body escalate when I relay what was said about Petra's chances.

"Let's not get ahead of ourselves," he tries to encourage me in between shallow breaths. "If Lazaro thinks she's useful, that works to her advantage."

"Yes, but Petra can only take pain away temporarily. She can't heal his wife. It will only enrage him. Besides, the girl's father said it wouldn't matter anyway. He kills them for sport it seems."

We're running now. There's no time for stealth. There's no time at all. As we near the square, the sound of chanting reaches our ears like an airborne torture device, reminding us that a crowd of bloodthirsty fanatics are gathered around tools of murder, awaiting their next sacrifice. The chanting grows louder, and I can barely breathe as we race toward it, my heart beating through my chest as if someone is banging a massive drum inside my ribcage. Lanterns cast eerie stretched out shadows across the stone walls as we approach. The shouting is nearly unbearable now, the crowd moving and seething as one ravenous monster as we enter from the west side of the square.

"Where is she?"

My eyes dart around the perimeter, but all I see are grotesque, angry faces, deformed by hatred and disease. A sea of hopelessness, misery and evil.

One of the stakes has straw piled high at the base – straw that wasn't there mere hours ago. Someone is tied to the stake, covered in a black robe with a hood over her head, platinum blonde locks escaping from underneath it. Ice fills my veins.

Petra!

Lazaro stands on top of the gallows and addresses his subjects, cloaked in his black robe. The light from the sea of torches reflects off the balding part of his scalp. "Tonight, we cast out another of Satan's demons from this city!" It seems I can understand him as well, my potential working in its mysterious new way.

The crowd roars. *"Burn her!"*

Lazaro motions for silence by raising his arms. "This witch claimed to be able to heal pain. But we saw with our own eyes as she sucked the soul out of a child and her father. A soul-snatcher! Yes, we have heard of her kind. She is no healer, nor mage. She is a demon, nothing more!"

"Burn the witch!" A man shouts. The crowd erupts again.

"An ageless snake that charms with her ivory hair the weakest of men, then takes the soul for the dark one. But tonight, her dark magic will be vanquished. Tonight, she *dies by fire!*"

An arm rips the hood off the condemned prisoner to reveal Petra's unconscious face. The crown of her light hair shines in the moonlight like a beacon.

"NO!"

Erik covers my mouth instantly. "Don't Ev, or you'll join her!"

My eyes water. I see Petra's head begin to sway as she comes to. Slowly, her head lifts to behold the horrifying scene in front of her. Terror widens her swollen eyes. She looks beaten and bloodied, and too weak to struggle.

I rip Erik's hand off my mouth. "What have they done to her?" I ask him. "She's not fighting back! *Fight back!*" I mutter to myself.

But Petra's head just nods back down, as if she's drifting on the brink of consciousness. A man holding a torch moves closer to the stake, then stops to glance at Lazaro, awaiting his command.

This can't be happening!

An angry mob of at least sixty stands between us and Petra. How will we ever get to her in time, once that dry straw is lit?

My instinct propels my forward once more. Again, I feel Erik's touch, but this time, his hand spins me around to face him. He kisses me passionately, the way he kissed me on the shores of the Prismatic that night in Senna. His lips melt against mine as if welded together, the chemistry and adrenaline and sorrow and regret combing to create an addictive and soul shattering sensation. I feel his heartbeat against my shaking body before he pulls away to stare into my stunned face.

"I love you, Ev," he says calmly, a smile creeping over his face. I'm astonished at how serene he looks. *Why does this feel like goodbye?* "There's too many of them. If we have any chance at all, we need to attack on two fronts, but if they see me, they'll see both of us. Wait for me to steal that fire, then it's your turn. You know what you can do," he reminds me, holding my head in his hands and looking at me intently. "I'll buy you time. It's the only way."

"*No!* Absolutely not! I'm not losing you again," I insist as I try to hold on to him.

But his hand slips out of mine. He's allowing himself to become shoved by the swarm of bodies, taken by them, like a leaf cast upon a dark, stormy sea.

"You're not losing me," he says, pulling his hood over his head as we're separated. "This is just the beginning Ev. I'll buy you as much time as I can. Trust yourself!" His voice drifts off and he vanishes before my eyes, absorbed by the sea of hate.

This isn't happening!

I'm alone. Helplessness sets in. The rage of the crowd is overwhelming. I manage to snap out of my shock and stand on top of a barrel to get a better view of Erik, but the mob has claimed him and he's nowhere to be seen.

From the corner of my eye, I glimpse Lazaro raise his arm again. When he lets it drop, the man standing near Petra moves the torch down to the straw, igniting it. The crowd cheers as the flames begin to crackle.

Suddenly, the flame vanishes, leaving only smoke in its place. A confused Lazaro motions for another torch to light the straw. Petra's head droops down again, as if attached to a paperweight. Fire ignites at her feet once more. I hear a whimper, then a louder cry.

Then again, the fire goes out, but this time, I see the millisecond-long flash of light that preceded its extinction.

Petra begins to struggle against the ropes that bind her to the stake, as if finally grasping the gravity of her situation. A third time, the flame vanishes when ignited, only on this occasion, Lazaro's eyes are on the crowd.

He knows.

He's one of them. A Vulturian, trained to sniff out Wakers and extinguish potential. He notices Erik's arm extend at the same time I do, seconds before a barely noticeable flash of light shoots into Erik's palm.

"Another!" Lazaro cries. *"An accomplice! Seize him!"*

Bodies begin to move toward Erik's location.

No! Run!

He's drawn them away, bought me time. I know it's consuming him, to hold on to so much energy, and my heart shatters as I watch him fall to the ground at the front of the bloodthirsty crowd. What is he waiting for to release it?

I try to focus so his risk is not in vain, the love that I felt earlier, the potential that broke down that door like it was made of paper…I need to find it again.

But the sight of Petra and now Erik being taken renders me useless, pulled in all directions and going nowhere, my mind seizing in frustration, my potential already depleted by the night's events.

I try again, and finally something stirs inside. Something familiar and powerful. Just as I'm harnessing it someone jostles the barrel I'm standing on and I lose my concentration, followed by my footing. I hit the ground hard on my shoulder, the same shoulder I injured sliding down that stupid muddy slope near my aunt's bunker. Whatever healing may have occurred, I feel it being undone, and I wince in agony as I struggle to get back on my feet.

I rise to see Lazaro staring into the face of the apprehended man who has thwarted his plans.

"Demon!" He cries over the murmuring crowd, his eyes bulging with ire. "Are you a demon, boy?" he asks, a smirk of sadistic satisfaction replacing his snarl. The mob has now seen first-hand the 'dark magic' Lazaro claims to fight. It will only fuel his madness and add legitimacy to his cult of death, and he knows it.

Erik keels over in pain. *Let it go,* I beg him silently. But his arms are being held back by Lazaro's henchmen.

"Now," Lazaro cries, raising up his arms, "you *both* will burn." The Vulturian drops his arms, and another torch lights the straw. The world comes to a standstill around me. All that moves are the flames beneath Petra's feet. I hear each individual crackle as I block out every other sound.

A light catches the corner of my eye, and I turn to witness the most incredible sight. Erik has released the energy after all. A light explodes from his mouth, the tail of it a brilliant flame. He looks like a human dragon, fire pouring out and engulfing the cloaked villain that stands next to him. Lazaro burns like a matchbox, arms flailing as he runs blindly into the crowd, setting others in his path ablaze. The henchmen release Erik in panic, and he collapses to the floor, rid of it all.

The world comes into focus again.

Now!

I summon my potential with the feeling of hope and pride that soars through me. The crowd of bodies that stand in my way fall like dominos, the path to Petra clear. I step on backs like they're steppingstones, rushing toward her. The fire under her feet grows hungrier, but I manage to put it out. Another torch lights the straw, the evil unwilling to surrender. I put it out again and keep moving forward with unquenchable purpose.

Petra raises her head, although her eyes remain closed. She smiles and begins mumbling something over and over. I squint to make it out, as her lips look dry and barely open. But finally, I figure out what she's saying.

Carpe Noctum. Carpe Noctum.

The smell of Petra's burning flesh stuns me out of my focus. Our eyes meet, and she speaks to me though no words leave her mouth. *I'm ready, Everest. Let me go.* Her face looks so serene, almost as if she's taking away her own pain. Where's Petra, the warrior? *Fight,* I scream at her inside. I need her to want to live, so she can try to escape it.

Two more torch bearers advance towards her. As I trip over more bodies in my haste, I notice Erik running toward me.

No, go to Petra. Save her!

But his hand is extended in my direction. He's yelling my name, his eyes wide and panicked. I summon my potential to try to extinguish the new flames, when suddenly, I feel my hair being yanked back with violent force. As I fall back, Erik lunges forward. He's almost at my side, reaching for something behind me. The back of my skull hits the cobblestones hard. I cry out in agony and look up to see Erik taking hold of a large, muscular arm wielding a giant axe. The world spins as Erik battles the stranger, the axe directly above my abdomen. Suddenly, it falls out of the man's hand and out of my field of vision. I feel something wet splash onto my face and a burning sensation rip through my bruised shoulder.

The city shrinks around me, enclosing me like a tomb. My fingers soak in a pool of blood as I lie on my back, unable to move. *Is it my own blood or someone else's? Where did the axe fall?* I can't see Petra from the ground, only the top of the stake, where a flame is now raging. *Maybe she got away. Maybe it was enough.* The smell of burning flesh poisons the night air. I choke, refusing to breathe it in until I'm fighting for air. Dread settles into my bones. *It wasn't enough. This can't be the end. This can't be happening…*

A hand grabs my injured shoulder. Stars dance in front of my eyes. Angry, spitting faces rush toward me with yellow teeth and bloodied lips. I look for Erik but can't find him. Reluctantly, I inhale a breath of the tainted air. A stabbing pain pierces my shoulder and spreads to the back of my bruised skull. Flames erupt around me, bodies hit the ground, war rages. Macardi was right: this is a battle we couldn't win.

I flinch again as another stabbing pain erupts in my skull. The stars above twinkle with contradictory peace and beauty compared to the scene unfolding around me.

"Petra…I'm sorry," I whisper as tears well up in my eyes. An explosion of light rocks the square, accompanied by a thunderous roar, and my world is swallowed by shadow.

About the Author

Aneta Torchia has a B.Sc. in psychology and criminology and a Master's degree in criminology from the University of Toronto. Her interests include human behavior, ancient history, metaphysics, the mysteries of the universe, and the untapped potential of the human mind. She writes literary, suspense, and fantasy fiction, children's picture books, and non-fiction with a focus on societal issues and well-being.

anetatorchia.com | theprismbooks.com

Find out what happens next…

THE PRISM SERIES BOOK 3
FINDING AEONIA

theprismbooks.com | theluminarypress.com

theluminarypress.com
info@theluminarypress.com